W9-DDK-720

The Finest Creation

The Finest Creation

JEAN RABE

A Tom Doherty Associates Book   TOR®   New York

THE FINEST CREATION

This book is printed on acid-free paper.

Book design by Jane Adele Regina

A Tor Book
Published by Tom Doherty Associates, LLC
175 Fifth Avenue
New York, NY 10010

www.tor.com

Tor® is a registered trademark of Tom Doherty Associates, LLC.

Library of Congress Cataloging-in-Publication Data

Rabe, Jean.
    The Finest creation / Jean Rabe.—1st U.S. ed.
       p.   cm.
    "A Tom Doherty Associates book."
    ISBN 0-765-30820-7 (acid-free paper)
    EAN 978-0765-30820-7
    I. Title.

    PS3568.A232F56   2004
    813'.54—dc22

                                                                    2004049828

First Edition: November 2004

Printed in the United States of America

0 9 8 7 6 5 4 3 2 1

FOR BRIAN THOMSEN

editor

~

friend

~

cat-fancier

~

and fellow Green Bay Packer fan

Acknowledgments

While I typed away on this manuscript, I received encouragement from my husband, Bruce, who provided names for a few of the characters, and from my friends Andre Norton, Beth Vaughan, Janet Pack, John Helfers, and Annette Leggett.

I am grateful to them.

The Finest Creation

1 · A Fine Pair

The world holds its breath when the Finest Court convenes~waiting, waiting for a word of wisdom, an emissary . . . some hint of redemption that, like a summer shower, will nurture a parched soul.

~Patience, Finest Court Matriarch

A blue-gray mist lay deep across the meadow and spiraled up trees that looked like slashes of charcoal on an ashen canvas.

"Congratulations, young one, on your appointment as a shepherd." The sonorous voice carried well through the thick mist. "It is a privilege to guide and guard one of the Fallen Favorites, one of the people of Paard-Peran."

The speaker stepped near a clump of willow birches, careful not to stand on exposed roots that he couldn't see this morning but that he knew from memory were there.

"When ages ago the Creators discovered that the people of Paard-Peran were not perfect, they established the Finest Court to help. The Court names shepherds to secretly guide the most beloved of the people—the ones the Creators call the Fallen Favorites. You should feel quite honored in your role of shepherd, young one. You could have a significant impact on your charge and therefore on all of Paard-Peran."

"Honored? Oh yes, I am indeed that. And I am more than that. In fact, I am . . . I . . ." The scents of clover and violets, damp from the mist, were strong and pleasant this day. He paused and inhaled deep, savoring the fragrance and the chance to gather his thoughts. After a long moment, he continued: "I am deeply honored, happy. And I am overwhelmed that the Court selected me to guide someone on the course to salvation, and perhaps to have an effect on the world. Though I admit I am puzzled how I can do this without my charge knowing."

"Your work is hidden."

"I know . . . I must act in secret. I must guide and guard, nudge when necessary, but never actually force. But to help someone without their being the slightest bit aware . . . it will be difficult."

"At times."

"It will be like living a life in shadows."

"You are privileged to live such a life."

"I know. I am truly honored. But above all of that I am nervous. You see . . . I am uncertain of myself. I don't know if I am up to the task. Oh, I hoped to be named a shepherd at some point. I just did not think it would happen this soon."

There was a loud snort. "Young one, the members of the Finest Court would not have granted you the responsibility if you were not ready. The greatest minds rule the Court, and they do not name shepherds on a whim. I am confident that much thought went into your selection."

There was the sound of pacing and the anxious clicking of teeth. "I understand that."

"Or so you try to tell yourself."

"I *do* understand. And I am excited about my new responsibility. I feel so proud and delighted and a dozen other things I cannot . . . at this very moment . . . put into words. I know I am fortunate to be leaving the lands of the Court tomorrow for the country called Galmier, fortunate that I will be given a charge. But this work is so terribly, terribly important. So much depends on how I guide that charge. What if I'm not . . ."

"You are a Finest, and you are prepared for this. Fresh from the Finest Court and ready to accept your mantle of protecting and redeeming one of the Fallen Favorites. You will be helping someone whom the Creators fancy." Another snort, this one clipped and sounding more like a chuckle. "But it will take your best effort."

"Everything I have."

"No, young one. It will take everything you are."

A pause. "Who will be my charge?"

"Patience, young one."

"Who?"

A silence slipped between the speakers, the only sound their breathing and the soft shush of the faint wind against the birch leaves. It was several minutes before the sonorous voice again cut through the misty air.

"When I was named a shepherd a long time ago, I was worried if I would be up to the task. I didn't fully understand my charge, didn't understand any of them, I suppose. I wasn't certain what to expect. It was all a great mystery that unraveled before my eyes. And I admit that even after all these years, my charge still can surprise me."

"How long have you been a shepherd?"

"Ah, young one, for more than two decades the King of Galmier has been my responsibility."

"The King—an impressive charge. And more than two decades—a long time. Who is to be my charge?"

He seemed not to hear the question. "I shepherded others before the King. Before he was crowned I watched over a wise woman from the Godspires. There was the leader of a fishing village on Minau-Pia, where the swift Cutter River meets the Esi Sea. I fondly remember twin sages from an island with no name. They looked and sounded so identical none but me could tell them apart. I threaded my way through the Winyan Range with an astrologer—in the days when astrologers were considered good. And in the beginning of my time as a shepherd, there was a handsome blind priest from the Sunsummit Mountains of Gredel-Saba. He had a kind heart. For well more than a hundred and seventy years I have guided and guarded the Fallen Favorites, moving from charge to charge when each no longer needed me and before curious eyes could notice I was not aging. But now the years wear on me. I am tired, young one, and soon it will be time for me to return here, to the lands of the Finest Court forever. I have earned it."

"But before that time comes . . ."

"I will escort you to the country of Galmier in Paard-Peran. There you will meet your charge."

"And just who is to be my charge? Who in all of Paard-Peran am I to shepherd?"

2 · Wedding Finery

The beetle matched the color of the flower shoots it crawled among, making it difficult to be noticed. But it had a couple of dark specks on its back, and that helped. And when Kalantha looked closely, she could see thread-fine antennae twitching curiously. The beetle was the size of her thumbnail, but it would likely double or triple in size, as each summer she watched larger beetles just like this one explore her favorite garden. It would grow with the roses, merrybells, and chrysanthemums that were planted in the narrow beds against the Temple.

There were other insects out this spring day—mourning cloaks; lacy brown butterflies with jagged, butter-colored edges; shield-shaped stink bugs; two-spotted ladybirds that were the smallest beetles to make their home here; and a trio of pygmy blues, tiny butterflies practically the shade of the periwinkle tunic Kalantha wore. Kalantha studied insects with far more enthusiasm than she applied to studying theology and history or perfecting the various embroidery stitches she was consigned to learn. Insects were much more interesting to the ten-year-old, and her friend Morgan the gardener was a most engaging teacher.

Kalantha watched the beetle a few moments before squatting—especially careful not to get dirt on her tunic and hose. She rested the back of her hand flat on the ground in the beetle's path. The insect paused only briefly before crawling onto her palm, and Kalantha drew it near her face so she could better see it.

"A rose beetle," she decided, as she stood. "One who nibbles on the undersides of the softest leaves." Its feet gently tickled her. "I think you will like this garden. And I . . ."

"You look lovely this morning, Kal." Morgan surprised her, approaching silently and towering next to her. The old gardener wore an apron, and there were gloves sticking out of his pocket—signs he was going to start potting in the arboretum.

"Thank you, Morgan. But I'm not dressed so fine as my brother, I think."

Kalantha looked past the beetle and across the garden, and through an archway in the Temple's east wall. Her brother Meven was inside, speaking with the Bishop. Only three years older than Kalantha, he was more than a head taller and was an adult as far as she was concerned, as he was shrewd, seemed ever so serious, and always watched out for her. He habitually dressed in somber colors, no reds, blues, or greens ever intruding to provide a bit of brightness. This morning he wore a voluminous black shirt with a leather lace up the front. His trousers, the palest pair he owned, were fog gray, spotless now though Kalantha knew they wouldn't remain that way. They would soon be spattered, as the ground would be muddy where they were going, and they had a long ride ahead of them. She'd chosen earth-colored hose for just that reason. The mud spots would not show as easily. Meven was indeed smart, she thought, but he didn't know much about nature.

Kalantha couldn't hear the Bishop and her brother, but she suspected they were talking about religion or politics. It was all they ever seemed to discuss—when they weren't praying. Meven prayed even when the Bishop wasn't around, and Kalantha fully expected him to pursue a religious life.

"Aye, your brother is indeed dressed well this morning, little Kal." Morgan brushed at a smudge on his apron. "But I think the mud from the road will show easily on those trousers of his."

She smiled at his comment. "He has an even fancier change packed," she said. "One so very deep brown with ivory buttons, and with a silk mantle that falls to his ankles. It's for the wedding. He fussed over his clothes all last night. A half-dozen outfits he is bringing, everything good that he has."

"And you?"

"My best damask dress for the wedding, pale red like the ladybirds. A spare dress and hose, and one of those horrid wimples, as the Bishop says I must wear a hat in the city. Oh, and a cloak in case it rains or turns chilly." She returned her attention to the beetle in her palm. "I don't want to go, you know. It's going to be boring. Ceremonies and parties, remembering to use forks and to nod and smile and to always always always say please and thank you."

"It's only for a matter of days. You should be back in plenty of time for your eleventh birthday. It will give me time to find you a present—and hide it somewhere so you can't find it."

"But I will miss the first trillium blooming." She sighed, her breath fluttering the soft cinnamon-colored curls that hung halfway down her forehead. Her hair was long, braided in one thick strand that fell to her waist, and tied with a white ribbon. Her hair matched the color of the freckles that dusted her cheeks and the bridge of her nose and that were more numerous on her arms and the backs of her hands. She thought the freckles made her look even younger than her ten years, but Morgan often told her they suited her, and, coupled with her green eyes, made her look mischievous—which he claimed she most certainly was. She was not fat, but neither was she slender like her brother. "Pudgy," her brother called her. "Healthy," Morgan pronounced, as he grabbed her doughy fingers.

"I really don't want to miss the first trillium blooming. And if I go I will not be able to help you pot the old man's beard or thin the firethorn hedges."

"I can manage well enough myself, Kal. Besides, I should think you'd be excited about this trip." There was a touch of mirth to Morgan's voice. "You've been sequestered at the High Keep Temple ·nearly all your life. Time you got out and saw some of the world."

"I've been out many times before."

"Aye, to the village of Fergangur. And with only your brother for company and the Bishop and a few of his men for an escort. You've been no farther."

"I like living at the Temple, Morgan. It's peaceful here."

"Funny. You're not a peaceful soul, Kal. A little trouble-maker you are."

She scrunched her face, drawing the freckles together. "I don't get into trouble, Morgan. Not much anyway. And certainly not this week."

He shook his head and playfully wagged a finger.

She grinned impishly. "Besides, only you notice. Bishop DeNogaret and the others don't pay much attention. It's Meven they're always concerned about. Meven this. Meven that. Meven. Meven. Meven."

Morgan scowled. "Kal, your brother is a fine young man. He's bright."

"Stuffy."

"Studious," Morgan corrected.

"Always has his nose in a book . . . when he isn't praying."

"He's devout."

"Much too serious."

"Bishop DeNogaret appreciates his piety. He is fond of your brother."

"Meven loves the Bishop. Talks about him all the time. Meven's with him whenever possible . . . whenever the Bishop doesn't shoo him away."

"Getting away will be good for your brother. Some different scenery and people. It could be good for you, too."

"Maybe it'd be good for him, but not for me. I don't want to leave. I like working in the garden with you." A pause. "Even if I do get into trouble once in a while." She glanced through the window and at the Bishop again, her guardian. The reed-thin man dressed even more starkly than her brother did, everything the color of ashes. Often his complexion was tinged with gray to match. Notwithstanding the Bishop's frail appearance, he had a commanding presence—which Kalantha felt despite the dozen or so yards that separated them. And because she so respected him, she always felt small and somehow humbled when she was with him. Her brother didn't seem to have that problem and appeared relaxed in the Bishop's company.

They were praying now, Meven and the Bishop, heads bowed respectfully and arms flush against their sides.

Kalantha giggled because the beetle was tickling her palm, and she transferred it to her other hand. Morgan shook his head, thinking she was laughing at her brother and Bishop DeNogaret.

"Respect your brother, Kal. He might pursue a religious life. It would be an honorable and selfless profession. He's well versed in the Temple doctrine, knows it better than many of the acolytes twice his age. He's reverent, well liked by everyone here."

A butterfly suddenly caught Kalantha's attention, and she thrust Morgan's conversation to the back of her mind. She'd heard him expound on Meven's many virtues often enough to know the words by heart. But this butterfly was one she'd not seen before, and so it deserved all her concentration. Its wings were eggshell white, with pale orange scalloped edges and yellow oval spots parallel to its body. Her eyes followed it, from one flower to the next, intently studying how it moved and fed, and how its long feelers constantly twitched.

"You are like that butterfly," Morgan was saying.

Kalantha was too preoccupied to register the words.

"Beautiful and delicate and vulnerable. Flitting from one thing to the next, never staying on one topic long, too easily distracted."

She shuffled along the edge of the flowerbed. When she glanced up, she could still see her brother and the Bishop through the window, and she could better watch the butterfly. It was feeding on the tallest blooms now, circling, hovering, and dipping down. She glanced at her hand to make sure the beetle was still there.

"What did you say, Morgan?"

"Or perhaps you are like a grasshopper. Jumping from one thing to the next, finding trouble here and there. Good that there is only one such as you here, Kal. A multitude of grasshoppers can ruin a crop."

"Pardon, Morgan?"

"So unlike your brother, you are." He gently rested a hand on her shoulder.

The butterfly flew away from the flowers at that moment and started across the lawn. Kalantha tried to watch it, but quickly lost sight when it climbed against a white shed. With a sigh, she returned her full attention to Meven and Bishop DeNogaret. She felt a little guilty that she was tarrying in the garden and wasn't praying with her brother, asking the gods to watch over them on the journey and to bless the upcoming wedding of her cousin, Prince Edan of Galmier, and his bride. For a moment, she considered joining Meven and the Bishop, which would be the proper thing to do. But she had waited too long. They were raising their heads now, and the Bishop had his hand on Meven's shoulder. A moment more, and Meven was leaving the chapel.

"Bishop DeNogaret is not coming with us," Kalantha told Morgan.

"Aye, I'm well aware."

"I'm surprised he's letting us go to the wedding without him. We've never been away on our own. But the Bishop said it wasn't his place to attend such festivities," Kalantha explained. "He said that another priest was presiding and so he should keep his distance. The principal Bishop of Nasim-Guri will be performing the wedding ceremony."

Morgan chuckled. "The politics of religion."

Kalantha shrugged. "There are enough other people going, though, so I don't suppose Bishop DeNogaret will be missed. Lucky for him. Too bad I can't stay behind. I shouldn't think they'd miss me either. They don't even know me." Her shoulders dropped and she released a breath, fluttering her curls again. Then, dividing her attention between the beetle still cupped in her palm and the path along the flowerbed, she turned and made her way to the front of the Temple, where a small entourage was gathered. There were eight of the Bishop's men, all with flowing cerulean capes, and half of them in chainmail shirts. The one in the lead had a yellow and blue pennant with the bishop's half-moon emblem on it. There were horses for her and Meven, and three stocky horses to carry packs—one was laden down with satchels filled with her and Meven's clothes, food, and a few wedding presents Bishop DeNogaret had selected for them to give.

Morgan had been following her. "It's a reasonable escort,"

he pronounced. "Though I would have thought Bishop DeNogaret would have assigned more men to accompany you."

Kalantha tossed her head. "Meven told me there will be many more, a grand parade when we join with my cousin's party south of Fergangur and Tolt. The King was supposed to be with us, too."

"The King is your uncle, Kal. High time you met him."

"I suppose. But I will not have to worry about that today. Bishop DeNogaret said the King has fallen terribly ill and is staying behind at the palace. Would that I could stay behind too." She saw Meven come out of the Temple. He was walking straight toward her. He'd cut his reddish-brown hair short this morning and had put on a rope belt, dyed black and decorated with carved wooden beads. She had such a belt too, but wore it only on worship days. Bishop DeNogaret gave the belts to them, and the beads were for counting prayers.

Meven's lips were curved upward ever so slightly, the closest thing to a smile Kalantha had seen him manage. His shoulders were square, and his chin was tipped toward the sky. Overly thin, his face was all angles and planes, which helped give him a stern countenance. But his dark eyes flashed, and that told Kal he was happy and looking forward to this trip. Morgan was right, Kalantha decided. Meven needed this outing. Some time away from his studies and the austere confines of the Temple might make him a little less serious. For that reason alone, she would try her best to enjoy this venture. The Bishop stood in the shadowed entrance to the Temple, watching Meven, then visually inspecting his men. The one with the pennant nodded a greeting.

"You must be on your way, Meven, Kalantha." Bishop De-Nogaret's voice was deep and strong, incongruous to his years and his aspect. Kalantha liked listening to it. "The presence of my men will keep any bandits at bay, and you'll join with the

King's men soon. It will be a formidable force. Take care of each other and make me proud of you."

"We will, sir," Meven was quick to reply. "We promise."

"Enjoy the festivities, children," the Bishop added. "And Meven, make sure your sister does not eat too many sweets."

The Bishop's men shifted their horses into a double-file formation, with Meven and Kalantha's horses, followed by the packhorses, in the middle.

"Indeed you should be going," Morgan said, barely loud enough for Kalantha to hear. "The sooner you are on the road, the sooner you will be back home. And then I will tell you all about the first trillium flowering."

Kalantha bent to release the beetle at the side of the path. "And about the old man's beard, how many cuttings you made of it while I was gone."

"Of course."

Meven stepped to her side. "C'mon, Kal. Don't you dally." He looked down at the beetle and shook his head. "Ugh." Then he ground the ball of his foot on top of the insect. He did not notice her forlorn expression. "I'll take the ugly brown horse," he said. "You can have that pretty spotted pony. It looks gentle."

"I do not want to go," Kal whispered.

~ ~ ~

There were fifty of the King's men, nearly all of them soldiers of a similar height and build, wearing chain-mail hauberks that gleamed in the midafternoon sun. Everything looked the same—their striking green tabards, polished full helms, and inlaid scabbards and broadswords. Even their boots and gloves were identical. Their postures were rigid, their jaws set, and their eyes were trained ahead. Not one of them spoke. To add to the military uniformity, their mounts were of the same breed, well-groomed noriker war-horses, dark brown with wheat-colored manes and tails, and with featherings at the hooves. It was every bit the regal parade Meven told Kalantha it would be.

The few attendants who were not soldiers—a scribe, three grooms for the horses, and an attendant for Prince Edan—wore exceptionally fine traveling attire and rode at the back of the procession. Even they were on the specially bred norikers. There were packhorses too, and these were massive heavy drafts, all chestnut with light brown manes. The people and animals were intended to look impressive . . . Galmier's foremost representatives decked out for the royal wedding in the neighboring country of Nasim-Guri.

Prince Edan was dressed in a more stately manner than anyone else was, and his horse was singular, inky black and with a long mane braided and decorated with silver beads. It was wearing cuirboille barding, a heavy leather painted with beeswax, and it had a crinet of fluted plates around its neck with a gap for its mane to hang free. The Prince caught Meven staring at the animal.

"It's a glavian, cousin. This horse is unequaled among all those in the royal stable. My father's prized stallion. He's several years older than me."

Meven was skeptical. "You are eighteen. Are you saying that horse is twenty years old?"

"Hah! At least twenty-five, and likely twenty-seven or twenty-eight I would think, as my father could ride him right away." Edan stretched forward in the saddle and scratched at the horse's ears. "My father named the horse Nightsong when it was presented to him by a noble in my father's court twenty-five years ago. It was the day my father was crowned King. The horse is in remarkable condition for his age. Don't you agree?"

Nightsong stood sixteen hands high and had elegantly sloping shoulders, a deep, broad chest, and a straight back. His legs and neck were long and muscular, and his head was large and exceptionally attractive. His eyes were expressive, and his ears were small and obviously alert, twitching one way and then another as the procession continued at a quick pace along the road that paralleled the westernmost branch of the Sprawling River.

"Maybe someday, years and years from now when I am crowned King, I will have a fine horse such as this," Prince Edan mused. He thrust his shoulders back and tipped his face up. "Dark and sleek, fast and with a spark of intelligence in his eyes. Well-mannered and a pleasure to ride. Or . . . perhaps I will have one even finer."

And who shall have me?

The words had a weight to them. And though they were spoken quite clearly, they were not heard by Prince Edan, Meven, or any other person in the procession. *Who am I to shepherd, Steadfast? When will you tell me?*

The words were directed to the impressive glavian beneath the Prince.

Who?

Patience, young one.

3 · The Finest Creations

The Finest shall wear the forms of horses, hiding in the open, while keeping close to their charges.

~*Paard-Zhumd, son of the creator-god*

Who am I to watch over, Steadfast? The Prince who rides you? Is he to be my charge?

Patience, I say, the glavian urged. The elegant black horse shook its head, the silver beads in its braided mane clinking like wind chimes and sparkling in the sun. *Everything in its time, Gallant-Stallion.*

I have patience, the big horse persisted.

But perhaps not enough, young one. The glavian's telepathic voice had a commanding quality that demanded attention. *I will announce your charge soon.* The glavian turned his head ever so slightly, and his eyes were unblinking when they met Gallant-Stallion's.

How is it that they cannot hear us, Steadfast?

The glavian snorted, the sound filled with exasperation. *We Finest talk in several ways, Gallant-Stallion. In this, what we call 'hidden speak,' our minds form the words that are passed between us. We use this when we are with the people of Paard-*

Peran. They cannot know that we are anything other than common horses, else we would not be able to secretly guide them. Too, we can talk to the animals of this land, using the nickers and snorts that horses make. And there is, of course, the verbal speech that I prefer. We can speak just like the people of Paard-Peran, though in tones richer and perhaps more meaningful.

I prefer that best, too, Gallant-Stallion replied. *I like to truly hear your voice, Steadfast. Still, I don't completely understand . . . if we can hear with our minds, why can't the people?*

Another exasperated snort. *The Creators gifted us with the ability to hear the thoughts of other Finest. People are not able to hear thoughts.*

Neither can we hear their thoughts, it seems.

No. We were not meant to intrude on the thoughts of people. Neither should we intrude on the thoughts of horses or birds or dogs or any other of the Creators' creatures.

Why?

Steadfast paused. *Because we do not need to,* he said after a moment. *Not to do our work.*

And our work is very important, Gallant-Stallion said. *Terribly important.*

Steadfast paused again, and as their course took them around a bend in the road, he quoted from the Finest Court canon. '*. . . and the Old Mare said: The Creators saw that people were imperfect and had failed the tests lain before them. People had to be cast out of paradise, and for this the Creators were sad. Even though people had fallen, they were still the Creators' favorites.* '

The road straightened again, and Steadfast looked to Gallant-Stallion to continue the passage. The big horse complied: '*Still, the thought of the cruel, yet deserved, fate that stretched before people distressed the Creators. So rather than abandon people, the Creators molded 'the Finest,' creatures far more perfect than people, destined to help them in their toils.'*

Steadfast finished it: *'The Finest are people's guides and cus-todians, tasked to help them along the path back to perfection. The Finest are the preservers of the Fallen. Fleet of hoof, strong of back, and loyal of spirit.'*

For several moments the big horse regarded the impressive glavian. When the shade of a stand of tall locusts fell across the road, Steadfast looked impossibly black to Gallant-Stallion, a piece of a starless night sky given life and come to ground. *You are a legend in the Finest Court. Your name, Steadfast, is spo-ken with great respect.*

Steadfast nodded at the compliment.

And yet the man upon your back calls you Nightsong.

Steadfast is my true name, the one given to me by the Finest Court. Just as Gallant-Stallion is your true name. People call me what they will. They most certainly will devise a name for you, too. As I said before, they haven't the divine ears to hear us, brother, and so they cannot divine our true names.

Steadfast and Gallant-Stallion continued their secret discus-sion as Prince Edan's procession increased its speed on the road that bisected the branch of the Sprawling River and the Galmier Mountains. It was evident the Prince was not pleased with the time they were making and called to the soldiers up front to go faster. Some of the norikers had started to sweat from all the hours of travel, and there were specks of foam on the lips of the packhorses. But the pace was only a trifling ef-fort to Gallant-Stallion and Steadfast.

Steadfast talked about *this glorious day*, with the wind bringing all manner of interesting aromas to him. He liked the scent of the wildflowers the best, particularly the dark pink ones with the soft smell of a new spring. The tall purple ones that looked like arrows stuck into the ground had a sharper fragrance, and the tiny yellow ones practically hidden in the grass smelled like drops of honey. Together they formed what he called 'nature's bouquet,' a concert of delights that settled pleasantly in his mouth.

Gallant-Stallion stretched out with his senses in an attempt to feel what Steadfast was talking about. There were flowers in the Finest Court, but they were somehow different than these and to him smelled sweeter and more intense. Still, there were other odors here that were appealing to him—the earthy scent of the moss and ferns that clung to life on the swollen riverbank. Even the water had a smell to it, a peculiar but not unpleasant one that he had difficulty describing. He let it rest on his tongue and began to enjoy it. There was a patch of the tall purple flowers Steadfast had spoken of. Gallant-Stallion drew that odor deep into his lungs and decided he didn't care for those.

Suddenly the mood was broken and Gallant-Stallion slowed, as Meven pulled hard on the reins and directed him around an especially large puddle. He was puzzled, as the puddles felt cool and the mud soft against his hooves. Why did the young man want to keep him from this small pleasure?

Despite all my training in the Finest Court, it will take time to fully understand them. Gallant-Stallion tossed his head.

I constantly learn new things about them, Steadfast said. *Even after twenty-five years, my current charge can surprise me.*

As you say, Steadfast, the King of Galmier is your charge, and yet you are here with his son. Are you worried about the King?

When Steadfast didn't respond, Gallant-Stallion continued. *Why are you not with the King? He is your charge.*

The glavian's eyes grew dark.

Gallant-Stallion pressed the issue. *The King,* he began. *Is he dying? Is that why you will return to the Court? Or am I to shepherd the King in your place? Have you spent too many years with him and fear discovery?*

Steadfast lowered his gaze. *The King is ill, though he will re-*

cover from this malady. But he no longer needs a shepherd. It was only in the early years of his reign that others sought his crown and he needed protecting. He rules wisely and has no enemies. His son will start a family soon and eventually will take over the joined countries. I could have left the King years before now. But I am fond of him. I enjoy his company.

The road narrowed here, and so the procession went single file for nearly a mile. The Finest did not resume their discussion until after the road widened again and they were side by side.

Then if not the King, Steadfast, am I to guide his son the Prince?

Steadfast made a wuffling sound and flicked his tail. *So fresh from the Court! I swear I will teach you some measure of patience, Gallant-Stallion. Perhaps I will not reveal your charge until after the man upon my back is wedded. Perhaps not until we are home in the King's stables. Perhaps not until the day my tenure is truly done and I leave for the Finest Court. Or perhaps I will tell you tomorrow. But certainly not today. Patience.*

Gallant-Stallion let out a loud snort, to which Meven responded: "My mud-colored horse even sounds ugly, Edan. What a funny-looking beast I am riding."

~ ~ ~

They started early the next morning. Kalantha and Meven were riding next to Prince Edan. The Prince, though speaking to both of his cousins, was truly talking only to Meven. The two seemed to have become good friends in a short time, and they had years of catching up to do. Kalantha slowed her pony and drifted far enough behind them so that their conversation was lost in the rhythmic clopping of the horses' hooves. She looked to the west, where the Galmier Mountains reached high into the sky. There were a few gray clouds hanging over them today, and Kalantha thought it might be raining there. The air smelled damp.

"I wish my father were here riding Nightsong," Edan told Meven, as he urged the procession to adopt a faster pace. They would have to travel forty miles today and the day after to cross over into Nasim-Guri and to its capital of Duriam, where the wedding would take place. Edan explained there would be few stops, as he had dawdled days ago in the hopes his father would get well enough to travel. Now time was precious. It would be bad politics to show up late for one's wedding, the Prince said.

"Meven, I've been told that our fathers were the closest that brothers could be. When your parents died while visiting Uland ten years past, my father took it very hard and made arrangements for you and Kalantha to live with Bishop DeNogaret in the High Keep Temple. He knew you would be better cared for there than in the palace. My own mother gone, he had enough on his hands trying to raise me and run this country."

"I know all of that," Meven said. "Bishop DeNogaret told us."

"But now that you're older, things could change," Edan continued. "Maybe it's time you came to live at the palace. It is more beautiful than the Temple."

Meven shook his head. "I would like to see the capital someday, but I've studies to tend to and . . ."

Edan looked surprised that Meven would prefer the Temple to a palace. "Then you must at least visit. I insist. The Bishop's books and lectures can be postponed for a month or so." Edan gave his cousin time to think. He glanced to the east and across the river. The land was lightly forested there, with tall black ash trees that favored the moist soil of central Galmier.

"Well, yes, a visit then," Meven said after a few moments'

consideration. "If Bishop DeNogaret agrees to it. Until now, I've never been anyplace beyond Fergangur."

"And that is a very small village. It isn't much to see."

Meven shrugged.

"So you shall see our capital, cousin, and every room of the palace, and the royal stable where we keep the norikers. Nightsong has a stable to himself. And you'll see our most impressive gardens with the topiary and the hedge maze. I will show you everything. It is long past time we got to know each other well. We are all that remains of the Montoll family." Much softer and a touch sadly, he said: "Until I have a family of my own and extend the line." Prince Edan rolled his shoulders and worked a crick out of his neck. "In fact, dear cousin, I will arrange for your visit right after the wedding. . . ." He paused and drew his lips into a thin line. "I will bring my bride to the palace, where we will make our home. She will settle in quickly, I hope. Then I will insist that you and Kalantha come stay with us for a time. The King—my father and your uncle—will properly meet you. We will have a grand time of it."

"This wedding," Meven prompted. "It isn't your idea, is it?"

"You didn't know?" Edan gave out a nervous laugh. The Prince stood in the stirrups and looked around the soldier in front of him. All he could see was the back of another soldier and another beyond him. After a moment he sat back in the saddle. "I haven't met my bride, dear cousin. All I can tell you is that she is Princess of House Silverwood, the ruling family of Nasim-Guri. It is all a political arrangement between her father and mine. I had no say in the matter."

"No say? Politics involved with your marriage? For years I have studied government and . . ."

"You are bright, Meven, but delightfully naïve. Be glad that your father was the younger brother in the royal family of

Galmier, else you would be Prince instead of me, and you would be riding along this muddy road to marry a girl who could very well look like a portly toad."

Meven made a face, then instantly slipped into a stoic mask, fearful he might have insulted his royal cousin.

"The marriage will effectively join Galmier and Nasim-Guri, in time creating the largest country in all of Paard-Peran," Edan continued. "You see, by Nasim-Guri's laws, its King must be male. The King of Nasim-Guri has no male heirs, and so by custom when he dies his lands will fall to his eldest daughter's husband."

"And that will be you."

"In three more days it will be me. And since we've so many miles to go, we must be quick if we are to make my wedding." Edan closed his eyes and shook his head. "Pray that there is something pretty about her, cousin, for she is young and will likely live a very long time."

Meven made an attempt to cheer him. "I can't imagine a princess not being pretty. But even if she does resemble a portly toad, she'll be better looking than this." Meven flicked the reins. "Bishop DeNogaret bought two horses last week for pulling our wagons and working the field. Why he gave me the ugliest one to ride to your wedding is a mystery."

"Perhaps he had no others available."

"I rather believe he is making sure I stay humble. I might be too prideful if I rode a horse such as Nightsong or even one of those beautiful norikers."

Prince Edan studied Meven's horse, and after a few moments pronounced it "sturdy" and an "old breed." "I believe it is called a 'punch,'" he said. "Or a suffolk-punch, from an ancient region of the same name. I know a bit about horses, and that one should prove a good worker. Even if he is a trifle ugly. At least his eyes are kind."

"Maybe your Princess will have kind eyes, too."

Edan let out a deep chuckle. "Indeed I must visit with you more often. Pity Bishop DeNogaret would not consent to letting you leave the Temple before this occasion. He's far too protective of you."

They passed the next few miles in relative quiet, the Finest and their riders, with Meven taking time to absorb the countryside. Galmier was also called Fenland by its residents, as the river that spread through its heart made the ground marshy, particularly in the spring after the last patch of snow had melted and the rains came. Meven saw stretches of standing water and places near the bank on either side where the river was well up the trunks of the ash trees. Everything would be drier in the summer and through the first part of the fall, he knew. But it was early spring now, and so the river had swelled its banks and Galmier was at its wettest.

Even parts of the raised road they traveled were dotted with puddles. Where he and Kalantha lived in the High Keep Temple, it was usually dry all year round. The land was simply higher in the north and near the mountains, and the river did not stretch far enough to make flooding a worry. The capital city of Nadir in the east, where the palace was located, was also on higher ground. Had the wedding been in drier times, Prince Edan likely wouldn't have met Meven and Kalantha on the road south of Fergangur and Tolt. The Prince's procession would have taken a direct route across country, not staying to the roads and saving considerable time. Meven was certain Bishop DeNogaret would not have let him and Kalantha go to the wedding on their own—not even with eight of the Bishop's men for company. It was simply too far away, and the Bishop was indeed sometimes too protective of his charges. "Good that it is the wet season," Meven whispered. "And that Prince Edan had to take this road. Good for Kal and I."

Meven found that later in the afternoon puddles appeared more frequently on the road, and one section was nearly washed out. And though he was annoyed that his trousers were thoroughly speckled with mud, and dusted with dirt that had blown from the infrequent dry spots, he was quietly relishing the change in scenery from the Temple grounds. The variety of trees was amazing. Kalantha pointed out that the predominance of black ash was giving way to stringybarks, willow birches, walnut, bitternut, hickory, sourwood, and alders. The latter she said were a bit like birch trees. An abundance of birds gathered in the highest branches. Along the ground an occasional fox and plenty of squirrels scampered.

"I've been thinking, cousin Meven." Prince Edan's voice cut over the clopping of the horses' hooves and the shushing sound the soldiers' tabards made in the growing breeze.

Meven nearly asked him, "Thinking about what?" as Edan had not continued. But he waited. Bishop DeNogaret had taught him that patience was an essential virtue. After a few minutes, the Prince went on.

"I've been thinking that when you come to visit, I will make certain that you are given a noriker."

Meven fought to hide his excitement. "And Kalantha?" He glanced back at his sister riding the pony. She seemed preoccupied with staring at the mountains. "In my heart I could not accept one if . . ."

"Kalantha will have a noriker, too, of course."

"Then I look forward to riding one of those beautiful, beautiful horses." He leaned back in the saddle. "It will be a fine change from sitting atop this ugly punch."

UGLY? A PUNCH? THIS CAME FROM GALLANT-STALLION. *I AM not so majestic as you, Steadfast. But ugly?*

Nearly sixteen hands high, Gallant-Stallion was the color of wet clay and had a wide forehead and a thick neck. His chest was very broad, and his hindquarters powerful looking. But his legs, though muscular, seemed overly short for his heavy frame, and there was no attractive feathering around his hooves. His mane was short and coarse, black streaked with chestnut. His tail had been bobbed so it wouldn't have to be groomed.

The boy on my back thinks I am ugly! He thinks I am funny looking!

What that boy thinks of you is none of your concern.

Gallant-Stallion could not contain his irritation. *Meven thinks those . . . horses . . . are better looking than I. Better in all ways than I. Steadfast, I am a Finest. Not a common horse. I am better than those norikers and . . .*

No, you are not. You are not any better, Gallant-Stallion. You are merely different. Those horses, they are loyal. They work hard and do everything they should. But unlike us, they are not aware of the past and the future. They live only for the moment, and as a result they cannot have any significant impact on people or the world.

But they seem so simple compared to us, Steadfast.

We are no better than they. And you have no cause to be arrogant. It is true they do not have our intellects, or our cares or our responsibilities. Some of them toil for people, like the norikers. But some are wild and run where they want, living unfettered. You think they are simple creatures. But they can enjoy Paard-Peran in ways we can never.

GALLANT-STALLION HAD LOOKED AT THE NORIKERS BEFORE, but now he truly *looked* at them. Beautiful animals, they had a form more graceful and regal than his own, but were not so powerfully built. He could communicate with them if he desired; as one of the Finest he understood all the languages of Paard-Peran. But theirs was a crude language, snorts and wuffles that meant food or danger or other base concepts. Now they seemed to be wanting water and rest. They had been carrying these men for more than nine hours now. It was normal for men to stop and eat, but these men had paused only long enough to dig through satchels for food—for themselves, which they ate while they continued on their way.

The horses had had but a few minutes to eat the coarse grass that grew on the side of the road, and to drink from the puddles. The men had not been so kind as to take them to the river's edge where they could drink their fill. The men were too busy, in too much of a hurry. There had been a couple of other brief pauses, as some of the men went into the trees to relieve themselves, then quickly returned. And there had been talk from the grooms at the back of the party about stopping. But the grooms had been keeping their voices low, and Gallant-Stallion knew the Prince could not hear them.

Several minutes later, however, someone grew bolder.

"The horses are getting tired, Prince." This came from one of the soldiers who rode ahead of Prince Edan and Meven. "We should give them a rest. We have been pushing them too hard."

"Time is short and valuable." Edan shook his head and scratched the glavian's neck. "Nightsong is managing just fine. As is the punch. Oh . . ."

Suddenly the punch wasn't doing fine. The big horse snorted and shook his head, spittle flying in an arc. He slowed, despite Meven urgently nudging him in the sides.

"Cousin Meven, I think I have been pushing everyone too hard."

"Sir . . ." The lead soldier had whirled his horse around and was coming toward the Prince. "The village Hathi is only a few miles ahead. We could stop there for the night."

Prince Edan nodded. "Rest the horses and ourselves. Take a bath." He looked at the back of his hands, smudged with dirt. "Take us to Hathi, then."

"Thank the gods," Meven said in a hush. "I am so stiff."
The lead soldier returned to the front of the procession.
The punch stopped snorting.

YOU ARE CLEVER, GALLANT-STALLION, STEADFAST SAID. *THE horses and the people will get an earlier rest this day.*

And I will get something to drink, Gallant-Stallion returned. *As you say, Steadfast, I am no better than the norikers and pack horses. And I find I have something in common with them.*

Steadfast brightened at the notion that his young protégé had learned something. *And what is that commonality, Gallant-Stallion?*

Like all the creatures in this cortege, I am terribly, terribly thirsty.

4 · Hathi

The world of people is one of hierarchies and confusion. The poor are the most numerous and have the least power, the rich are the fewest and hold sway. The poor and the rich consider themselves vastly different, one from the other. It is good the Finest have keen enough vision to realize that the poor and the rich are the same creatures.

~*Gray Hawthorn, Finest Court Patriarch*

The setting sun painted the thatched rooftops of Hathi a molten yellow. It was the only thing bright about the village, which consisted of roughly three dozen small buildings, nearly all of them made of wood and practically the same color as the damp earth that spread out between them. The few buildings that were stone were a dismal gray, and they were squat, looking like tortoise shells cut here and there by a window or cloth-covered doorway. All the dull hues ran together, making the village look poorer than it likely was, and seem beaten-down though everything was reasonably kept up.

There was a simple livestock pen, and it held a half-dozen milk cows and a few sheep. From the sounds the animals made, Gallant-Stallion could tell they were content and well cared for. A smaller pen farther away was filled with mud-speckled chickens, all of them plump to attest that they were fed plenty. To the east were two narrow farm fields that had been turned for planting, the rows filled with water. And to the west, be-hind one of the homes and so not easy to spot, were frames where deerskins were being stretched.

The people wore the colors of the village—tunics and trousers of browns and grays, and a few shirts that years past were white, but were now a dingy, dark yellow. Their clothes for the most part were in good repair and clean, but there were obvious off-colored patches and shiny spots where the fabric was wearing thin. There was only a smattering of people milling about when the procession came into the village. But within a few minutes the entire village turned out.

The people were chattering, the buzz at first sounding like a swarm of insects to Gallant-Stallion. He focused his senses to cut through it all.

"Is it the King? The King must be with them fancy people."

"The soldiers are wearing the King's colors. And look at the horses."

"Not the King. I seen the King once some years back. No one's old enough there to be the King."

"His son, then. See the fancy, fancy man on the big black horse. That must be Prince Edan Montoll. I'll wager three hens that's the Prince."

"How beautiful they all look!"

"Maybe they'll stay awhile. Wag their tongues an' tell us all the news of the kingdom."

Most of the words were favorable and the voices filled with couched excitement and awe. But there were ill-meant things, too.

"He's come to tax us. Bleed us dry."

"Come to take our land, he has. Come to take everything we got."

"Look at them all so rich and mighty paradin' among us."

"I spit on 'em, I do."

Fortunately, Gallant-Stallion could tell that the latter were in the minority, and those speakers were quickly hushed by others. The Finest let his other senses come into play. There was the damp smell that permeated much of Galmier this time of year, and there was a trace of fetidness from the fields—the old crops rotted and turned under, fertilizing the rich soil. He could smell something delightful he couldn't at first put a name to.

Bread baking, Steadfast told him.

Gallant-Stallion memorized the scent and breathed it deep, let it lie on his tongue. Somewhere there were flowers—lilacs, he thought. Perhaps there was a vase of them in one of the homes, a gift to the woman who lived there. He couldn't see any flowers amid all the drabness. Maybe there were lilac bushes behind the homes. And there was the strong scent of the cows and sheep and the dung that had been left in the pen. The people had a scent too, much different than the smell of the soldiers, Prince Edan, and the others. It reminded him a little of the odor of the damp earth, but it was mixed with the ripeness of sweat and hinted to him that these people did not have the opportunity to bathe as often as those in the royal procession.

Some of their faces were streaked with dirt, particularly the smallest among them. And it was the small ones that were the most excited about their royal visitors. Questions and dreams tumbled from their lips.

"I will be a King's soldier someday," one wide-eyed child vowed. He was stroking a small, dirty mongrel. "I will look as fine as that!"

"I will ride a horse like that one!" A little girl was pointing at Steadfast. "There is no more beautiful horse in all the world than that one."

"Why are they here?" This was a question repeated by several of the youngsters, and even a few adults.

No one answered that question.

The norikers were 'talking' too, wuffling their pleasure at stopping, smelling water lying in the fields and smelling the fresh river nearby. The grass was tall and inviting near the riverbank, and they nickered their desire for it. Gallant-Stallion saw only two horses in the village, at the far end tethered under a big lean-to that served as a stable. Horses were not common to poor people, he knew, and so this village must have been doing well if it had them to help with the fields.

At the back of the procession, he heard the Prince's attendant whispering to the scribe. The two felt sorry for the villagers living under these conditions. "Poor" was repeated so many times Gallant-Stallion lost count. The attendant and scribe were spoiled by palace life, the young Finest thought. As a whole, the people of Hathi were obviously not sorry for themselves. They appeared healthy, and most of them were cheerful, and they had manners enough to keep a respectable distance from the mounted cortege that ran down the middle of their village.

The lead soldier dismounted and stiffly walked back to the Prince. He kept his voice low. "I will secure us lodging for the night and have them put your father's horse into what amounts to their stable. The horses can be watered, graze and . . ."

A slight gesture from the Prince cut him off. Edan spoke in a conspiratorial whisper. "There is no inn."

"Of course not, sir." The soldier shook his head. "Hathi is a small village, but the people will take us in. I've been through here before and . . ."

"I'd rather sleep in the muddy field than in one of those rat-infested hovels."

"Yes, Prince Edan."

"Ask them how far to the next village."

"No need. I know this part of Galmier well. The next village would be Cote d'lande, Prince Edan. It is quite a bit larger, but it is more than a dozen miles down this road."

Gallant-Stallion sensed the puzzlement of the young man on

his back. Meven seemed surprised the Prince didn't know much about the villages in his own country, and he felt disappointed that Edan didn't want to stop here. Meven nervously rubbed his thumbs across the reins as he looked back and forth between Edan and the villagers.

"Is there an inn?"

"In Cote d'lande? Yes, Prince Edan. As fine as the one in Bitternut. But it is getting late, and it looks like it could rain at any moment and . . ."

"Then we'd best start on our way to Cote d'lande immediately."

While the muted conversation continued, the villagers grew anxious.

"Why won't they speak to us?" an elderly woman wondered.

"What are they talking about?"

"Are they off to war? There's so many of them."

"That's not an army." This came from the man who claimed to have seen the King. "There's not near enough of them for it to be an army."

"Aren't we stopping here?" Meven asked Prince Edan a little too loudly.

The Prince narrowed his eyes and whispered back: "I reek, cousin. I want a warm bath, a good meal, and a soft bed tonight."

"It will be well past dark before we would reach Cote d'lande," the soldier offered.

"Then we'd best be on our way." Edan straightened in the saddle and raised his voice to address the villagers. "Good folks of Hathi. I am Prince Edan Montoll and I am bound for Duriam to wed Princess Silverwood of Nasim-Guri. The union will make our countries stronger. Give us your blessings, good folks."

"Meven . . ."

Meven turned in his saddle so he could see Kalantha. It was the first word she'd spoken in a few hours.

"Meven . . . why can't we stay here? I'm tired of riding this pony. And I'm hungry. I smell bread."

Meven shook his head and drew a finger to his lips.

"I'm really hungry."

The Prince turned in his saddle too, and he scowled at Kalantha, lines of consternation etched on his brow. Then he waved to the people on each side of the road. "Perhaps I shall bring my bride through your fine village on my return trip home," he suggested. Then he motioned for the soldiers to move.

Applause and good wishes filled the air, and the village leader stepped forward and thanked the Prince for taking the road through Hathi on his way to the wedding.

The boy with the small, dirty mongrel frowned. "I wish they would stay awhile. I would like to talk to the soldiers."

Kalantha mouthed to her brother: *I'm hungry, Meven.*

Moments later, Hathi was behind the royal procession, and the horses were loudly wuffling their displeasure at not tasting the sweet-smelling river water that was so close or sampling the lush-looking grass that surely would be delicious. The sky was growing darker, from the lateness of the day and the deepening bank of gray clouds.

STEADFAST, IF IT IS THE PRINCE I AM TO SHEPHERD, MY TASK is formidable.

The ink-black horse said nothing.

The Prince is too concerned about wealth and appearance, and he does not care much about others of his kind. His manners are lacking. He is very discourteous. Those villagers would have put him up for the evening. Or perhaps I should say would have put up with him.

Gallant-Stallion waited, but Steadfast remained quiet. The

elder Finest had his ears trained forward and appeared to pointedly ignore his companion.

The Prince was disgusted by that village, Steadfast. I could sense his attitude before he uttered a word. And he breathed so shallowly while we were there . . . like he was afraid to pull the villagers' air into his lungs. Like he was afraid of catching something. Those people were hardworking. I would say that deep down those villagers are no different than the Prince. The Finest Court teaches us that. But there is a difference, Steadfast. The villagers are gracious where the Prince is rude.

The road narrowed beyond Hathi's fields and angled more to the west. Its course was closer to the mountains now, and so the land was darker still, as the peaks were cutting the last of the sunlight. The shadows were quickly claiming the land, and a soft rain started.

Kalantha reached behind her and tugged her cloak free from a pack. She wrapped it around her and put the hood over her head.

The Prince simply lacks compassion, Steadfast finally said. After a moment, he added: *For those considered beneath his station, it seems. However, he holds his father in high regard, and he has good feelings toward his cousins.*

They were moving at a good pace, despite being spent and hungry and thirsty. The rain was coming a little harder. The clouds covered the last rays of the sunset and gave everything a dull gray cast. The rain felt good to Gallant-Stallion, though it was cool. However, the nickering of the soldiers' horses behind him revealed they wanted to be where it was dry and where there would be no men and packages upon their backs for a while. Too, the horses continued to wuffle about their thirst and hunger, their hooves dragging in the mud as they went.

Gallant-Stallion gave a heavy snort and tried to shut out all the complaints. *It is the Prince for me, isn't it, Steadfast? That arrogant man is to be my charge. He certainly needs a shep-*

herd. He needs someone to guide him down the path of righteousness and courtesy and . . .

Patience, was Steadfast's reply. *Patience, Gallant-Stallion.*

THERE WERE ONLY A FEW PATCHES OF SKY THAT SHOWED BEtween the clouds, and these were turning the pale purple-blue of twilight. The stars would be coming out soon, the two Finest knew, and the wedding party was getting closer to Cote d'lande.

Gallant-Stallion and Steadfast were listening to the conversation of Meven and Prince Edan now. The cousins were speculating again about what curious-looking animal the Princess would resemble and how good a warm bath would feel followed by a hearty meal and soft bed. How good it would be to smell something other than sweat and mud and the air filled with the threat of rain.

The Finest were smelling the sweet clover that grew in profusion to the east, and listening now to the river that was growing wider and moving faster the farther south they traveled. The river made more pleasant sounds at the moment than the two young men, who continued to compare the Princess to all manner of animals.

At length a different noise intruded, steady and muffled, a soft thundering like a herd of distant horses pounding across the ground. It was a few minutes before the men heard it too, and before Prince Edan straightened in his saddle, trying to spot the charging herd. But the shadows hid the approaching horses.

The lead soldier called for everyone to stop, else they blunder into the path of the herd.

The horses nickered nervously, and Steadfast made a low neighing sound in an attempt to calm them.

HOW MANY HORSES? GALLANT-STALLION ASKED. AND WHY are they running? What has frightened them?

Perhaps they are merely running for joy, Steadfast returned. *Trying to out-race the storm. I tried that once, a long time ago, with a daring astrologer on my back.*

How many, I wonder. It sounds like a lot, but it is too dark to catch sight of them. Maybe they are on the other side of the hills. Maybe . . .

THE SHADOWS TO THE WEST DIVIDED, TAKING ON LIFE AND seeming to flap like a cape blown loose in a strong wind. There was a sudden flash of lightning, showing that the wave of black was a force of dark men on dark horses rushing toward the Prince's procession. Dark cloaks fluttered against the dismal, deepening sky and competed with the sound of racing hoofbeats.

"Move!" The lead soldier raised his arm and pointed forward. Then he dug his heels into his horse's sides. None of the horses needed such encouragement, however, as they were all bent on escaping the approaching army.

"Death!" came a strangled cry from somewhere in the mysterious charging forms. "Death comes!"

5 · Shadow Slayers

The father of the gods bequeathed his life to create the world, pulling out his own heart, naming it Paard-Peran, and setting it to float in the heavens. His son and daughter mourned his passing, their flood of tears becoming the oceans and seas and rivers, and their grief and memories taking physical form to populate the world as animals and men and women.

~*The Old Mare, from the Finest Court canon*

*S*teadfast! *An army rides on us! We are attacked!* Panicked, Gallant-Stallion shouted the obvious to his companion. *Assassins! What should we do?* The young Finest had not expected trouble, not with Steadfast beside him and fifty armed soldiers on war-horses. This was to be a wedding party, he thought, but the wave of strangers fast approaching could surely turn it into a funeral procession. There was no mistaking the mysterious men's intentions. They were bent on slaying Prince Edan and all of the rest. *Steadfast! What are we to do?*

Steadfast didn't answer, as the veteran Finest was also caught off guard. He glanced at Gallant-Stallion, then tossed his head this way and that, trying to take everything in.

Steadfast, where did these men come from? Gallant-Stallion was trying to quickly absorb everything, too. He knew there had been no hint of trouble, and he'd thought the thundering horses merely a wild herd on the run, likely frightened by lightning that had touched down. He had not expected an enemy army, and he knew Steadfast hadn't anticipated one either. And just where had this army come from?

Was there a spy in the village of Hathi? Gallant-Stallion did not remember anyone looking suspicious or seeming out of place. Had the assassins been hiding in the homes? If the Prince had stopped in Hathi, would the assassins have ambushed the wedding party as it settled in for the night?

And when the Prince ordered his entourage to instead continue, had the assassins silently left the village, following and waiting for evening to fully descend?

Right before the attack there'd been nothing unusual in the growing breeze and the cool rain, no distant whispers from the dark men who were now racing toward them. The attackers must have done something to cover their scent, as even though they were coming closer, Gallant-Stallion still could not smell them. There was only the damp mustiness of the ground, the fresh scent of the rain, and the smell of the horses and the people he'd been riding with for hours and hours.

For one brief instant Gallant-Stallion considered that since he couldn't smell them, perhaps they were not really there. Perhaps they were some ephemeral dream given life because all the people and all the creatures in this wedding party were so very tired and thirsty. The assassins were merely shadows in the storm that were playing tricks on his weary eyes.

But they had a sound to them, the soft pounding of hooves as they closed the distance, the flap of cloaks. Thunderous noise, but not the sound of thunder. They did not speak, not beyond those first words: "Death! Death comes!" Who was directing them? They must be real! So where in the mass was the lead assassin?

Steadfast . . . what am I to do?

LIKE INK SPILLED FROM A BOTTLE, THE MYSTERIOUS ARMY spread out from the shadows of the mountains to the west and now from the trees to the east. They were moving to surround the wedding party. The night continued to hide their details, even from the keen senses of Steadfast and Gallant-Stallion. All the two Finest could see were the black forms of men, so vague it was impossible to tell how large they were, or how old, if they were armored, and if they wore faces they'd seen in Hathi. There could be women in the mix, as all of them were cloaked in black garments as dark as their horses. Coal-dark slashes raised into the twilight sky above them were likely swords coated with weapon black to keep the blades from gleaming in the scant remaining light.

The wind abruptly picked up and the rain fell harder, and the air was filled now with the flapping of the assassins' cloaks and the soldiers' tabards. Lightning flashed again and again, and the ground rocked with thunder. The silver beads in Steadfast's mane clacked furiously, and Gallant-Stallion's coarse mane whipped into his eyes.

At last Steadfast spoke: *Gallant-Stallion, we must run!*

There seemed to be more than one hundred assassins, Steadfast guessed. Too many for the King's soldiers to handle. But the darkness hid the foe's exact numbers and so there could have been twice that many. The veteran Finest was overwhelmed for only a heartbeat more, cursing himself for not anticipating the danger and for being too old to act instantly once that danger appeared. Then he leapt into action and shot toward the east.

Gallant-Stallion, I must protect Prince Edan, he shouted. *I must get him to safety, then return to help the rest. Flee with the Prince's cousins!*

~   ~   ~

No, Nightsong! We stay with the soldiers!" This came from the Prince, who pulled back hard on the reins with one hand, and with the other drew an ornamental dagger from a sheath at his side. He began slashing at the air in an attempt to keep the attackers at bay. "Stay close to the others, Nightsong! Don't run! We stand our ground with my father's soldiers! We fight!"

But Steadfast ignored the Prince. The baffling enemy had taken all of them by surprise and was far too numerous to contend with. Soldiers were going to die, and the elder Finest didn't want the Prince dying with them. He reared back, and the Prince was forced to throw his efforts into staying on and keeping hold of the dagger. Hooves flailing out at the wall of closing assassins, Steadfast managed to push one assailant back, then another. He charged forward, intent on finding a gap in the press of murderous bodies and getting the Prince a safe distance away.

The lightning flashed again and again, showing dozens of the mysterious black men and horses. Thunder rocked the land, and the rain pounded down harder.

Save them, Gallant-Stallion! As I will save Edan! Steadfast shouted with his mind as he galloped away. *Be fleet of hoof and save the Prince's cousins! We will find each other when the threat is passed!*

"Nightsong! We stay with the soldiers!" the Prince bellowed. "Nightsong, stop! Don't run!"

~ ~ ~

Gallant-Stallion could tell that "Nightsong" wasn't stopping, and so he whirled to also escape, nearly unseating Meven, who was calling for his sister. The boy couldn't see her through the dark chaos, but Gallant-Stallion could. The pony Kalantha was riding spooked and tossed her to the ground, then fled into the midst of the black-cloaked attackers.

Gallant-Stallion glanced between a narrow break in the press of bodies and the fallen girl. He could get the boy away now and be certain to save one of the cousins. But Steadfast told him to get both cousins away. He could get the boy cleanly away, if he . . .

By the Creators! Gallant-Stallion cried. Before he could act, the gap he'd spied closed, and the swarm of assassins moved closer still.

"Kal! Kal!" Meven's hands were clenched so tight on the reins that his fingers were growing numb. He was looking frantically for his sister, and though she was only a few yards away, he still couldn't see her. There was only the shifting wave of blackness and the pounding of the enemy horses' hooves.

Other sounds filled the night: the shush of steel being drawn as the King's soldiers met the assassins' charge; the whistling the soldiers' blades made as they sliced through the air and at the attackers; the bark of the lead soldier ordering some of his men to fight and ordering others to fall back and find the Prince; the alarmed cries from the grooms; the frightened whinnies of the packhorses; and finally the voice of Kalantha, so hard to separate from everything else.

"Meven! Edan!" she cried. "Meven! Meven!" Terrified, her words came so fast they sounded like a hornet's buzz. "Meeeeeeven!"

Save both the cousins. Gallant-Stallion surged forward, reaching down with his head and snapping his teeth shut on the back of her rain-drenched tunic. The muscles in his neck straining, he picked her up off the ground just before she would have been trampled by a fleeing packhorse, and he flung her to the side where Meven could reach her. Meven dropped the reins and clamped his legs tight to stay on. He flailed out for her, grabbing her and pulling her close and settling her in front of him. Then he reached around her for the reins just as Gallant-Stallion spotted another break and bolted past one of the assassins. Fast as the wind, he galloped in the direction of the foothills, assassins trying to swarm him as he went.

It doesn't feel right, Gallant-Stallion thought as he ran. *I have heard stories of foul-tempered men who steal and kill. And I have heard about men making war on each other. I thought it would smell different, sound different, and be different. This doesn't feel right. I don't smell . . . men.*

But Gallant-Stallion didn't have time to study the assassins; he needed to escape them. The young Finest sped through blackest black, trusting that he was heading west, where the Galmier Mountains stretched. The enemy had become an inky hallway he cut through. In an instant their billowing cloaks were not just whipping at his sides, they were flowing above him and cutting out the rain and the few patches of twilight sky. He couldn't see the storm's lightning for their cloaks, but he heard the subsequent thunder, the vibrations racing through the ground and into his feet. The wind picked up to blow the cloaks away, battering him and painfully sending rain into his eyes. The air felt close and heavy and oddly musty, and his tongue grew thick in his parched mouth. His lungs burned from his efforts. Effectively blind, Gallant-Stallion was forced to rely on his other senses to guide him. He tried to thrust the tremulous voices of Meven and Kalantha to the back of his mind.

Meven rammed his heels against Gallant-Stallion's sides, demanding he go faster and take Kalantha and him from this chaos. Kalantha clung to the Finest's neck, fingers digging in and face pressed so close that Gallant-Stallion could feel her warm, ragged breath.

Steadfast! Gallant-Stallion shouted. *Where are you?* He expected an answer, as he was certain the elder Finest could also separate the sounds and hear him, and could not be too far away. Gallant-Stallion continued his charge and listened hard for Steadfast's reply. He wanted to hear that Edan and Steadfast were all right. He suspected that Edan was to be his charge, and he didn't want to lose him and fail his assignment from the Finest Court before his work had begun. *Steadfast! Can you hear me?*

All the horses were 'talking,' the neighs, whinnies, and snorts all filled with dread and uncertainty. The packhorses especially were terrified; they were screaming in pain and fear and calling for help. The norikers, however, were bred for the possibility of war and their fear was controlled and laced with excitement.

Gallant-Stallion heard the soldiers shouting. One voice giving orders, others cursing at the enemy, some calling out for Prince Edan, one yelling that he and his horse were badly wounded. Gallant-Stallion thought he heard Prince Edan shouting for Steadfast to stop.

The pounding of the assassins' horses' hooves continued, markedly distinct from the hoof-sounds of the norikers. It indicated to Gallant-Stallion that the assassins rode a far different breed. The pounding filled the air all around the Finest and threatened to drown out his superb senses.

He barely heard a thump to his left, a horse going down. It was followed by another, and the strangled cry of a soldier who was pinned by his horse. The rain hammered even harder, a *rat-a-tat-tat* that added to the cacophony. Gallant-Stallion heard something else that he couldn't identify, and at that moment he also sensed something he couldn't explain that sent a shiver down his back. It was a presence, palpable and evil, and it chilled him to the bone.

Steadfast! Where are you? Steadfast, answer me! Gallant-Stallion knew only the elder Finest would be able to hear him. His desperate words in hidden speak were lost on all the soldiers and assassins. *Steadfast!*

"Meven, I'm scared. What's happening?" Kalantha was yelling to be heard over the ruckus. Her voice was shrill and almost painful to Gallant-Stallion, who was straining hard to hear the elder Finest. "Meven, where's Edan? Meven!"

"It'll be all right, Kal." Meven spoke loudly, and though there was a tremor in his voice he tried to sound confident. "I'll take care of you. We'll get out of here and find Edan." Again he ground his heels into Gallant-Stallion's sides. "C'mon," he told Gallant-Stallion, not really believing the horse could understand him. "Get us out of here! Hurry!"

There was an agonizing scream, and Gallant-Stallion recognized it as the voice of one of the grooms. It was followed by another scream and another, these voices he didn't recognize and so guessed they were from the soldiers who were dying— or hopefully the assassins.

"Death comes," a rasping voice said, so close to Gallant-Stallion it sounded as if the speaker was just behind him. "Death death death comes!"

The words were repeated by the other attackers, becoming a haunting chorus that rose to a near-deafening pitch: "Death comes. Death comes. Death comes." There was another word, or perhaps part of a song. "Fala." Repeated over and over like the summer drone of cicadas, it sounded: "Falafalafalafalafalafala." The slurred word mixed with the shouts and the screams, the boom of thunder, and the interspersed cries of "Death comes!"

The presence he felt rushed closer, and the evil somehow intensified. Gallant-Stallion galloped faster, putting distance between himself and . . . what? The lead assassin? Was that the evil he felt? Faster and . . . suddenly he couldn't detect the evil presence any longer. Perhaps he'd outrun it.

Kalantha's heart was hammering so wildly Gallant-Stallion could feel it against the back of his neck, and the sweat from her fear and the scent of the blood all around him stung his nostrils. His hooves continued to tear up the muddy ground, just as Meven continued to drive his heels into Gallant-Stallion's sides.

"Hurry!" Meven shouted.

All at once a sharper pain intruded. One of the attackers had caught up and slashed Gallant-Stallion's back. Another slashed at his legs. Someone hiding in the blackness in front of him sliced his chest. Meven must have been struck too, as the young man yelped and shifted back in the saddle, pulling Kalantha with him and almost toppling them.

Gallant-Stallion slowed for just a moment so Meven could regain his balance. "Are you all right, Kal?" Meven asked his sister. "Kal!"

"Fine," she mumbled. "So scared. Meven, are we gonna die?" A moment more: "Meven? Are you hurt?"

"I'm hurt a little. But it's not bad." Again Meven assured her they would be all right, that the big ugly horse was taking them away from the mysterious attackers. It was a gang of assassins from Nasim-Guri, he told her. "A band of killers hired to keep the Prince from marrying the Princess."

Gallant-Stallion thought that might well be the case. They were not terribly far from the Nasim-Guri border, and he'd listened to the Prince and Meven's discussion about the marriage being politically motivated. Cruel politics might well have provoked this attack. Someone who did not want the countries joined.

Steadfast! Gallant-Stallion tried one last time. *Where are you?*

At last came a response, but not what he was looking for: *Save the cousins! Flee while you still have breath!*

Gallant-Stallion was trying to do just that. *Steadfast, where are you?* He tossed his head to the side, trying to see behind him. He saw nothing but the blackness of the enemies' cloaks and horses. Faintly, and in the distance, he thought he saw a pair of shiny, cold eyes. It was a fleeting glimpse that made his massive frame shudder. But then the eyes were gone and there was only the utter darkness and the constant thundering of hooves and the pounding rain. He realized Steadfast was likely too far away to hear him, especially over the chaos. Besides, how could Steadfast know where he was in this blackness? Gallant-Stallion wasn't certain where he was himself.

He wondered if he might be running in circles, as there seemed to be no end to the dark and no let-up in the sound of hooves and men screaming, and in the howl of the incessant, buffeting wind. And through it all came the assassins' dirge: "Falafalafalafala. Death comes. Death comes!"

Gallant-Stallion was struck again in the side, a thin blade it felt like, cutting long, but not deep. He knew Meven was hit again as well. The boy tried unsuccessfully to swallow a cry of pain. He hunched protectively around his sister and dropped the reins, and he stopped jabbing Gallant-Stallion with his heels.

Maybe the young man was seriously hurt this time, Gallant-Stallion thought.

Keep them safe, he thought he heard Steadfast call once more. It was a whisper, because of the distance or because it was muffled by the press of bodies. Or perhaps he'd imagined it. *Keep them safe, young one.* No! Not imagined. It was Steadfast's voice he dreamed hearing. *Gallant-Stallion, keep your . . .*

Where was Steadfast? Behind him, certainly. In the midst of the attackers? Beyond them and headed east toward the safety of the trees and the Sprawling River? Steadfast's voice sounded so very distant, and at the end he couldn't hear it at all. Neither could Gallant-Stallion smell the elder Finest. The odors of sweat and fear and blood from all around him were too overpowering.

He redoubled his efforts to plow through the dark army. And after what seemed like forever, he was rewarded when he burst out onto open ground. He blinked furiously to make sure he really saw the mountains straight ahead of him, the foothills so achingly close. The night sky was overcast, but there were a few clear, dark blue patches here and there between the clouds. The wind had slowed considerably away from the throng of assassins, but the rain continued. For just an instant, as he kept on running, he tipped his head up and let the blessed rain spatter into his mouth.

"I can see!" Kalantha said. "Meven? Meven!"

Gallant-Stallion felt Meven twist in the saddle, and he cast his own head back, too. Lightning arced down. Free of the wall of black created by the gang of attackers, the Finest finally could get a look at what was going on back there. He saw a cloud of shifting shadows that circled around where the wedding party was, the assassins effectively corralling the Prince's wedding procession. When lightning flashed again, Gallant-Stallion could make out the vague figures of the dark men on horses, but again everything was too indistinct to reveal details that might identify them or tell precisely how many were in their ranks.

The assassins' horses looked different, Gallant-Stallion decided. They looked like horses, but their legs appeared thicker than normal, or in some cases thinner. The necks overly long or short. They weren't like the common horses the Finest had been around, and certainly not like the norikers, which were fairly uniform in appearance. The assassins' horses didn't seem right, Gallant-Stallion thought. They were unsettling. Again, he shuddered.

What if those horses and the assassins were *truly* different? The Creators were responsible for the Finest. Were there other supernatural creatures? Gallant-Stallion had heard tales that there could be. The attackers didn't feel *right* to him—even though there was nothing right to begin with about attacking the Prince and his people.

No time to puzzle it all out, Gallant-Stallion decided. And certainly not worth the risk to return to the battle for a closer look. Such curiosity could prove fatal to him and the cousins.

The lightning came again and again. Some of the wedding procession horses were scattering—norikers who'd lost their riders, a few of the pack animals, one of them limping terribly. A lump at the edge of the assassin band was a fallen noriker. Smaller lumps were downed men—soldiers or assassins or grooms, Gallant-Stallion wasn't going to stay around to determine which. Had others tried to break from the procession when the assassins came? Soldiers and attendants? Some of the Bishop's men? Had others successfully escaped?

Get the cousins to safety, he remembered Steadfast telling him.

He craned his neck back to the west and lengthened his strides. He was going remarkably fast for a creature of his build. His short legs were tremendously powerful, and they churned up the earth as he went. The foothills, he decided. He'd leave Meven and Kalantha somewhere in the foothills then double back and find Steadfast and the Prince. The hills were swathed in shadows, but they were not so dark as the swirling band of attackers, and so Gallant-Stallion could make out a narrow path that ran between two hills. He headed toward it.

Within a few heartbeats he was running down the path, the shadows of the mountains swallowing them. He could still hear the battle behind him, the clinking of swords, the moans of the dying, horse hooves hammering against the ground, the shouts of the King's soldiers, the angry rumble of the storm's thunder. Since some soldiers yet lived, there could be hope,

Gallant-Stallion thought. The soldiers must be formidable to have lasted so long anyway. Maybe they could drive the assassins away.

Hide the cousins, then return for Steadfast, he repeated. He slowed his pace out of necessity, as the path narrowed and turned, and there were ruts and rocks everywhere. The passage widened for a dozen yards and climbed, then became so thin he could barely fit through it. After a few more turns, the path headed straight west and was climbing higher into the mountains. Flashes of lightning helped illuminate his way.

Meven had taken the reins again and was tugging hard on them. "Horse, stop," he demanded. He tugged hard again and Gallant-Stallion complied.

There was a crevice to their right, and that was what had drawn Meven's attention. The young man slipped from the saddle, groaning slightly from his injuries. He helped Kalantha down and pointed her toward the crevice. Then he tugged on the reins to get Gallant-Stallion to follow them. The Finest had every intention of returning to the site of the battle, but he would make sure Meven and Kalantha were safe first.

"Meven, those terrible men . . ."

"They're far away," he told her.

"You're hurt and . . ."

He shook his head. "I'm not hurt bad. Honest. I'm going to be fine."

Gallant-Stallion could see the slashes across Meven's left arm and leg and could smell the blood. Kalantha couldn't possibly see just how many slices her brother had. But none of the cuts were deep, as were none of the ones on Gallant-Stallion. Meven would indeed be fine. The Finest suspected the assassins were also hampered by the darkness and so were swinging their thin blades imprecisely—fortunately for Meven and Gallant-Stallion.

And hopefully fortunately for some of the others, Gallant-Stallion thought. *Steadfast!* he hollered, knowing that as keen as the elder Finest's hearing was, he was likely well out of earshot.

"Do we have to go in there?" Kalantha hesitated outside the crevice. She couldn't see inside it, and the blackness made her shiver.

Gallant-Stallion could smell an old staleness. The crevice had served as the home to some animal. A large cat of some kind, probably. But the animal was long gone and there was no trace of anything recent.

"We have to hide, Kal," Meven urged. "In case they come looking for us."

"They're not going to want us," she argued. Kalantha crossed her arms around her chest and shivered from fear and the cold. She'd lost her cloak somewhere along the way. The rain was cool, and the wind, which found its way down this path, was adding to the chill. "You know they were after Edan. He's the Prince and is important. Maybe they thought the King was with us, and it was the King they were really after. They wouldn't want common people like us." She paused. "Do you think Edan got away?"

"I'm sure he . . . I don't know, Kal." Meven decided not to lie to her. "I couldn't see anything. Just get inside. It's dry in there. And no one will see us. We'll be safe."

She finally relented, and he followed. Gallant-Stallion saw them disappear. He was too wide and too tall to fit, and so he backed away. And when he heard Meven softly chattering to her, the Finest quietly retraced his steps. He stopped when he reached the spot where the foothills ended and the stretch of open ground began.

A great display of lightning showed that the assassins were still there, but there didn't seem to be as many of them. At first Gallant-Stallion thought quite a number of them had been killed, and he made a move to rejoin the remaining soldiers and help them fight. But he stopped with the next flash of lightning. It revealed that while indeed there were fewer attackers around the remaining soldiers, the rest had scattered. Black riders were spreading out in all directions, with several coming straight toward the foothills.

They were methodical in their movements, and so he got the idea they were searching for something. The Prince? Steadfast must have gotten him to safety. But where?

Despite the lightning, Gallant-Stallion couldn't see as far as the trees to the east. And he still couldn't make out any details about the attackers. He stepped deeper onto the path in the foothills, fearful that the lightning might also reveal him. He wouldn't search for Steadfast, he decided, not at the moment, not while there were assassins about. Some were definitely coming in this direction, and he needed to make sure Meven and Kalantha were protected.

So he quickly returned to the crevice and waited. Gallant-Stallion shut out Meven's voice. He was still reassuring his sister that they were safe. And the Finest shut out the wind that whistled down the passage in the hills and each boom of thunder that followed the lightning flashes. He concentrated on everything else. Faintly, he heard a whisper: "Death comes!" Faintly he heard the pounding of hooves. And after an hour or more had past, there was nothing more.

6 · The Aftermath

The violence people inflict on one another is at the same time terrible and inconsequential. Terrible in the pain and suffering that results. But inconsequential in the fact that the world goes on nevertheless. Unlike people, the Finest are incapable of warring against one another.

~Patience, Matriarch, from the Finest Court canon

Meven and Kalantha were sleeping, and the storm was finally abating. Gallant-Stallion thought about slipping back to the scene of the attack, curious whether the assassins and soldiers were still fighting and if he might be able to help. He wanted desperately to know more about the assassins and to figure out what wasn't *right* about them. But above all of that, he felt an obligation to protect Prince Edan's cousins, and he worried that if he left them, even a lone assassin might arrive and slay them.

He wondered if the Prince's wedding party—those who had survived the onslaught—had traveled on to the next village. Was anyone looking for the cousins? Was Steadfast looking for him?

Steadfast! he called.

No answer.

Once more he considered retracing his steps. He was so uncertain what to do. *If Steadfast were in my position, he would know. I am too young, too inexperienced. The Finest Court should have chosen another shepherd. Where is Steadfast?* Gallant-Stallion snorted in frustration and repeatedly called for Steadfast in hidden speak. *Too far away to hear me. East by the river with Prince Edan, who is likely my charge.*

So he stood on guard outside the crevice for hours, unmoving and vigilant, legs stiff and aching from the wounds of last night, his mind worrying over the possibilities and pondering whether Steadfast was searching for him.

Meven crawled out of the crevice at dawn, rubbing at his eyes, grimacing and rolling his shoulders.

"C'mon, Kal," he said. Reaching back into the crevice, he tugged his sister out. The two were filthy, from the dirt inside of the crevice and from the mud and blood that had spattered them earlier. Nothing about them looked royal or the least bit civilized. Indeed, they resembled grubby, cast-off urchins with streaked faces and tangled hair.

"We've got to find Cousin Edan," Meven told her.

"I know." She shuffled toward Gallant-Stallion.

"I'm sure he's worried about us," Meven said as he helped her up. "Afraid we were killed by those horrid assassins or that we got lost."

"We are lost," she told him. She rubbed at the dirt on the back of her hand, only managing to spread it around. "And he's probably *not* worried, at least not about us. Meven, he might be our cousin, but we just met him. He's going to get married to a princess, and someday he's going to be King. He's got more important things on his mind than us. Simple, unimportant us." After a moment, she added: "But I am worried about Edan. I'm worried about Bishop DeNogaret's men, too. And the soldiers."

Meven opened his mouth to argue that Edan did indeed care about them, then thought better of it. With some effort, he got on behind her. Meven was stiff and sore, and despite managing to sleep a few hours, he was still tired. He grabbed up the reins, gave them a flick, and gently nudged Gallant-Stallion in the side. He had noticed the horse's cuts, and so was being careful. "Horse, we're going back to find our cousin."

"Wherever *back* is," Kalantha said. "We're lost."

"I'm not . . ." Lost, Meven was going to say. But again he kept from arguing, and he flicked the reins harder. Now wasn't the time to argue with his little sister.

"We're lost. And nobody will care that we're lost," she continued.

Gallant-Stallion let Meven direct him, as the boy wanted to go precisely where the Finest did. Gallant-Stallion took the path that led them here, finding only a trace of his hoofprints from the night before—the rain had washed most of the tracks away. He paused where the foothills ended and the open ground began. And he cautiously peaked out around a mound of earth—one last check to see if any attackers remained. There wasn't a hint of a single assassin, but the aftermath of last night's attack was evident on the open ground. The sight struck both the cousins and the Finest hard.

The early morning sky was lightly overcast, and a thin blanket of fog covered the ground, giving an eerie cast to the landscape. Two horses stood amid the carnage. Bodies of horses and men were strewn everywhere.

Gallant-Stallion moved closer. He walked slowly, ears forward and eyes darting everywhere. The silence was spooky, and so he focused on hearing *something*—anything. There was a slight breeze, and it ruffled the tabards of the fallen soldiers and rustled the leaves on the trees to the east. Beyond the trees was the river, and he could hear and smell the water. Close by, there was a pecking sound, which he couldn't place, and the wuffling of the two horses grazing ahead.

"Faster, horse," Meven said. Again, a gentle nudge. He shook the reins for emphasis.

"It looks bad, Meven. Real bad."

Meven glumly nodded. "I think everyone's dead, Kal."

"Maybe not. Maybe we'll find someone alive. We have to find Edan. I'm sure he got away. Maybe other people escaped, too . . . just like we did."

Gallant-Stallion plodded forward into the fog. The ground felt comfortably cool against his hooves, and had the circumstances been different, he would have allowed himself to enjoy the sensation. But the air was strong with the acrid scents of blood and death. And he looked down into the mist to see body after body of horses and soldiers. Everywhere skin was striped with narrow slashes and dotted with puncture wounds, proving that Gallant-Stallion had been correct: the assassins were using thin-bladed weapons.

"Maybe Edan's on his way to his wedding. Maybe he's sending some soldiers back here to . . . clean all of this up," Kalantha continued to chatter.

The pecking noise eluded Gallant-Stallion. It grew slightly louder the deeper he went into the fog. But he couldn't see what was making it.

"Maybe he's sending word to Bishop DeNogaret. The Bishop would worry—about you at least, Meven."

Finally the source of the pecking became clear to Gallant Stallion—birds. They were predominantly crows, and they were feasting on the dead. Most of the birds took flight when Gallant-Stallion neared them, but some were stubborn and warily continued to eat.

Meven was quietly counting the soldiers and the Bishop's men. Kalantha started calling out for Edan. Gallant-Stallion didn't call for Steadfast. He didn't have to. He saw the elder Finest at the edge of his vision. Steadfast was dead, tendrils of mist wrapping around his once sleek and muscular body.

Gallant-Stallion walked toward the elder Finest, careful not to step on any of the fallen men or trip on the dead horses as he went. He listened to Meven, still counting. Twenty, he was up to, of the King's soldiers. All eight of the Bishop's men were dead. Gallant-Stallion made his way beyond the greatest concentration of bodies to the two standing horses. Both of them made wuffling sounds; they seemed happy to see Meven and Kalantha; hopeful they would be given some direction. One was a packhorse from the High Keep Temple, the other was one a Bishop's man had ridden.

Gallant-Stallion wuffled back, asking the horses to stay there, hoping they understood. Then he was moving past them and through to where the greatest concentration of bodies lay, slowing as he approached Steadfast.

Forty of the King's soldiers, Meven counted.

Somehow Gallant-Stallion knew all fifty of the soldiers were dead, Meven just hadn't seen them all for the fog. The bodies of the grooms and the scribe and the Prince's attendant were there, too. And everywhere lay the bodies of the once-beautiful norikers.

"Edan!" Kalantha saw the Prince.

He was lying twisted near Steadfast, like a broken, discarded doll. He was covered with the thin slashes and puncture wounds—just like Steadfast was. Meven and Kalantha slipped from Gallant-Stallion's back and went to the Prince.

"Edan!" Kalantha shrieked again. "Meven, he's dead."

Meven didn't say anything. He just grabbed his belt, fingers flying across the wooden beads as a whispered prayer spilled from his trembling lips.

Kalantha was shivering as she knelt next to the body and tried to straighten it. She sobbed openly, the loudest sound on the field. Through a gap in the mist that blanketed the Prince, she saw his ornamental dagger, the blood on it showing that Edan had at least wounded an assassin before dying. She grabbed the pommel and tugged it free from Edan's fingers, clutched the dagger to her chest. Her shoulders shook from crying so hard.

Meven knelt next to her and draped an arm around her. The fingers of his free hand continued to flutter across the wooden beads. When he finished praying, he gently kneaded her shoulder.

"Kal, don't weep so. It's like you said, we really didn't know him." Instantly he regretted his callous words. She wasn't crying *just* for the Prince, he knew. She was crying for all the dead. Neither of them had seen a dead body before. And there was just so much death. The magnitude of it finally struck him and tears rolled down his face.

While the cousins wept over Prince Edan, Gallant-Stallion stared at Steadfast's body. *How could the elder Finest be dead? Strong and swift and incredibly wise, how could he be dead? More than one hundred and seventy years he had walked Paard-Peran. How could he be dead now? It wasn't possible. It could not be!*

Yet, it was. The inky body on the ground in front of him was riddled with so many slashes and punctures—killing Steadfast obviously hadn't been easy. There'd been too many assassins. Even the elder Finest couldn't find his way through all of them to reach safety. Gallant-Stallion realized just how lucky he and Meven and Kalantha and the few horses that had escaped were.

So thanks to fate, I live, Gallant-Stallion mused sadly. *Luck let us live*. He glanced at the body of the Prince. Meven and Kalantha had straightened him. It looked like he was sleeping. Kalantha still clutched his ornate dagger.

"You should leave that." Meven pointed at Edan.

Kalantha shook her head and took the sheath from Edan's belt and attached it to her own belt.

"Kal . . ."

"No, Meven. I'm keeping this."

"To remember Edan by," Meven said sadly. "All right, Kal. You can have something of our cousin's as a keepsake."

"No, Meven." She shook her head and choked back a sob. "Something for protection. You better get a weapon, too. Just in case more of those terrible men come. Take one of the soldier's swords."

Meven was running his fingers across the beads again.

"Meven, those soldiers aren't going to be needing those swords ever again. Take one."

It was his turn to shake his head. When he finished another prayer, his fingers, still trembling, reached to the Prince's hands and worked free a large ring. He cupped it in his palm. It was a thick gold band set with a smooth ruby. On one side was the Montoll crest.

"You're the Prince now," she said, eyes wide with the revelation. "You're next in line for the throne of Galmier."

The words struck Meven hard and caught Gallant-Stallion's attention.

The Finest's ears perked up and he recalled Steadfast's last words: "Take care of your . . ." *Charge.* Steadfast was going to say: *Take care of your charge.* Steadfast knew he couldn't escape, that he was dying, that the Prince was dying or already dead. And he knew that Meven would be the next Prince of Galmier. Meven was Gallant-Stallion's charge. The young Finest would be Meven's secret shepherd.

Meven was standing and helping his sister up. "These bodies should be buried, Kal, but we can't do it. We've nothing to bury them with, and it would take too long. We've got to hurry back to High Keep and tell Bishop DeNogaret what happened here. He'll get word to the King. The King will send people to bury everyone."

A large crow cawed loudly, and a few smaller ones took flight. The large one was defending its find of a plump soldier.

Kalantha wrinkled her nose at the bird and tried to smooth her tunic. "I know there are too many bodies for us to bury. But shouldn't we at least take care of Edan?"

"Bishop DeNogaret will have it taken care of. C'mon, we've got to start back now."

She continued to stare at the big crow. "All these dead soldiers, Meven. . . ." The fog was starting to lift, and they could be seen in more grisly detail. But it would be some time before all the fog burned away to reveal everything. Kalantha cupped her hand over her nose and mouth.

"This road is oft-traveled, Kal. Someone will be along soon and find them, certainly before we can get back to High Keep. And word will likely reach the King of Nasim-Guri, too."

"I didn't want to go," she said, her voice muffled by her hand. "I told Morgan I wanted to stay at the Temple. I wanted to see the first trillium bloom."

"Kal . . ."

"But Morgan said I had to go. This was going to be a grand outing, he said. It would be good for you, he said. You were going to enjoy yourself and get away from your studies and prayers. All these people dead." After a moment: "Meven, do you think anyone else escaped?"

He took another look at the carnage, quickly passing over the bloodiest of the bodies, eyes lingering on the few defiant crows. "No, Kal. I don't think anyone else made it through this." Meven took Gallant-Stallion's reins and pulled him toward the two remaining horses. "We've got two good horses here we can take back to High Keep. We can leave the punch here. Awwww . . . no."

Meven scowled as he got close and noticed the horse that one of the Bishop's men had ridden—the one he had intended to take for himself—was obviously lame. That was why it was still here, he thought. The packhorse was here because its dropped reins were beneath a soldier's body, effectively keeping it in place.

"We'll have to leave that good horse," he said to himself, looking at the lame one. "We'll have to keep the punch." Then he started taking some of the satchels off the packhorse and looking inside. "Wedding gifts," he pronounced. "The ones the Bishop selected for us to give." These he left on the ground, save for a silk scarf that he wrapped around a gash on his arm.

Then he started searching through the packs of the nearby downed horses. "Nothing. Nothing. Nothing worthwhile here either. Wait . . . here's a few changes of clothes. Probably Edan's." They were of exceptionally fine material with embroidery on the collars and beads on the cuffs. This satchel of clothes and one filled with food he hooked to the back of the packhorse's saddle. He found two full waterskins that he hooked to Gallant-Stallion's saddle. Finally, he freed the reins so the packhorse could move. "Up you go, Kal."

Kalantha was still looking at the bodies. "All of these people, dead. We could be dead, too." After another moment, she let him help her up onto the packhorse.

"C'mon, horse," Meven said to Gallant-Stallion. He made a move to get in the saddle.

"Meven, you can't keep calling him 'horse.'" She patted the neck of her own mount. "This is Fortune, for it was fortunate he made it through the fight and lived."

"Fortunate for us he got his reins caught, you mean," Meven said. He got on Gallant-Stallion and pointed him north, nudging him down the road that would eventually lead to High Keep.

"He probably doesn't like being called 'horse,' Meven."

"Fine, Kal, I'll name him." He paused and rubbed at his eyes with one hand. With the other, he ran his fingers across the reins.

"Well, Meven . . ."

He held the reins in both hands now. "This is Rue."

"Rue?"

"Yes, Kal. I've named him Rue. It's a perfect name. What a rueful looking beast this is, this big, ugly punch of a horse."

7 · A Gathering of Evil

The creatures of Paard-Peran were given function. The smallest were little more than ornaments, serving as food for the larger, swifter animals. Birds provided songs, fish splashed in the rivers to add to the melody of the world. Horses, among the most noble of the creations, served people.

People served their own purpose and at the same time served no one. Though most of them revered the gods, their reverence was not enough, for they were the most flawed of all the beings. They lied to each other, coveted one another's possessions, and the darkest of them slew their brethren in anger and for greed.

The son and daughter gods knew they would have to help the people of Paard-Peran . . . or banish their souls from their father's heart forever.

~The Old Mare, from the Finest Court canon

Little of the afternoon sunlight filtered down through the thick canopy of Nasim-Guri's vast Old Forest. No greater variety of trees could be found anywhere in Paard-Peran, and nowhere did they grow as large or live as long. There were stringybarks well more than a thousand years old and more than two hundred feet tall. And there were walnut and pecan trees nearly ten feet in diameter, with reed-thin branches that intertwined like clasped fingers. In places, clump birches grew so close together they practically formed a living wall. And in a few sections, red oaks and hickories grew a dozen or more feet apart and had plenty of room to spread their limbs.

Hardly any animals searched for food on this forest floor. Most preferred the less dense and more hospitable woods that were scattered elsewhere throughout Nasim-Guri and the bordering countries.

There were plenty of birds above the floor, however, as they delighted in the lofty branches and the lush foliage. The birds' calls filled the Old Forest. It was pleasing music to the assassin named Fala.

Overhead, Fala heard the stately and powerful wingbeats of a bustard, a big narrow-necked bird prized by hunters for its sweet meat, but safe in the Old Forest. Hunters stayed away from this place. Fala didn't particularly care for it either, though he had little choice in the matter this day and so tried to make the best of this eerie environ.

As an unnecessary precaution, Fala kept to the abundant shadows cast by the great trunks and listened intently as he went, focusing in particular on the songs of the orioles and larks. Then the shrill cry of a large starling intruded, off-key and dissonant and giving him pause. The bird was upset that Fala had moved directly below its nest. Fala watched the bird for a few moments, taunting it, then eventually wended his way deeper into the woods—where the light became so diffuse it appeared to be evening.

"Follow me," Fala hissed. "All of you stay close. He waits for us."

His fellow assassins were silently creeping behind him. They moved slowly, and he accommodated them, as they were all exhausted from the previous night's foray against Prince Edan's entourage.

Deeper still into the ancient trees they went, where the Old Forest became a world of grays and blacks, the darkness shifting only slightly when a gust of wind stirred the high canopy and therefore caused the shadows below to move. The floor became thick and soft with the shredded, rotting husks of long-dead trees. Stumps jutted up here and there like canted tombstones, and the assassins carefully, and by memory, picked their way through them. The farther the band traveled, the more intense the scents of the Old Forest became. The odor of rotting wood was the strongest, as there was so much of it. But there were also the smells of the damp earth and mushrooms and something that had recently died nearby.

"He will rejoice when he hears our news," one of the assassins said.

"Pray that he does," Fala cautiously returned. "Pray hard that he is made happy by the death we inflicted."

They passed a tree so old its name had been forgotten, and then a tree with exposed, gnarly roots that radiated outward from its trunk like a tangle of bloated snakes. There was a veil of spiderwebs they hadn't intended to disturb, but did. It took them a few minutes to brush all the webs and spiders away and resume their course. There was a string of murky, foul-smelling pools they skirted, and a large patch of mushrooms they walked through, a few of the assassins in the rear tarrying to pluck some of the most tender ones.

"Fala." The word came from behind the eldest of the Old Forest's giants and made all the assassins stop. The huge, half-dead tree marked the very heart of the dark woods. "My lieutenant brings me news, I hope. Good news." After several silent moments, the speaker stepped from behind the trunk so that he could scrutinize the assassin band and allow himself to vaguely be seen in the shadows.

Fala respectfully edged closer, while his fellows remained several cautious yards behind him. The most nervous among them shifted back and forth on their feet.

"Good news, yes. There was much success," Fala announced. He locked his legs and stood straight, head up to show his pride. He knew that despite the darkness, his overseer could clearly see him. "We brought much death upon the wedding party."

The overseer came near and stared into Fala's cold, shiny eyes. "Much death I am certain," the overseer repeated. His voice was deep and soft and slightly raspy. But it wasn't a weak voice, and it commanded the assassins' attention. "Still, Fala, it was not enough death. Was it?"

Fala swallowed hard and lowered his head. He fought to suppress a shudder. "No, not quite enough. Not everyone who rode with the Prince died."

A longer silence took hold, and Fala stepped back to join his fellow assassins. His overseer remained motionless, watching Fala in particular, but eventually and almost imperceptibly moving his eyes to take in each of the assassins. After what seemed like an eternity, he spoke again.

"Explain your success, Lieutenant Fala. And then tell me of your failure."

Fala raised his head and again looked up into the overseer's eyes.

"We went to village Hathi in the country to the north. It was where you said the Prince of Galmier and his followers would stop for the night."

"And . . ."

Fala shook his head. "They were not there, none in the Prince's party. None of their horses were in the paddock or in the stable. To be certain we thoroughly searched the village anyway. They were not anywhere. But we eventually found a woman and her son who would talk to us."

"Go on."

"She said the Prince came into the village, but he did not even bother to get off his horse."

"Suspicious? The Prince was suspicious something would happen if he stayed in the village?" The overseer paced in a tight circle. "Something, someone tipped him off that there would be danger."

Again a head shake from Fala. "No. Not suspicious of us. The woman said the village was spoiled milk to the Prince's royal palate. He could not stomach the meager place and did not want to sleep in one of their straw beds."

"Too beneath him." The overseer stopped pacing and came

to stand in front of one of Fala's assassins. "I should have realized that the village was too beneath him."

"Yes," Fala answered. "Beneath him. The woman said the villagers were most disappointed. The Prince and his men stayed only a few minutes, then they continued on the road. She said the Prince was asking one of his soldiers about Cote d'lande."

"Another village," the overseer said. "Much larger. More pleasing to his palate."

"I decided to strike the Prince as soon as we could reach him. I could not risk him making it to the next village."

"Wise of you. Cote d'lande is much larger than Hathi. Too many people there," the overseer noted. "In Cote d'lande others could have come to the wedding party's aid and could have stopped you and your kin. You were wise indeed, Fala."

Fala nodded at the compliment. "We found them as the darkness and the rain came. They were still on the road, blessedly well short of Cote d'lande. The horses were tired and slowing, and we rushed in."

"We surrounded them," volunteered one of the assassins.

"It was glorious," said another. "We brought death."

"Death to the Prince."

"Death came to all of the soldiers."

Many of the assassins joined in then. Their voices had a similar quality, a harsh whisper wrapped around the edges, and they all spoke happily of death. It made the eerie, shadowy Old Forest seem a perfect setting for their dark meeting.

Fala managed to speak louder than the others, though his first few words were drowned out by the assassins' chatter. ". . . and we swept around the Prince and his men so none could escape. We were a tightening noose."

"But some did escape," the overseer stated. "You said so."

"Two," Fala answered. "And at first we thought them unimportant. Grooms or other servants of no concern."

The overseer cocked his head, imploring his lieutenant to explain further.

"The Prince was our first mark," he said. "As you directed that he be. We fought through many soldiers to reach him. He wounded three of us before he went down. Him and his beautiful horse, slain."

"It was a sweet death," one assassin cooed.

"You wanted his horse dead, too," another assassin cut in. "All of the horses. You said . . ."

". . . that I wanted nothing left alive," the overseer finished.

No one spoke for a handful of minutes. Leaves rustled overhead, and from the south came the throaty mating call of a button quail. A hawk of some kind was flying just above the canopy, its shriek sharp and high-pitched.

Fala finally continued: "Unfortunately some horses escaped, overseer, but not many. They were not as important as the Prince."

"No. Clearly they were not."

"And they were not as important as the other heir to the throne."

"Fala . . ."

"Overseer, it is our failure. The two people who slipped through our grasp . . . one is the next heir. They were not servants as first we thought. But we did not discover that until morning when we searched the corpses. All the servants were dead and accounted for. But the Prince's young cousins—those were the two who escaped. The boy cousin is the next heir."

The overseer closed his eyes, and Fala trembled.

"The Prince died," Fala repeated hopefully. "We killed him first."

"Which pleases me." Still, the eyes were closed.

"The rains came harder as we fought, and there was lightning. And the lightning was forcing back the night."

"I understand, Fala."

"The lightning threatened to reveal us. You wanted us unseen. You demanded that no one be able to identify us."

"But the cousins did not die, and I demanded that, too." The eyes opened wide, and in that instant the hawk overhead shrieked shrilly again.

"We missed only two of our marks, overseer."

"Yes, Fala. You missed them."

"If the Prince and the others had stopped in the village Hathi . . ."

"But they did not."

Fala shook his head. "And so we failed."

"And so an example must be made of your failure."

"Yes." Fala turned and looked into the eyes of his assassins. "An example." He scrutinized each of them for several moments, as much as he could given the darkness of the deep Old Forest. Then he selected two, and in an instant slew them. "Two of my band for the two cousins who escaped."

Fala watched his overseer strut before the remaining assassins. "Good that the Prince died, Lieutenant Fala. And good that the soldiers died, too."

"And the Bishop's men. The grooms," Fala cut in. "Good that we killed them."

"Death came to them all," one of the assassins said.

"Swift and painful," said another.

"And so must death come again," the overseer pronounced. "To the two you missed."

Fala stepped up to the overseer and once more looked into his wide eyes. "We will find the royal cousins. And we will not fail this time."

The overseer retraced his steps and disappeared behind the eldest tree.

After a time, making sure the overseer was not coming back

and had nothing else to say, Fala led the assassins from the deep part of the Old Forest. "We must not fail him again," he told them.

"Death will come," the assassins answered.

8 · Return to Hathi

The first men were among the bravest, and their courage kept the good gods of the world~who numbered five now~from casting all men into oblivion. "Their spirit is strong," one of the gods said. "And so we must create a guardian who is stronger and who is near to our own image. We shall call that guardian Mare."

~*Blackeyes Longmane, Finest Court recorder*

Hurry, Rue. We've a long way to go." Meven held the reins loosely in his right hand. The fingers of his left were running over the wooden beads on his belt. "Grant us a swift and safe return home," he prayed. "Watch over us and keep our minds and the road clear. Bless cousin Edan and all the soldiers who died, and hold their spirits close." This last part he'd said many times since they'd discovered all the bodies. "Move faster, Rue." He shook the reins, and dug in gently with his heels for emphasis. Then he looked back to make sure Kalantha was following.

She was a dozen or so yards behind him on the packhorse, still staring over her shoulder at the carnage. Crows had returned to pick at the remains, and she hollered at them in the wasted hope they would fly away. She'd made sure they would have a hard time getting to Edan's body, as while Meven had been going through the packs, she'd covered Edan with three blankets and the pennant with the King's colors, and weighted everything down with swords. Despite her repeated urgings, she couldn't get Meven to take one of the swords for protection.

He wasn't skilled with a sword, he told her, and so it was only something heavy to drag along.

Neither would he agree with her about what to do with Edan's body. Kalantha wanted to take it with them, but Meven said he was unsure of customs with the royal house. Should the Prince be buried at home? Or was he to be buried where he fought and died? If it was the latter, he shouldn't be moved. If it was the former, there might be some stately way to take his body back, perhaps in an ornate wagon pulled by norikers. Wrapped in blankets and draped over the rump of a horse might go against the King's wishes and therefore do more harm than good. Besides, he said carrying even one body with them would slow them down. That was the real reason Meven left Edan behind—added weight on either horse would make the trip take longer. Speed was essential.

"Meven, I don't think that leaving him . . ."

"Kal, we've been over this before. You really have no say in the matter."

"Customs are foolish things, Meven," Kal told him. "I don't want to leave him there. I don't want to leave any of them for those nasty crows."

Meven said men made the decisions in Galmier, at least all the important ones. And since he was the Prince of Galmier now, his decisions carried even more weight. All of the bodies would stay where they were, and she would have to accept that.

"Kal! We need to hurry," Meven pleaded.

"All right! I'm coming." One last look over her shoulder at the grisly site, then she urged the packhorse a little faster. It was a futile gesture, as the horse was tired and sore, its hindquarters and forelegs crisscrossed with slashes. It moved, but not quickly. "Do you think that other horse will be all right, Meven? The one we're leaving behind?"

"It'll be fine, Kal. It's lame is all, and that's why we can't take it with us. But it'll be all right." Softer, he said: "If someone comes across it and tends to its wounds, it will be all right. Maybe." A pause. "May the gods grant us swift passage home and keep us safe on our journey." He released the prayer beads and reached into his pocket, touching Prince Edan's ring. Kal suggested he put it on, as he was the Prince of Galmier now. But there'd been no formal ceremony to name him Prince, and so the ring stayed in his pocket. Meven wanted to follow proper protocol in the matter. Besides, he considered the ring Edan's, and he intended to present it to the King along with the satchel of Edan's fine clothes. "Hurry, Rue. We must get home as fast as possible."

Gallant-Stallion adopted a gait that would not outdistance the packhorse. He whinnied to the horse, encouraging it to go faster. It whinnied its refusal and laid its ears back in a threatening manner that suggested it not be pushed. Hungry. Tired. Thirsty. Hurt, it said.

Fine, Gallant-Stallion thought, realizing it was an accomplishment to just make it move. It doesn't understand that the urgency for speed is more important than its desire for a comfortable walking pace. *Fine. Fine. Fine,* he repeated, deciding in the end that since the packhorse was not going to go faster, he couldn't leave it and the girl behind. Besides, the deliberate pace was comfortable for him, and a small part of him decided that it wouldn't hurt to take things slow for just a little while— despite Meven's constant heel-jabbings.

Gallant-Stallion let his thoughts wander to the previous day's events. It should have been a time of happiness for him— spending time with the legendary Steadfast and gaining an important charge, the new Prince of Galmier. Instead it was a time of dread. Could he have done something to save Steadfast and Prince Edan? If he'd spent more than a few short weeks on Paard-Peran would he have been better prepared? Why hadn't he been paying more attention that night? If he'd been alert, he might have noticed the assassins earlier and warned everyone. It was all so tragic and wrong. Certainly there was something more he could have done. But what?

Then something began to fester at the back of Gallant-Stallion's mind. Something about the site of last night's attack didn't sit right with him. The site, the assassins . . . Not that there was anything right about the slaughter anyway. But something was . . . definitely wrong. He couldn't puzzle it out right now, and he couldn't return to the scene to study it further. He was sure Meven would have no part of going back. That probably wouldn't do any good anyway, he thought. He could picture everything precisely. Indeed, he believed he might never forget the ghastly images. Steadfast would have noticed the problem, Gallant-Stallion was certain. Why couldn't he pinpoint what was out of place?

And how could Steadfast be dead? One of the greatest of all Finest, admired, his name spoken with reverence. More than one hundred and seventy years Steadfast had walked on Paard-Peran, and now he was dead by assassins. Just as Meven was going to report Edan's death, the Finest Court had to be told about the slaughter and Steadfast's death, Gallant-Stallion decided. He was the only Finest who knew of Steadfast's death, and therefore it was his responsibility to make the report. Too, he wanted the Finest Court to know that Meven, the new Prince of Galmier, was his charge. And he wanted them to bless the partnership. So he needed to return to the Court as soon as possible.

But returning just wasn't possible at the moment. He couldn't leave Meven and Kalantha—not until he got them back to the High Keep Temple and safe in Bishop DeNogaret's care. When they were with the Bishop, he could return to the Court. Then he would rejoin Meven after a few days and shepherd him for as long as necessary.

Meven was praying again, for Edan's spirit, for the King who had lost a son, for Kalantha and Galmier. He even prayed for Rue and the packhorse to go faster. He continued praying for more than an hour until the village Hathi came into view. It was midmorning now, no trace of the ground fog remaining, but also no trace of the sun. The sky, which had teased them with a bit of blue earlier, was now heavily overcast, hinting at another spring downpour. Meven could smell the rain coming.

They rounded a curve in the road, and could better see Hathi. The two village horses were under the lean-to, and they had company—a saddled noriker. Gallant-Stallion broke into a trot. Meven was also excited, and was jabbing the horse with his heels.

"Kal!" he called back to her. "One of the soldiers survived after all. C'mon, Kal!"

"Fortune, hurry!" She tried to make the packhorse go faster, but couldn't hope to keep up. Meven was at the noriker and off Rue before she reached the edge of the village. He was inspecting the horse, happily noting it wasn't injured—not a scratch on it. He motioned for Kalantha to catch up, then he rushed into the nearest home without waiting for her.

Gallant-Stallion started talking to the noriker.

What did you see at the battle? Did you see the assassins up close? How did you manage to escape and get here? He gave a frustrated snort when the horse nickered its confusion.

Battle. Fight. Assassins, Gallant-Stallion said, trying simple concepts. *Remember the fight? All the blood and death? People crying in pain?*

The horse whinnied that it was trained for fighting.

Yes, fighting. The great fight last night! The slaughter on the road south of here.

The horse whinnied that it didn't understand what Gallant-Stallion meant.

All the death!

Death? It asked him to explain the word.

Death. The end of everything.

Nothing has ended, the horse replied, adding that the food and water certainly hadn't ended. The oats were good and it was willing to share.

Simple, simple creature, Gallant-Stallion said to himself. *Why can't you comprehend? Where is your rider?*

The noriker lowered its head to the food trough and wuffled that it was done talking and was going to continue eating. It wuffled that there was plenty of hay and tasty oats and repeated that it was willing to share if Gallant-Stallion was hungry.

Gallant-Stallion was hungry, but he had more important concerns.

Kal slid from the packhorse's back and tugged it toward the lean-to and the other horses. It finally picked up speed when it saw the water buckets and the food trough, and she tied its reins to a pole where it could reach the hay and oats.

"Are you thirsty too, Rue?" She put a water bucket close to the packhorse. "You're not tied up. You can come get some water here. And . . . Meven?"

Gallant-Stallion looked past her to Meven, who was staggering out of the home. He was wiping at his eyes and gesturing to Kalantha, palms out as if to keep her away.

"Stay there, Kal," he warned, when she made a move toward him. "Stay back and take care of the horses." Then he ducked into another building. He was inside only a few moments, then he was out and running into another.

Gallant-Stallion left the lean-to and walked to the road that led through the center of the village. There wasn't a soul outside, save Meven who stumbled from one cottage and into another. Where were all the people? They wouldn't all be inside, he thought. Not at this time of day. He should have noticed right away that there were no people outside. But he was weary, and because of that his senses were dull. He'd stayed awake all through the night, and through the previous night when he was on guard with Steadfast. And though he was almost indefatigable, the lack of rest was taking its toll. Even a Finest needed to sleep.

"Meven?" Kal watched as he dashed into another cottage. "What's wrong? Are the people gone?"

Gallant-Stallion realized that indeed they might all be gone. He didn't hear them, didn't hear anything—not beyond the breeze rustling the thatch of the homes, the swish of the noriker's tail as it kept away flies, Meven's footsteps as he ran from home to home. He didn't hear the people.

"Meven?" Kalantha stood next to Gallant-Stallion and watched her brother come outside again. This time he doubled over, clutched his stomach, and retched. "Meven!" She hurried toward him.

"Stay back, Kal."

"Meven!"

"I said stay back!"

She ignored him and ran to him. "What's wrong? Are you sick? Meven . . ."

"They're dead, Kal. All the people are dead. All of them. Every last one of them. Dead as Edan and the soldiers."

Gallant-Stallion sniffed the air. He smelled the rain coming and the damp earth, the livestock in the pen, and the horses behind him. And under that, he smelled death, a scent that was so familiar to him after what had happened last night. It was an almost sweet, cloying odor, and it was muted because the dead villagers were inside the homes.

"Lying in the beds, sitting at dinner tables, on the floor. They're dead. All of them. Killed just like Edan and the soldiers were killed. The assassins were here." He wiped at his mouth, then grabbed her shoulders. "We need to get out of here, Kal. We must get back to Bishop DeNogaret right away."

"Why?"

Meven sputtered. "Why? Because the Bishop has to know. He'll send someone to the King and tell him about Edan and the soldiers and this village. Bishop DeNogaret will know what to do."

She shook her head. "No, Meven. I mean why were these people killed?"

Meven seemed to be staring at the cottage across from him, but his mind was elsewhere, whirling with the possibilities. "I don't know why the assassins killed all these people," he said after several moments. "Kal, we need to . . ."

Kalantha was glancing at the homes Meven hadn't searched. "We have to check them all," she said. "Just to be certain that everyone's . . . dead."

Meven closed his eyes. "I know. I know, Kal. But I'll do it. You stay with the horses."

"Meven, you don't have to protect me all the time. I'm not a baby. I can help, I'll . . ."

Meven pushed her toward Gallant-Stallion. "Kal, it's not about protection. There's just no reason both of us have to see this. It's horrible. No reason both of us have to do this. I'll be quick." Then he was dashing across the road and into the next closest cottage.

Two buildings later, he found someone alive.

9 · The Darkness Came

The minds of the Finest are strong. There is no room for madness. The minds of people, however, allow lunacy to take a firm root.

~*Steadfast, veteran Finest*

The soldier had been one of three traveling the road early this morning on a regular patrol of the region. They'd come across the slaughter, and immediately two of the soldiers headed back to the capital city of Nadir to report to the King and to summon a detail to bury the people. The third remained behind to start gathering the bodies and to search for clues about the attackers. The soldier had found the lone Hathi survivor only minutes before Meven and Kalantha arrived.

The woman had been hiding under the bed she was now sitting on. Her bare arms showed the same slices made from the assassins' thin blades. Her clothes were practically shredded, and the soldier had put his cloak around her.

The soldier sat next to her, and Meven and Kalantha sat across from them on a crude bench. Gallant-Stallion hovered near the window and listened in.

"The darkness came," the old woman began. Her wide, wild eyes darted back and forth between Meven and Kalantha.

"The night," Meven supplied. "You mean the night came."

She nodded. "And the darkness came with the night. Night. Night. Night came. The darkness was alive, riding in and hissing that death was coming. The darkness killed my friends."

"The darkness. You mean dark men? They were the assassins on horseback," Meven said. "They were dressed in black, weren't they?"

"Yes. Yes. Dark assassins," she said. "They came into our homes while we ate dinner." She rocked back and forth and made a smacking sound with her lips.

"After Prince Edan and the soldiers came though here?" This came from Kalantha. "That's when the assassins came?"

Another nod. "After the Prince. Prince Edan. High and mighty Prince. After he left."

"And before the rain?" Kalantha persisted.

Gallant-Stallion was pleased with the girl's questions, as he wanted to know precisely when the assassins struck.

"Yes. Yes. After the high and mighty Prince and before the rain." The woman dropped her gaze to her lap and fiddled with a loose thread on her skirt. She started rocking from side to side now, jostling the soldier. "They were looking for Prince Edan Montoll, they were. From house to house to house to house them assassins went looking for the Prince. Prince Edan." She tugged the thread free and started working on another. "But they didn't find the Prince. He was gone. Gone. Gone. He wouldn't stay here. Didn't like our homes, he didn't. Nothing wrong with our homes. Nothing. Nothing."

Meven leaned close to Kalantha and whispered: "I think she's mad. Maybe driven mad by the assassins."

"Or maybe she always was that way," Kalantha returned in a hush.

"Didn't want to stay here, the Prince didn't. I heard Elmer tell them assassins just that—that the high and mighty Prince turned up his royal nose at our village and went down the road to Cote d'lande. Nothing wrong with our homes, there isn't. 'Cept now there's no one to live in them. Elmer's dead. Poor Elmer. All of 'em are dead." She tugged free another thread. The soldier made a move to hold her hands, but she batted him away and went back to work.

"But you didn't die," Kalantha offered. She smiled a little, but the woman wouldn't look at her. Her gaze was fixed on the thread she was tugging.

"No. Not yet. But I will," the woman said. "Everyone dies." She raised her gaze and met Meven's for only a moment, then she returned to the task of unraveling her skirt. "But I didn't die last night. Everyone else but me. The darkness came with the night and tried to kill me. I was outside when them assassins came thundering down our road. They cut me all over. All over. All over. See?" She paused and thrust out an arm so they could better see the cuts.

"You need tending," the soldier offered.

"They cut me," she continued, pulling her arm back and finding the thread she'd been worrying on. "Just like they cut that young man there." She pointed to Meven, whose arms were also crisscrossed with cuts. There was a deeper cut on his leg. "But he's young. He heals faster than me. Faster. Faster."

"Tell us about the assassins," Meven said. He edged forward and reached out a hand to touch her, but she recoiled. Meven settled farther back on the bench. "Can you tell us anything about them?"

"They were cutting on me, they were, and I ran in here and hid under the bed. They started cutting on someone else then. Couldn't see anything under the bed, but I could hear 'em."

"The assassins?" Meven asked.

"Yes. Yes. Them assassins. I could hear them. In their scratchy voices they were asking about Prince Edan, and they were killing the people who wouldn't answer them. Asking about Prince Edan and his cousins. Asking. Asking. And then they were killing even the people who did talk and who told them the Prince had went down the road to Cote d'lande. They were killing everyone but me."

And his cousins, Meven mouthed. *They didn't kill us.*

"Cousins?" Kalantha asked aloud. "You heard the assassins ask about the Prince's cousins?"

"I done told you that, girl," the woman said. She pulled another thread loose and slapped her knee. "Told you. Told you." She raised her voice. "Can't you hear? They asked about Edan and his cousins."

"Sorry," Kalantha said.

"You should be sorry," the woman went on. "Sorry that Elmer died and Isamu and Jackie and Tendrik and Neecha and Kaerek and Les. Sorry for all of them. Sorry. Sorry. No one to feed the cows now. Tendrik always fed the cows and the horses." She got a faraway look in her eyes then, and a lone tear slipped down her cheek. "I don't like to feed the cows. So the cows will die like Elmer and Les did. The sheep, too. And the chickens." The woman stopped tugging on the threads and fixed her gaze on a cloak that hung on the wall. Like everything else in the cottage, the cloak was worn.

Clay cups and plates were strewn on the floor, and the other bench was tipped over. A pot of beans was on its side on the table, and flies were feasting. At first Meven thought this cottage was free of death. But a halfway open curtain separated this room from a sleeping room. He saw a pair of feet and a pool of blood, and he quickly sat back to block the view from Kalantha.

"Why do you think the assassins killed all these people?" Kalantha asked her.

"Why?" The woman drew her face into a point, giving it a painfully pinched appearance. "Why? Why indeed?"

"I mean, if they were looking for the Prince . . ."

"And the cousins!" The woman raised her voice and her finger for emphasis. "The Prince *and* his cousins, them high and mighty fancy folk who were too good to stay in our village."

The soldier took a turn: "But if the Prince and his cousins had stayed in this village, they would be dead, too."

"Yes. Yes. Dead," she said. "Everyone dies. But maybe them assassins would've only killed the snooty royals and left us hardworking people alone."

Meven shook his head and dug the heel of his boot into the dirt floor. "They would've still killed all the people of Hathi."

The old woman raised an eyebrow. "Oh, you think so?"

"I know so," Meven countered.

So do I, Gallant-Stallion thought. *They would have killed all the villagers anyway. Like they killed all the soldiers, the grooms, the scribe, the Prince's attendant, and the horses.*

"The assassins didn't want to leave a single witness behind. They didn't want anyone to be able to identify them," Meven said.

"But I saw them!" the woman cackled. "I survived, and I saw them! Saw them!"

Kalantha leaned forward. "What did they look like?"

"Yes, just what did they look like?" the soldier pressed.

The woman's eyes narrowed. "I already told you. Are you deaf? The darkness. The darkness. All of 'em looked just like the darkness. Every last one of them assassins looked just like the night."

Meven drew the soldier outside the cottage, where he related every terrible detail about last night's attack on Prince Edan's wedding party. Gallant-Stallion watched them closely. No wonder the noriker didn't understand what Gallant-Stallion had been talking about. The horse hadn't been with the procession when it was attacked. The soldier said Meven was correct to leave all the bodies undisturbed, as the King would want to deal with it and would want his wisest men to investigate the scene and probe for clues to the assassins' identities.

"I will ride to the King immediately and tell him." The soldier had a long face, and it exaggerated his forlorn expression. "Prince Edan was loved in Nadir. The people will take it hard. The King will be heartbroken, and the news might push him deeper into his illness. I do not look forward to telling him about his only son's death." He adjusted his tabard and rolled his shoulders. "You said you were with the wedding party when the assassins came. Did you see the Prince die?"

Meven shook his head. It was all so dark, he remembered, and Rue took him and Kalantha away. Saved them. "That woman in there," Meven said. He was uncomfortable talking about grief and the battle and wanted to change the subject. "You'll have to take her with you."

"No. Definitely not." The soldier offered no further explanation.

"She can't stay here. Not by herself. She's . . . mad."

"That's not my concern. She's a commoner." The soldier pointed down the road to his noriker. "I'll leave immediately for the capital. I'll ride as fast as I can."

Meven was fumbling in his pocket. "Wait."

The soldier wasn't waiting, and was striding toward his horse. He obviously considered Meven a commoner, too, and not worth spending any more time on.

"I certainly look like a commoner," Meven said to himself. He stank and his clothes were filthy. "I said wait!" Meven hurried to catch up, and he thrust the ring at the soldier. "I said my sister and I survived the attack. But I didn't tell you who we are."

The soldier stopped and looked at the ring. "That's . . ."

"The Prince's ring."

"Galmier's crest." The soldier pointed to the raised gold symbol on the side. "Where did you . . ."

"I'm Meven Montoll, Edan's cousin and the King's nephew. Edan's dead and that makes me the Prince of Galmier now."

The soldier's eyes grew wide, and he took a step back. "One of the cousins the mad woman spoke of?"

"Me and my sister Kalantha. We were going to watch Edan wed the Princess of Nasim-Guri. And now we'll see him buried."

The soldier bowed slightly at the waist. "Prince Meven," he said. There was a measure of respect in his voice now. "You should come with me to Nadir. Your sister, too. The King will want to . . ."

"No. We're not going to Nadir just yet." It was Meven's turn to refuse. "But you have to take that woman with you. She's not right, and she can't stay here alone."

"I can't take her to Nadir. She's common, mad, and . . ."

"But you can take her to the next village up the road, Bitternut. The people there can look after her." Meven put the ring on. His fingers were slender, and he had to wear it on his thumb. He made sure the soldier saw it again. "This village has two horses. Load one of them up with her things, anything else she wants to take from this place and will be of use to the people who take her in. Put her on the other horse and take her with you."

The soldier looked at the ring once more, then at his noriker and the horses near it. He sighed loudly.

"That big one with the cuts on its leg is my sister's." Despite its injuries, Meven knew it was a better horse than the ones belonging to the village. "The punch is mine until I get a better one."

"I'll see that someone takes the old woman in," the soldier said with a shake of his head. "Where will you be going, Prince Meven? I need to tell the King."

Meven thought about that a moment, and rocked back on his heels. "Tell the King we'll come to Nadir . . . after a while. I've someplace else to go first."

The soldier tipped his head questioningly, but Meven didn't supply any more information. Then Meven spun on his heel, nearly bumping into Gallant-Stallion. "Rue! You follow me too closely!" He slipped around the horse and darted back into the cottage. "Kal, we're leaving. Find yourself a few changes of clothes."

The soldier gathered up the mad woman and a few sacks of cloaks, mugs, pots, and tools. After a quick good-bye to Meven, he was on his way.

From one of the other cottages Kalantha claimed a few skirts and tunics and two pairs of boy's trousers that looked like they would fit her. She stuffed them all into an old leather satchel. Then she opened the pen so the cows and sheep could range freely. She threw out grain for the chickens, then opened their pen, too.

"Kal, we don't have time for that."

"If we leave them in there, Meven, they'll starve. They might starve anyway. Bet they're so used to people feeding them. But at least they'll have a chance." Then she went to the well and pulled up the bucket.

"Kal, we must be going."

She ignored him.

"Kal!"

Her tone was almost angry. "Fortune and Rue are tired, Meven. Look, Fortune's sleeping now. They need to eat and drink and rest just a bit. I'm tired. But more than tired, I'm dirtier than I've ever been in my life. I can't stand my own smell." She tugged off her tunic, the one that was once the color of the pygmy blue butterflies that danced in her favorite garden. She tossed it on the ground. Then she drank deep from the bucket, upended the rest over her head, drew up more water, and started scrubbing.

"Kal, we're in a hurry," Meven muttered. "The day's half gone." He would have pointed to the sun to prove his point, but clouds were everywhere. "It's going to rain, Kal. The rain can wash you."

She continued scrubbing, using a scarf she'd found in the cottage.

"Kalantha!"

"Meven, even if we left right this very moment and rode like the wind, we wouldn't make it to the next village by nightfall."

So? he mouthed.

"And we're not staying here. Not with all these bodies. Are we?"

"No."

"Then we'll be sleeping on the ground, or in some black crevice like last night." She waited for him to argue. When he didn't she added: "And I'm going to sleep clean." She continued scrubbing, so fiercely her skin was turning bright pink.

She was trying to rub off more than the dirt, Meven knew. She was trying to rub out the memory of the assassins and all the bodies and every bad thing that had happened since they'd left the High Keep Temple. She would be eleven years old in just a matter of days, too young to have witnessed what she did.

He knew he was too young, also.

"I didn't want to go," she said to herself. "I should have stayed with Morgan and the Bishop." She left her old leggings behind in favor of one of the pairs of boy's trousers. She put on a tunic when she was finished. The clothes were not nearly as fine as what she'd discarded, but they were clean and smelled faintly of soap, and that pleased her a little. To Meven: "I'm going to find me a cloak. And a blanket or two for sleeping tonight. It won't be stealing. Not now anyway." She worked to tighten her braid and stuff the loose hairs in. "A cloak and something to eat, and a bar of soap if I can find one. I'm going to take some oats for Fortune. Then I'll be ready. And . . . your highness . . . you'll just have to wait for me."

Meven thought about ordering her to forget the cloak and

the food and to leave with him this very moment. He was the Prince after all, and he'd heard Edan order the soldiers around enough. But he knew she was in no mood to pay any attention to him.

So he waited until she started her search for a suitable cloak, distressed as she entered a cottage that had slaughtered children inside. Then he went to the well, discarded his own clothes, drank his fill, and began to scrub. When he was finished, he fished about in the pack he'd rescued of Edan's clothes and picked out the least ostentatious thing he could find. It was a dark green tunic and leggings, of expensive material and lavishly embroidered with lighter shades of green— leaves and vines marching their way around the collar and cuffs and up the sleeves. It was a little too big, and the most colorful thing he'd worn in recent memory. But it was better than whatever he could find in this village of the dead. He'd intended to give the clothes to the King.

"But what good would that do?" he said. "Edan can't use them anymore."

Gallant-Stallion watched Meven and Kalantha and listened to everything but their banter. He wasn't going to let anything surprise him again. There would be no more assassins sweeping in to take him unawares. But there *could* be more assassins out there, somewhere. He thought about the mad woman who claimed the assassins were asking about Prince Edan *and* his cousins. The assassins wanted all the royals dead, and they didn't want to leave any witnesses. If they found out that Meven and Kalantha had escaped the slaughter, they might come looking for them.

But what were the killings for? To prevent a marriage? If that was all that it was about, Meven and Kalantha should be safe. But what if there was more to it? Gallant-Stallion wondered if the Finest Court might be able to help him think it all through.

"All right, Meven. I'm ready," Kalantha announced. She had retrieved Fortune from the hay trough and had a basket filled with bread and dried meat. She hooked a sack of oats to Fortune's saddle.

Gallant-Stallion had just enough time to take a long drink from a bucket before Meven climbed up and took up the reins.

"Off to High Keep," Kalantha said, as she prodded the packhorse into moving down the road.

"High Keep? I don't know about that," Meven said, as he came even with her. "There's Nadir to consider, too. I haven't decided just where we're going yet. I'll figure it out after Bitternut."

Kalantha gave him a puzzled look. "I want to go back to Morgan and the Bishop."

"We'll see, Kal."

Gallant-Stallion kept his ears pointed forward, listening, and he sniffed the wind. If he paid close attention, he would learn everything the wind knew.

10 · Bad Dreams

All creatures dream. Even the Creators let apparitions flow behind their closed eyes. Nightmares, however, only seem to trouble people and old dogs.

~The Old Mare, the first of the Finest

Rue's gait was easy, and certainly not as fast as Meven wanted to go. But this time Meven didn't push the big punch. The new Prince was well aware that Kal's tired packhorse wasn't capable of traveling at the speed the punch could. Too, the horses needed more rest, and so did he and Kalantha. But Meven wanted to put some distance between them and the village of the dead, which meant they would travel until dark. Sometime tomorrow they would reach the next village to the north—Bitternut. He couldn't seem to get the images of all the slain people of Hathi and the dead soldiers out of his mind. Edan's ashen face in particular loomed large.

Kalantha hadn't spoke since they'd left Hathi more than an hour before. She alternated between looking at the sky, which kept threatening rain but so far hadn't produced any, and looking to the east at the trees and the swollen river. She was absently combing her fingers through the packhorse's mane.

Meven's stomach rumbled, and his head ached. He hadn't

eaten since yesterday afternoon, and though he was hungry, the notion of food didn't appeal to him. Still, it was good Kal thought to take bread and meat from the village. He should have thought to fill a waterskin or two. Had Kal taken care of that? They would eat when they stopped for the night, as it would be necessary to keep their strength up. If she hadn't brought water, they'd go to the river. The horses would probably like that.

Meven closed his eyes. Rue was heading straight down the road, and so Meven trusted the horse and allowed himself just a moment's rest. It was only going to be for a minute or two to ease his tired eyes, he told himself. He wouldn't let himself fall asleep. The road was uneven, and he'd been riding so long that the saddle was uncomfortable and would certainly keep him awake. But Rue's gait was steady, and the rocking motion was relaxing. Despite his best efforts, Meven's head nodded forward, and the reins slipped from his hands.

In his dream he was back at the High Keep Temple. He was in Bishop DeNogaret's study. It was one of Meven's favorite rooms at the complex. Warm-looking wood was everywhere— the massive desk, the table and chairs, the chandelier that held the thick beeswax tapers that were made by acolytes at the Temple workshop. The bookcases that lined the walls were of the same wood as everything else—rich mahogany polished until it gleamed and carved with curving lines and flower petals. The Temple for the most part was simple in its furnishings, and lacked even some of the comforts he'd noticed in the Hathi cottages. There were no cushions on any of the chairs, and the mattresses on the beds were thin. There were no pillows, just folded blankets for their heads. The Bishop believed that it was important to pamper the mind and the spirit, not the body.

But the Bishop's study seemed to be an exception. The chairs were crafted in such a way as to be very comfortable, the table at a perfect height for reading, and the chandelier provided so much light that studying was easy on the eyes. Meven hadn't always been allowed in Bishop DeNogaret's study. In fact, when he and Kalantha had been brought to the High Keep Temple—when he was just five and she three—they were allowed in only a few of the rooms. They were cared for by all of the acolytes, laws were laid down, a regimen established, and their education started immediately. There was little time for play, but even that was part of the schedule.

The Bishop insisted that they both learn to read. They were not commoners, Bishop DeNogaret said, and therefore they would be keenly educated. Reading was difficult for Meven, but he was infinitely eager to please the Bishop, and so he struggled for a few years until he finally mastered the skill. And recently he had begun to study the ancient languages, which he considered convoluted and unnecessarily flowery.

Older than Kalantha, Meven had more deeply felt the loss of their parents, and the Bishop quickly became a father figure to him. Kalantha got along well enough with the Bishop, but she was never as close to him as Meven was. Instead, she formed a bond with a commoner, the Temple gardener. The Bishop didn't seem to object; he said Morgan was a good, hardworking man, and he had things to teach.

But from almost the time Meven had set foot in the Temple, he'd latched onto Bishop DeNogaret. It was easy to admire the Bishop—smart, commanding, respectful of all those around him. A supremely religious man, the Bishop had sworn to never marry and to give all of his love to the Temple and the five good gods of Paard-Peran. But the Bishop managed to save just a little love for Meven.

It was three years ago, on Meven's tenth birthday, that Bishop DeNogaret finally brought him into the study. The High Keep Temple had a library, and Meven had been allowed into that almost right away. The High Keep library had many more books than the Bishop's study, but the library was not so impressive as far as Meven was concerned. The furniture was not so beautiful or comfortable, and the light was not as bright to read by. The books in the Bishop's study were more interesting to Meven, perhaps because they belonged to the Bishop or because some of them had oiled leather bindings that were dyed rich reds and greens and which had titles embossed in gold leaf. Some had edges that were rubbed with gold, and a few were written by the Bishop. The books on one shelf had a musty smell because they were so very old. Books on another shelf were new, just copied by the acolytes. Overall, the books in the study were in better condition than most of the ones in the library, though that was probably because not so many people handled and read them.

One book in particular was Meven's favorite: *Sulene's Guardians.* It was about the five good gods of Paard-Peran and how they managed to overpower the world's two evil trickster gods in a fierce fight for custody of the Sea of Sulene. The evil gods sought to claim the largest sea and turn it red with the blood of all the sea creatures that lived there. That would ruin the coastal villages that relied on the sea for food. The Galmier Mountains were born of the good gods' victory, the book said. The mountains were coaxed up from the flat earth so the people of Galmier could climb their peaks and see to the far end of the bright blue Sea of Sulene and watch the whales come to play off the Skarnhold harbor.

A small passage in the book talked about the heart of Galmier, where most of the Sprawling River spread. The evil gods knew they were losing their battle for the Sea of Sulene, and so they wanted to leave something behind to vex the good gods and their worshipers. They chose to leave their mark on Galmier, causing its heart to be wet and inhospitable much of the time and causing the spring rains to be heavy and the river to often swell its banks and flood the farm fields.

Meven liked the book for the story, but more so for the way

it felt in his hands—heavy, but not overly so. And he liked the way the words were printed, the first letter on every page an elaborate, swirling work of art. There were pictures, too, incredibly detailed, of the sea creatures.

"It's yours, Meven." Bishop DeNogaret held out the book when Meven came to the study, summoned on his twelfth birthday. "I know you enjoy it so. I want you to have it. I've never given you a birthday present before. But perhaps now is the time I should start making a tradition of it." The Bishop was smiling, and he rarely did that. Meven couldn't suppress the smile rising on his own face.

"Mine? *Sulene's Guardians?*"

"A birthday gift, Meven."

Meven shuffled forward, his eyes never leaving the book. The weight of it felt so good in his hands when he took it from the Bishop. "Such a gift," he said. "I don't know what to say."

Bishop DeNogaret patted Meven on the head. "Say that you will take good care of the book and read from it often."

Meven nodded and clutched the book to his chest. The leather felt warm against his fingers. "I will read from it every day." He took the book back to his room and placed it on a high shelf where Kalantha wouldn't be able to reach it without a considerable amount of work. It wasn't that he didn't trust his sister—he did trust her, and he loved her dearly. But this was the first birthday present the Bishop had given him, and so it was special. He knew the Bishop must have struggled to give him this book, as the Bishop had sworn to only love the gods, and had never given presents before. Meven knew he and his sister were making it difficult for the Bishop to keep that vow, and he realized that through the years the Bishop had come to think of them as his children.

Meven spent the rest of his birthday with Bishop DeNogaret. It was a day for history, the Bishop told him, and so they poured over maps of Galmier and Nasim-Guri, and they dis-

cussed the politics of the realms. The Bishop said it was important that Meven learn all about the government and Galmier's
line of kings. Meven was part of the royal family, and as such
had an obligation to discover his heritage. He wouldn't have to
worry about ruling, though, the Bishop told him, which was a
blessing. The Bishop said the King had a son, Edan, who would
one day wear the crown.

"What about Kal?" Meven asked. "She's part of the royal
family, too."

"A treasure," the Bishop called Meven's sister. "And if the
world were different, she would have a more prominent place
and would study the government. But the world is not different, and so her choices in life are limited."

Meven realized what the Bishop was talking about. Women
were relegated to households and farms, and at best could
achieve some measure of prominence in religious roles. Kalantha wasn't interested in politics—or religion, it seemed. She
was interested in plants and animals and spending as much
time as possible in the Temple's gardens.

"If I ever had a hand in government, I would change things,"
Meven told the Bishop. "I would make it so my sister could do
whatever she wanted."

That same year the Bishop gave Kalantha a birthday gift,
too—a simple but pretty coral necklace he'd purchased on a
trip to Nadir. The next year he gave them the belts with the
carved wooden prayer beads.

On a wintry day a few months ago the Bishop confessed to
Meven that when King Montoll originally asked him to be
their guardian, he'd refused. He said he wasn't prepared to
watch over children and was far too busy with his Temple du-
ties. But the King insisted, and so he relented. Now the Bishop
had come to think of the three of them as a family. Maybe it
wasn't wrong, and maybe he hadn't pushed the limits of his

vows, the Bishop said. Maybe the gods wanted him to have a family.

The dream changed and Meven was on the road to Prince Edan's wedding. He was missing Bishop DeNogaret and the Temple already, but he was excited at the prospect of traveling to the neighboring country. He could so clearly see the Bishop, telling him and Kalantha to make him proud. He couldn't remember his own father's face now, or his mother's. But he was very young when they died and so was not angry with himself that he couldn't remember.

"So much death," he mumbled in his sleep. The image of the Bishop vanished, and in its place was the pale face of Edan, eyes closed and face marred by cuts, so pale in death. Edan's face loomed larger, until it was giant-sized. Meven tried to shut his own eyes, to block out the image, but Edan only grew larger still, as big as a mountain now. Meven watched Kalantha struggle to put the blankets over Edan's body. It took so many blankets this time because the Prince was so large. "So much death everywhere."

"Meven!"

Suddenly it felt like he was falling. His eyes snapped open and he grabbed at Rue's neck to keep from slipping from the saddle. He was trembling all over.

"Meven, you fell asleep." Kalantha looked worried. "I think you were dreaming. You were mumbling Edan's name. We have to stop, Meven."

He shook his head. "We have to get back home, Kal. We have to tell the Bishop about everything that happened." He cursed himself for still shaking.

"We will tell the Bishop. And Morgan! Morgan must know, too. But we have to stop for a while first."

"It's only afternoon. We have hours before dark."

Gallant-Stallion slowed and whinnied for the packhorse to

stop. The horse was happy with the suggestion, and it looked toward the river and the inviting water and tall grass.

"The horses are tired, Meven. You're exhausted." She made a huffing sound. "We're stopping. Over there." She gestured toward the river. There was a stand of willows and black walnuts directly east.

Before Meven could argue, Gallant-Stallion started toward the trees. *Follow me*, the Finest told the packhorse. It was quick to comply.

"All right, Kal," Meven said. He fought back a yawn. "But we're just stopping for a little while. A very little while. We've a long way to go. I'll watch over you while you take a nap."

Kalantha blew the curls off her forehead. "You need a nap more than I do."

Meven didn't argue, but he had no intention of resting. He didn't want to fall asleep again. He was afraid he'd see Edan and the soldiers.

11 · Thorns and Lilacs

The gods decided that men's guardians would be the greatest creatures to walk Paard-Peran, but they would not be without limitations. Protectors of the best of men, they would not be able to speak to men. They would advise subtly, watch carefully, and they would try to steer their charges down the path to salvation. They would not force, for men must have choice. And they would have their own celestial home. The Finest creatures would dwell from time to time in the Finest Court.

~Pureheart, first stallion of the Court, from the Finest Court canon

Large vases filled with daffodils and lilacs sat to either side of the podium, from behind which Bishop DeNogaret preached. Picked this morning by the gardener Morgan, the flowers sweetly scented the air and added a splash of color to the otherwise drab worship room. From the benches to the floor, wall panels, the Bishop's robes, and even most of the worshipers' clothes, flat earthen shades were everywhere.

It wasn't a regular worship day or service, and so there were only a few dozen in attendance. For the most part they were commoners from the village of Fergangur and from the farmhouses scattered near the Temple grounds. A trio of minor nobles who owned land to the northeast could be picked out by their fine cloaks and well-styled hair. They sat in the front row. Morgan sat at the very back, dirt-caked boots tucked under the bench.

"Moments ago a ceremony began in Nasim-Guri," the

Bishop said. "Our beloved Prince Edan Montoll is wedding the Princess of House Silverwood. Though we are far from Nasim-Guri and its capital of Duriam, our hearts and hopes are with these two young people. Their union will ultimately join our countries and make our land strong. Pray with me that the gods will bless their marriage."

Bishop DeNogaret continued the service, detailing Prince Edan's life from his birth to the early loss of his mother, through his childhood, and to his most recent visit to the High Keep Temple. The Bishop briefly mentioned that his wards Meven and Kalantha Montoll, of whom he was quite proud, were with the Prince. And he explained that the Prince would be immediately bringing his new wife to Nadir, where they would live at the palace.

"But they will not be content to remain within its thick marble walls," the Bishop said. "The Prince told me that this entire country will be their home, and they intend to regularly travel it. In fact, I will present them to you in this very room. The Prince intends to show his wife all of Galmier within their first year together, and he will bring her to High Keep. You can personally meet them—before our summer ends."

A lengthy sermon on love, commitment, and family followed, as the Bishop seemed reluctant to let the congregation leave. When he was finally finished, he announced that the wedding ceremony was no doubt over by now, and that Galmier had a Princess to embrace. All but a handful filtered out. The three nobles remained, and they were quick to get Bishop DeNogaret's attention.

"There is a dispute," one of them began.

"Between the northern borders of our lands and an estate claimed by the crown of Uland."

The Bishop bowed his head as if he were praying. Morgan, who still sat at the back, knew this was the posture the Bishop adopted when he was deeply thinking. The gardener glanced down and saw that quite a bit of dirt had fallen off his soles. He knocked off more and pushed it all farther under the bench where it couldn't easily be spotted.

"History will show that the land clearly belongs to you and not to the country of Uland," the Bishop said. "I have volumes filled with maps and family lineages. We will make your claim factually undisputable, and I will speak to King Montoll about adding his influence to help resolve the matter. Uland is not as large or strong as Galmier, and its King is an old, frail man."

The nobles courteously thanked the Bishop and arranged to make a sizeable donation to the High Keep Temple. Morgan watched them leave. He'd seen them here before, but not regularly. They only seemed to show up when they needed something. And on this trip they were leaving much happier than when they'd arrived. Morgan learned long ago that attending worship services could do more than improve one's spiritual side.

Two boys remained, twins from a farm west of Fergangur. They normally attended with their parents and older sister. Morgan moved up to a closer bench and listened attentively.

"You know Rosaree, our sister," one brother began. "She is sick, Bishop DeNogaret. Very sick."

"She burns with a terrible fever," the other explained. "It started three days ago and shows no sign of letting up. Mother sits at her bed constantly and thought that you . . ."

"Say nothing more. I will pray for Rosaree," the Bishop said. "And I will come to your home tomorrow and we will all pray together."

The brothers left after answering the Bishop's questions about Rosaree's skin and alertness, what she'd been eating, how strong was her fever, and other things that might help pinpoint the malady.

"Morgan?"

The gardener stood and nodded respectfully to the Bishop. "I will be happy to go with you in the morning." Morgan had been with the Bishop enough years to anticipate what he would ask. "I've several herbs that might help, and I'll prepare some blends this evening."

"Rosaree Woodard is Meven's age," Bishop DeNogaret said. "Thirteen. And she has the carmine fever, I believe. Your herbs might help. You have the healer's touch."

Morgan ran a hand through his thinning hair. "The carmine fever is bad."

"Rare in one so young."

"But young people are strong, Bishop DeNogaret. And she is a good girl. I will try my best."

"And I will pray that the gods assist you." The Bishop patted Morgan on the shoulder. "There is always hope while there is breath." They stood face to face, arms flush at their sides and heads bowed. The prayer was a long one. "I look forward to your company on the trip, Morgan."

"Bishop . . ."

Bishop DeNogaret raised an eyebrow.

"Bishop, I . . ."

"Morgan, the lilacs you placed in here this morning. And your presence throughout the service. You want to speak to me about something, don't you?"

Morgan gave an exaggerated nod.

"The lilacs are among Kalantha's favorites," the gardener said. "I was trimming them just before sunset yesterday, and I noticed that one of the bushes was dying. It had been so healthy the day before."

"And you took this as an omen?"

He glanced around the Bishop and to the flowers by the podium. When he looked at the lilacs he thought of Kalantha. "An omen? Not by itself. But last night I had a horrid dream. More like a vision, I think, as I was awake part of the time."

The Bishop's usually implacable mask melted into a concerned expression. A tip of his head encouraged the gardener to continue.

"I saw Kalantha being swallowed by a black cloud. Maybe falling in a pit. Maybe getting lost, separated from the wedding party late at night. I rarely have troubling dreams. And I can't imagine why . . ."

The Bishop reached out and took Morgan's hands. "And that is precisely it, my old friend: your imagination. Do you know I almost didn't let Meven and Kalantha go with the Prince? I worried over the prospect for days and prayed to the gods for guidance. They are young, Morgan, but they are smart and protected. And if we do not let them explore this world, if we keep them tightly tied to this Temple, we will ultimately lose them."

The Bishop sounded confident, but there was a faint twitch at the corner of his eye.

"You miss them," Morgan said.

The Bishop released the gardener's hands and closed his eyes. "They are dressed in their finest clothes, Morgan. Listening to music and watching Prince Edan and his bride dance. And no doubt your Kalantha is sampling everything sweet on the table, and stuffing her pockets when no one is looking. Meven will tell us of their grand adventure when they return in four or five days. And my men will provide great details of the wedding and of the Bishop of Duriam's delivery of the marriage ceremony." He walked down the aisle between the benches and out of the worship room.

"Aye, you miss Meven and Kal very much," Morgan said softly, as he followed the Bishop.

The sun was out, though there were rain clouds to the south. Bishop DeNogaret stood near the garden and watched the worshipers head down the walk, some to their horses and carriages. Most of them would be walking the few miles back to their homes. The Bishop was intently watching a middle-aged couple.

"Tara and Willum Reed have not donated to the Temple in some time. Yet they come to nearly every service. They walk five miles each way."

Morgan didn't answer. He was usually unaware of just how many goods and coins individuals gave to the Temple.

"They do not live terribly far from the Woodard farm. And so it would not be much out of our way to stop there after we visit Rosaree. Tara and Willum Reed are among the poorest in the congregation. And they must be on especially hard times, else they would have donated. Can you make arrangements to have a few bushels of food and some lengths of cloth on our wagon in the morning?"

"I'll see to it, Bishop."

"A vase of the lilacs, if we can keep them from tipping over, would also be welcome." After a moment, he added: "Two vases, I think, one also for Rosaree and . . ."

"Bishop DeNogaret!"

The Bishop and Morgan whirled to see a young acolyte rushing out of the Temple. "Bishop DeNogaret, someone is in your private study. A visitor, he says."

"My study?" There was the tiniest hint of ire in the Bishop's voice.

"Until tomorrow morning, Bishop DeNogaret." Morgan was walking toward the lilacs, wanting to check on the dying bush. There seemed to be some improvement, though when he scratched his fingernail on a high branch, there was no trace of green. He made a note of which bush to take cuttings from in the morning, then he moved on to the roses. It was almost too early for them to bloom, though there were plenty of plump buds on the bush that would produce large flowers the color of a sunset. The bush had thick, healthy stems, well grown out from the late fall pruning. Of the roses, this was Kalantha's favorite, and she had checked on the bush just before her trip. When it bloomed, she liked to float three or four newly opened buds in a small bowl in her room. There might be a few ready for her when she returned.

"Ouch!" Morgan pulled back and saw blood on his thumb. That wasn't like him, to be so careless that he was pricked by the thorns. Not only was he typically especially careful, but his fingers were thick with calluses. The thorns shouldn't bother him. Was this an omen, too? he wondered. Something to validate his worries about Kalantha and Meven? Something to make him remember the dream of her being swallowed by a black cloud?

12 · A Gallant Shepherd

The Finest come to cherish the Fallen Favorites, too. Though rarely will a shepherd confide that a charge has become an ally and friend.

~Steadfast, veteran Finest

*S*teadfast, what would you make of all of this? Edan dead? Meven the Prince now? Me the shepherd of Galmier's new Prince? Gallant-Stallion spoke plainly, as if he were talking to Steadfast, but in truth he was just speaking out loud to himself. He missed the elder Finest, even though he'd only known Steadfast for a short time. He missed the company of one he could truly communicate with. The packhorse thought and 'spoke' too simply to carry on a reasonable conversation with. And while Meven and Kalantha often spoke, it wasn't to him— they thought him nothing more than an unassuming creature that could not understand much of what they said.

Gallant-Stallion was surprised that he liked Meven. The Finest hadn't been sure what he would think of people. He'd studied their history in the Finest Court and thought he understood their passions and foibles. He knew that many of them were motivated by power and wealth, not realizing how transitory those things were. And he knew a strong, moral nature was far more important, and that virtuous convictions and a lack of prejudice would carry a person farther than a chest full of gold and a lengthy title. It was written in the Finest Court canon that "Character served people beyond this life. Wealth only weighed down their spirit."

Gallant-Stallion in general considered people inferior, but not without merits and certainly not without promise. And he realized that people were necessary to the existence of the Finest. If the five good gods did not believe that people could be saved, the Finest would not have been created. So it was up to Gallant-Stallion to 'save' Meven by guiding him down a righteous path and helping him to become an exemplary leader of men. If Gallant-Stallion did his job, Meven would influence other men—ultimately hundreds could be redeemed.

The Fallen Favorites, Steadfast. That is indeed what the gods consider people. Gallant-Stallion well knew why they were considered "fallen." They made war on each other over pieces of land or over slights. They killed each other for profit or revenge. They betrayed each other, stole from each other, lied to each other and did all manner of other horrible things. They'd fallen far. *But there is good, too, Steadfast. I can see it in Meven. I saw it in some of the soldiers who rode with us. Some men try to help each other. I understand why the creators love some people. I am pleased with my charge.*

Gallant-Stallion studied Meven. The young man indeed had much to recommend him: He was protective of his sister, determined to do the right thing—even though he was unsure at the moment just what that was, and he respected his guardian the Bishop. So far Meven had shown no evidence of greed, and he cared for strangers. When Meven ordered the soldier to take the mad woman safely away from Hathi, Gallant-Stallion was delighted. No wonder the gods favored at least some of people. Only one thought troubled him: Meven considered Gallant-Stallion rueful-looking.

Meven had eaten his fill and was struggling to stay awake. He made sure Kalantha was comfortable and that the pack-horse and Gallant-Stallion were tethered to a fallen tree at the river's edge. Their saddles straddled the rotting trunk. The grass was sweet here, and the water cool and welcome. And though Gallant-Stallion didn't like the idea of being tied up, and had almost instantly figured out how he could get free, he was content for the moment. The veil of a weeping willow brushed his back, and he found the sensation pleasurable. The tree's roots extended well into the river, and he tried imagining how far out they went and what fishes swam among them.

Willows and black walnuts predominated where they rested. And the veils of the willows obscured the view to the west where the road and the mountains stretched. The river was really the only thing Gallant-Stallion could get a good look at. It was wide and appeared murky because of the rain clouds reflected on its surface. Its course was straight here, and so it had a good speed. Gallant-Stallion knew it was an old river, as elsewhere its course twisted and turned and slowed considerably, the mark of an aging river that was meandering more with each decade. He liked the sound of the water as it rushed by and swirled against the tree trunks and stands of cattails and spring reeds. And he liked the breeze as it came across the water and picked up a bracingly cool feel. In the space of several minutes, Gallant-Stallion decided that this river was one of the best things about Paard-Peran, and that Galmier must be blessed to have it spreading through its heart.

Gallant-Stallion decided to allow himself a few hours' rest, the sound of the precious river quickly lulling him to sleep. He dreamed he was back in the Finest Court, delighting in the company of other Finest—young who had not yet received charges to shepherd and elder ones who had engaging tales to tell of their time in Durosinni, Blagdon, Aroon, Qadiar, Farmeadow, or other countries on Paard-Peran.

Tell me about one of your charges. Gallant-Stallion dreamed he was talking to Steadfast.

Which one?

The twins you mentioned.

Steadfast's eyes loomed close. *Their company was stimulating and amusing. They were smart, among the brightest and talented men I'd ever met. They worked for the betterment of the people around them, spending winters in the poorest coastal villages. But they also put too much effort into confusing people—pretending to be each other. Truly no one could tell them apart.*

Except you, Steadfast.

Each had a distinct scent. And one's left eyebrow was a few hairs thinner.

Gallant-Stallion snorted in glee. *So you shepherded more than one Fallen Favorite at the same time. It must have been trying at times. Have others done this?*

Some have watched over many more than two. Steadfast raised his head, and his ears pricked forward. *Gallant-Stallion, wake up!*

The young Finest was roused from his dream just as night came. It had been much longer than he intended to sleep, but he had to admit the time did him good. He felt better than he had in the past two days, and the soreness from the wounds the assassins inflicted was gone. He took a deep drink from the river and noticed that Meven and Kalantha still slumbered.

He decided he would free himself and wake the new Prince, as Meven wanted to be on his way. But he paused after he pulled loose his reins, relishing the sensation of the willow leaves gently tickling his back. The veils still obscured the road.

They also obscured the black figures that moved north along it. Though Gallant-Stallion couldn't see the figures, he smelled the dried blood that must still be clinging to their thin blades, and he heard their whispers: "Falafalafala," "Cousins," and "Not fail." Gallant-Stallion stood motionless and found himself praying that the packhorse would not make a sound, that Meven and Kalantha would remain asleep, that nothing would happen to draw the assassins' attention in this direction.

His mind whirled with the possibilities of what to do should the assassins come this way. Snatch up Meven and cut across the river? Gallant-Stallion was a strong swimmer and could likely outdistance the assassins' horses. He could carry Kalantha too, as the packhorse would shy away from deep water and in any event could not keep up with him. And then where would he take the brother and sister?

"Falafalafala. They came this way."

"Tracks," one said. "Falafala, there are tracks."

"Down the road," another suggested. "North, Fala."

"Falafalafala, death will come to the cousins. With death we succeed."

Gallant-Stallion's chest burned, and he realized he was holding his breath. He strained to hear the assassins, their voices growing softer and softer until the breeze playing with the leaves drowned them out.

Don't come closer, the Finest seemed to will them.

And they didn't. They continued chattering about the cousins and death, and they continued north. When Gallant-Stallion thought they were finally gone, he waited an hour more before moving, just to be certain. He'd been breathing so shallowly he felt lightheaded and dizzy, and he nearly stumbled when he moved toward Meven.

Steadfast, what am I to do? The assassins search for the new Prince, and he does not know it. He didn't hear them or smell them, and I cannot tell him that the assassins moved north searching for him in the night. He cannot hear me. But maybe he will notice their tracks on the road. He is a clever young man. Gallant-Stallion wanted the counsel of other Finest and again thought about returning to the Court to speak to the most seasoned members there. Perhaps there would be someone in the next village who would watch over Meven and Kalantha, just long enough for him to make a brief journey to the Court. Meven might not even know his "Rue" had been gone.

I need guiding, Steadfast. Just as my charge does. He mulled over various courses of action for another hour or more. The rain interrupted his musings.

Meven and Kalantha woke as the deluge began. It was in the early hours of morning, before dawn and just as the sky was lightening. Meven cursed loudly. He was angry with himself for sleeping so very long, and he was quick to get them back on the road and heading north.

Gallant-Stallion inspected the road. *No trace of the assassins' tracks,* he said. The downpour had obliterated any hint, even to his keen eyes. *No proof the assassins were here. Meven won't know how close he was to danger.*

Unless the assassins stopped in the next village, he thought. There might be some trace there. But if that were the case, would it be a village of the dead, too? Just like Hathi? A shiver raced down Gallant-Stallion's spine.

~ ~ ~

They reached Bitternut just as most of the villagers had settled down to their evening meals. It was drizzling now and had rained on and off all day. There were swaths of mud and puddles everywhere, and the air was filled with the moldy smell of hay and thatch. But there was no scent of death, and that was what Gallant-Stallion was concentrating on. He picked up the odors of roasting pig and boiled potatoes, and the coveted scent of fresh-baked bread. Conversations spilled out of windows and mugs were clinking in fellowship. If the assassins had come here, they'd left the villagers alone.

Bitternut was considerably larger than Hathi, and the homes radiated outward from a cluster of small businesses, the streets looking like the spokes on a wheel. The circle-shaped village likely had nearly three hundred residents, and the stable Meven was leading them toward looked sizeable.

"Let's stay here tonight, Meven." Kalantha slipped from Fortune's back and tugged the packhorse to the stable doors. "It's a nice village. And we could sleep in beds. And we could get something to eat. I've never been hungrier in my life."

"I remember a small inn from when we came through here with Edan," Meven said. "Next to a tavern, I think. We could get something warm to eat there."

Kalantha's smile reached her eyes.

Gallant-Stallion had not seen her so happy, and for the first time since the attack Meven seemed relaxed. The Finest suspected it was the thought of being among people again and being closer to home that was easing their moods. Two more days of travel and they would be back at the High Keep Temple. If he did not have an opportunity here to slip away to the Court, he would at the High Keep Temple.

Meven was rummaging in the pack of Edan's clothes. He retrieved a pair of dyed-blue leather gloves, a hammered silver cloak pin, and a tan hat that had glass bead trim, a row of small feathers, and the King's crest in dark brown embroidery. Meven offered the gloves to the stable master in exchange for feeding and keeping the horses for the evening. He told Kalantha he intended to use the hat to pay for their meal and hopefully warm cider, and the cloak pin would more than cover rooms and baths for both of them.

"We'll come for the horses very early in the morning," Meven said. Then he and Kalantha were hurrying down one of the spoke roads toward the center of the village. They were running and ducking under awnings as they went, and doing their best to avoid the puddles.

"Beautiful," the stable master said, as he ran his fingers over the soft leather. "Beautiful, beautiful gloves." He took the reins and led Gallant-Stallion and Fortune into the barn. It was large and clean, filled with hay and smelling of oats and earth. Gallant-Stallion was placed in the stall nearest the door, and the stable master pulled a rope across the front—something that would not keep the Finest in. Fortune was in the stall opposite him.

"Oats, water, and hay," he said. He patted Gallant-Stallion on the neck and went across the aisle to scratch Fortune's nose. "Looks like you've been traveling awhile, lathered up a bit you are. Got a farrier coming by in the morning to look at the rest back there. If your riders don't take you 'fore then, I'll have the farrier look at your hooves, too. These gloves are fine, fine and new. Worth your board and a visit by the farrier."

He stepped back and took a good look at the packhorse. "I'd say you're about six years old, judging by the wear on those teeth. Your big friend over there, three, maybe three and a half." He pointed to Gallant-Stallion. "Good condition, the both of you. But your legs and bellies are all muddy. It's all this spring rain."

He felt the soft leather of the gloves again, then carefully folded them and put them in his pocket. "It's my dinnertime, fellows. But after I'm done I'll come back and clean you up. Fine, fine gloves." He drew a rope across Fortune's stall. "Fresh oats coming right up for the both of you. Then it's dinner for me. Hope Bethany made me a pie."

Gallant-Stallion immediately liked the man. Not because of the promise of food, though the Finest was certainly hungry. But because he had kind eyes. The stable master was a caring man, he could tell, and by his touch Gallant-Stallion knew he respected animals as well as people, and he bothered to talk to them. If the rest of the folks in this village shared this man's traits, Meven and Kalantha would be safe tonight. But Gallant-Stallion was frustrated that his charge would be out of sight. As powerful and smart as Gallant-Stallion was, he couldn't join them at the inn. His body presented limitations. Perhaps he wasn't meant to be with his charge all of the time.

Meven was thirteen, and from the Finest's studies he knew some boys of Meven's age or a year or two older went off on their own. However, from conversations Meven had had with the Prince, Gallant-Stallion knew that Meven had been cloistered at the Temple and hadn't the experiences or perhaps skills to be out on his own. He lacked a worldly maturity. Still, Meven was bright and could likely take care of himself—Gallant-Stallion hoped. He wondered if Steadfast had worried when the King was elsewhere.

Steadfast, there were many things you should have told me, Gallant-Stallion mused. *How often did you return to the Court for counsel? And do I have time to seek the Finest Court's counsel now? While my charge and his sister sleep?*

Gallant-Stallion ate some of the oats and continued his musings. He noticed that Fortune was also eating, and was making a snuffling sound that he was both thirsty and content.

All he worries about is himself, Gallant-Stallion observed. *His comfort. Simple creature.*

It is an important thing for horses, for most of the world's creatures, came another voice. *Food and water and a dry place to stay.*

Gallant-Stallion's head shot up and his wide eyes flitted around the stable. It wasn't a man's voice, it was clearly another Finest. There were nine other occupants of the stable. In a row extending back from Fortune were three chestnut cobs, resembling heavy horses but actually relatively small and known for jumping. Near Gallant-Stallion were two warmbloods, riding horses renowned for their speed and hard hooves. One was a bay and the other a pale gray that was almost white around the neck and withers. The warmbloods had nickered their greetings to Gallant-Stallion and Fortune when they first arrived at the stable. There was also a mule; a mud-brown cutting horse that was well-proportioned and nearly fifteen hands high; and two ponies. The pony Gallant-Stallion could best see was a muscular, dun-colored halflinger with a mealy muzzle and a flaxen mane. The other was in the very back where the shadows were deep. This one gave a shake of her head and moved into the aisle between the stalls. No rope had been stretched across her stall.

The old pony clomped along slowly and deliberately, her head bobbing up and down as she eyed each horse she passed until she came even with Gallant-Stallion. Dappled gray, she had a finely-shaped head and an arched neck that was graced by a long white mane. Her tail stretched to the top of her striped hooves.

You are a young Finest, she observed. *And one I have seen come through Bitternut only once before.*

Gallant-Stallion closely regarded her as questions tumbled through his mind. A Finest here? Who did she shepherd? Had she known Steadfast?

I am Mara.

I am Gallant-Stallion, he answered. *The young man I shepherd calls me Rue.*

Rue. A pretty word. The stable master calls me Old Woman. He knows I have seen many years. He thinks I am well more than twenty. She drew back her lips, the approximation of a smile, and revealed worn-down teeth that were slanted forward. *He is wrong, Gallant-Stallion-called-Rue. I am nearly two hundred.*

He lowered his head in respect, and she stood nose to nose with him.

Did she know Steadfast? he wondered again.

In a manner, I did.

Gallant-Stallion hadn't spoken. He took a step back. *I did not speak. How did you hear . . .*

I have gifts, Gallant-Stallion-called-Rue. Your thoughts and speech are both heard by my very old ears. Every Finest has a gift. She tossed her head, and her white mane looked like a mass of delicate spiderwebs. *I knew the Finest Steadfast. I met him many years ago when he came through this village, a King on his back. I saw him pass through here again days ago. And you were with him.*

He is . . .

Dead. You told me as much when you came in here. You grieve fiercely, though you hardly knew him. I grieve, too. The death of a Finest is a somber thing.

Without meaning to, Gallant-Stallion related how Steadfast, the Prince, the soldiers, and all the horses died. Through his eyes, she saw the wave of assassins and Gallant-Stallion's flight to the foothills. She was with him under the veil of willows when the assassins passed by on the road last night.

The assassins did not come here, she said. *But they have not given up. They still hunt.*

How do you know that? There were other questions spilling from Gallant-Stallion's mind.

I have gifts that I cannot explain, she repeated. *But because of those gifts, I know that the dark assassins want the one Steadfast selected as your charge. Too, I know that you wish to go to the Finest Court, and that you cannot risk leaving your charge at this juncture. The Finest Court could help you, its counsel is flawless. You have not been long from the Court.*

A few weeks, I have been on Paard-Peran.

Fifty years since I last visited the Court. Perhaps I will see the Court again before I die. It is a perfect and beautiful place, but not so interesting as Paard-Peran. And there is no one to shepherd in the Court.

Who do you . . .

I shepherd this entire village, Gallant-Stallion-called-Rue. At first I shepherded its headman. But when he died sixty years past, I received the Court's blessing to shepherd all the people here. I became so attached to all of them.

Gallant-Stallion's eyes opened wide. He hadn't thought a Finest could have more than one charge. But he remembered that Steadfast once shepherded twins. And he thought he dreamed that Steadfast said other Finest had shepherded more. Like this Finest. *Mara, don't the people in this village . . .*

Wonder at my longevity? Some. Those who have frequented the stable through the years do. The stable master certainly does. But he says nothing to the others to fuel suspicion. And he speaks often to me.

Does he know . . .

He knows nothing of the Finest or our Court. He does not know that we guide men on the path to perfection. But he thinks me special, a magical Old Woman. And I consider him a good man.

Gallant-Stallion's curiosity grew, but the old pony finally threw off his questions.

If your travels take you through Bitternut again, I will tell you more about myself and all the people here whom I guide and guard. I will tell you of other Finest who traipse through this piece of land the men call Galmier. But there are more important things to concern you now.

The assassins, Gallant-Stallion thought.

And your charge, Mara said.

What can you tell me? Any counsel you can give will be treasured.

The old pony threw her head back again, the spiderweb mane flying in the fading light that was coming in through the stable doors. *See through my eyes, Gallant-Stallion-called-Rue.*

I don't understand. I . . . But suddenly he did understand.

Mara's eyes seemed to grow impossibly large and impossibly dark. All trace of white disappeared, and even with his acute vision, he could not see her once-amber irises. A moment later clouds appeared in her eyes, gray-bellied rain clouds that flashed lightning and brought at first a steady rain, and then torrents.

Her eyes became Gallant-Stallion's world, growing to fill his vision. The sheets of rain became a wall of fog, and then the fog burned off and there were trees everywhere. The trunks stood resolute like soldiers, and there were hundreds of them, all tall and straight and filled with birds. He tried to hear their song, but all he heard was the shushing sound Fortune made eating oats from a bucket and the gentle nickering of the cutting horse. Gallant-Stallion blinked and the birds were gone, the trees were shedding their leaves, and the trunks were melting into the ground, becoming tombstones. A mist hung low around the stones' bases. There were words on the markers, but Gallant-Stallion knew only the spoken languages of men and creatures and could only read the mystic symbols in the Court's canons.

The markers grew and the mist floated above the ground. In an instant the tombstones were mountains touched by low-hanging clouds. There were shadows darting around the foothills. As Gallant-Stallion watched, the shadowy forms grew more distinct and looked like men on horseback.

The assassins search in the foothills of the Galmier Mountains, he said.

Will search, Mara answered. *You look at the future.*

The mountains crumbled and Bitternut took their place. It was night, and the shadows were slipping around the buildings and heading toward the center of the wheel-shaped village.

The near future. Tomorrow night maybe, she supplied.

The shadows darted down the road to a smaller village. Fergangur, Gallant-Stallion recognized. Then the High Keep Temple sprung up, casting long shadows that writhed and grew into tall, dark trees. There were faces between the trunks. Bishop DeNogaret and his acolytes, soldiers whose eyes were closed in death, faces of children and adults Gallant-Stallion had never seen before. One of the faces came to the front. It was featureless like a lump of clay at first, but then it formed angles and planes, a shock of dark hair grew and eyes opened.

Meven.

Your charge is an important one, Mara said. *And will bring hope to the people of Galmier . . . and pain to those who spread evil.*

Stars formed around Meven's head, spun in a circle and formed a chain.

A crown, Gallant-Stallion said. *He will be King.*

The stars spun faster and faster and climbed higher, glowing like the sun. Meven's face and all the other faces behind it melted like wax and pooled on the ground, looking like flesh-colored lakes. In the span of a few heartbeats the lakes turned blue, thinned, and became streams that fanned out and formed a river. There were trees again, black walnuts and locusts, willows and more.

Everything is confusing, Gallant-Stallion said.

My visions come clearer with the passing of time, she replied.

The image changed again and the trees shed their leaves and branches. Small homes grew on top of the trunks. The river grew wider and wider and rose until it was nearly even with the homes. People's faces appeared in the windows and looked out the doors. They were tanned-skinned, and several had sunken eyes. Only a few were smiling. A moment more and night descended in the vision, and the homes became mountains. A host of stars twinkled down, and for a moment Gallant-Stallion allowed himself to enjoy the scene. Suddenly a piece of the sky pulled loose, shook off its stars, and fluttered toward Gallant-Stallion. Then there was total blackness.

What does this mean? Gallant-Stallion asked.

Mara provided no answers, only more pictures.

There were ponies running across a stretch of tall grass that was shadowed by mountains. They were beautiful ponies with wild-looking eyes. One was black, reminding him of Steadfast. The bare legs of a man were interspersed with the horses' legs, and before Gallant-Stallion could look more closely to see if there were more men, the grass gave way to a sea of blood.

The red darkened and became like coal. Then the black receded and Mara's head came into view. She stepped away, and in the waning light coming in through the barn door, she looked like molten silver.

Glimpses, Gallant-Stallion-called-Rue. Pieces of the past in some cases. Looks at what the future might hold, depending upon your actions.

So cryptic, he said.

She dropped her head down, then up in an embellished nod. *I offer things that are clear and things that are indefinable and puzzling. Things I can easily figure out, and things that haunt me with their mysteries. Such is one of my gifts.*

I do not know what it all means.

She snorted, the sound similar to a chuckle a man might make. *Maybe you are not meant to know. Or maybe you must find out to help your charge. Gallant-Stallion-called-Rue, again I tell you this: Your charge will play a vital role in the future of this country, and perhaps in all of the world. The specifics are not revealed to me. At least not right now.*

So you might learn more? Gallant-Stallion's voice was hopeful.

Death and life await you, Gallant-Stallion-called-Rue. If

you survive the challenge fate casts in your path, return to me. When time moves forward, I can provide more guidance.

"Old Woman!" The stable master stood in the doorway, a pail in each hand and a length of cloth draped over his shoulder. A brush stuck out of his pocket. "You visiting with the newcomers?"

The stable master came forward and set the buckets in front of Gallant-Stallion's stall. Then he retreated to the doorway and pulled a lantern down from a hook. After a few moments' fumbling, he coaxed a light.

"The missus fixed a blackberry pie for me," he said. There was the hint of a stain on his upper lip for proof. "Grandly tasty. I'm going to have me another piece later tonight when she's reading to the boys." He unhooked the rope from the front of the stall, dipped the cloth in the bucket of water, and started cleaning the caked dirt off Gallant-Stallion's front legs. He had to rub hard in a few places.

"You go on back to your stall, Old Woman. I'll come give you a good brushing when I'm done with our visitors."

The pony looked intensely at Gallant-Stallion, and for a brief moment he saw clouds and shadows racing across her eyes. *Until you come to Bitternut again,* she said. Then she swished her tail and returned to the far end of the stable, meeting the gaze of each horse as she went.

13 · Buried Plans

The Finest Court shall be a pasture, with thick green grass as far as the eye can see. It shall be dotted with ponds and streams filled with cool, clear water, and there shall be stands of perfect trees. This is where the Finest shall gather and grow, where they shall learn about men and all the creatures of Paard-Peran, where they shall discover their crucial role in the world and in deciding the fate of men. The Court shall be home and school and above all paradise. And we shall visit from time to time to run with our Finest creations.

~*Paard-Zhumd, son of the creator-god*

The farrier cleaned Gallant-Stallion's and Fortune's hooves long before Meven and Kalantha arrived at the stable. The two had slept well into the morning, enjoying the most comfortable beds they could ever remember and eating their fill of eggs, sausage, and honeyed biscuits at breakfast. Kalantha had seconds.

Meven asked around at the inn about the King's soldier and the mad woman, thinking this would be the closest village on the soldier's route to Nadir, and the one he suggested the soldier leave her at. He wanted to make sure the soldier indeed had put her in a reliable person's care, and wanted to look in on her before leaving. The people at the inn knew nothing about the soldier, however.

So Meven asked again at a boardinghouse and at a tailor's that were on the way to the stable. But no one he talked to had seen a soldier and a woman ride through. Maybe they had cut across country, Meven thought, and stopped somewhere else.

Or maybe he took her to the capital. But with all the rain, the former seemed unlikely, and with the soldier's attitude, the latter probably was out.

"You have fine horses," the stable master told Meven as the young man approached. He saddled Gallant-Stallion and Fortune and brought them out of the barn. "Nice day today for riding." He looked up at the sky. "No rain for a change. It will be good traveling weather for you. Road might still be muddy, though."

Meven took Gallant-Stallion's reins. "Do you have any horses for sale? Something that would be faster than that packhorse? I've some things to barter with. Maybe something better than this ugly punch?"

Trade me? Steadfast, the Prince cannot do that. I am his shepherd! Gallant-Stallion snorted loudly, and Meven wrinkled his nose in response.

The stable master scratched his head. "That packhorse's a fit animal, young man. And the punch is young and healthy and obviously strong. Can't say that I have anything better. Most of the horses here belong to the people who live in the village. The cutting horse is from a man passing through."

Meven brightened. "Did you see a soldier pass through, too? With a woman in raggedy clothes? Very early yesterday or late the day before?"

"A soldier? One soldier?" The stable master's face clouded, and he slowly shook his head. "There were soldiers several days ago, the Prince's wedding party. They didn't stay, though. Went onto Hathi as I understand it."

"Not *soldiers*," Meven corrected. He dug the ball of his foot into the ground. "One *soldier*, riding a noriker. He would have been here yesterday most likely. He had an older woman with him."

"Friends of yours, young man?" Meven didn't notice the hesitation in the stable master's voice.

Kalantha moved up. "We were with that wedding party, and the Prince was killed south of Hathi. Meven is the Prince of Galmier now, and he was just checking on the soldier. Meven'd given him an assignment."

The stable master shifted his weight from one foot to the other. "The Prince dead? And you the new Prince? You don't look like . . ."

Meven pulled the ring out of his pocket and put it on his thumb. He took a deep breath and prepared to tell the man all the grisly details about Edan's death, and the soldiers who were likewise assassinated.

"I hate to tell you this, Prince," the stable master said, the hesitation thicker. He was standing straighter and his shoulders were back, as if knowing that Meven was the Prince was cause for being at attention. "But Garvin Kigley and his sons found a lone soldier and a woman dead early yesterday morning. He figured it happened sometime during the night. The bodies were on the road just a wee bit south of here, around the bend in the road. Their horses were killed, too. Sliced up bad, all of them were. No trace of who killed them. Maybe robbery was the reason. Garvin said they didn't have much on them, so they might have been robbed. Some bags of tattered clothes, chipped dishes and such. If you want to talk to Garvin, I can find him for you. Garvin figured it was bandits . . . they prey on travelers from time to time."

Gallant-Stallion glanced into the barn behind him, to the far corner where Mara was. The pony bobbed her head. *Life and death, I told you. Death and life await Gallant-Stallion-called-Rue.*

Gallant-Stallion recalled the visions she gave him. And he remembered that he heard the assassins moving down the road the other night while he and Meven were obscured by the veil of willow leaves. The assassins must have found the soldier and the mad woman and killed them. They might have thought the soldier a straggler from the wedding party, or they might have recognized the woman as being from Hathi. In either case, they didn't want anyone alive able to identify them.

Meven shook his head in disbelief. "Dead? The mad woman *and* the soldier? Both of them dead?"

"Both of them, sir. Was she some relation? A friend?"

"No. Just someone we met."

The stable master scratched Gallant-Stallion's neck. "They've been buried, and the horse carcasses drug into Carlen's field. Can't leave bodies out in the open to rot. The soldier's things are at the Bell Cow's. He's telling folks around here to take care on the road . . . in case it's bandits."

Meven raised an eyebrow.

"The village leader. We call him the Bell Cow. I can take you there."

Meven shook his head again. "Dead. The woman and the soldier." His eyes narrowed and he clenched his fists. "No one has a right to hurt us or the people we know. We've done nothing wrong," he said.

The stable master realized Meven wasn't talking to him. He gave the reins of the packhorse to Kalantha. She touched the horse's mane and gave a faint smile of thanks; Fortune had been brushed so that his hair felt silky.

"We've hurt no one," Meven continued. "We've never been away from the High Keep Temple. We've not offended anyone. We've not stolen from a soul or lied. There's no reason someone would want to kill us. No reason."

"Kill you?" The stable master's curiosity was piqued.

"They're still after us," Kalantha said as with some effort she climbed up on Fortune. She was achy from the long ride yesterday and was too full of breakfast. "The assassins who killed our cousin Edan, and who killed the soldier and the mad woman—they want us, too." She looked to Meven. "It's just like the mad woman said. The assassins want us dead."

Meven's jaw was set in a firm line and the veins stood out on the sides of his neck.

"And you're wrong, Meven. We did do something. We were born into the Montoll house."

And the assassins want to eliminate the entire royal family it seems, Gallant-Stallion said in hidden speak, wanting the Finest pony to take note. *All of the Montolls dead, don't they? But for what reason?* He expected a reply from Mara. But she remained silent, and she slipped farther back into her stall where Gallant-Stallion couldn't see her any longer.

"But who wants us dead?" Meven was fast on Gallant-Stallion's back and was turning him north toward the High Keep Temple. "Who?"

"Sir? Is there anything I can do to help?" The stable master jogged after them. But Meven urged Gallant-Stallion into a fast trot, and Kalantha pushed Fortune to keep up. The stable master was quickly left behind.

Meven took the main road that cut through the small cluster of businesses and past the inn with its blessedly soft beds and delicious food. The road continued through a row of stone-and-thatch homes, then past a few small farms. To the east, behind a livestock pen, Meven could see the village cemetery. There were two fresh mounds, and one was marked by the soldier's sword.

When the village was out of sight, Meven directed Gallant-Stallion off the road and to the west.

"What are you doing? That's not the way to High Keep!"

"We're going to High Keep, Kal, but we're not taking the road. Our original plan is buried just like the soldier and mad woman are buried." There was a quaver in his voice, as if he wasn't quite sure of himself. "We can't take the road. Edan, the soldiers, the mad woman. They were all killed on the road, and all of them at night. We're getting as far from this accursed road as possible."

He sped up, and Kalantha kneed the packhorse to make it

go faster than it wanted. It whinnied its protest only once at the pace, and Gallant-Stallion tried to tell it to cooperate. Fortune finally sped up a little. He seemed more agreeable than usual since his brushing this morning and fussing-over by the farrier.

"That soldier," Meven said when Kalantha finally came even with him. "Before he died he might have told the assassins where we were going. That's another reason we can't afford to take the road."

"I don't think you told him about High Keep."

"I'm not sure. I think I tried not to tell the soldier anything. But I'm really not certain, Kal. And just to be safe, we're taking the long way to the High Keep Temple." He continued talking, and Gallant-Stallion knew it was to bolster his own confidence and to justify his new plans.

"I know we've never been on our own before. But we've got some of Edan's things we can barter with on the way. Most of these villages don't use coins—they just trade goods and services. I've studied geography, Kal. High Keep's north of the Galmier Mountains. If we cut west through the mountains and travel north up the coast, we'll find High Keep when the mountains end. It'll be easy. We go west, then north, keep the mountains on our right once we're through them. Won't take us much longer than if we took that road."

Kalantha's face took on a troubled mien. Meven was afraid she was going to argue with him. But she sucked in her lower lip and stayed quiet, looking even younger than her scant years.

"My birthday's in a handful of days, Meven."

He didn't reply to that. "We'll find another village, maybe with an inn just like last night. Soft beds to sleep in. It'll be fine, Kal. You'll see." He was staring at the mountains as they went. "We'll find a pass through these mountains. It won't take us much longer to get to High Keep this way. We just have to get away from the road. And be far, far away from it when night comes."

It was a good plan, Gallant-Stallion thought—likely as good a one as he would have come up with. The foothills here were larger than the ones to the south where he had escaped with Meven and Kalantha during the assassins' attack. They were more than three hundred feet tall in places, and the mountains that started behind them were at least five times that height. The foothills were shades of brown and were lightly forested, and the rocks that littered the ground were rounded and therefore of softer stone than what made up the Galmier Mountain range. There was a smooth-flowing, sluggish stream just to the north, and Meven guided them toward it.

He let Gallant-Stallion and Fortune drink as long as they wanted, and he filled two waterskins he'd bartered for in Bitternut. Kalantha took a few minutes to wash her hair and twist it into a fresh braid. Then they were traveling again.

"More than one hundred individual mountains make up this range, Kal," he told her. Meven wasn't trying to impress her with his knowledge of Galmier's geography, he was just chattering to pass the time and to keep her mind off the bad things. "A dozen are a good two thousand feet tall, and one rises almost five thousand feet. I wonder how they managed to measure it?"

"Sister of the Stars," Kal said of the lone giant. She looked up and to the south where the massive mountain reached. Its top was hidden by clouds.

"Born on the day the good gods saved the Sea of Sulene," Meven added. "Legends say if a man with a pure heart fasts for days as he climbs all the way to the top, the gods will answer any single question he asks and will grant him eternal life."

Kalantha kept looking at the giant. "Do you think we're pure of heart, Meven?"

He directed Gallant-Stallion around a section of loose rock, not wanting the shards to hurt the horse's hooves. "Of course we are."

She thrust out her chin. "Then I think we should climb the mountain. You can ask why the assassins want us dead. And I'll ask who the assassins are. We could reach the top by my birthday if we start now. But I'm not going to do the fasting part."

Gallant-Stallion thought that wasn't a bad idea either on the face of things, but he couldn't climb very far up that mountain. And after thinking about it a moment, he doubted the gods would really answer their questions. The gods rarely spoke to the ones who led the Finest Court. Why would they talk to Meven and Kalantha?

"The whole Sister of the Stars thing is a legend, Kal. Doesn't mean it works. Did you ever hear of anyone talking to the gods . . . and getting an answer? And we're not about to waste the time trying to find out if it'll work for us." Meven's voice had a serious tone, reminding Kal of the Bishop when he was gently scolding them for one reason or another.

"I'd like to think it works," Kalantha said. She didn't have to guide Fortune around the skree; the packhorse somehow knew it would hurt his feet, and so he followed Gallant-Stallion. "And I think I'll see for myself if it does." After a moment, she added: "Someday. If the assassins don't get us and when Bishop DeNogaret lets us leave High Keep again. I will climb the Sister of the Stars. But I think the fasting part is silly."

Gallant-Stallion suspected both youths knew that after this wretched adventure the Bishop would keep a tight rein on them when they returned. However, Meven's new title might force the young man to go to Nadir. Would the Bishop go with Meven and Kalantha? Gallant-Stallion hoped so. Meven could use as much mentoring as possible.

The mountains teemed with plants, with the bulk of them growing at the lower elevations. As they picked their way through a winding, climbing pass, Gallant-Stallion could smell the heady scent of wildflowers. Seas of yellow and purple blooms were spread throughout the hills. Higher up there were blotches of white—snowblossoms, he believed they were called. The Finest Court provided an incredible education about Paard-Peran, but Gallant-Stallion hadn't paid especially close attention to the naming of things. And flower labels were not terribly important to him.

But he recalled the names of some trees, which he found slightly more interesting. Pines and oaks grew on the exposed, relatively dry slopes. Basswood shrubs grew in sheltered coves, where he suspected the trapped soil was rich. Hemlocks were plentiful along the stream, which they were paralleling at the moment.

A variety of birds roosted in the hemlocks—starlings, predominantly. But there also were bluebirds, bright yellow finches, black-shouldered kites, and jays. The latter squawked loudly as they passed by.

Meven was quiet now, and Gallant-Stallion could sense that he was thinking. There was a lot on the young man's shoulders, and he probably hadn't comprehended just how his life was going to be changing. Someone his age should not have to handle such responsibility.

And that's why I am his shepherd, Gallant-Stallion thought. *Because he cannot manage all of this on his own.*

Gallant-Stallion knew Meven eventually would have to live at the palace in Nadir. Would Gallant-Stallion be given Steadfast's private stable? he wondered. And how would the young man, so tied to the High Keep Temple, weather all of the pomp and the courtly responsibilities? It was all too much for someone who was only thirteen.

It was late afternoon by the time they'd found another pass. This was one that climbed even higher and appeared to wend its way west through the Galmiers. They were better than five hundred feet above the country's plain when Kalantha spied a relatively flat, grassy area a few dozen feet up and to the north.

She slipped from Fortune's back. "Stop here, Meven." Then she was climbing up a rock face that was jagged enough to provide her ample hand- and footholds.

"Kalantha!" Meven ground his teeth together and clutched the reins so tight that Gallant-Stallion could feel the tension in the young man's arms.

"Mountain laurel," she hollered down. "Morgan showed me drawings. It's beautiful. This place is called a heath bald, Meven. It's a miniature prairie. And there is huckleberry and sand myrtle and . . ."

"I don't care what it is and what's growing on it, Kal. You've got to come down . . ."

"Wild dewberries. I was right. There are wild dewberry plants all over. Hundreds. And the berries are just getting ripe. I'm hungry, Meven. Aren't you?"

"There are more important things to do than eat," Meven countered. "You wouldn't be so chubby if . . ."

"We didn't barter for any food in Bitternut, Meven," she called down. "They're not my favorites, but they're the first berries of spring. There won't be any strawberries and raspberries for quite a few weeks, maybe a month or more. Aren't you the least bit hungry?"

Meven slid off Gallant-Stallion and looked furtively around for something to tie the reins to. He growled when he saw there was nothing. "You stay here," he said. "Understand, Rue? You stay here." He pointed at Fortune and gave the command again, then he fumbled around in the pack of Edan's clothes and pulled out a silk cloak. He scrabbled up after her. "We'll put them in this, Kal," he said.

Gallant-Stallion was pleased. Meven and his sister were resourceful and were thinking ahead.

"We have to pick all of them," he heard Kalantha tell Meven. "The horses will like the berries, too." She showed him the milky white berries, and said that the ones with a little pink blush to them were the ripest and would taste the best.

Even from where he stood, Gallant-Stallion could tell that the berries smelled sweet. He was very pleased at the prospect of sampling them.

It was nearing sunset when the path took them higher still. The rocks were painted with an orange glow, and there were bits of crystal and minerals exposed that sparkled like gold beads. Gallant-Stallion glanced back and around Fortune. The Sprawling River far below and behind was glistening silver and was spread like an opened hand through the center of the country. The Finest considered it the most beautiful view of Paard-Peran he'd seen so far, though it was not near so magnificent as the land of the Finest Court. Still, it was worth admiring, and he noticed that Meven and Kalantha were pausing to take a long look, too.

"I wonder if it looks even prettier from the Sister of the Stars," Kalantha said.

"Looks peaceful," Meven pronounced. "I think I could enjoy it up here if the circumstances were better. C'mon, Rue. We have some light left. Don't get all tired on me yet." He thumped the Finest in the side and directed his attention back to the path.

They were high enough up that Gallant-Stallion could tell the air was thinner and crisper. The vegetation here was different, as the rugged mountains were steeper and there was less earth trapped in coves. There were small spiraea bushes and spreading avens, and rock lichen was plentiful. Farther up there were stands of pines.

"It's going to take us days, isn't it, Meven? Not just a little bit longer like you first said. We won't make it to High Keep in time for my birthday. There'll be no special dinner. All the trillium will be . . ."

"I thought we might find an easy trail through here, Kal. Something that cut right through. And, yes, it could take us a couple of days to get to the other side. We'll just celebrate your birthday a little late."

She seemed less disappointed at that thought. "It's all pretty up here, Meven. Think the Bishop will let us come back?"

Meven started to say yes, but he couldn't lie to her. "Not for quite a while, Kal. And I'm not sure I want to go out for a while either. This hasn't been a good outing." He dropped his right hand to his belt and ran his fingers across the beads. "And I forgot to pray last night." Meven made up for that, praying until the sun was gone from view and the sky took on a purple-blue cast.

They'd found another pass, one that branched from this one and cut down and a little to the north. It had higher, sheerer walls, and Meven thought it might be promising. But it was narrow at its mouth, and it would be a tight squeeze for the Finest.

"We'll try it in the morning," Meven said. Then after he'd dismounted and started to loosen the saddle, he said: "No. Let's go ahead and try it now."

"It's getting dark, Meven. I think we should stop here."

"C'mon, Rue." He was in front of the Finest and started leading him through the narrow part.

Fortune nickered his reluctance, but Kalantha was tugging him along. "I don't think it's a good idea either, Fortune. It's too dark. But Meven's as stubborn as a bull."

Gallant-Stallion scraped his side, and Kalantha scolded her brother for picking this trail. Fortune rubbed against the rocks, too, but it was not so tight a fit for the packhorse, and Kalantha had pulled loose the satchel and was carrying her makeshift sack of berries to help.

Several minutes later the path widened and became a grassy bald that looked like a small valley with high walls. A pass continued to the west beyond this, but even Meven agreed it was too dark to travel farther. Meven took the saddles off Fortune and Gallant-Stallion and let them graze.

"Nothing to tie them to," he said, looking around. In truth, it was getting difficult to see a lot of details, and so he really couldn't tell if there was a suitable outcropping to twist the reins around.

"They won't go anywhere, Meven. They'll stay with us." She sat on a flat rock, opened Edan's cloak and started eating the berries. "So good," she pronounced. "Come have some." When she'd eaten her fill, she put a few handfuls in a well she made in her tunic and shared with Fortune first, then Gallant-Stallion.

The Finest relished the taste and committed it to memory. He would help Kalantha find some more of these tomorrow.

"Up here, Kal." Meven had climbed partway up the wall of the pass and was stretched out on a grassy ledge about a dozen feet above the valley floor. It was protected by an overhang that helped cut the cool night breeze.

Kalantha patted Fortune. "I was going to stay down here with you," she said. "But I can look out for you from up there. Now don't you wander off anywhere. My brother would be very upset." She was quick to join Meven and stretch out, pulling her heaviest blanket over them.

The stars began winking into view when Meven rose and retrieved another blanket and two cloaks. The air was truly cold now and chased away all hint of spring. Meven was shivering as he patted Fortune and Gallant-Stallion before returning to the rocky shelf and his sister.

He could make a good ruler, the Finest thought, with more

life experience. *And so, Steadfast, I must keep him alive long enough so he can someday wear the crown. And he must not think about selling me again.* But to keep Meven safe, the Finest knew he would have to discover who the assassins were and why they were after the Galmier heirs—and all the witnesses to the attacks. Politics were involved, and wealth, he was certain, as he'd learned from his training in the Finest Court that greed for wealth and power were the prime motivations of evil men.

Gallant-Stallion would have liked to look at the scene of the soldier and mad woman's death. There might have been some crucial clues there—clues he had missed at the site of Edan's death. But it had been raining, and so anything of note could have been washed away. Like the assassins' tracks to Hathi had been washed from the road when Gallant-Stallion and Meven were hidden by the willow leaves.

Steadfast, I am smart and my senses are keenly honed. But there are clues I am missing. The site of the battle should have yielded clues. His mind reached back to that horrible night when the assassins surrounded them so quickly and killed Prince Edan and all the soldiers. There was something about the battle that still seemed . . . wrong. Something he'd noticed about the field of the dead the next morning that didn't fit. *Something out of place and I cannot see it.*

Neither did Gallant-Stallion see something now that was darker than the shadows in the small valley and darker than the twilight sky. He was preoccupied with his puzzle.

There was rain that night, Steadfast. Plenty of it. But . . . in the morning when we came upon the dead soldiers I saw hoofprints. Faint, but they were there. The rain hadn't taken them all. His eyes grew wide and he stamped a hoof. He finally realized what had been bothering him and what was wrong about the site of the battle. *There were not enough tracks! The ground wasn't torn up. And it should have been. There were so many assassins on horseback that they should have ripped up the earth when they charged in and circled. The rain would not have obliterated it all. So how could the assassins' horses not have left tracks? What if there were no horses?*

But there was the thrumming of horses charging that night, Gallant-Stallion recalled. Soft at first, like the sound that intruded now in his musings.

Again that sound!

He wuffled a warning to Fortune, but the packhorse was oblivious to the approaching danger. Then he gave out a high-pitched whinny meant to rouse Meven and Kalantha.

A moment more and the darkness moved closer and the sound of hoofbeats grew louder.

Not hoofbeats, Gallant-Stallion said. He whinnied again, as piercing a sound as he could make. Fortune whinnied his displeasure at being wakened. Kalantha sat upright and Meven began to stir.

"Fortune?" Kalantha was looking for the packhorse. "What's wrong?" She cocked her head. "Horses coming?"

The sound was *like* hoofbeats, but not hoofbeats. The soldiers' horses were moving the night of the attack and were adding to the cacophony, and so everything seemed to sound like hoofbeats to Gallant-Stallion. But there was nothing to compete with the sound now, nothing that might confuse things.

The Finest's ears shot forward and his eyes scanned the pass leading from the valley. Nothing. He twisted and looked at the pass they'd come through. Nothing there either. What was that sound?

"Kal, what's going on?"

"I'm not sure, Meven. I hear something. Sounds like horses. Meven, I think . . . Meven!" Kalantha glanced up.

Bits of black, like torn pieces of fabric fluttering in the breeze appeared above the top of the cliff. The pieces hung suspended for an interminable moment, caught perhaps by a gust of wind. Then they moved, flowing together in groups until they were no longer pieces, but men with billowy cloaks that whipped about in them. They stood poised at the top of the cliff face above Meven and Kalantha, more than a dozen of them, slashes of black above them were swords poised to strike. Then they poured down the rocky wall.

"Assassins!" Meven croaked. He could manage no other word, as his mouth had gone impossibly dry.

Meven could hear the muted thundering of horses' hooves, just like he had heard them the night of the attack on Prince Edan. But there were no horses. There were only the mysterious men.

Like spiders they skittered down the rocks, paying no attention to gravity and heading straight toward the cousins. Their cloaks continued to billow about them, and coupled with the darkness made it difficult to make out any details.

"Falafalafala. We find the cousins. We kill the cousins."

"Death comes!"

14 · A Living Blackness

A shepherd has been known to sacrifice his life to save his charge. Though noble, this has never been the wisest course of action.

~*The Old Mare*

Fortune's ears pulled back and his eyes narrowed, finally perceiving the threat. He rose up in fear and bolted, taking the pass ahead that led from the small valley. Gallant-Stallion reared back too, but in anger. He galloped toward the cliff face, his hooves striking rocks as he tried to climb to reach Meven and Kalantha. He fell back as the black figures closed.

Gallant-Stallion recalled one of the visions Mara had given him. It was a chunk of the night sky shedding its stars and dropping on him. What he was seeing looked just like the vision, ink spilling over the cliff face and running down to envelop his charge. It was the dark assassins come to slay the cousins and himself. Mara had foreshadowed this very attack!

"Run!" Meven shouted. He'd managed to find his voice again, though there was a tremor in each word. "Run, Kal!" He grabbed Kalantha's hands and lowered her over the ledge. "Climb down and run!" But his rash act surprised her, and she couldn't get a purchase with her feet. Her legs dangled free. "Kal! Get a hold of something!"

"Let go!" she shouted. "Drop me!"

"Too far to fall!" Meven changed his mind and tried to pull her up, but she wriggled in his grasp.

She was able to pull one hand free of his and jam it into a crevice. "Let go of me! Run yourself!"

Meven did let go just as she found a small outcropping to stand on and just as the first black figure reached him. As she started to climb down, the first assassin struck Meven, and he howled in pain and surprise. In the next instant, the blackness seemed to swallow him.

"Meven?" Kalantha couldn't see what was going on. She hung indecisive below the ledge for just a moment, then she climbed back up so she could see him. But all she saw was a cloud of black, darker than the shadows and moving in and out as if the cloud was one entity and was breathing. She clung, frozen, the terror taking hold, eyes searching for some trace of the men she'd seen climb down the rocks.

It wasn't until she heard Meven cry out that she blinked and forced herself to move. Climbing down and running away would be the sensible thing and might keep her safe. Meven cried again and she instead crawled closer to the cloud, chest tight and gasping for air. A piece of the cloud broke away, just as she thrust her hand into the blackness, trying to find her brother.

She brushed against something soft and felt a rush of air against her skin. Then she felt a jolt of pain, as her arm was stabbed. She pulled back, but instantly thought of Meven again, and this time, sobbing in fear, she shoved both hands into the darkness and fumbled about until she'd found her brother. She gave him a strong tug, and he rolled with her, dropping over the ledge and falling as she barely managed to hang onto the rocks, legs dangling free. "Meven!"

He didn't answer her, but started rolling when he hit the

ground. He headed toward the Finest, and he didn't look back. She began to scrabble down the cliff face, her chest tighter than ever, just as the black cloud swarmed over the ledge and descended with her.

As it moved, it divided into two shapes, four, a dozen. They looked like men again with billowing cloaks. Then they seemed to shatter into fragments of black glass. Some of the fragments fluttered around Kalantha, but most took flight toward Meven.

By the Court! Gallant-Stallion cursed. *The assassins are not men, they are birds!* He charged forward until Meven was under him, then he reared back again, hooves flailing out at the approaching enemy, heart hammering in excitement and fear.

He saw distinct shapes in the darkness—bats, blackbirds, black-shouldered kites, black redstarts, warblers, and woodswallows. That's why there had been no hoofprints from the assassins' horses—the assassins hadn't been riding horses. They were all birds and bats, flying in tight formations to make themselves look like cloaked men on horseback. It was why he could make out no features that night during the attack on the wedding party, and why the 'horses' looked *different* than any breed he'd seen before. They weren't horses. But the night, the storm, and the chaos helped conceal their true forms then.

Birds! Gallant-Stallion shouted, as his hooves struck one after another and sent them to the ground. He shook his head and started snapping, his teeth clacking shut on birds and bats. He clamped down hard and felt their bodies break and their blood spurt into his mouth, then he tossed them aside and snapped at more.

His mind raced as he went. Was Meven all right? And Kalantha? She was running toward him, arms waving in an attempt to keep the birds away. But her arms and face were covered with cuts; the Finest could see this and knew she must be hurting terribly. And he could smell her fear, so strong it nipped at his nostrils.

"Kal!" Meven seemed to be all right. He crawled out from under Gallant-Stallion, awkwardly got to his feet, and hobbled to meet her. He hugged her tight and pulled her down to the ground with him, just as the Finest came to them, flailing away at the birds with his hooves.

"Kal! They're not assassins, they're birds," Meven said, the tremble still thick in his voice.

She held him tighter and gasped for breath. She was shaking fiercely. "B-b-birds. Men. It doesn't m-m-matter. They *are* assassins, Meven. And they're going to k-k-kill us."

The Finest continued to strike out with his hooves faster and faster, and he snapped at the air, hoping to catch more of the hateful creatures in his mouth. They were attacking him now instead of the cousins, as he was proving a threat to their plan.

"Kill the horse," one of the birds said. "Kill it quick."

"The horse first," came a clearer voice. "Deal with it, then the children."

Gallant-Stallion wished Steadfast was here at his side, both for the elder Finest's strength and so he could witness the birds' vile antics. They were not normal birds, they were too vicious and smart and they were clearly capable of speech. Perhaps they were to normal birds what the Finest were to common horses, Gallant-Stallion thought. The Finest Court must learn such beings exist! He vowed to stay alive so he could report this atrocity of nature.

"Kill the horse, I say!"

"Yes, Falafalafala."

"Kill it now!"

Gallant-Stallion saw the speaker through a gap in the black wings. It was a large inky hawk with shiny eyes. The shiny, cold eyes he'd spotted during the attack that night. He sensed evil emanating from the bird, and the hair on his back stood up.

"The horse!" the hawk repeated.

"Yes, Fala. The horse."

"Falafalafala says kill the horse."

I think not! Gallant-Stallion shouted as he charged toward the hawk and away from the cousins. The hawk hovered a few feet above the ground, certainly within his reach. *I think I will kill you instead!*

"M-M-MEVEN, THEY'RE TALKING. THE BIRDS!" KALANTHA untangled herself from her brother and watched the birds coalesce into a cloud again and swarm around Gallant-Stallion. The Finest was leading the birds away from the brother and sister and pursing a bird that stayed separate from the cloud. "And they're going to kill your Rue!"

Meven pointed a shaking finger in the opposite direction, toward the western pass out of the valley. The stars provided just enough light so they could see the way. "We have to get out of here, Kal. If we don't run, we're dead."

"But Rue . . ." She gave a sad look over her shoulder at the blackness that had swallowed Gallant-Stallion. She could see nothing of the punch now. Then she helped support Meven and hurried to the pass. He'd hurt himself in the fall and couldn't walk quickly.

"I think I broke my leg, Kal."

"We'll tend to it later," she said. "After we're safe."

BEHIND THEM, THE BIRDS WERE SCREECHING. THE SHRILL chorus was bouncing off the rocks and echoing eerily. There were so many birds and bats that their beating wings sounded like the muted pounding of horses' hooves. The Finest continued to defy them, rearing back again and again, lashing out with his hooves, biting them, driving them into the ground, trying to reach the hawk.

"Death comes!" a raven cried.

"Kill the horse for Fala," another said.

"Death to the horse! Then to the cousins."

"We will not fail!" the raven shouted.

You will fail, Gallant-Stallion told them. *Vile creatures, you will not get my charge.* He knew they couldn't hear him, but he shouted at them nonetheless. The words helped keep his mind clear and kept him from thinking about the pain that coursed through his body.

They were jabbing at him with their needle-sharp beaks. Some were flying by, raking him with their talons. It was talons and beaks, not daggers and thin-bladed swords that were responsible for killing Edan and the soldiers. He might have seen that, had he not been so sure that men were responsible for the slayings.

You will not kill Meven! But Gallant-Stallion wasn't sure of that. As powerful as he was, he doubted he could drive all the birds away. There were just too many of them. At least he was managing to lessen their numbers, and he was buying time for Meven and Kalantha. The ground was littered with crows, starlings, bats, and more. He feared he would join them.

"Its eyes," one of them said. Gallant-Stallion knew it was the big hawk talking. "Blind the horse and it cannot cut us so."

"Falafalafala says blind it. Blind it then kill it."

"Death comes."

Gallant-Stallion slammed his eyes shut and tried a new tact. Like a wild horse working to throw a rider trying to tame him, he whirled and bucked, reared back and smacked anything within his reach. All the while he tossed his head from side to side, using his strong jaw as a club. He was no longer frightened of them; he was beyond that. He was angry and desperate, and oddly, above that, curious that such birds could exist.

The birds continued to stab and claw at him, and one raked him particularly deeply along his neck. But the Finest did not give in to the pain. He felt a hotness against his sides and on his withers, and he knew it was his own blood. He wondered if Steadfast had suffered so before he was taken down. And he wondered just how long it would be before he joined the elder Finest in the land where spirits dwelled. He suspected it wouldn't be too long, as he was tiring.

When he sucked in great gulps of air, it felt hot and left a coppery taste in his mouth. Each breath seemed harder to take in than the last, and his chest felt on fire—despite the chill night air. His strong legs were feeling weaker and weaker and were becoming so heavy they were hard to lift. In the back of his mind he saw Steadfast lying dead near Prince Edan. He saw all the norikers dead, the soldiers dead. He wondered if anyone would find his body. But he also saw Meven and Kalantha, pictured them sleeping on the ledge, then climbing down when the assassin birds came. He had to last awhile longer, he told himself—long enough for Meven and his sister to find a safe place to hide.

But was anyplace safe? he wondered, as he continued to buck and whirl, summoning the last of his strength to furiously strike the malicious birds. They would be able to eventually find Meven and Kalantha because there were birds everywhere. Gallant-Stallion remembered seeing blackbirds in the trees along the road past Hathi before the first attack came, and most recently in the mountains where Kalantha and Meven picked dewberries. They might have been spies for the assassin flock. There might be more spies elsewhere. And if that was the case, Prince Meven would not be safe on his own anywhere— he would need a Finest to shepherd and guard him.

The only way to ultimately make Meven safe would be to slay all of these birds and discover who was commanding them. Certainly the birds hadn't come up with this plan on their own. They were puppets, malicious, hateful, and hurtful, and someone had given them the power to speak and was directing their every action.

So Gallant-Stallion would have to live if Meven was to live. He reached deep inside himself and found a reserve of energy he didn't know he possessed. The Finest nurtured it and channeled it, and imagined his legs growing stronger and his hooves sharper. He flung his head back and forth faster and faster and felt the birds break against his jaws.

"The horse kills us," one of the birds called. "He will not fall!"

"Death comes to us," cried another.

"The cousins," came a third voice, this belonging to the big hawk called Fala. "Leave the horse and find the cousins. They run!"

"Cousins," the birds said. The word was repeated until it sounded like the buzzing of a bee swarm. "Kill the cousins."

Then suddenly Gallant-Stallion didn't feel the birds against him, and the jabbing and scratching stopped. The sound of their wingbeats retreated, and he risked opening his eyes. The birds were flying down the pass to the west, where Fortune had fled long minutes ago and where the Finest had caught sight of Meven and Kalantha running. One bird was higher than the rest, the big hawk with the shiny, cold eyes. It was herding the assassin flock like a dog herding sheep.

Meven! Gallant-Stallion called to the new Prince, though he knew his voice was lost on men. *The assassins come, Meven!* The Finest charged down the pass, barely registering the dozens of dead birds that littered the valley floor and that he trampled. He'd killed so many of them. But there were still so many left.

His sides and legs screamed in protest, the wounds on them opening wider as he ran. His chest felt impossibly hot and his head throbbed. Gallant-Stallion had never been in such agony before; the wounds he'd suffered in the first battle were nothing compared to what he was suffering now. The Finest Court had not prepared him for anything like this—pain had been only a word before, not something real and overwhelming. Instinct told him to retreat, that there was nothing he could do to stop the assassin birds. Why should he die with his charge?

But Steadfast had stayed to the end, so loyal to Edan he'd been, and Edan wasn't even his real responsibility.

It is what the gods created the Finest for, Gallant-Stallion said as he continued to rush headlong after the black cloud. *To save the Fallen Favorites.*

The mountain pass twisted and turned, but continued to go toward the west. For a few moments the Finest lost sight of the birds, as they flew over a rise rather than slow their pace to fly around a bend. But he saw them again when the pass straightened and became wider, and then opened into another valley, this one much larger than the one they'd tried to spend the night in. The bulk of the assassin flock was well ahead of the Finest now.

Meven was in the center of the valley, clinging to his sister while at the same time trying to protect her. He was using himself as a shield, and the birds were swarming him.

Gallant-Stallion forced himself into a gallop, the earth churning up in clumps behind him. He leapt as he neared the cloud and managed to strike out at the outermost birds. Then he sped around the cloud and struck at it from the opposite side, setting his gaze on Meven.

"Rue!" Meven called. "Help us!"

Gallant-Stallion heard his own heart pounding, heard the thrumming of the assassin-birds' wings, heard what passed for the sound of thundering hoofbeats, heard Meven continue to call for him. He reared and slammed his hooves into the birds darting in at his charge. He whirled and bucked and again thrashed so violently that his head and neck and entire body became a bludgeoning weapon he was wielding against the birds.

He heard the soft thumps their bodies made when they struck the earth around him. And he heard the big hawk call for them to again concentrate on the Finest.

"Kill the horse," the hawk ordered. "Kill it this time, and then the cousins will be ours."

"Death comes to the horse," an assassin answered.

Gallant-Stallion kept flailing away. He was in a maddened frenzy, no longer really thinking about what he was doing, just pummeling and kicking and stamping and biting. The birds shrieked in anger and agony, and more and more of them fell. The Finest's heart hammered louder, competing with the sound of their beating wings and the thundering of hooves.

"Retreat," the hawk ordered. "Another day."

"Death another day," the assassin birds answered. "Death comes another day."

"Fala says retreat. Falafalafala."

Gallant-Stallion felt the breeze their wings created as they left him, then felt a coolness—the night air clear around him. He felt a sense of relief, and of pride that he'd managed to save his charge. He felt an intense concern about the supernatural birds. And then he felt himself falling, finally succumbing to his wounds.

Meven hobbled toward him, Kalantha helping him along.

"Rue." Meven brushed at the Finest's mane, matted with blood. "He saved us, Kal. This big ugly horse saved us. And I had thought about selling him. We'd be dead if I had."

Kalantha touched the blaze marking between Gallant-Stallion's eyes. "But he couldn't save himself, Meven."

15 · Scarlet Haws and Water Plums

It is a matter for the Court Elders to determine the pairing of a Finest to a Fallen Favorite. It is a partnership that will challenge the Finest and benefit the Fallen one, and both should be better and stronger for it.

~The Finest Court canon

Death will next come to you," the hawk called to Meven and Kalantha. He and a trio of his assassins circled the brother and sister and the fallen Finest, then shot toward the sky. They followed the rest of the malevolent flock up and over the cliff face, just as the pounding of hooves became almost deafening.

"Are more evil birds coming?" Kalantha hugged Meven and waited for the sound to bring more assassins.

The hoofbeats were genuine this time. Galloping into the valley came a herd of mountain ponies. There were well more than a hundred of them, snorting and rearing. With each snort, the ponies' breath puffed in miniature clouds that hung like fog in the chill spring air. They stamped and tossed their heads, and they practically filled the valley, within moments surrounding Meven and Kalantha and Gallant-Stallion.

Roughly half of them were spitis, dun and gray ponies with pronounced jaws, large heads, and short necks. The rest were chestnut-colored huculs with small ears and active eyes; dark brown and black fells with long, thick manes; heavy-framed roans; and shaggy-coated highlands with dorsal stripes. Even in the meager starlight, one pony stood out. Among the smallest, she nudged her way through the herd and came near Meven and Kalantha. When she snorted, her breath drifted away from her nose in an ethereal lacy fan.

The starlight made her black coat shimmer like it was liquid. She had an abundant mane and a tail that brushed the ground, and a deep, wide chest. Her gold-flecked eyes sparkled when she looked back and forth between Meven and Kalantha.

"First birds and bats, now ponies. This is utter madness! Have the ponies come to finish what the birds couldn't?" Meven spat. He tried to push Kalantha behind him, but she'd have nothing of it.

"They would've killed us already if that was their plan," she said. "They drove those horrid birds away, Meven. They helped us."

He shook his head. "Horses, ponies. They're animals, and none of them have the sense of a . . ."

Meven swallowed the rest of his words as the little black pony began circling them. Her lacy breath was coming faster now, and when she went behind Meven and Kalantha a second time, and was closest to Gallant-Stallion, she bent low and breathed on him.

Kalantha whirled to watch, while Meven divided his attention between the closest ponies in front of him. One of them was pawing at the ground, ears laid back as if in a warning, and the whites of his eyes showed.

I AM ARIÈG, THE BLACK PONY SAID TO THE FALLEN FINEST. *Can you hear me?*

Gallant-Stallion remained motionless. He felt like he was floating. He could see nothing—perhaps he was blind. He smelled blood and earth, the mustiness of birds, and faintly he smelled dewberries. The sweet taste of the berries still lingered on his tongue and warred with the taste of the assassin birds' blood. He thought he heard something, Meven and Kalantha talking, someone else calling herself . . . Arièg? He tried to speak, but he couldn't.

His voice was gone, and he knew the pain had taken it. The pain was intense and had stripped him of his impressive strength. It was taking his life, too. Gallant-Stallion knew he was dying, and he wondered if he would see Steadfast when he was gone from Paard-Peran. He wasn't afraid, as he knew every creature—even each Finest—would someday die. So the inevitable was nothing to be feared.

Steadfast, will I see you when I die?

Yes, Gallant-Stallion.

Steadfast! Gallant-Stallion wondered if he was already dead, and so could hear the veteran Finest.

You still must cling to life, young one, Steadfast said. *Though your hold on it is weak.*

Gallant-Stallion tried to see the veteran Finest, but all he saw was an utter blackness.

Will I still feel this pain when I die?

No, young one. All pain vanishes.

How can I hear you, Steadfast, if I am not yet dead?

A silence stretched out, and Gallant-Stallion repeated the question. *Steadfast . . . am I dreaming?* There was no answer, and so Gallant-Stallion decided he was dreaming, or hovering at the edge of consciousness. He thought he'd heard Steadfast's voice once before, the night they stayed by the river and he heard the assassins pass by on the road. But that had been a dream, too.

Wake up, Gallant-Stallion.

It might only be wishful thoughts that he would see Steadfast soon. Those thoughts gave him some succor, but he was profoundly disappointed and filled with sadness. His charge was the new Prince of Galmier. And because the assassin-birds had felled him, he had let both the Prince and the Finest Court down. Without a Finest to protect Meven, the new Prince likely would never reach High Keep; the assassins would be back. Would they kill Meven quickly, so he would not feel such pain?

Wake up.

Gallant-Stallion wondered if it was possible for the pain to get worse, and how long it might take for him to die. He hoped it wouldn't take too terribly long. He wanted an end to this suffering.

As he drifted, he felt a cold sensation intrude—something more chill than the night air. It brushed his neck and teased his ears. Then it centered on the blaze between his eyes. It grew colder still, like he imagined the feel of a stream in winter, and it swept through his whole body. His blood had become ice.

"Meven, the pony's doing something to poor Rue."

"What? What is it doing?" Meven turned so he could see the black pony, then whipped his head back around to keep track of the ones in front of him. "It's not doing anything. It's just smelling him. Keep away from it, Kal. Maybe we should leave." But his voice lacked certitude. "Can't see the way out of this valley, though. Too many ponies." Softer, not intending Kalantha to hear: "I don't know what to do." He dropped a hand to his belt, touched a bead, and began to silently pray.

The black pony continued to breathe on Gallant-Stallion, her fan-shaped breath hovering like mist over his prone form. Kalantha stared as the mist sparkled faintly like frost, then settled completely over the big horse. Ice formed around all the cuts and punctures.

"Meven, you better see what the pony's doing to Rue."

But Meven was intent now on the husky pony in front of him that was pawing the ground and snorting. There were a few others that were looking agitated, too. "Rue's dead. Don't worry about him. I think maybe we should try to leave," he said. "If they'll let us." He made a move to stand, but his injured leg wasn't cooperating. "I need your help, Kal."

Kalantha knew it was difficult for Meven to admit he was having trouble. She reached behind and touched Meven's back. "You really need to see this," she told him. "I don't want to leave yet."

"Do you always have to argue?" Meven took another quick glance and gasped when he saw ice all over the fallen punch. Then he put a hand on Kalantha's shoulder and put his weight on it, using her to help him get up. He leaned against her, then balanced on his left foot while she got up. "We have to get out of here, Kal. I don't like the looks of any of this."

"I don't want to leave yet, Meven."

The black pony was making a clicking noise with its teeth, its muzzle right over Gallant-Stallion's ear.

Do not leave us, she told him. *I sense that you are young and have time yet to give the world of the Fallen Favorites.* She directed her lacy breath over his eyes and ears and stretched her head down to the ground and breathed into his nostrils.

Gallant-Stallion felt the cold intensify. So cold! It was the stronger sensation now, and so the pain didn't dominate him anymore. He took a breath, and felt cold, cold air slip down his throat.

I am curious, the pony said. *The birds were vicious. Not like birds should be. You must not leave us, as no one else can tell me about the birds. I am exceedingly curious, brother Finest. You must live and tell me.*

The frigid air filled his lungs. He started shivering uncontrollably.

"Rue's moving, Meven."

Meven's eyes were again on a dozen ponies he'd seen pawing

at the ground and snorting. "I think the pass west is through those ponies with the ridges on their backs." Meven referred to the shaggy highlands, which were standing like soldiers, shoulder to shoulder several feet away. They appeared calm, and none of them were stamping on the ground. "Maybe we can get through them."

"Not yet, Meven." Kalantha couldn't keep her eyes off the punch.

The cold had thoroughly numbed Gallant-Stallion. The Finest wasn't in the slightest pain anymore, and so he thought he was unable to feel anything and was heartbeats from death. He waited, searching with his senses for Steadfast and other Finest creations who had passed on before him. Instead, he heard snorts and wufflings, all the sounds horses made, hooves stamping at the ground. He also heard voices, what sounded like Meven, and a voice that sounded memorable and haunting and that was urging him to live.

I must know about the birds, the haunting voice persisted. *Do not leave us. Tell me about the birds.*

It would be so easy to give up and slip away. It would be so very easy, Gallant-Stallion knew, to let go and find the place where spirits roamed in meadowlands beyond the bounds of Paard-Peran and the Finest Court. He would no longer feel so cold, and there'd be no fear the pain would return. But something in that cold sensation was keeping him from death and was somehow giving him the tiniest amount of hope.

Fight, the voice ordered. *Do not let my effort and energies be for naught. Fight for your life.* The voice sounded so distant.

Gallant-Stallion tried to answer, but his tongue felt too unwieldy and his throat had frozen. Even hidden speak was beyond him. *I am trying,* he wanted to say. *I do want to live. I need to stay with Meven and protect him.* There were questions, too. *Who are you? How can I hear you? Am I dreaming your voice?*

Fight. Do not give up. Find something to live for. The voice was a little stronger. *There must be something or someone you cherish.*

Gallant-Stallion thought of Meven and the wonderful dewberries, the incredible smell of bread baking and the feel of willow leaves tickling his back. He tried to draw strength from all the things he found good about Paard-Peran. And he concentrated on the other sounds that were becoming clearer to him.

The nickering and stamping of horses was the loudest and made Gallant-Stallion at first think he'd somehow returned to the Finest Court or was back among the norikers. At length, he realized it was a Finest speaking to him, the persistent and memorable voice telling him not to leave. But as he continued to listen, he heard Meven's voice too, and so he guessed he was still in the Galmier Mountains. The new Prince was talking about leaving the valley and finding a safe place to stay. Kalantha was talking, too.

"Meven, Rue's not dead! It's the pony, I know it. The pony did something to bring Rue back to life!"

Gallant-Stallion felt Kalantha's hands on him, welcome warmth against his frosty hide. He felt the unnatural cold gradually leaving him. It was replaced by the brush of the night air, cool this high up in the mountains this early in the spring, but not so cold as what he'd been feeling. He also felt the pain returning, though it was not nearly so intense as it had been when he fell. Now it was only a dull throb that suffused him, worse along his withers and neck where the deepest of his wounds were. He still smelled the mustiness of the birds and the acrid odor of blood, the faint scent of dewberries, Kalantha and Meven. Above that was the strong odor of horses. Lots of horses.

Where was he?

Not in the Finest Court.

Not with norikers—they were all dead, weren't they? Still in the mountains as he suspected; he could tell that from the thin crispness of the air he was deeply sucking into his lungs.

He remembered hearing the sound of hoofbeats, but thought at the time it was his mind playing tricks and that it was really the noise made by all the birds' wings. But it wasn't a trick and there really were horses. Lots of them. But where had they come from?

He forced open his eyes, half expecting to see an army of the King's men on war-horses, somehow all come in search of Prince Meven. Instead he saw dozens of mountain ponies, and one coal-black one that was inches from his head.

The black pony neighed loudly and stepped back. She tossed her head and fixed her gold-flecked eyes on Gallant-Stallion. *I did not want you to leave,* she said. *I want to know about the birds.*

Meven and Kalantha were talking at the same time, expressing their surprise at Rue's recovery. Kalantha kept insisting that the pony was responsible for healing Rue. The brother and sister's words were a buzz, and Gallant-Stallion pushed them to the back of his mind and concentrated on the Finest pony. With considerable effort he struggled to his feet.

You healed me?

To the best of my ability. Time will heal what I was not able to. The black gave a nod. *All of us have gifts, young Finest. The ability to heal others is mine.*

You are . . .

I am Arièg.

Thank you, he said. *I cannot begin to repay the kindness you have shown.*

I do not need your gratitude for using my gift. She raised her head, the hairs of her night-black mane swirling and catching motes of her frost-breath. *But I would have information from you. Curiosity is my greatest fault—peeping, prying, spying.*

It was his turn to raise his head in question. *You want to know about the assassin-birds?*

To sate my curiosity. Yes. Tell me everything about them.

Gallant-Stallion was slow in answering, and so the pony continued.

Curiosity. It is why I have no one to shepherd, young Finest. The Court discovered that when I was guiding a wise, promising boy from north of High Keep, I did not give him my full measure. I was far too curious about everything going on around myself and him. He was destined for great things, young Finest, but I failed him, and he slipped into obscurity. In a sense, I slipped into obscurity as well.

Then why are you here? Why are you not at the Court?

The Court gave me a humble role. I must aid travelers in these mountains until I have mastered my curiosity. When that happens I can end my penance and return to the Court. There I pray I will be given someone else to guide and guard. I will do better with my second chance.

Gallant-Stallion couldn't hide his astonishment. He'd never heard of a Finest failing in such a way. The Finest were created by the gods, and were better than people. Yet this one had a Fallen Favorite–quality—an intense curiosity—that had tainted her.

It has been nearly a decade since a Finest passed through the mountains who I could speak with. So while I am sorry at the circumstance that brought you to need my help, I am appreciative of your presence.

Arièg, I am called Gallant-Stallion by my Finest brothers.

An impressive name for one so young. Your charge must be significant, and your task must be momentous. You must tell me all about it. Please. But first, tell me of the birds.

Gallant-Stallion quickly retold the story of the first attack of the assassin-birds, and how Steadfast and the others fell. *I believe Steadfast would have assigned Prince Edan as my charge.*

But with Edan dead, Meven took that role. This young man is the Prince of Galmier now, and if I guard him successfully, he will become King.

Meven and Kalantha were still talking, both of them convinced now that the ponies would not hurt them and had—either accidentally or by design—helped save them from the slayers. Kalantha was gently prodding Gallant-Stallion's wounds.

"They're closing up, Meven. It's unbelievable."

Shepherding the future King, a consequential assignment indeed. Steadfast, who you spoke of, guided the King of Galmier.

You knew Steadfast?

Steadfast came through the mountains when the King was a young man and was intent on fishing in the village Windwane. Even Kings need a respite from their responsibilities, Steadfast told me. I did not see them return, which was a pity. I very much wanted to know what the King caught.

"Amazing," Meven said. He was running his hands over Gallant-Stallion, while balancing on his left foot and keeping an eye on the black pony. "I think you're right, Kal. I think the pony did something to help Rue."

"Magic," Kalantha decided.

Meven scowled. "Magic exists only in children's stories, Kal."

"As do talking birds."

Gallant-Stallion again pushed the brother and sister's words aside. He would pay close attention to his charge and Kalantha in a moment. But he wanted to speak more with Arièg first.

You healed me. Can you heal the Prince and his sister?

Arièg shook her head. *Neither is in danger of dying. They hurt, and their wounds are numerous. But none of the injuries are terribly serious. The young man has impaired his leg. He and his sister will live.*

But you can help them. Can't you?

A stronger shake of her head. *Listen to them. Already they think there is something special about me. I should have waited to tend to you until after they left. They thought you dead. I should have waited.*

I might have died if you had waited.

She ignored the comment. *The young man watches me closely. He is so suspicious. If I were to help them, it would remove all doubt in their minds. They would know I am more than a simple mountain pony. I am not to be discovered, Gallant-Stallion. They will live. None of us are to be discovered, no matter the cost.*

Gallant-Stallion gave a snort and tipped his head back. The stars were brilliant in the cloudless sky, and directly overhead was the formation of Paard-Zhumd, eldest and most revered of the world's five gods. *You said the Finest Court bid you help travelers until your curiosity was conquered.*

They will live, Arièg repeated. Her eyes had an angry spark. *The boy and girl are hurt, my charge especially.*

I cannot be found out. You should appreciate that, Gallant-Stallion.

I appreciate that you want to know about the birds.

Arièg's eyes grew wide and her nose flared. Her breath came faster, lacy fans of mist touching Kalantha, who was closest.

"It's cold!" Kalantha squealed. She jerked back, but Arièg followed her, breath coating her arms and neck, rising up to cover her face. Kalantha stood still, quickly understanding what was happening. The slashes were closing and the ache was lessening. She stepped away from Gallant-Stallion and held her arms out so the black pony could better breathe on her.

"Kal, what're you . . ."

She waved Meven off and tipped her chin up, where there were several ugly red welts.

She knows I am special, Arièg said. *I have removed all doubts and now risk the wrath of the Finest Court. Now tell me of the birds.*

The birds tried to make us think they were men on horseback, flying in a formation to look like such. We thought the men had cloaks flapping in the wind. And the beats of their wings sounded like the thundering of horses' hooves. The night helped to make them convincing.

Tell me more. Arièg continued her ministrations as Kalantha turned so the pony could heal the backs of her arms.

"The cold's not so bad, Meven. The pony's healing me. It *is* magic." Her teeth were chattering, and she turned so the lacy breath could touch her everywhere she was hurt. "The pony *did* help your horse. She helped me. She can help you, too."

Meven remained cautious and skeptical and kept his distance.

Tell me more about the birds, Arièg pressed.

Meven first. He is my charge.

Arièg stepped closer to Meven, some of the ponies behind her moving in closer, too. *They are curious like Arièg,* Gallant-Stallion thought as he moved sideways to keep as many back as he could.

Kalantha locked her arm with her brother's and nodded toward the black pony. "Don't be afraid, Meven."

"I'm not afraid. I just don't like any of this, Kal." He leaned on her, and he didn't resist as she walked toward the pony with him in tow.

Arièg chilled the distrustful Meven, bowing her head and spending the longest time breathing on his leg. Meven shivered visibly. He kept his eyes on the pony, glancing up only once when Gallant-Stallion snorted a warning to keep the curious huculs back. After a few minutes, Meven leaned away from Kalantha and tested his leg.

"She healed you, too." Kalantha brushed at her brother's

cheek, where scratches had already scabbed over. "A magic pony, this black one is."

"It's not right," he whispered. "My leg can't be healed like this. It's broken." But the tension left his face and he was breathing more easily. He put more of his weight on his still-sore leg and reached forward to stroke the pony's neck. "But somehow it's not broken now. Thank you," he said.

Kalantha was nose to muzzle with Gallant-Stallion. She reached up and touched the blaze between his eyes. "I think you're magic, too," she said, loud enough to make certain Meven heard her. "You saved us when those awful birds came. Rue is a very good name for you. Those birds are ruing the day they came upon you."

16 · Birthday Haw

The Finest Court has never erred in pairing a shepherd to a Fallen Favorite. The Finest Court is incapable of making a mistake in this area.

~*Pureheart, first stallion of the Court, from the Finest Court canon*

Six days later there wasn't a trace of stiffness in Meven's leg. All of his cuts had healed, as had nearly all of Kalantha's. However, she had a ropy scar on her neck that Meven knew wouldn't go away. It was where one of the largest birds had sliced her deeply. Every time he looked at the scar, he thought of the assassin-birds and how close both of them had come to dying.

"It's my birthday today, Meven."

"I know, Kal." He brushed a strand of hair out of her eyes. "Happy Birthday, sister." He gave her a broad smile, but she didn't return it.

"I'm eleven today. Morgan was preparing a present for me. And Bishop DeNogaret would have had the cooks make roast pork and sweet potatoes. There might have been a cake."

They were sitting beneath a scarlet hawthorn, or scarlet haw as Kalantha called it. There was a stand of the smallish trees in a valley to the west, between where the Galmier Mountains ended and the foothills began. The hawthorns had toothed leaves and an abundant amount of small, fragrant flowers. Kalantha explained that the flowers would turn into fruit that could be eaten in the late summer to early fall.

"It won't be very sweet. Not like cake," she said. "Or so Morgan taught me. But birds like them. We can eat the berries, too. And over there is a water plum." She was pointing to a large, lone tree that leaned over a wide stream. "It should have fruit at the end of summer. But not so much fruit as these trees. Sweeter, though, and very juicy."

The trunks of the scarlet haws were covered with a thin gray and scaly bark. And the branches, many of which were low to the ground, were dotted with hundreds of inch-long thorns.

"The scarlet haws'll help keep us safe," Kalantha said, pointing out that the tree they sat under practically enveloped them like a leafy cocoon. "Those evil birds will have a harder time getting at us here because of the thorns."

"Smells nice," Meven admitted. "Happy Birthday, Kal." He paused, then added: "As Prince of Galmier I present you with this beautiful scarlet haw for your birthday."

She finally smiled.

He peered out between the branches at the herd of mountain ponies. His big punch towered over them. Fortune was there, too. They'd found the packhorse two days ago, his reins stuck in a crack between two boulders, preventing him from going anywhere. Meven put their saddles and satchels in a crevice in the nearby foothills. He could see it across the stream.

"Meven?" Kalantha was looking straight up, fixing her gaze on a clump of flowers. "I know I asked you this yesterday, and maybe the day before, but why do you think birds would attack us? Why would they be capable of killing people, just like real assassins kill? And how can they talk?" Before she gave him a chance to answer, she went on: "Morgan told me that some birds can talk—parrots, he called them. They mimic what people say. He showed me wonderful drawings of them and said that they're native to the islands of Farmeadow and Gredel-Saba and that wealthy people in Nadir have some in cages in their homes. But the birds that tried to kill us weren't parrots. And they were *talking*. They weren't mimicking anything."

Meven shrugged. "I don't know. We went over this, Kal. Yesterday. The day before, and the day before that. I don't know." It was something that was vexing him, this puzzle he couldn't work out. But Kalantha wasn't looking at his face, and so she couldn't tell just how much he was bothered by it all.

She kept staring at the flowers and started twirling her fingers in the grass. A part of her mind was elsewhere. "I have to know, Meven." She twisted a particularly long blade around her thumb.

"I want to know, too, Kal."

"I *have* to know." She found a weed and began pulling it out.

"We'll have plenty of time to think about it," he announced. "We're not going home for a while."

He finally had Kalantha's full attention. "What do you mean? After Bitternut you said we'd cut through these mountains and then head north until we saw High Keep. You said we'd just celebrate my birthday a little bit late. Now that we're feeling better aren't we going home?"

Meven vehemently shook his head. "I want nothing more than to return to the High Keep Temple and see Bishop DeNogaret again. But that's the one thing we can't do, Kal."

"I don't understand."

"Yes you do." Meven crawled out from under the tree and stood. He brushed his hands on his trousers. "The assassins were after Edan, and not only did they kill him, they killed all the soldiers with him, the Bishop's men, the grooms, horses . . . everyone and everything. They would've killed us if we hadn't gotten away that night. And they tried to kill us again, and nearly succeeded. If we were at the High Keep Temple . . ."

"The birds might come there. They'd kill Morgan and Bishop DeNogaret, too."

"All the acolytes," Meven added. "They'd kill everyone. And maybe they'd finally get us in the process."

Kalantha finished wrestling with the weed. Victorious, she crawled out and joined him. "So to keep all of them safe, we have to stay away."

"For a while anyway," he said. "For quite a while, I should think. Until we're sure the assassins have given up or figured we've died or just forgotten about us."

He walked toward the herd, and she was quick to catch up. "So where will we go?"

"We stay here, away from any village and away from the roads. Maybe move around the mountains for a while. Probably not stay in any one place too long. And we stay away from people. I don't want anyone else to die because we were near them."

"Won't the Bishop be worried about us?"

Meven stopped in his tracks and stared at the toes of his boots. "He'll probably think we're dead, Kal. Someone's going to get word to the King about Edan and the soldiers. And word will get to the Bishop, too. The Bishop and Morgan will think we were killed with Edan."

Kalantha trembled and she took Meven's hand. "Morgan. I don't want Morgan to think I'm dead. He's my friend and . . ."

"There's no other way, Kal. Think about it."

They stood quietly for several minutes, and Meven gave a gentle squeeze to his sister's hand.

"It's not what I want. I want to see the Bishop. I want to meet the King. I'm the Prince, Kal. I'd like to enjoy being the

Prince." He dropped her hand and ran his fingers through his hair. He thought about his precious book, *Sulene's Guardians*, on a high shelf in his room. Would the Bishop give it to someone else? "I'm sure the Prince is supposed to . . . be doing something important for the King and Galmier. I know I have responsibilities. But all of that is going to have to wait. I know this is a lot for an eleven-year-old to handle, but . . ."

"I'm only two years younger than you, Meven. And I can handle anything."

Two and a half, he mouthed.

Kalantha tipped her face to the morning sun and let out a deep breath that fluttered her curls. "I understand. You're right. It's the right thing to do. It will keep them alive." A moment more and she added: "And maybe it'll keep us alive, too. The birds might not think to look for us here. They'll think we're heading to Nadir or High Keep or someplace where there are people. If we stay with the ponies, we might stay alive. And the birds just might forget about us."

They walked toward the herd, and at the same time Gallant-Stallion came toward them. He'd been telling the black pony everything he knew about the assassin-birds, and in particular that a big black hawk named Fala was leading them. Arièg followed Gallant-Stallion, asking him now about High Keep, where she had lived decades ago with her charge.

What is it like now? Are there new buildings? Do many people come to worship? Is the orchard doing well? The yellow apples were my favorite.

Gallant-Stallion said he hadn't been there long enough to notice such things about the Temple grounds. But he knew the orchard still existed.

"It won't be forever, Kal, staying away from High Keep." Meven was trying to lift Kalantha's spirits. "Just for a while."

"Until we think it's safe to go home. Until they've given up or forgotten."

"Yes."

"I'm going to miss my friend Morgan." Kalantha reached up and scratched at the blaze between Gallant-Stallion's eyes. "But I think it might be fun to live with horses."

Meven dug the ball of his foot into the ground. "Fun. It will be . . . interesting." His voice didn't sound like it would be fun. "I'm wondering what we'll find to eat tonight. We ran out of those dewberries yesterday."

"I'll take care of that, Meven. Morgan's been a very good teacher."

~ ~ ~

Dinner wasn't pleasant, and Meven ate only because he was famished and knew he had to keep his strength up.

It consisted of various roots found along the edge of the creek and near the water plum. They were either chewy and tasteless or tough and sour. He ate quickly and fought to keep from gagging. He could tell Kalantha wasn't enjoying it either, but she didn't complain and seemed to be stomaching it better.

"We'll look for different roots tomorrow," she said. "And some more of those dewberries. And maybe we can catch some fish."

17 · Eyeswide and the Horse Between

And the Old Mare decreed that the paradise called the Finest Court would be governed by Elders and led by a Matriarch and a Patriarch. These being the first fourteen Finest the gods created. As time claimed them one by one, they would be replaced with those Finest who distinguished themselves in the world of men. But always the first fourteen would be held in esteem, and their names spoken in reverence.

~The Finest Court canon

Fala took the lead and ushered his band south, rising above the Galmier Mountains where the air felt thoroughly wintry. Though he could well tolerate it, he abhorred the cold. And as it found its way beneath his feathers, it fed his already vile temper. There was a warmer course to travel, but flying above the mountains was the most direct and therefore the fastest means of reaching the Old Forest. He would have preferred to follow the passes and valleys in the mountains and the foothills, where the air would be more to his liking and the hateful wind would be cut. Unfortunately, such a route would take far too much time, and Fala was in a hurry.

Several of the blackbirds and crows were chattering about the cold, but mostly they were talking about the significant losses the assassin band had suffered at the hooves of the big horse. They speculated that two of them would be killed because again they had been unsuccessful in slaying the cousins.

They debated which two Fala would select to slay, and a young crow questioned whether Fala might kill even more in his anger. Fala listened to them and to the wind whistling by his ears, and though he found both sounds bothersome, they helped a little to take his mind off the horrid cold. Not all of the assassins could talk, which Fala considered a blessing. Only some of the blackbirds and crows were so gifted. The others were simple creatures who had just enough sense, malice, and cunning to follow his orders and to fly in the artful formations that hid their true nature.

"Horse." Fala spit the word out like it was a rancid piece of meat. The large horse had managed to kill a few hundred of his flock. While Fala still had a substantial number of assassins remaining, the horse had cut his force noticeably and therefore crippled the assassins' effectiveness. Fala cursed himself for not bringing his entire flock to bear against the cousins and their horses. But who would have thought one horse could cause so much devastation? And had he brought every bird and bat, would it have made a difference?

"Foul horse!" Fala could not remember when he had been so angry. Not even watching the horse finally fall helped to quench his ire. Neither did knowing that he dealt the horse one of his most significant injuries, slicing deep along the brute's withers, perhaps dealing the killing blow all by himself.

"So many dead." Fala had lost assassins before, though usually to his own beak and claws, in response to the flock failing at some task and he being told to make an example. A few were lost each winter when the temperature dipped too low, fewer were lost to illness. But he'd never lost so many at one time, and never before to a single foe. "Accursed horse."

"Falafalafala." One blackbird flew nearly even with the lead assassin, staying only a little back to be respectful. "Who will you slay? Who among us will pay for our failure?"

"How dare you?" Fala sneered. The hawk beat his wings faster and shot past the blackbird. He watched the mountains below, the stars providing ample light to reveal the peaks and the scant thin pines that grew so very high up. He saw a flash of silver, a mountain stream that tumbled into a narrow falls near the Sister to the Stars. Then he was flying beyond it and the falls. In the height of summer he liked that part of the mountains the best. When the overseer sent him on missions through the Galmiers, he inevitably found his way to the falls where the water splashed him gloriously. It was better than rain—finer and spattering him from all directions. During the day, the light hit the falls and created a dazzling array of shimmering rainbow colors. And at night, everything the water touched looked silvery. The hawk loved things that sparkled. But he only dallied at the falls in the hottest part of summer. At other times of the year the spray from the falls was too cold for his comfort. He would look, but never touch at those times.

"Falafalafala . . ." The blackbird had managed to catch up.

Fala cawed loudly to reiterate his rage at being interrupted. He thought the blackbird would sensibly leave him alone. But it was young and foolish, and above that it was persistent.

"Falafalafala . . ."

"I heard you." The hawk seethed that one would dare intrude on his thoughts. He didn't have to turn his head to see who was speaking to him. His eyes were perched in such a manner in his head that he could see practically all the way around. He called the blackbird Voiteh, after a grizzled, meddlesome warrior the band slew a few years past. Though this Voiteh had seen only two summers, the bird was one of Fala's best assassins, having a taste for blood and a fondness for the most nefarious assignments. The young blackbird knew it wouldn't be selected for slaughter, and so felt comfortable about pestering Fala.

"Falafalafala . . ."

"I do not know who will die, foolish Voiteh," Fala said finally. In fact, he didn't know how many the overseer would demand in retribution. He hoped not too many, as he didn't like to see his band's numbers cut further. The more assassins he could command, the greater the chance for success. The overseer would groom more for him, but not until sometime this coming summer when the eggs would start to hatch. The overseer could somehow sense which babies would grow into dutiful and capable additions to the flock. They would be taken the moment they could fly, and the overseer would somehow 'improve' them. But that point would be months away, and it likely would be a year beyond that before the new birds were big and healthy enough to be useful. And so Fala prayed to the dark gods that not many of his band would have to die today because they failed to kill the royal cousins.

The big hawk had considered staying in the mountains and waiting for another opportunity at Meven and Kalantha. But the ponies were too numerous for Fala's depleted force to take on. And likely because of their numbers, the ponies could not be spooked. So the assassins would have to wait until the herd and the cousins parted ways. The cousins might well stay with the herd for a few days for safety, and the overseer expected an immediate report from Fala. *Immediate*, Fala told himself, as he increased his speed. Returning to the Old Forest on time—despite their failure—was likely a better alternative. The overseer hated to be kept waiting even more than Fala hated the cold.

It was early the following morning when Fala and his evil flock reached the heart of the Old Forest. He cherished the dark, twisted woods that mirrored his heart, and he basked in the stillness of the air. In this part of the woods, the great trees held any wind at bay and trapped all manner of interesting smells. Fala couldn't fly in the very center of the woods. The branches were so interwoven in places they looked like spiderwebs that most certainly would entangle him and his fellows. He didn't mind walking in this place, as the rotting branches, often damp, felt good against his claws, and usually there were tasty grubs and beetles to eat along the way. Today, however, he had no appetite.

"Falafalafala," Voiteh whispered. "Who will you . . ." The blackbird stopped in mid-sentence when the band reached the oldest tree and the overseer stepped out from behind it.

The overseer was an impressive owl, standing more than two feet tall from his dark yellow talons to the tips of the feathers that curled above his head like an old man's eyebrows. His beak was the shade of ivory at the end, darker near the base, and it opened and shut in time with each breath. His eyes were his most striking feature. Seeming overly large for his head, they were perfectly round and unblinking, bronze around the outer edge and darkening to a velvety black in the center. They took in Fala and each of the assassins, held them as surely as if all of their claws had taken root.

The eyes loomed larger and focused only on Fala now.

Were they late? Fala wondered. Had the overseer been waiting long? By the breath of the dark gods, don't let him order too many slain, he prayed. Don't let him slay me for this failure.

None of the birds spoke for several minutes while the overseer continued to stare at Fala. The silence was especially unnerving to the youngest and least experienced of the assassins. The scent of their fear was heavy.

"Eyeswide." Fala finally spoke and risked calling the overseer by his name. The black hawk added a head bob in an animated greeting. "Again we failed you, Eyeswide, though we slew the big horse that was between you and me."

"Between you and me?" The overseer cocked his head, the gesture meant to pull more information from the hawk. "Between?" The owl's voice was thin and soft and held a trace of hoarseness. It sounded as if he had to force the words out of his throat. Perhaps because of the effort it took the overseer to speak, his voice commanded respect and invited no interruption. "What do you mean, Fala?"

The hawk swallowed hard and searched for the right words. "Between you and me. Wiser, stronger, more powerful than me, but a far, far lesser creature than you."

"A creature between us. An interesting way to look at a Finest." Eyeswide stepped even closer to Fala. The owl's breath ruffled the feathers on the hawk's face. "But then you haven't the vaguest notion of what a Finest is, do you?"

The owl was larger than the hawk, in girth and height. The feathers that covered his body were a mix of beige and white, darker at his throat and lightest at his talons. His wings were various rich shades of brown striped with white and threaded here and there with thin lines of black. His head was his most striking feature, white around his beak and above his large eyes. There was a reddish brown stripe that fitted around those eyes like a bandit's mask, and a darker shade of feathers at the top that looked like a skullcap. Eyeswide swiveled his head one way and then the other, practically spinning it all the way around.

"I knew you were coming here to tell me of your failure." The owl looked for a reaction on Fala's face, and was pleased when he found none.

"I watched you," Eyeswide continued. Keeping his wings tight to his body, he made a gesture like a man rolling his shoulders. Then he leaned first on his right talon, then the left. "From the vision pond I saw your attack on the royal cousins fail."

"Yes, we failed," Fala admitted. "But at least we managed to slay the horse between you and me."

Some of the blackbirds trembled, worried that Fala might select them to be slain in the retribution they were certain was coming. An old crow tried to hide behind a young black-winged kestrel.

"But before the horse fell, he took down many in your assassin band," the owl said. "Many many many that I had spent time and effort enhancing. The ground was covered with their bodies. Dozens and dozens. I watched this."

Fala nodded and turned his head slightly so he could see directly behind him, where the assassins were gathered into one black mass. His eyes flitted from one bird and bat to the next, beginning his assessment of each one and trying to decide who to kill.

"And worse than failing to kill the cousins," Fala admitted, "they saw us and know that the slayers of Prince Edan and the soldiers were not men. *This time the cousins saw us.*"

"And you worry that the cousins will tell someone of importance."

Fala nodded.

"Who would believe children who have never been beyond High Keep before?"

It was Fala's turn to cock his head.

"No one who matters would believe them, Fala. And not a single adult saw you."

"Then you are not angry? You will give us another chance, Eyeswide?" There was hope in the hawk's voice, and he stood a little taller.

"Dismiss your flock," the owl said. Again he rested his weight on his right talon, then his left. It was a gesture that Fala knew meant the owl was contemplating something. "Perhaps tomorrow I will have something else for them to do. None of them need die today."

Fala opened his beak in surprise.

"I said dismiss them. Do it before I change my mind."

Fala whipped around and spat out instructions. He wanted

the band to regroup in the morning at the stand of willow birches north of the Old Forest's heart. The birds and bats left quickly, walking from the twisted woods, then taking flight as soon as the branches thinned. The beating of their wings sounded like faint thunder. The noise should have been louder, Fala knew, but the horse had cut the numbers and so also the sound.

"Eyeswide . . ."

"Yes, Fala?"

The hawk studied the owl. "You *are* angry at our failure."

Eyeswide gave a low throaty hoot, which Fala knew to be a 'yes.'

"And yet you did not order me to slay . . ."

"The horse between you and me inflicted a great loss to our assassins, Lieutenant Fala."

"So many dead," Fala said. There was a hint of sadness in the hawk's voice. Both he and Eyeswide knew it wasn't because Fala cared for any of the individual fallen birds and bats. It was because his force had been weakened, and therefore his own power had been shaved. "Never have I lost so many, Eyeswide. Good that particular horse did not fight when we attacked the wedding party south of Hathi. Good that he fled. He well might have thwarted . . ."

"A powerful horse," Eyeswide observed. "A singular creature with a strong mind and body."

"A hateful, thankfully, blessedly dead horse."

The owl let out another hoot, longer and mournful and meaning 'no.'

18 · The Vision Pond

The good gods created the Finest and established the Finest Court. But while those gods were busy, their two evil brothers created a dark animal with a heart as black as their own. They gave it feathers and flight and made it look like an owl.

~Paard-Zhumd, son of the creator-god

Fala's beak dropped open in surprise. "I killed that horse! I felt its blood on my claws. I watched it fall."

"The horse is still between you and me." Eyeswide fixed an unblinking stare on the big hawk. For several minutes neither spoke, then finally the owl turned and retreated behind the oldest tree. Though only scant light found its way through the Old Forest's dense canopy, it was more than enough for the owl to see by. His course took him through a section where the trunks grew so close they resembled a stockade wall. He squeezed between them and continued on.

Behind him Fala stared at the oldest tree. "Not dead? How could the brute not be dead?" The crow had hated the horse first because of its strength and intelligence—because it was a greater creation than he. Then Fala hated it because of the number of assassins it killed in the mountain valley. Now the crow hated the horse because it was not dead. Somehow it had survived the attack—Eyeswide said so, and Eyeswide was never wrong. Fala suddenly hated the horse more than the cold. More than anything. He turned his back on the oldest tree and slowly and wrathfully left the heart of the woods.

Where Eyeswide walked the floor was thick with the shattered bones of birds, husks of dead insects, thousands of fallen leaves, and rotted wood. It felt springy and gave a bounce to the owl's steps. The only sound here was what he made—his talons brushing softly over the loam, the clicking he made with his beak. The trunks seemed to keep any other sounds from entering, which caused the place to feel even eerier than the rest of the Old Forest. However, the owl embraced his ghoulish surroundings and spent most of his time here. He reached the center of a circle of stringybarks and stood at the edge of a stagnant pond. He called it the vision pond. There was a dull green film on the water, and as Eyeswide watched it, the green grew as bright as the shade of new grass.

Faint motes of white and yellow appeared in concentric circles, and the rings slowly rippled outward. Eyeswide stretched a talon into the water and gently stirred it. He hooted long and low, and as the sound trailed off the pond became still again. All trace of green vanished. It was black now, shiny like a mirror.

"Show me the cousins," Eyeswide said. He bent until his beak could reach his talon. A quick slice and a thin line of blood appeared on a scarred claw. He let a few drops of blood fall into the water. "Show me the ones called Meven and Kalantha Montoll."

Images instantly appeared. At first they were ghostlike pieces of fog. But as Eyeswide patiently waited, they became more substantial.

"The boy and his sister," Eyeswide said.

Meven was in the forefront, kneeling at a stream and splashing water on his face. Kalantha was behind him, using her fingers to comb Gallant-Stallion's mane. All around them was the herd of mountain ponies, at least a hundred and fifty strong.

The small black one was at the edge of the image. Eyeswide had watched this pony last night after the assassins' failed attack. He had uttered a string of curses when the pony healed Gallant-Stallion and the royal cousins. "So the punch and the pony are both detestable Finest creations," the owl had muttered. "The new Prince has a powerful guardian. And I am forced to devise a new plan."

The owl watched the royal cousins now until well into the evening, and looked in on them over the following few days while he worked out all the intricacies of his scheme. He would need Fala and his depleted flock to carry out his plan, and he would need to add to the flock if there was to be a chance at success. Normally he chose hatchlings, but the Finest had dealt a serious blow to his vile band, and so he would have to recruit adult birds and bats he would otherwise overlook. He would recruit more than he ever had before. And he would have to enhance all of them.

It was nearly two decades ago that Eyeswide enhanced Fala, giving the big hawk the gift of speech, a long lifespan, and a sentience that was nearly the equal of any man. But the owl made sure the hawk was not his own equal, and using his magic and threats, he engendered a fierce loyalty in Fala.

Eyeswide augmented all the birds and bats that had come to be part of his assassin band. Each was *between* a normal creature and Fala—in strength and intelligence—and each was imbued with loyalty to both Fala and Eyeswide. So Fala was better than the assassins, but could never equal Eyeswide. There was a hierarchy to be preserved, and a fidelity to ensure. The owl could not have a subject that would flee when conditions became threatening. He needed subjects who would fight to the death for him.

At one time Eyeswide also had been a normal creature. But that time was many decades past. The Remorseful Time, he called it, days of simple existence. Like Fala, he had been "improved," but this power came from the twin dark gods of the world. Eyeswide was proud to consider himself "god-touched" and greater than any Finest.

Those dark gods were called Iniquis and Abandon—the names given them by Peran-Morab, sister to the eldest god Paard-Zhumd. The two supreme gods named the world after themselves, calling it Paard-Peran. Eyeswide thought that terribly haughty of them. There were three other "good" gods, Eyes-wide had learned from his considerable studies—Kazak, Salcor, and Kladrub. They were the offspring of Peran-Morab's union with one of the first men. Some believed Iniquis and Abandon were also her children from that union, disowned when they became too unruly and mischievous for her to manage. Legend claimed that a final child, Shetl, died in the battle between the good and dark gods over the Sea of Sulene. Shetl was said to have fallen in the final moments of the battle, dealt a killing blow by Iniquis, and turned to stone by Abandon. The peak became known as the Sister to the Stars.

There were Temples throughout Paard-Peran devoted to the five good gods. There were even a few Temples in the larger cities that were dedicated to a single god, this usually Paard-Zhumd or Peran-Morab. Eyeswide had no interest in these places. However, he had visited a hidden Temple to Abandon and Iniquis on this very island continent, and another on the small island of Farmeadow. Eyeswide had discovered the latter through his use of the vision pond. Despite the impressive architecture of the hidden Temple, Eyeswide found the twisted heart of the Old Forest to be the best shrine to his dark gods.

Of all the gods, Eyeswide respected only Iniquis and Abandon, considering the five "good" gods weak and uninteresting and therefore not worth praying to. He believed their greatest accomplishment was the creation of the Finest. But even that was not good enough to win his veneration, as he knew a Finest was not his equal.

Iniquis and Abandon had formed a far greater creature in Eyeswide. And the Finest Court that Iniquis and Abandon had told him about? That was a pasture of futility as far as the owl was concerned.

"An ill-fated Finest, that horse between myself and Fala," he humorously mused.

It was by Iniquis that Eyeswide was given speech and wisdom. Abandon gifted him with uncannily fast flight, and the ability to enhance other winged creatures. Iniquis's tears formed the very pond Eyeswide stared into now. And Abandon gave the owl a mystical ability that let him use the pond as a window so he could look in on anything and anyone he wanted. Apparently the dark gods liked to work together, Eyeswide thought.

"Show me the horse between."

The image on the pond shifted and Gallant-Stallion filled the stagnant water's surface.

"Not a pretty horse," Eyeswide noted with some satisfaction. But then none of the Finest were so comparatively beautiful as himself. "Indeed, it is ugly."

Gallant-Stallion was surrounded by the mountain ponies, who were grazing on the grass and sweet clover. He was watching one in particular, the small black who had healed him. But he didn't watch that pony long. It was clear to Eyeswide that Gallant-Stallion did not take his eyes off Meven for more than a few minutes at a time.

"Indeed, you guard the new Prince well," Eyeswide said. "Slayer of my precious assassins, you are careful of your charge."

The owl stepped back from the pond and the mirror-black finish instantly turned into its familiar dull green film.

"You ugly horse between. You forced me to change my plans."

19 · Running

Salcor and Kazak painted the Finest. The first fourteen were snow white, absent of color and considered perfect and pure. But Salcor said such creations stood out in the world of men, and the Finest were to be secret shepherds. Kazak painted the fifteenth Finest the color of the earth. He gave the mare a mane of coal black with eyes to match, and he decorated her with white stockings. Salcor added a gray dappling to the sixteenth, making this Finest look like patches of fog. The seventeenth was a canvas of browns, black, and white. The two gods continued their work, adding diversity and making some into great stallions more than sixteen hands high, while turning others into small, delicate ponies. No Finest creations beyond the first fourteen were wholly white like snow.

~The Old Mare, the first of the Finest

Meven's bare feet pounded across the meadow, and he sucked in great gulps of air. His sides were aching, he'd been running so hard, and his dark hair was slick with sweat and lay flat against his head and neck. His throat felt on fire and his right heel pained him—somewhere he'd picked up a tiny rock or sliver of wood, and each time he slammed his right foot down, it felt like a pin jabbing him. He should stop and remove the rock, put his foot up and rest for a while. That would be the sensible thing to do—before he really hurt himself. But he couldn't afford to stop, he told himself, and so he fought against the annoying pain. He had less than a mile to go now, and if he slowed even a little Kalantha would pass him by.

She did better at these longer races, and he worried that if he picked an even lengthier course she just might beat him. Meven risked a glance over his shoulder. She was only a few yards behind him, her hands made into fists and her arms swinging furiously at her sides. Kalantha's face was petal pink from exertion, and she was making a strained huffing sound. Her puffed-out cheeks reminded him of a chipmunk's, all full of nuts. Meven thought she looked comical, and he stifled a chuckle. But he noticed that her eyes were deadly serious and were fixed on a point ahead and above them—where the meadow narrowed and turned into a pass between sheer walls of dark gray rock.

He couldn't call her pudgy any longer. She was lithe and taller and so unlike his sister who used to shuffle around the halls of High Keep and dig in the gardens.

At the very top of the pass, where the clover and grass stopped, was a small tablerock that marked the end of the race. It was a route they'd been running every day for what he guessed might be close to two weeks. There had been other courses, but this was the most demanding that he had devised. This was also the greatest number of days they'd spent in any one place in the Galmier Mountains, and so they could run this course over and over.

It had started on an off-handed dare early last fall, Meven challenging his sister to a simple race along a stream many miles south of here. The loser would have to scrub clothes in the stream. Subsequent races they wagered on let him avoid all sorts of chores. It had been no contest in the early days, even when they struggled through knee-deep snow on their sporadic winter runs. He always easily bested her. But now, come late summer, he really had to work to stay ahead. And so what had started as a simple dare to avoid one night of washing clothes had turned into a rigorous, exhausting competition.

He was still taller than she, even more so than before. His long legs were conducive to running, and that gave him an advantage. Kalantha said he'd grown fast like a dandelion in the time they'd spent with the mountain ponies. Meven guessed that time was a little more than a year and a half, but certainly less than two—everything was still green, though the shortening days and cooler night air suggested fall wasn't far away. They'd left High Keep for Edan's wedding very early in the spring, and in the first three months since Meven relegated them to the mountains, he kept track of each day by putting marks on one of their leather satchels. But then one morning he forgot to make a mark, and then a few days later he forgot again. After a third or fourth lapse he decided to give up on the practice entirely.

The days were blending together for him anyway, and he started counting the passage of time based on the flowering of trees, the size of the insects, the temperature, how quickly night came, and where the constellations of the gods hung in the sky. It wasn't precise, but it gave Meven enough of a general idea to satisfy himself.

Meven was no longer skinny—his legs and arms were muscular, and his endurance was considerable. When he ran, veins stood out like strands of yarn on his neck. His fingers were thicker, and he was wearing the royal ring on his middle finger now. It was too small for his thumb. He wondered what Bishop DeNogaret would think of him—going from a young man who got winded climbing the stairs in the Temple's bell tower to someone who ran miles every morning and frequently climbed sheer rock walls just for something to do. His hair was long and shaggy, and he thought it looked somewhat like the punch's coarse mane. He no longer sported a pale scholar's complexion. His skin was tanned, and he mused that he might look like the barbarians of Farmeadow. But after he got cleaned up, cut his hair, and into some appropriate clothes, he thought he might turn the heads of many a young woman.

Kalantha regularly used the ornamental dagger to crop her hair short. It stuck out from her head in all directions, resembling stunted sage grass. It wasn't the rich cinnamon color anymore, as the constant sun had lightened it so much that it looked a dusty wheat-blond. She'd tangled her waist-length hair one too many times in the branches of the scarlet haws last year, and cut it in frustration one summer morning. Meven saw her hacking away at it every few weeks now, when it grew long enough to rub at her neck. The Bishop wouldn't let her do that after they got back to High Keep. Young women were supposed to fuss over their stylishly long hair and trim it with beads and ribbons.

Kalantha was tanned too, her arms and legs slightly muscular—an uncommon build for a proper young woman. And though she hadn't taken to rock-climbing as Meven had, she loved to run. Sometimes she ran by herself, which worried Meven, as he liked to keep an eye on her. But when she slipped away early in the morning while he was still sleeping, he certainly wasn't able to argue with her. Oh, he scolded her later, even telling her that he was the Prince of Galmier and he was ordering her not to disappear on him ever, ever again. But it didn't do any good. Sometimes she ran with the mountain ponies, and he would watch the herd move like a wave across a meadow or valley, looking at their legs and finding Kalantha's bare legs amid theirs—and proudly noting that she could keep up for quite some time with the smallest of them.

Meven knew he wouldn't have been able to stay away from civilization so long if she hadn't been with him. Indeed, he would have starved out here. She learned to be self-sufficient, as skilled as any veteran woodsman. She taught herself how to catch fish with her hands and to make fires to cook them over; learned where to find the best fruits and nuts; and discovered what roots were fit to be eaten and would keep the longest and did not taste too, too horrible. She'd even made a storehouse of food for the worst part of winter when the stream practically iced over and the fish went to deeper water somewhere. And she'd caught more than a few rabbits since the snow melted by fashioning clever traps.

She endeavored to share her survival skills. Meven honestly gave it try, but found he was best suited to picking berries and water plums. He could not master the other tasks, and so left them to his resourceful sister. He knew he was much more suited to life in a village, or more preferably at High Keep or someday Nadir, where food could be had for coins or bartering and where there were stacks of books on government, history, and religion to study. He was a savant, not a naturalist, and he missed the Temple and Bishop DeNogaret. Meven ardently wanted to return to the comfortable surroundings and the friendship he once shared with the acolytes and the Bishop. And he wanted to visit the King and officially be crowned Prince. It was time the Bishop and the King knew that he and Kalantha were alive. Meven couldn't begin to imagine how far behind he'd fallen in his studies and how many long, long nights he'd have to put in to catch up to the schedule Bishop DeNogaret had established for him.

The Bishop and his private study . . . Meven mused. Might he find books on sentient, evil birds somewhere on one of those wonderful shelves? Maybe there'd even be a book on other gifted animals, such as the small black pony able to heal injuries. He planned to discuss the birds with the Bishop at the first opportunity. Perhaps the two of them could figure out how such creatures could exist and who might be controlling them. He and Kalantha discussed the birds almost every evening, agreeing that some*one* had trained them and was behind the attacks. It was just a matter of finding out who.

"Birds are not smart enough to come up with such vile plans on their own," he frequently told her.

"Maybe they're magic," she returned. "Bad magic."

There were always birds around everywhere in the moun-

tains, even in winter. And to this day they made Meven nervous—
there were three flying overhead now. But these were jays, and
so could be dismissed. There'd been no monstrous-sized flock,
no overly large hawk with shiny eyes, and no other dark bird
had shown any peculiar interest in him or Kalantha since the
night of the attack in the valley. Part of him thought he might
have dreamed the whole thing, and he might have been able to
convince himself of that if there hadn't been that ropy scar on
Kalantha's neck.

But there had been small flocks of blackbirds—Meven had
spotted them on the two previous occasions he thought about
returning home and started down a trail through the mountains. The flocks had been spread out on the rocky ledges over-
looking the various paths that cut through the Galmiers and
along the road that led north and paralleled the western coast.
Each time their presence made him tense and caused him to go
back to the mountain pony herd. They'd not seemed malicious,
none of them had spoken, and he couldn't be sure they were
even paying attention to him. But he thought it better to be
cautious. Kalantha never objected to staying with the ponies;
she seemed to enjoy life better here than at High Keep, even
though the living was rough and winter had been almost un-
bearable. It had been months since she'd even mentioned the
Temple or Morgan the gardener. She talked about individual
ponies, various butterflies and beetles, and the shape and color
of leaves. He suspected she could stay here forever, and that she
really didn't care if they ever went back.

But it wasn't up to her. Men were in charge, Meven had been
taught. They made the rules, they held the positions in government. And he was older, and so she would have to abide by his
decisions no matter what. Kalantha would never be able to
make any rules, or truly amount to much, he thought. Still, he
fiercely admired her, and wondered if he might be able to do
something to change her lot in life when he was *officially*

crowned Prince. And if not then, he could change things when he eventually became King. Kalantha deserved better than practicing the embroidery stitches she would be forced to learn when they returned to the Temple at High Keep.

He wondered if Bishop DeNogaret would allow them to continue running each morning.

"Kal!"

She shot past him, arms still flailing away, cheeks round, and face as red as he'd ever seen it.

"Kalantha!"

She didn't answer him, as that would take effort and might somehow slow her down. In a heartbeat she was several yards ahead of him. And though he tried to catch up, she lengthened her lead and for the first time left him well behind.

Kalantha reached the tablerock first, climbed up, and stretched out. She turned her head to the sky and gasped for breath. She didn't say anything when Meven joined her, though her wide smile struck him as gloating.

"Congratulations," he panted. He crossed his right leg over his left knee and twisted his foot so he could see the bottom. There was a red, festering welt on the heel, and after he brushed away a little dirt he saw a thick sliver of rock. "Ugh. No wonder you won, Kal."

She frowned at the slight, but still didn't say anything.

"Let me borrow your knife."

Kalantha pulled the ornamental dagger out of its sheath and passed it to him. She always wore it at her side, affixed to a belt she'd made from woven horsehair. The dagger was a remembrance of Edan, but more than that, it was a tool she used all the time.

Meven started worrying at the sliver, grimacing from the pain he was inflicting on himself, but refusing to let out a whimper or ask her for help. If he really hurt himself, he'd visit the black pony and coax her to heal him. "I've been thinking,

Kal. We'll start back tomorrow," he said. "Probably should have started back days and days and days ago. I've just been cautious." And the weather's been so nice and warm, he added to himself. It was easy to enjoy the mountains in summer.

She was studying something on the opposite rock face, perhaps a pattern in the striations. She wiped the back of her hand across her forehead.

"Maybe it was wrong of us to stay out here so long, Kal. But we needed the isolation to keep our friends safe. There was no sense in Bishop DeNogaret dying by the assassin birds." Softer, he said: "I wonder if the birds killed the King? Did they get everyone in the royal family?" He dropped his hand to his belt and said a brief prayer. The belt was gray now, the black dye having faded. Some of the carved beads were missing, and others were chipped. Would the Bishop give him another such belt? Meven vowed to pray several times each day when he returned to High Keep. He sometimes forgot to pray here. "It'll be nice to use some soap. Better to get some shoes that fit."

Kalantha smiled faintly at this.

They had outgrown their shoes months ago, and had consigned themselves to going barefoot or wrapping leather and cloth around their feet when they were traveling across ground that was scattered with rock shards or when they were moving under the scarlet haws, where fallen needles were plentiful.

It was a sliver about the size of one of those haw needles that he finally pulled out of his heel. "Ugh," he repeated. He looked down toward the herd, searching for the magical black pony. "We definitely need to get some shoes and clothes." What few articles they had left were ragged and threadbare and wholly unpresentable as far as he was concerned. They certainly wouldn't be enough to pass another fall here, let alone another winter.

Kalantha was wearing a long tunic she'd taken from Hathi. It fell to just above her knees and was marred by small holes and snags. She had one pair of trousers left that were serviceable enough, but they were wool and she didn't wear them in this warm weather. Meven, however, rarely went barelegged, as it wasn't 'civilized,' he told her. He had on a rosy-colored pair of leggings, embroidered down the side with ochre thread that swirled into the semblance of vines. He hated it because it was so bright. His lace-cuffed shirt was a faded blue, but not faded from the sun as the fabric was a knobby silk that was intended to look that way. The shirt had a matched pair of fancy blue leggings that he had ruined rock-climbing in the spring.

"We look silly," he said. "I'd be too embarrassed to go back to High Keep like this. Actually, I'm worried about anyone seeing us this way. I'm the Prince. And Princes do not look like this. But I figure we'll cut east through the mountains and find Bitternut on the other side again. Better that than taking our luck due north with a village we've never been to. Bitternut should be safe, since we've been away from people for so long. I've a gold chain of Edan's we can use to get some clothes and shoes. And I have two silver belt buckles in my satchel. Maybe we can spend a night or two in those soft beds at the inn while we get cleaned up. And by the gods get a thick piece of roast beef and potatoes with butter. A hunk of mince pie." His mouth watered at this prospect. "A big mug of cider." He'd had nothing to drink but water since the beginning of their self-imposed exile.

"And most important, Kal, we'll ask around about what's going on in Galmier. We might find out about the King. Might hear if anyone has been attacked by flocks of birds." He was formulating an argument to coax her into leaving the mountains willingly. "It really is time we stopped running. Why, we can even . . ."

Kalantha crawled off the tablerock and started down the meadow pass toward the herd. "Why wait for tomorrow, Meven? It's still early in the day. Why not start back now?" She looked over her shoulder. "I've got some good-byes to say first."

~ ~ ~

Kalantha went from one pony to the next, not trying to pet all of them, but making sure to visit the ones she was especially fond of. She lingered at a spotted hucul and combed her fingers through its silky brown mane. "I will miss you, Nugget. But I will remember all our sunset runs."

She moved to another, this one of the highlands. "You'll have to reach the water plums all by yourself, Pudge. I'm sure you can do it. Just stretch as far as you can." The stocky pony nuzzled her hand, then rubbed its face against hers.

"Midnight, maybe I'll come back to the mountains and find you someday. We can count the stars together again."

"There you are, Mud-Bug. Want your ears scratched?" The roan pony bent its neck and waited for a tickle. Kalantha rubbed its ears for several minutes. "I'm going to miss all of you." She let out a deep sigh, and the roan pony looked up into her watery eyes. "I think best friends have four legs, not two," she said. "And I wish I didn't have to go home. But I *do* have to go home. I suppose it's my duty. For Meven."

She lingered at the small black pony. "You're magic," she said. "I can't pretend to know how you heal others. I don't think I should know. I think it should always stay a secret, always be magic." She brushed at a twig that was caught in the pony's mane. "I promise I won't tell anyone about you. If others knew they might try to catch you and put you in a pen and force you to work your magic for them. You should always run free."

Perhaps, Arièg, when the Finest Court relegated you to these mountains they were not punishing you after all, Gallant-Stallion said. The big punch had been following Kalantha, wanting to hear what she said to each pony. Meven was near enough that the Finest could see him and didn't have to worry. The Prince was keeping a little distance, though, obviously waiting for Kalantha to be finished with the black pony so he could get his foot healed.

"You've become a very good friend to me, magic pony," Kalantha continued. "But I won't even tell the Bishop or the gardener about you."

Gallant-Stallion had discovered that Kalantha had an affinity toward all animals, and he admired her kindness and humanity. *Arièg, perhaps this assignment in the mountains was your next charge—shepherding all the travelers this way. You have shepherded Kalantha well. Perhaps there really was no punishment intended for your curiosity.*

There had been times when Arièg had disappeared from the herd, and Gallant-Stallion suspected she was elsewhere in the mountains, healing a man or a creature who had been injured. The pony offered no explanation for her absence.

I treasure this girl, and I wish she were not leaving, Arièg said. *I love her just as I have learned to love these mountains.*

There is always beauty here, Gallant-Stallion told Arièg. There is also cold weather, he thought. The big Finest wasn't fond of the snow, or the scarce food that was available in winter. Despite his enjoying Arièg's company, and feeling that Meven and Kalantha were comfortably safe with the herd, he was looking forward to going back to High Keep or to Nadir, where there would be a warm stable, plenty of food, and more men to watch and study.

The Finest pony nickered softly into Kalantha's ear. *May the good gods watch over you,* Arièg said. *May they keep you kind and wise and gentle. And may your journey one day lead you back here.* The pony knew Kalantha couldn't hear the words, but she said them anyway.

And may you, Arièg, conquer your curiosity.

That, Gallant-Stallion, might well be an impossibility. Arièg stepped back, and she and Gallant-Stallion watched Kalantha continue her good-byes. Meven came forward, got Arièg's attention, and pointed to his foot. *Kalantha talks to the ponies like she would talk to a person. While her brother considers them just animals. Considers me just an animal, too, though one able to tend his wounds.* The Finest pony bent to begin healing Meven's heel.

The mountain ponies *are* animals, Gallant-Stallion thought. There is a great gap between them and us. Their thoughts and desires are painfully simple. Still, they are graceful, hardy creatures that mean no ill to each other or to men.

Steadfast, I begin to understand why you admired them, Gallant-Stallion said. He was talking to himself again, though under the guise of addressing Steadfast. *Simple animals they may be, but there is a stateliness about them. Perhaps all creatures . . . no, not all creatures are to be respected.*

The assassin-birds are creatures, too, he mused, abruptly changing his thoughts. And there is nothing in all of Paard-Peran to recommend them.

Gallant-Stallion and Arièg had tried to puzzle out the attack of the birds the past many months. Arièg relished the mystery that she said "tickled her curiosity." In the end, even after all this time, all she and Gallant-Stallion could determine was that someone had controlled the birds—there would be no reason for crows, blackbirds, and bats to act so viciously on their own. Only a man with some strange, arcane power could have granted them speech. The gods would not have done it, both Arièg and Gallant-Stallion agreed. The gods created the Finest and established the Finest Court. They would not have also created malicious, killing birds. The gods wanted men protected, not destroyed.

I will miss your company, Arièg, Gallant-Stallion admitted.

At High Keep, there are no other Finest Creations. I will have no one to talk to.

And I will miss your conversation.

Gallant-Stallion tossed his head, his coarse main fluttering in a breeze that had picked up. *I must confess to you. I am also a little inquisitive, Arièg.*

The Finest Pony gave a playful snort and pawed at the ground. *And so you want to know . . .*

The charge you left behind, the one you did not shepherd when your curiosity got in the way at High Keep.

The boy who showed so much progress and promise? The one who could have become something special?

Gallant-Stallion gave a nod.

Men do not live so long a time, Gallant-Stallion. And so he is likely dead. Arièg's voice was thick with regret. *If he were alive, he would be an old, old man. I don't recall much about him, other than that he liked flowers—odd for a boy. His name was Morgan.*

20 · Bitter Bitternut

I understand why they are "fallen," as they steal, lie, kill, and commit other acts not in the name of survival, but in the name of what they believe is self-advancement. It was good the gods did not accidentally give the other creatures of the world these traits. The other creatures are blessedly too simple to know that there is a world beyond this world where their spirits will drift when their lives are done. Men are not so simple, and so they know that such a place exists. But they do not realize their nefarious practices will keep their souls out. All the simple animals are warmly welcomed in.

~*Stoutspirit, seventeenth Finest*

Gallant-Stallion picked his way along a winding mountain path they had not traveled before. Meven had selected it, saying it looked like it went straight east—and if it instead twisted and turned in another direction, they'd just find a different trail to take. Meven wanted to go to Bitternut because he would remember some of the people, and he could make himself look presentable by getting new clothes before going to Bishop DeNogaret. The Finest considered Meven a resourceful young man and was happy with the plan.

So Gallant-Stallion would make certain they didn't end up north of Bitternut by closely keeping track of just where they were going, relying on his innate sense of direction. Gallant-Stallion wanted to visit Bitternut perhaps more than Meven did. He wanted to speak with Mara, the Finest pony that was hopefully still in the stable. She was old, he thought, and it had been more than a year and a half since he had seen her. Would she still be alive?

Steadfast, I hope with my heart that she is still there.
Gallant-Stallion wanted to tell Mara that the visions she gave
him on their first meeting had come true, at least some of them.
The wave of darkness was the attack of the assassin flock. The
image of someone running with horses was Kalantha playing
with the mountain ponies. Gallant-Stallion was amazed that
Mara had predicted the attack and the fact that the cousins
would live with the ponies. He wanted to see if she had any
more predictions, and if he could puzzle them out before they
came to pass. *Steadfast, I hope that . . .*

*She is still there, Gallant-Stallion. And she will be happy to
see you.*

The Finest nearly unseated Meven as he whipped around
looking behind him. There was only Kalantha on the packhorse, no sign of any Finest. Who was talking to him? He
whirled again, then stopped abruptly.

Steadfast? It sounded like Steadfast to Gallant-Stallion. But
the elder Finest was well more than a year and a half dead.
Steadfast! Is it you? Where are you? Steadfast!

Meven kneed the Finest. "Rue! Be careful! What're you doing?" Meven thumped Gallant-Stallion with his heels for emphasis. Then he furtively looked around to see if his horse had
been spooked by birds. "Don't stop so suddenly!" When he
dug his heels in again, Gallant-Stallion felt a stab of pain.

The young Prince had changed in the time away, the Finest
knew. Physically he was much stronger than before, and the
heel jab honestly hurt.

Patience, he told Meven, even though he knew the young
man couldn't hear him.

I used to tell you to have patience, Gallant-Stallion.

And I used to hear you only in my dreams. Am I going mad?
Gallant-Stallion kept watching for Steadfast as he continued
slowly on the trail. Could a Finest return from death? Was it re-

ally Steadfast? Or was it another Finest, and he merely thought it sounded like Steadfast? Could he indeed be going mad?

He stretched out with his senses. There was the odor of damp earth that was trapped in low places in the rocks, and the small, mossy plants that grew there; there were the scents of Meven and Kalantha and the packhorse; and there were still some summer flowers he could smell, clinging to life in the last warm days. He did not smell another creature. Still, he felt something different in the air, a cool breeze that had suddenly sprung up.

You are not touched. I am with you in spirit, Gallant-Stallion, Steadfast finally replied. *I am beyond Paard-Peran and the Finest Court. But I am not so far that I cannot look in on you from time to time. I listen when you speak to me. But it is easiest for me to speak to you in dreams.*

Gallant-Stallion had so much to ask. He didn't know where to start.

You have done well for your charge, my brother. I sense that the Court is proud of you. And you have much yet to do. Your charge has grown in form and mind. Pray that it is enough for the times ahead. The future is filled with challenges and dangers.

What? Gallant-Stallion practically shouted. He tossed his head, and drew another heel jab from Meven. *What is ahead, Steadfast?*

I know the future, Gallant-Stallion, but I cannot reveal it. I can advise you, but I cannot influence the outcome of anything. The Creators will not allow me to interfere.

Steadfast, will there be . . .

The breeze was gone as suddenly as it came, and Gallant-Stallion discerned that the spirit of Steadfast left with it. He felt elated and sad at the same time—joyous to know for certain there was something beyond this life, and disappointed that

Steadfast didn't stay long enough to answer at least some of his questions.

But there is Mara. Steadfast said she was still alive. *I will speak with her.* He picked up his pace, as he'd become sure-footed in the mountains. The packhorse was having some trouble keeping up, but despite its laziness it had no desire to be left behind.

The mountains looked different in the late summer, or perhaps it was merely that the Finest had not seen this section of them. They were rugged and steep here, with one sheer wall of the pass made of stone as white as snow, and the other comprised of bands of gray and rosy granite. There were a few needle-thin trees scattered in wells of dirt, and there was a large weeping hemlock towering high and to the south, the tree seeming to defy nature to exist where it was. On a ledge to the north perched a falcon by a nest; its pointed wings and narrow tail marked it as a peregrine. Meven saw it too, but paid it little notice. It was mostly shades of brown and so was not to be feared. Only black birds had been in the malevolent flock. The falcon's mate circled overhead, then flew to an opposite ledge when Gallant-Stallion was well beyond their nest.

The trail wound south then straightened to the east again, and Gallant-Stallion had to slow when they came to a section with a steep incline. The packhorse had considerable trouble, and Kalantha got off and helped encourage him. Rock shards were plentiful, and Kalantha grimaced with each step.

"Good shoes, Meven," she said. "I want a pair of good, sturdy comfortable shoes."

At the top, the trail opened into a narrow meadow filled with small spruce and carpeted with thick moss and tiny yellow flowers. She was happy to walk barefoot through this, getting back on the packhorse only when Meven chided her that she was slowing them down.

They stopped late in the day when Kalantha spied a hedge-like row of berry bushes. The scattering of berries she found were mixes of deep reds and purples, and they were clustered in threes and fours. She'd not seen them before. There were plenty of bird droppings on the ground around them, and an angry-looking bluebird was screeching at her. The bluebird's scolding, and her guessing that the birds had already picked most of the fruit, told her the berries were safe. Meven was in a hurry, but he knew they couldn't make Bitternut in one day. So he helped her pick them. They ate nearly as many as they gathered, finding the fruit pleasantly sweet.

"Better than water plums," he pronounced with a smile.

Kalantha took a few leaves and pressed them in a strip of cloth in her satchel. She'd already pressed several leaves there from different berry bushes, intending to tell Morgan about them. "Better than dewberries, too," she said.

"I think that any berry is better than a dewberry, Kal. You only eat those when you're desperate."

Gallant-Stallion listened to Fortune. The packhorse softly whinnied its desire for some of the fruit. But Meven kept the gathered berries with him, and so Fortune and Gallant-Stallion were disappointed.

It was two days later that they reached Bitternut, the trail from the mountains coming out farther south than Meven had expected. But it did not take them long to reach the village. They could smell evening meals cooking everywhere, and they watched men hurry down side streets on their way home to dinner. The sun was still well up—it stayed light for quite some time even in the late summer.

"By the gods of Paard-Peran, it is so good to see people," Meven breathed. "I am so tired of being around nothing but horses."

Kalantha scowled at his remark. "Ponies, Meven, and they were very good to us. Very good company."

"It's very good to be on our way home." He was quick to

stable Gallant-Stallion and Fortune, promising the stable master he would be paid in the morning.

"Or the morning after that," Kalantha told the man. "We might be in town two days."

The stable master remembered them, commenting to Meven on how much he'd grown, his eyes lingering on Meven's bare feet. It looked like he wanted to say something else, perhaps ask them about their appearance, but he didn't.

"Please groom them," Meven added. "The punch has a terribly snarled tail."

The stable master gave a nod. While Gallant-Stallion and Fortune were in excellent physical condition, there were burrs in their manes and tails, and dirt was caked on their bellies and legs.

"I will take very good care of your horses," he said.

Then Meven was striding down a spokelike street that would take them to the small business district. He walked on a wood-planked sidewalk, which was kinder to his feet than the gravel-littered street, and he slowed only so Kalantha could catch up. She was dawdling by looking at everything.

Glass in shop windows was rare in villages, but a pot seller near the inn had one. It was a long, narrow window behind which vases, plates, mugs, and the like were displayed on an equally narrow set of shelves. Kalantha and Meven caught their reflections in the window and stopped.

"I'm taller than before," Kalantha said. "Definitely taller, and thin." She didn't quite come up to Meven's shoulder, but she noticed a difference in herself. She'd been by this window when they were in the village the first time, and today she was eye to eye with a row of tavern mugs. "Five feet," she guessed. She smiled and turned this way and that, seemingly not bothered by her ragamuffin clothes and the dirt on her face and arms. "Wouldn't you say I'm five feet tall? Maybe a little more. And I don't have so many freckles."

Meven nodded in agreement. He guessed he was about six feet—an impressive height for a fourteen-year-old. He grinned. "I must have grown at least six inches."

"I said you grew like a dandelion. Should've believed me."

"Couldn't you have picked something other than a weed to compare me to?"

One corner of her lip turned up. Her face was as brown as the clay in the pots, and had lost much of its roundness. Her cheeks were more pronounced, and her ears stood out because of her hair. She was twelve now.

"Bishop DeNogaret isn't going to like my hair." She fingered it, discovering that while it was short all over, it was also terribly uneven.

"He's likely to keep you inside the Temple until it all grows out and is pretty again." As soon as he said it, he realized it was the wrong thing to say. It was the truth, he thought, but she didn't need to hear it at the moment. And she certainly didn't need to hear it from him.

She frowned and stomped away from the window. "You got that gold chain with you? I remember the inn having a bathtub. I'm going to soak for an hour."

Meven hurried past her, reaching into his pocket for the chain.

There was a well-dressed man at the inn, sitting behind a desk and writing something on a sheet of parchment. Meven didn't remember him from the previous visit.

"Good afternoon." Meven got the innkeeper's attention.

The man smiled, but it didn't seem genuine. His eyes roamed over Meven and Kalantha, fixing on their dirty bare feet.

Meven pulled out the chain and asked for Kalantha's dagger, then he indicated a few inches he intended to break off. "Will this do? Two rooms, and a bath for each of us. A few meals."

He was a middle-aged man with a careworn face. Rheumy

blue eyes continued to scrutinize Meven and Kalantha. "This's gold, this chain. Thick and very valuable. Who'd you steal it from?"

Meven backed up as his mouth dropped open in surprise. "Steal? You accuse me of stealing?" Every inch of him showed that he was offended.

The man's eyes narrowed, and he jabbed a finger at the chain. "I own this place, and I won't take stolen goods. And I won't rent rooms to thieves. No matter how much gold they have." He sniffed the air. "Filthy, stinking thieves."

Meven dropped his hands to the table, fingernails digging into the soft wood top. "I am not a thief. I am, however, the Prince of Galmier. And I will not be talked to in this manner."

The man raised an eyebrow and gave out a clipped laugh. "The Prince. The high 'n mighty Prince of Galmier? Not at all possible. The Prince . . ."

"I am the Prince of Galmier."

The innkeeper's fist came down on the table, knocking over a vial of ink, which he quickly righted. Meven was startled. "A thief and a liar, you are, young man! If you don't leave right this very moment, I'll call for the Bell Cow and his men. You can take your ill-got booty with you now or you can be thrown in the Bell Cow's cellar." Again, he jabbed a finger at the gold chain.

Meven's jaw clenched, and the veins on his neck stood out. "Listen, you disgusting, miserable . . ."

"Young fool, there is no Prince of Galmier! Prince Edan Montoll died two years come next spring. All's left is the King, and he's not faring well. Don't you sully the Prince's name, you wretch!"

"Wretch?" Meven sputtered. "Fool? Thief? Is there anything else you'd like to call me?" His face turned blood red in anger. "The punishment for your insolence should be considerable!"

"Thief. Wretch. You heard me. Get out or I *will* call the Bell Cow. And your punishment . . ."

"C'mon, Kal. We'll never be back to this place. Ever. We'll go straight to High Keep. And after I meet with the King in Nadir I'll make sure this man pays dearly for his insults." He whirled and started to leave, but Kalantha grabbed his arm. "Pays dearly, I say, Kal!"

"Stop. Please. Stay here for the horses, Meven, if not for us. We've ridden Rue and Fortune hours and hours. They've got to be more tired than we are. We can't push them any more today." She gave a pleading glance to the innkeeper. "He's truly who he says he is. Look, sir, it's a long, long story how we've come to be like this." She gestured to her clothes and her hair. "How we've come to look so raggedy."

"Yes, a very long story of how we've come to be in this pitiful village and in your pathetic inn," Meven added. "All right, Kal. For the horses. Believe me, if we had somewhere else to stay tonight, we'd stay there. I'd sleep on the ground if I wasn't thinking so much about a bed. But Kal's right. We can't push the horses any more at the moment. Can't afford one of them to come up lame and useless when we're so close to home. And so we're forced to spend the night in your stinking sty of an inn."

"Meven!" Kalantha knew her brother was angry with the innkeeper; she was also, but apparently not to the same extent. She'd never heard Meven talk so foully, and it scared her. It reminded her of Edan when he wouldn't stay in the village of Hathi because he considered it too beneath him.

But Meven's vulgar language seemed to convince the innkeeper that he really was the Prince, or at least some kind of royalty. That, and Meven slapping his open hand down on the table so the Montoll ring clearly showed. The innkeeper stared slack-jawed at it.

"Yes, Prince Edan is dead," Meven said. "His slayers tried to kill us, too. We've been in hiding to save ourselves and our friends." Each word had a brittle edge to it. "I'm Edan's cousin, the King's nephew, and I'm next in line for the throne. And I will not be talked to . . ."

"M-m-my deepest apologies . . ."

"Prince Meven Montoll."

"Your highness . . . Prince M-m-meven." The man added a bow. His fingers twitched nervously and he continued to stammer. "I-I-I meant you no slight. I-I-I-I just . . ." He shook his head. "Your highness . . . the way you look . . . no shoes . . . the w-w-w-word around the country . . ."

"What word?" Kalantha interrupted.

The man shook his head again. "That the royal family is all but gone. Prince Edan dead, the King ill, and . . ."

"How ill?" Meven demanded.

"Worse than ever before." The innkeeper shrugged. "Word is that he is dying. Listen, I'm so very sorry I called you a thief. I truly had no idea that . . ."

Meven snarled, cutting the man off. Kalantha could tell her brother's anger was lessening, though, as the red was leaving his face and he was not breathing so hard. She put a hand on his arm.

"Meven, we *do* look like beggars. You can't blame this man for thinking us thieves—or worse. And we've been away for some time. Everyone probably thinks we're dead, too." She dropped her voice to a whisper. "The Bishop and the King, they don't know you're alive. And I thought we were going to keep our news secret until we reached High Keep."

"I intended to, Kal. But I didn't intend on being accused of thievery." Meven turned his attention to the man. "You say the King is dying?"

"Rumor is he's very, very ill. They say he won't recover this time, and that he won't make it through the coming winter." The innkeeper stood and walked from behind the desk. He bowed again, this time bending nearly all the way over. "Truly, your highness, I am sorry for my thoughtless words. Please forgive . . ."

Meven pointed to the gold chain on the desk. "As I asked before, how many links? Two rooms, two baths, and some meals."

The innkeeper picked up the chain, momentarily admiring it. "You are my guests, Prince Meven. . . ." He looked pleadingly to Kalantha. "Princess . . ."

Kalantha shook her head. "No Princess. We're not married. And I might be part of the royal family, but I'm not royalty. I'm his sister. Call me Kal."

"Prince Meven, Lady Kal. You are my guests. Stay as long as you like, dine as my guests. It is the least I can do given what I've said." He handed the chain back to Meven. "My guests."

"All right. We'll stay here tonight."

"Maybe two nights," Kalantha cut in. "We need to get ourselves cleaned up and get some new clothes. The horses need considerable grooming and . . ."

"And we're very hungry and tired," Meven finished.

"I'll show you to your rooms."

"You shouldn't have talked to that man like that," Kalantha said so softly Meven barely heard her. "It's not like you."

Meven didn't reply.

21 · Through Mara's Eyes

Each Finest will have at least one gift, something that sets him or her apart and that will benefit shepherd and charge. Each Finest must nurture and develop this gift and realize it comes from the Creators.

~Peran-Morab, sister to the eldest god

Gallant-Stallion remembered the cozy feel of the stable. It was clean, like it had been during his previous visit, and the open doors invited the warm breeze inside. Fortune nickered that he was tired and his hooves were sore, and he nickered his great pleasure at being here. The stable master held an apple for him, which he finished in two bites. Then the packhorse began eating from his trough as soon as grain was put in front of him.

Simple creature, Gallant-Stallion thought for the hundredth time. *I will never fully understand you.*

Gallant-Stallion had learned to prefer the wilderness, even though it was difficult to get his fill in the deepest part of winter. He appreciated the lack of boundaries and the absence of doors and fences. More than that, he valued being able to keep his eye on Meven all the time. But he was here and not in the wilds, and so he decided to find something good about the place. The stable held the rich scent of the earth, the musty scent of hay, and a mix of pleasant smells—fresh oats and early apples that were mounded in wicker bushes. He could smell all the horses in the stalls, and the pony named Mara, too; she had a softer odor, and it held a hint of spice.

I knew you would return, Gallant-Stallion-called-Rue.

The stable master gave Gallant-Stallion an apple, filled his trough, and made sure there was plenty of water within every horse's reach.

When he was gone, the Finest pony left the far corner of the stable and walked down the aisle between the stalls. She looked to each horse as she went, making a wuffling sound that some of them responded to. Only four of the horses were familiar to Gallant-Stallion from his previous stay—warmbloods and cobs. The rest of the stalls were filled with bretons, heavy drafts, morabs, and cutting horses.

I saw it in a vision that you would come back shortly before the snow.

The snow is months away.

Indeed. The pony's gold-flecked eyes seemed to loom larger, and Gallant-Stallion couldn't look away. *You came here with your charge?*

Of course. No doubt you saw Meven outside these doors. Gallant-Stallion instantly thought of the Prince, who had told the stable master he could be reached at the inn. Gallant-Stallion didn't like being separated from Meven, but the Finest unfortunately knew his limitations in a village. Again he wondered if it would be like this at the High Keep Temple and at Nadir. How often would he be with Meven? It had to be the same for other Finest, not being with their charges all of the time. How did they handle it?

Yes, I saw the new Prince. Your charge looks well. No need to worry so.

I do not worry. Gallant-Stallion could not look elsewhere, he was so consumed by her eyes. The gold flecks seemed to be dancing like fireflies. *Much*, he added.

The gold flecks sparkled brighter. In an instant it was night and he was galloping across a grassy field, stirring up golden fireflies as he went. His hooves touched down so lightly it felt as if he floated above the ground and that he might take flight at any moment. The field gave way to woods, but the fall-dressed trees were far enough apart that Gallant-Stallion did not have to slow. It grew increasingly chilly and marshy the farther he went, and trees that were once narrow—birches and stick pines—became thicker and shorter and sprouted cottages atop them. The fireflies swirled all around.

I've seen this before.

A vision from your earlier visit, Mara said.

Gallant-Stallion recalled it was indeed similar to some of the cryptic images he'd seen when he looked into her eyes more than a year past. But there were differences in this vision—he didn't see the faces looking out the doors, and the leaves were no longer green. Still, there were soft lights coming from some of the windows, indicating the presence of people.

What you see has not yet come to pass, Mara continued. *Your travels have not yet taken you there.*

Taken me to a place where houses grow atop trees? It was humorous, absurd, and unsettling to Gallant-Stallion. But certainly no more unsettling than her vision of the blackness that had become assassin birds. As he continued to watch, the trunks thickened and the cottages disappeared into them, as if they were being swallowed. The bark became stone and spread to form a wall he could not get through. His hooves futilely struck against it. The wall grew taller and taller, curved and became a tower. The fireflies winked out, replaced by bats that spun away into the night.

There was a crack of lightning and Gallant-Stallion felt rain falling hard upon his neck. Thunder boomed and the stone wall melted into muddy ground that in a few moments faded into nothingness. Mara was standing in front of him again, and the gold flecks in her eyes no longer danced.

I don't understand.

She snorted long and shook her head, and Gallant-Stallion got the impression she was disappointed in him. *You do not understand the horses of this world. You do not understand your charge. There is much in general you do not understand.*

I do not understand your visions.

You do not fully understand the horses because you are not like them, she said. *You do not fully understand your charge, or any of the people of Paard-Peran for that matter, because you are not one of them. You can study them, run with them, and listen to them. But you cannot be them, and you have not yet acquired the imagination to pretend to be them. You do not understand my visions because you do not yet have the eyes to truly see them. And so to you they are scattered glimpses of the future that are both a warning and an enigma.*

Gallant-Stallion tossed his head in frustration.

I am not disappointed in you, she said, sensing his thoughts. *And do not allow yourself to become disappointed and disheartened. You are young, and like your charge you have more growing and learning to do.*

Gallant-Stallion looked past her and across the aisle, to where the packhorse was. Fortune had eaten his fill of the oats and was drinking now.

Can you . . . He looked into Mara's eyes again and focused on the gold flecks. *Can you show me a vision of my charge? I want a hint of what the future holds for Meven.*

His words trailed off as the gold specks twinkled like stars. He expected the world to fall away again and to receive another cryptic image. But after a moment Mara's eyes became dull.

I didn't see anything.

Mara nodded. *I had nothing else to show. The one you safe-guard was with you when you galloped across the marshy field, and again in the woods where you ran to the homes growing on trees. I see nothing beyond that. That future is too far away.*

Gallant-Stallion recalled feeling a weight on his back in the vision. So Meven was riding with him.

Your charge is destined for greatness, she said. *If you are strong enough to face the growing evil and keep it at bay.*

What evil? Gallant-Stallion shouted the words.

The King is very ill. You safeguard the very future of Galmier and the lands beyond it. After a moment, and as she backed away, Mara added: *Pray to the good gods of this world that you are up to the task, Gallant-Stallion-called-Rue. I do not believe a Finest has ever in the history of this world had a more important mission.*

Gallant-Stallion watched the Finest pony retreat to the far corner of the barn and meld with the shadows. He could smell the musty hay, the sweet oats and the apples. He could smell the odor of the other horses and of the earth beneath his hooves. But he could no longer smell her.

~ ~ ~

Sometime during the night word spread that the Prince of Galmier was staying at the inn. People bowed when Meven came down for breakfast, and the serving girl was especially re-spectful and doted on him to the point of it being annoying. They were given the large table in the center of the room, and there were cushions on the seats. Bowls of fruit, bread, and cheese were brought, quickly followed by plates of steaming eggs and sausage, and mugs of tea and cider.

"It makes me uncomfortable, Kal," Meven admitted. "All this attention, the little nods, the bowing. Everyone's eyes on us. Really uncomfortable." He gestured with his head to indicate a young couple at a nearby table intently watching them. "They probably wonder why the Prince of Galmier is dressed like a beggar and has no shoes."

"*You're* uncomfortable? I felt uncomfortable yesterday, the horrid way you talked to the innkeeper. I was so embarrassed."

"He talked poorly to us."

"He had an excuse. We did look like thieves."

His face grew flushed, and he drew a finger to his lips, trying to get her to talk more softly so the eavesdroppers wouldn't overhear. "I'm not sure what came over me yesterday. I looked for him a few minutes ago to tell him I was sorry, but the cook said he's not in yet." He stuffed a forkful of eggs in his mouth and closed his eyes. "This is so very, very good. I missed having hot, salted food. I always appreciated what we had at the Temple, but I never realized *just* how fortunate we were until we lived with those ponies. I'm never going to live like that again."

Kalantha drew her lips into a thin line. "You'll apologize when you see him? The innkeeper?"

Meven nodded and stuffed in several more forkfuls of eggs. The first of his words were muffled because he had so much food in his mouth. "I was tired when we got here yesterday, so mad when he called me a thief and a liar." He swallowed the eggs and reached for a sausage. "No one had ever accused me of those things before. I'm a religious man, Kal. Whoever would accuse me of theft? Of lying?" After filling his mouth again, he took a deep pull on a mug of cider to wash it down. "I can't remember ever being so angry. And I know that was wrong, the foul words I used. I prayed for forgiveness last night. I won't let myself get that angry again." Softer still: "I'm sorry I embarrassed you."

"So you're truly ashamed?"

Meven drained his mug and thumped it on the table, a signal

for the serving girl to bring him another. "Yes. Look at my eyes, Kal. I barely slept last night I was so ashamed." He had dark circles, like on the nights with the ponies when he had nightmares about the assassin-birds.

"We'll find the innkeeper later today," she said. "You'll feel better when you tell him you're sorry."

That afternoon Meven bartered for shoes and a few changes of clothes for each of them. The clothes were new and better made than he expected from a village, but they were not as fine as he would have preferred for his reunion with Bishop DeNogaret. And nothing was as nice as anything he'd worn from Edan's satchel. However, the dark colors suited him. "We needed more than one change," he told Kalantha, "because we've grown, and none of our old clothes at the Temple will fit us well enough. We'll have to make do with these until we can have more tailored."

"None of *your* clothes will fit," Kalantha corrected. She knew most of hers would still fit fine, but they would be a little shorter. And she could always add trim to the wrists of her tunics and blouses and to the hems of her dresses and skirts to make them longer.

Meven tried to get her a hat, but Kalantha would have none of it. "Not even a scarf, and certainly not an ugly wimple."

"The Bishop might make you wear one," Meven scolded. "Actually, I'm pretty certain he will." *Your hair looks terrible*, he mouthed.

"But I don't have to wear one until then."

Meven knew she'd not been cheery since they came into Bitternut, and her mood had worsened in the hours here. First yesterday—after his comment at the pot shop's window about her staying indoors at the Temple until her hair grew out. Then after his exchange with the innkeeper. Meven said he was sorry for both affronts, and told her he was kidding on the matter about her hair. But Kalantha had fixated on the notion of being sequestered until her hair grew. He worried that she would give him the glum treatment all the way home.

"So I've talked foul to an innkeeper and upset my dear sister. Is there anyone else I can aggravate?" He closed his eyes and imagined he saw Edan on the exquisite glavian. Edan was visually inspecting the village of Hathi and the rag-tag collection of residents. There was a disgusted look on Edan's face when he considered the peasants. "I don't want to be that kind of Prince."

"What did you say?" Kal tugged on his sleeve.

"I said we'll spend one more night in the inn, then first thing in the morning we'll be on the road to High Keep. You'll get to see your friend the gardener very soon." He hoped she would smile just a little at that prospect, but she didn't.

"I'm going to look in on Fortune and make sure he gets groomed," she said. "I'll be ready to leave at dawn." She hurried down the closest side street before he could protest. Her pockets bulged with berries she'd taken off the breakfast table, and Meven knew they were treats for the packhorse.

He strolled down the opposite side street, looking at business signs and in open doors and windows and nodding back or smiling to everyone who acknowledged him. He didn't see two haggard-looking men following him.

22 · Lessons

I spent two decades among the Fallen of Paard-Peran, and I shepherded only one man. In those years I discovered that he and I liked the autumn the best, and both of us treasured rosy apples. The world was at its most colorful and delicious then. The people, however, were not at their best.

~*Patience, Finest Court Matriarch*

Fortune nickered his pleasure over the apples this morning and the berries Kalantha brought him yesterday. The packhorse didn't complain about the pace Gallant-Stallion set and seemed happy to take in the sights along the road that led north out of Bitternut. *Home*, he said to the Finest. *Going home. Wonderful home.*

Whether Fortune had picked up the notion of going home from Kalantha or simply got it in his head from the direction they were traveling on the road didn't matter. Gallant-Stallion was simply pleased not to have to coax the packhorse to speed up. Gallant-Stallion was surprised the packhorse remembered this road and remembered High Keep for that matter. But maybe all creatures considered someplace home and kept it in their heart. For Gallant-Stallion, that place was the Finest Court. He hoped he would have a chance to return there for a visit as soon as Meven was safe at the Temple.

How long will I have at the Court? Gallant-Stallion wondered. *Meven will have to go to Nadir, likely soon.* Meven had talked to Kalantha enough about the matter of Nadir and the palace, that it was well ingrained in the Finest's head. Meven would have to be officially crowned and would have to meet the King.

Meven was discussing that matter again right now, though it was a one-sided conversation. Kalantha wasn't talking back.

"I bet we won't be at the Temple too long," Meven said. "With the King being sick—terribly sick, according to the people in Bitternut—we'll have to go to the capital. Probably a few days, maybe a week at best at the Temple, then we'll go with Bishop DeNogaret to see the King. By the gods, Kal, the King can't die. If he does, I'll be crowned King. And I don't want that." *At least not yet,* he mouthed. *I'm too young.*

Meven continued to chatter, and Kalantha nodded occasionally. It was clear her mind was somewhere beyond this road and that she wasn't paying attention to him.

"High time we met our uncle anyway, Kal. He'll want to know exactly what happened to Edan and the soldiers. And he'll want to learn all about us. He hasn't seen us ever, Kal. Well, Edan said the King saw me when I was a baby. But our parents moved north, and the King never saw me again. Edan said our dad never cared for the royal life, and didn't want to be near the palace. So the King never saw you. Aren't you excited about meeting him?"

She shrugged and twisted her fingers in Fortune's reins.

It was dry. There wasn't a single puddle near the road that Gallant-Stallion could smell or see. The climate was changed from when he'd come down this road with the wedding party more than a year and a half ago. The Finest appreciated the altering seasons, and he found the migration of the birds and the slight shift in the trees' coloration interesting. The warm air brought him the scent of the river and the late summer flowers, which, while not as fragrant as the spring blooms, had a soft tang to them that teased his senses. The warm breeze played with his tail and mane, felt especially good drifting over his withers, and it held no trace of dampness. Summer here was different than in the mountains, somehow not as intense, as if the flatness of the land deadened some of the sounds and did not attract as much wildlife.

Gallant-Stallion could hear birds, one making a clacking sound he'd committed to memory because of its oddness. A knobby hornbill, Kalantha had called it. The bird was somewhere in the trees by the river, and she was looking for it also, hanging as far over in Fortune's saddle as she could. The Finest wished he could see it. He'd spotted a pair only once before, and that was a few weeks ago in the foothills of the Galmier Mountains. The hornbill was a large bird, purple and blue with a large yellow beak that curved like a piece of mushfruit and was crested with a scarlet knob. Kalantha had explained to Meven, and thereby to Gallant-Stallion, that the birds were not native to this island-continent, and had been brought here more than a century ago by a merchant family who traded with the barbarians of Farmeadow. They were scarce in Galmier and only lived here in the summer and very early fall. They preferred warm weather and went as far south as possible when the leaves started to turn.

There were several blackbirds flying overhead, but they didn't seem to be following the road. Gallant-Stallion could tell by the way that Meven sat in the saddle that he was watching them, too.

Steadfast, to be concerned so by a dozen tiny birds is shameful of me, Gallant-Stallion said. He thought, perhaps, that the spirit of Steadfast might talk to him. *Have the assassin-birds given up?* Mara's vision didn't reveal any birds, not even a trace of the black hawk. *Have we been away long enough? Whoever controls the evil birds . . . does he think Meven dead? And what is the danger ahead Mara hinted of?* There was no ghostly reply from Steadfast, and so Gallant-Stallion lapsed into silence, listening to Meven chatter and finding that Kalantha, like Steadfast, wouldn't answer any questions.

The road narrowed and ran by a stand of maples and pin oaks that cast a long shadow across their path. Gallant-Stallion suddenly stiffened and stopped, picking up the scent of something new. Men, two distinct odors and close enough that he could smell them without effort. But he couldn't see them. There was the scent of two horses also, these smelling of sweat as if they'd been ridden fast. Gallant-Stallion didn't like it that they were out of sight.

"Rue! Move!" Meven flicked the reins and jabbed Gallant-Stallion with his heels.

Stop, the Finest told the packhorse. *Stay here.*

The packhorse complied, wuffling its curiosity.

"Rue!" Meven leaned forward in the saddle, and laying up against Gallant-Stallion's neck spoke loudly in his ear. "Listen you stubborn punch. Move!" He jabbed harder with his heels, then sat back in frustration. "Kal, I don't know what's wrong with this ugly horse."

"Fortune's not moving either," Kal said. "I think something's wrong."

The men's scent is coming from the stand of trees, Gallant-Stallion decided. It might be nothing, travelers resting in the shade. There weren't any birds directly in the area, and that much was good. What to do? he wondered. Hurry past or retrace his steps and come this way later?

Steadfast, I'm not sure what to . . .

"What's the matter, young things? Your horses don't want to take you any farther?" A thickset man of Kalantha's height stepped out from behind the largest maple. His face was weathered, and there were deep creases around his eyes. "Are they dead tired? Or can't you control them properly?" The man was rumpled looking, in worn trousers and an overlarge shirt with voluminous sleeves that fell halfway down his hands. His hair was stringy and hung past his shoulders, and he had the start of a straggly beard.

There was something about him that was familiar to Meven. Perhaps he'd seen the man in Bitternut.

"There's nothing wrong with our horses," Meven said.

I shouldn't have stopped, Gallant-Stallion said. *I should have sped up and not been so cautious. This man means no good and I should have spirited Meven from this place. But if I had sped up, the man might have chased us on his horse. Men,* the Finest thought. He smelled two of them. Where was the other?

"We're going to be on our way now," Meven continued. He jabbed Gallant-Stallion with his heels again, and the Finest plodded ahead warily, telling Fortune to follow.

"You're not bein' very friendly, young sir. Not friendly at all. A Prince should be friendly to his lowly subjects." The man walked quickly to keep up with them and grabbed at Meven's trouser leg. "I should think the Prince would be ridin' a fancier horse," he continued. "And should be dressed fancier, too. I would've thought the Prince a fancy, fancy man."

So the man was from Bitternut, Meven thought. Had to be from that village to know he was the Prince. "C'mon, Rue. You have to get moving. Let's get . . ."

There was a *thwup* sound.

Kalantha screamed as Fortune fell. She managed to jump free barely in time before the horse could pin her. "Meven!"

A quarrel was lodged in the packhorse's throat. Fortune kicked his rear legs once, then lay still.

"Fortune, oh please no." Kalantha suddenly seemed oblivious to the rumpled man, to everything but the dead packhorse she crawled to. She sobbed so hard her shoulders shook. "My friend Fortune. My very best friend."

Gallant-Stallion stood motionless, taking everything in,

shocked by the unfounded slaying of the packhorse, and concentrating on the rumpled man. The second man was in the stand of trees, armed with a crossbow that was trained on Kalantha now. The Finest saw him; he was noticeably bigger than the man on the road, who'd drawn a long knife, and he was wearing a leather jerkin that had daggers strapped to it. Gallant-Stallion suspected he might be able to get Meven away, though there would be a risk the man would shoot a quarrel at the Prince or himself—probably would have shot right away if the Finest had not stopped by the stand of trees. That had likely been the trap's intention—shoot both horses as Meven and Kalantha rode by, the Finest thought.

Meven slipped from Gallant-Stallion's back. He stood uncertain, looking back and forth between Kalantha and the rumpled man. Meven couldn't see the man in the trees, but he knew someone was there. The dead packhorse attested to that. Unlike Gallant-Stallion, he didn't know a quarrel was aimed at his sister.

"What do you want?" Meven asked.

The rumpled man stroked what amounted to his beard. "I figure the Prince ought to have gold on 'im."

Meven reached into his pocket and pulled out a length of gold chain. He'd spent more than half the links bartering for their clothes and shoes and paying the stable master.

The man laughed. "I told Keth back there that you weren't the Prince when we laid eyes on you in Bitternut. But Keth, he swears you're the Prince. Said word was all over town that the new Prince was parading around in commoner's clothes and was riding a big ugly horse."

"He's the Prince all right." The voice came from the stand of trees. "Look at his ring."

The rumpled man waved his knife threateningly and stepped up to Meven to get a closer look. Gallant-Stallion smelled the ale on his breath and the stench that clung to him like a second skin. "Yes, that's quite the ring, Keth. I'd say you're right. He's the Prince. Or if he ain't the Prince, he's a thief who stole that ring from the Prince."

"I *am* the Prince," Meven said. There was the slightest tremor in his voice. "But this is all the gold I have. You can have it." He dropped the chain into the brigand's hand.

"Not good enough," the rumpled man said. Still, he slipped the chain into his pocket. "I want that ring, too."

"Meven?" This came from Kalantha, who was standing now. "Why would they kill my horse?" From where she was standing she could easily see the man with the crossbow. She waved her fist at him. "You didn't have to kill my horse! We would've given you that bit of gold anyway. You didn't have to kill Fortune!"

"And the ring," Keth said from the trees. "That 'bit of gold' and the Prince's ring."

"And the Prince, too," the rumpled man added. "We'll take 'im. He's worth somethin'. We'll ransom him to the King. Little Princess here can go back to the palace and get us a nice chest of gold for 'im. If we think it's enough, we'll let her take the Prince home with her." He let out a twisted laugh. "Ain't that right, Keth? If it's enough gold he can go."

"Yeah, if it's enough. That's a good idea, Mica." Keth stepped forward now where Meven could see him, still keeping the crossbow aimed at Kalantha. He gestured with his head. "Princess, you get on that big horse and get riding to that palace and the King. And you tell him you need to bring a chest of gold to me and Mica. You bring it to that pot shop in Bitternut, you hear. And no tricks. No soldiers. Understand? You trick us, the Prince ends up just like your horse. Dead. Dead. Dead."

Kalantha stared at the crossbow, then dropped her gaze to Fortune's still form. "You didn't have to kill him," she whispered. "And you're not going to kill my brother." Kalantha was saying something else, but her voice was so soft.

"I figure the Prince there's worth lots o' gold, ain't that right, Mica?" Keth said. "The Prince being the last in line for the throne and all. Why, if something were to happen to the Prince, whatever would happen to this country? Who'd rule it then?"

"I'd make a right fine King," Mica laughed. "No taxes, I'd say. I'd bring all of the good-lookin' ladies to my palace. And I'd wear me lots of fine, fine clothes."

"Good thing for us you didn't have no soldiers with you," Keth told Meven. "We couldn't've sprung this trap if you'd had company. We couldn't've set ourselves up for lots o' gold."

Meven drew his shoulders back and thrust out his chin. "Kidnapping the Prince will get the both of you dead. Leave now and I'll . . ."

The ruffians laughed, spittle flying from their mouths. Mica grabbed his belly, he was laughing so hard. Keth kept his senses about him though, and shifted the aim of the crossbow between Meven and Kalantha.

"You heard me," Meven said. His hands were clenched, the knuckles white.

"Maybe I ought to shoot the other horse, too, and let the little Princess here walk to the palace for our gold."

Mica was rubbing at his chin again. "Don't want to wait that long for my gold, Keth. She'd be gone weeks and weeks, I think. She'd be gone so long she'd forget about the Prince, here. Nope, we don't shoot that horse. But maybe we shoot the Prince in the leg to show the girl here that we mean business."

Keth trained the crossbow only on Meven now, the quarrel pointed at his leg. "I wouldn't move, Prince. If'n you move, I might miss and hit you a little higher. Might kill you by mistake. Then we'd have to ransom your corpse."

ALL THIS TIME GALLANT-STALLION HAD BEEN THINKING. AND he'd been listening to the horses hidden behind the trees. They didn't care for their riders, and they didn't want to be here. They were nervous because they smelled the blood of the dead packhorse. And they were thirsty and hot; they smelled the sweet river that would quench their thirst.

Gallant-Stallion nickered to them. *Go to the river,* he said. *The water is cool and good.*

The men, they returned. *Beat us. Hurt us. Must stay.*

I will not let them hurt you, Gallant-Stallion persisted. *Please go to the river. Hurry to the river.*

One of the horses moved, tugging until it had loosed its reins. *Thirsty,* it told Gallant-Stallion. *Hot. Thirsty.*

The river water is so very sweet, the Finest urged.

THE HORSE STEPPED ON FALLEN BRANCHES AS IT CAME TO-ward the road. The noise distracted Mica, and he turned toward the stand of trees to curse at the horse. It wasn't what Gallant-Stallion had hoped for. He wanted the man with the crossbow to be ruffled. But Keth kept his hands steady, and the quarrel aimed at Meven.

"Stupid horse done got itself loose," Mica said.

"Won't go far. Leave it be," Keth returned.

SWEET, SWEET WATER, GALLANT-STALLION PRACTICALLY COOED. *I will not let them hurt you.*

The horse crossed the road and headed toward the trees to the east and the river beyond.

"DARN FOOL HORSE," MICA SAID. HE STARTED AFTER IT, AND Keth finally moved. He glanced toward his partner, and in that moment Gallant-Stallion acted.

The Finest charged Keth, knocking Meven to the ground in

the process to keep him safe. Keth fired the crossbow, the quarrel whizzing above Meven's prone form. Without pause, Keth reached for another quarrel and was notching it in place when Gallant-Stallion reached him. The Finest reared up and slashed out with his hooves.

Keth was quick and leapt to the side. He raced toward Kalantha while avoiding the horse's hooves. Suddenly, he swung the weapon on Kalantha and jumped behind her, using her as a shield against the big horse.

But Kalantha would have none of it. "You killed my Fortune," she hissed as she spun. Oblivious to the crossbow, she locked her eyes on his.

After a heartbeat Keth blinked, gaze flitting between her anger-etched face and the punch that had placed itself between Mica and the Prince.

"Mica, get around that horse and get the Prince!" Keth had looked away from Kalantha, and so he didn't see her reach for the ornamental dagger that was always at her side. And he didn't see her flick it toward him. It was an easy gesture for her, one she'd practiced when she was hunting rabbits or used when she was trying to get fruit too high up for her to reach.

The blade flashed forward and struck him in the chest. It was so sharp it went straight through the leather jerkin.

"Mica!" Keth's eyes were wide with shock. "Fool girl, what have you . . ." Red foam appeared on his lips and he dropped the crossbow. Then he pitched forward into the dirt.

In the same instant, Gallant-Stallion lashed out with his hooves at Mica. The brigand ducked and slipped around him, and was going for Meven. The Finest whirled and struck Mica in the chest and the head, hearing the crack of bones and watching the rumpled man fly backward from the force of the impact. Mica was dead before he hit the ground.

Meven was on his feet and running to Kalantha. "What . . . what did you do? By the gods, Kal, you . . ."

"Killed that man." She stared at Keth for only a moment, then she brushed past Meven and returned to Fortune. She knelt by the horse and stroked its mane. "But that man killed my friend," she said. Her fingers fluttered over the horse's neck and closed on the quarrel. She yanked it out and threw it to the side of the road. "And he would've killed you, Meven. They were desperate men, and they didn't really know what they were doing."

He looked back and forth between the two fallen men. "They just wanted gold, Kal."

"And if we'd had enough, they might've let us go on our way," she said. Kalantha's hands were over Fortune's wound, pressed hard in an effort to stop the bleeding, as if that act might somehow bring the horse back. "But when they saw how poor we were, they didn't know what to do. They came up with the notion of ransom. I'm sure that wasn't their original plan. Desperate men, Meven. They wouldn't have waited for a chest of gold to come. They would've panicked and killed you."

"You killed a man," Meven said incredulously. "I can't believe that you . . ."

"Taught them a lesson? Saved our lives?" Kalantha lifted her hands and held them in front of her face. They were covered with Fortune's blood. After a moment, she wiped them on her tunic. "I've nothing to dig with. How can I bury him?" She was talking to herself, not asking Meven.

Gallant-Stallion nudged Mica's body with a hoof, wanting to be sure the man was dead. Then he went to Keth to be certain there also. The Finest sniffed the air to make sure there were no more bandits. There was just the cutting horse still heading toward the river, and the one behind the stand of trees. And there was the scent of Fortune, and his blood that continued to seep out onto the road.

The threat passed, Gallant-Stallion allowed himself to grieve over the death of the packhorse. He'd considered it a simple creature, but it had truly been Kalantha's friend. And he allowed anger to well up. There was no reason for the man to kill the horse. Fortune had done nothing to offend them. The death had been to set an example and to increase the threat, the Finest knew. But the death was completely senseless.

He looked again at the men's corpses, certain their souls would never reach the pleasant place where spirits drifted. *Fallen,* he said. *Steadfast, so many, many of the people are fallen. And ones like these are not . . . cannot . . . be favorites of the gods. They are wretched, greedy things that should not walk on Paard-Peran. They are . . .*

Not all are like this, Gallant-Stallion. You know that. It was Steadfast's voice. It came with a cool breeze that played around the Finest's muzzle. *You were correct to stop on the road, Gallant-Stallion. Galloping by the men would have added to their desperation. More than Fortune would have died.*

Gallant-Stallion snorted, his eyes locked onto the pooling blood around Fortune's neck. *This was senseless.*

So many things are senseless when those who are truly Fallen are involved. You did well to save your charge, Gallant-Stallion.

The cool breeze was gone, and Gallant-Stallion knew that the spirit of Steadfast had left. Meven was tugging Kalantha up, and gesturing toward the Finest.

"Let's get going, Kal. There's nothing to be done about Fortune." Meven pulled a satchel free from the packhorse. It had Kalantha's clothes in it. Meven had bartered for them, and he didn't want them left behind. He swung the satchel up and affixed it to the back of Gallant-Stallion's saddle. "C'mon. The punch is big enough to carry both of us."

Kalantha stood defiant, hands on her hips, eyes still on Fortune. "I never wanted to go, Meven."

"We couldn't have stayed in the mountains another fall. You know that. Probably stayed longer than we should have."

She shook her head. "No. I never wanted to go to Edan's

wedding. I never wanted to leave High Keep." She bent and gave Fortune one last pat. "There's only been death since we left," she said. "And it was all supposed to be a grand outing."

"I wonder if these men had anything to do with the assassin-birds?" Meven mused.

Kalantha shook her head. "Just bandits. Stupid, desperate men. They weren't smart enough to be involved with the birds."

She stepped to Keth's body and tugged the dagger out, wiping the blade on the leather jerkin. Then she thrust it in its sheath on her belt and walked across the road.

"Kal, what are you doing? Time to be on our way. They might be common thugs, but maybe they have friends. And we should be long gone before those friends come by."

She disappeared into the trees, despite Meven's continued protests. He started after her, but stopped when she came back, leading a chestnut-colored cutting horse. She scratched the spot between its eyes.

"I figured they each had a horse," she said. Kalantha pulled herself into the saddle and rocked forward to get the horse going. "No use this one getting left behind."

Gallant-Stallion nickered for the cutting horse to follow him. *There would be food and water ahead,* he told the horse. *And there would be no more beatings.*

"Rue, let's get going." Meven held the reins in one hand. The fingers of his free hand were drifting between the few beads remaining on his prayer belt. He mumbled softly and dropped his head, trusting Gallant-Stallion to follow the road.

"What are you doing, Meven?" Kalantha asked. She was riding even with him.

"You killed a man," Meven said. "I'm praying for your soul."

23 · Back from the Dead

There is no nobler creation than a Finest. Dedicated to the salvation of the Fallen Favorites, molded to give men a final chance at redemption. In the meadowlands of the Court each Finest will seek counsel. Let them aid each other so that charge and shepherd can take the correct path. And when the Finest creations are finished with their worldly travails, may they gather in the Finest Court for fellowship and their reward.

~Paard-Zhumd, *on the formation of the Finest Court*

Tears spilled from Bishop DeNogaret's eyes, and he clutched his robe near his heart. He knelt and hugged Meven fiercely, then reached out with a trembling hand to touch Kalantha.

"By the gods, I thought you children lost to me forever," he said. "I thought you dead with Edan and my men. You are beautiful ghosts come back to me." He buried his face in Meven's tunic, and his words were garbled until he pulled his head back. "I prayed and prayed for your safe return. When they didn't find your bodies with Edan's, I thought there might be some small chance that you lived. But the months passed, and then more than a year, and I heard nothing. Oh, I prayed. Every day and night I prayed that you would come back to the Temple."

Meven returned the Bishop's embrace, and began to tell him of the slaughter of the wedding party, promising to tell everything at length later. Then he glanced at Kalantha. "Please pray with me, Bishop DeNogaret," he said. "While we were away Kalantha killed a man."

The Bishop's ashen face grew even paler.

"Killed him just two days past, Bishop DeNogaret."

Kalantha nodded.

"Tell me all about the painful ordeal, my child." The Bishop rose on shaky feet and brushed Kalantha's cheek with the back of his hand. "I will have the acolytes prepare dinner, while you tell me everything. Then we will meditate to help cleanse your spirit."

Meven did nearly all the talking as they sat in the Temple anteroom, with the Bishop interjecting questions from time to time. They all cried when Meven recounted the tale of the assassins' attack in considerable detail, then they cried again later when he told the Bishop about the second attack in the mountains. Though Meven didn't mention the magical pony, he spoke at length about the assassin-birds.

"I know it's hard to believe, maybe impossible," Meven said. "But the killers really were birds. And bats! All of them terribly, terribly vicious." He pointed to the ropy scar on Kalantha's neck. "They nearly killed us."

The Bishop dried his eyes on the sleeve of his robe and ushered them into the dining room. The acolytes were eating elsewhere tonight, as the Bishop wanted Meven and Kalantha to himself. He entreated Meven to continue their tale as they ate a simple stew washed down with goat's milk.

Meven even mentioned the roots they dined on beneath the scarlet haws and the mountain ponies they traveled with as protection.

"The King sent soldiers when Edan's wedding party did not reach Duriam. They found the remains of Prince Edan and the others, though they did not find you," the Bishop said. "We thought, perhaps, that you had fled into the woods. And we thought you died there, of starvation or to wolves. You were gone so very long."

"To keep you safe," Meven told him. "We stayed away to

keep the acolytes safe, too. And we stayed away hoping the birds, whoever controlled them, would think us dead or would forget about us." He explained how the birds killed everyone, even the mad woman from Hathi that they had come in contact with. It was clear the assassin flock wanted no survivors or witnesses. "But Kal and I are witnesses *and* survivors, and we can tell everyone exactly what happened. You believe me, don't you Bishop DeNogaret? About the birds?"

The Bishop nodded. "I know that you and Kalantha don't lie, Meven. Not everyone will believe your tale, however, because not everyone knows you and not everyone believes there is some magic in this world. So you must be careful whom you tell it to. You can't afford to have people think you mad."

"The King will believe me."

"Yes, because we will tell him together."

They talked all through the night and into the early hours of the morning, Meven finally explaining about the magical black pony—despite Kalantha asking him not to. He left out almost nothing—save for his vulgar exchange with the Bitternut innkeeper.

They slept only a few hours, and late the next morning, following baths and grooming by the acolytes, Meven and Kalantha resumed their meeting with the Bishop. Kalantha rarely spoke, unhappy that her dagger had been taken away and that she was forced to wear a scarf wrapped tight around her head to hide her short hair. Meven babbled on about all their experiences, and he finished with the tale of the two brigands on the road.

"Kalantha killed the big one," he said. "With that fancy dagger that had been Edan's. There was blood everywhere. He was threatening us. But there had to have been another way." After a length of silence, Meven added: "Will Kal be all right, Bishop DeNogaret? Will the gods forgive her?"

The Bishop put a hand on Kalantha's shoulder. "The gods

are forgiving, Meven. Kalantha indeed can be saved. It will take time to cleanse her spirit, though."

Kalantha finally met the Bishop's gaze. It was the first time since their reunion that she'd looked directly at him.

"My treasure, you will be all right, and I will help you get through this." The Bishop extended a hand, and she took it. He traced his thumb across a small scar on the back of her hand, then released her. "Pray with me." He placed his hands at his side and waited for her to copy the gesture. Heads bowed, the Bishop began a lengthy prayer with her.

Kalantha's feet were tingling from standing still so long. She wanted to move, and she wanted to be outside the Temple. She admired Bishop DeNogaret fiercely and she feared that he was disappointed in her—for her appearance, for killing someone. She wasn't worried about the condition of her soul or wasn't afraid that she had offended the gods by killing the brigand. She had convinced herself the killing was justified. But would she have to pay for it? Murder was a crime in Galmier. But did killing that man count as murder? Or was it as she believed—self-defense? She continued her musings, paying no attention to the Bishop's words. However, she noticed when he stopped talking.

The prayer was finally finished, she looked up, ashamed that she had not been praying with him. "Bishop DeNogaret, will I be thrown in some cellar for killing that man? Is what I did truly considered a crime?"

He shook his head. "The man was a robber, and you were protecting yourself, child." He paused and straightened himself as much as he could. He couldn't completely, because of the stoop in his shoulders. "The laws of this land will not call for you to be punished. But there is a penance required, a period of atonement that will be necessary. You took a life, Kal. And all lives are sacred."

"What penance?"

"That will take some consideration." He offered her a tight smile. "The acolytes are ready to measure you and Meven for new clothes. My, but you've grown, the both of you. And Kalantha, you are so slim! I sent one of my men to Fergangur for lengths of cloth. We don't have much here. And after you're done, Kalantha, you may spend some time in the garden with your friend, Morgan. He's been begging to see you. At dinner we will discuss your atonement."

Kalantha backed away, nodded respectfully, then hurried to the antechamber. The sooner she was measured, the sooner she could spend time with Morgan. They were just finishing with Meven, and she overheard him talking to a young acolyte holding up a length of gray cloth.

"I like dark colors," Meven said. "No reds or blues. Definitely no yellows or white. I like grays and browns. Black is fine. And I'd like some trim along the sleeves, some very nice buttons if you could. The Bishop says I will have to look my best when I am presented to the King."

Kalantha stayed in the doorway until Meven finished his instructions, then he headed for the library. She knew he wanted to find some mention of sentient birds in the Bishop's books. When the last of his footfalls faded, she took a deep breath, stepped forward, and held her arms out to the side. "I don't care what color of clothes you make for me," she said.

~ ~ ~

Twelve years old, you are! A young lady. You look beautiful, Kal." Morgan briefly held her close, then pulled off her scarf. He chuckled and ran his fingers through her short hair.

"The Bishop doesn't think I'm so beautiful." She put the scarf back on. "He says I have to keep my head covered until my hair grows to a 'respectable length.' That could take some time. Oh, how I hate scarves and hats. The acolytes are making one of those . . . those . . . horrid wimples for me."

For a moment, Morgan thought she might cry. The old gardener beamed at her, and that seemed to lift her spirits. "Bishop DeNogaret knows you're beautiful, Kal. He's just wrapped up in what's proper for young women. Do you know how much he missed you? He was certain you and Meven had been killed, and he blamed himself for it—for not sending enough men to protect you, for letting you go in the first place, and even for not being with you and dying at your side. For months there was a daily prayer vigil just for the two of you. He even rode to Nadir to talk to the King about the slaughter of the wedding party. And mind you, that was some sacrifice—Bishop DeNogaret leaving this Temple. I hadn't seen him travel past Fergangur in more than a decade."

Kalantha shrugged and turned her attention to the garden. Her fingers fluttered over a coral-colored rose bud.

"You look strong, Kal. Taller, thin. I missed you terribly, but I must admit it looks like the time away did you some good."

For the first time since reaching the Temple Kalantha smiled. "I liked running with the ponies," she said. "And all those wonderful things you taught me about the woods . . . about finding roots to eat, and about looking for berries that birds liked . . . that kept us alive. But sometimes I didn't like what I had to do just to live." She closed her eyes and remembered.

~ ~ ~

Kalantha was on her stomach in the tall grass, head kept down and breathing shallowly so she didn't spook her quarry. A plump white rabbit with long, graceful ears was a few yards away. It was nibbling on clover leaves, its nose twitching nervously.

Beautiful, she thought. Snow come to life. Its eyes were a brilliant blue, large and round and ever moving. Kalantha had crept upon it from such a direction that the wind would not carry her scent to the rabbit.

Its ears stood straight up now, and for an instant Kalantha thought she'd made a sound or the wind had shifted. But the rabbit turned its head, looking behind it, at something Kalantha couldn't see or hear. The rabbit stopped eating and bounded toward her, spooked by whatever was in the opposite direction.

Kalantha sprung up to meet it, aiming as she went and flinging the dagger hard and fast. The blade caught the rabbit in the side, and it fell. It didn't die instantly, and so she watched it twitch as she approached. She pulled the dagger free and slit its throat, crying as she did so.

"Beautiful creature," she said. Then she sat next to it and bawled piteously. Kalantha hadn't wanted to kill it, but fishing had been poor lately, and they needed something other than roots and berries. She stroked its fur, and continued to cry as she skinned it. She made a mess of it, she knew, as she'd never done something like this before. But when she was finished, she had a carcass that would feed her and Meven well this night. She used her hands to dig a small hole to bury the head and skin, then she took the carcass to the bank of the stream, where she'd gathered plenty of dry twigs.

Kalantha built a fire, as Morgan had taught her, and she fashioned a spit on which to cook the rabbit. Meven was overjoyed with the meal, but Kalantha only picked at it. In her mind's eye she kept seeing the creature alive and eating clover.

She prepared other rabbits for other dinners, most of these caught with traps she concocted. Eventually she was quick to eat them, along with the squirrels and groundhogs she caught.

But to this day, she still vividly remembered the large blue eyes of the white rabbit.

~ ~ ~

You grew up while you were gone, little Kal."

"I suppose." She bent and pulled out a weed. "Morgan, I feel more sorry for that rabbit, and the other animals I killed for food, than I do for that man on the road I . . ."

"All grown up, Kal." Morgan cut a rose and gave it to her. "You did no wrong in killing that man. Some folks are just evil, and there is nothing to be done for them. They can't be saved."

"The Bishop will decide a penance for me," she said. "So that I can be saved."

Kalantha didn't see Morgan's eyes fill with tears. The gardener bent to cut another flower.

~ ~ ~

Dinner this evening was more elaborate—roast pork and steamed potatoes, biscuits and honey, and grape juice. Meven couldn't hide his pleasure, and the Bishop did not protest his request for second helpings.

"In three days we will hold a service in your honor in the Temple," Bishop DeNogaret said. "Word is all around High Keep, the farms, and to Fergangur that you are alive and home. The people will want to see you. And they'll want to meet the new Prince of Galmier."

Meven washed his meal down with a full mug of the grape juice. He poured himself another. "And what about meeting the King?"

The Bishop nodded for an acolyte to begin clearing the table.

"Within the month you will be on your way to Nadir, with the King's soldiers for escort. I sent word to the palace about your arrival, and I asked for a complement of one hundred soldiers to take you to the King."

"One hundred?" Meven seemed both surprised and pleased.

"After the two previous attacks, we must be overly careful," the Bishop returned.

"You'll be coming, too?"

"Of course. I insist on presiding at your crowning."

"And Kalantha?"

The Bishop shook his head. He looked to Kalantha, and slowly shook his head again when she did not meet his gaze. "There is a sanctuary in Uland where select young women are given intensive religious schooling. I am making arrangements for Kalantha to go there."

Meven opened his mouth to protest, but stopped himself and waited for the Bishop to continue.

"After a few years, she can return to this Temple as an acolyte. It will be quite the honor for a young woman, pursuing a religious life."

Meven turned to her sister. She was studying a whorl on the tabletop. "I'm happy for you, Kal" he said. "Maybe we'll see each other when . . ."

"Bishop DeNogaret?" One of the Temple's eldest acolytes rushed into the dining room. "You have a visitor in your private study. He says he must speak with you immediately."

The lines on the Bishop's face appeared to deepen as he pushed himself away from the table. "Children, we will discuss the travel plans later."

24 · Foul Plans

Many of the Fallen have no chance at redemption, neither would they grasp at a chance if presented one. Like a pig enjoying a wallow in a mud pool, they enjoy wallowing in malevolence. The Creators were not careful enough when they shaped the people of Paard-Peran. They allowed malice and spite to be palatable to some.

~Arièg, Finest mountain pony

Bishop DeNogaret clenched his jaw as he glided through the Temple corridors toward his private study. He did not like interruptions, and if the visitor was not important, he would punish the acolyte who dared disturb his time with Meven and Kalantha. He was angry at far more than the interruption, however. He was quietly seething at the recent and unpleasant turn of events.

His hand twisted the doorknob, and he slipped inside, closing and locking the door behind him. Three beeswax tapers arranged in the center of a massive desk softly lit the room.

"I do not like being disturbed from my evening meal," the Bishop hissed.

"And I do not like to be kept waiting. I never like to wait for anyone or anything. But you know that." Eyeswide was perched on the back of the Bishop's favorite chair. The owl fluffed its feathers and rotated its head. "You sent for me, Master DeNogaret."

"Yes, yes I did. But I did not expect you until tomorrow." Bishop DeNogaret slammed his fist down on the desk, making the candles jump. The flames set the shadows to dancing around the room. "You failed, Eyeswide! The children live. They are here, in this very Temple! Your assassins were to kill them. It was agreed!"

The owl seemed nonplussed by the Bishop's ire. "They are hardly children anymore." Eyeswide's voice carried farther in this room than in the Old Forest. But it was still soft and harsh, and it still seemed like the owl had to force each word out of his throat.

Again the Bishop pounded his fist. "You were to kill them. I ordered you to kill them!"

The owl blinked and gave a long, throaty whooot. "My assassins killed Edan, as you demanded. They killed the soldiers and the attendants. They killed even your men, and nearly all the horses. They killed and killed and killed for you." The owl drew itself up, and the features on its crest came forward. "But, no, we were not successful in killing the royal cousins. Fate intervened."

The Bishop began pacing. There was little room to walk in the study that was crowded with shelves, a desk, and a long, impressive table. "I should have been told about your failure more than a year ago. In the name of Iniquis and Abandon, I should have been told!"

"My assassins thought the children likely perished in the wild. They found no trace of your Meven and Kalantha." The owl watched the candle flames for several moments before continuing. "It is obvious they moved around, and hence we did not detect them. Yes, my assassins failed. But they did kill Edan and all witnesses."

"Not all witnesses." The Bishop's words were almost painfully drawn out. "Meven and Kalantha saw the birds. Meven intends to tell the King about the 'birds who talk and slay.' We cannot be found out, Eyeswide. If we are discovered, all our plans are dashed."

"And you think an ill and befuddled King will believe him?"

"Someone might." The Bishop paused at the long table and looked at its polished surface, seeing a ghostly image of himself reflected there. "Someone certainly might believe him. They'll think astrologers are involved, perhaps. They'll think politics is involved, certainly."

"Politics lies at the root of this—and at the root of most things in Galmier."

The Bishop snarled and resumed pacing. "I have nurtured this plan for more than a decade, Eyeswide. I have put people loyal to me in key positions in the palace, in Nadir, and to the south in Nasim-Guri. It has taken a very long time to arrange all of this, and I will not be thwarted because your assassins could not handle the slaying of two children."

"They are hardly children anymore," the owl repeated. "But, as you say, they are here. Why not kill them yourself?"

He slammed his fist against the table this time. "You fool, my part in this must never be known! That is why I'd never personally raise a hand against them. There are too many people at this Temple not wholly under my thumb, too many watchful eyes here and throughout the kingdom. The cousins were to die far from me, where nothing could be traced back. Their parents died far from me, in Uland, where no connection was ever made. Ever. I limited the royal line with those slayings. I would have limited it further. The wedding was so convenient. They were all to be killed on the road. The Prince, Meven, Kalantha. Only the King was to be left alive."

"And now he is dying. An illness that this time he cannot recover from. Convenient."

"And arranged." The Bishop nodded. "Planned. All carefully orchestrated and carried out. My hands are clean on the King's count, too." He paced faster. "You see, Eyeswide, when the King learned of his son's death, and the suspected deaths of Meven and Kalantha, he decreed that rulership of Galmier would fall to this church with his own eventual passing. I would be King, sole custodian of this country. No heirs, he had no choice. But he has heirs, doesn't he? Meven is the Prince now, and in a few years old enough to marry and continue the line."

"And there is the girl to consider."

"Kalantha is of little consequence, though she must be dealt with to completely end the Montoll line. Men rule here. But Meven . . . Meven lives, and this was not to be!"

Eyeswide said nothing. He watched the Bishop pace and fume and rant quietly to himself. The old man was tiring himself, and the owl seemed to enjoy watching.

"This ruins everything, Eyeswide. All my plans are ruined."

The owl gave another *whooot.* "It ruins nothing, Master DeNogaret. It merely changes things. For the better, I think."

The Bishop stopped and came to stand in front of his desk, steepling his fingers on its polished surface and leaning across so his nose came within inches of the owl's beak.

"Yes, the girl must be dealt with, Master DeNogaret. And soon, to simplify things. But Meven, there is a potential here that you are not seeing." The owl stretched its short neck forward until beak and nose touched. "Here is what I think, Master . . ."

25 · Meven's Destiny

To see through the bad and find the good within a man's heart is a gift~and a responsibility~that each Finest creation possesses.

~*Firemane-Stormwithers, third Elder of the Finest Court*

Kalantha, my treasure, you are strong and smart." Bishop DeNogaret sat with her in the Temple anteroom. He wore white, and there was a pale blue sash wrapped around his waist and elaborately knotted. The garb meant he would perform a wedding later today.

Kalantha wondered if she knew the couple, and she nearly asked the Bishop just who was getting married. But from Bishop DeNogaret's expression, she could tell she was only meant to listen.

"You are far too smart to spend your life cooking and sewing and becoming some farmer's wife, growing plump and raising children. Oh, you might do better than that, for with Meven the Prince he could find some minor noble from Nadir who would wed you. And while that would likely provide some luxuries, you still would be expected to raise a family. And on top of that, you would have to learn all of the courtly graces. My dear, dear treasure, you are destined for something better than either of those fates."

He brushed a piece of lint from his sash, then smoothed an imaginary wrinkle. "Kalantha, the path I've chosen for you is more suitable and honorable. In time, you will be happy with my decision, and you will realize that I am right. You will one day thank me for this."

Kalantha sat opposite him, hands on her knees and fingers digging in. She fixed her stare on the Bishop's chin, not wanting to meet his eyes for fear she would crumple. She finally risked speaking: "Bishop DeNogaret, please, I want to live here, with you and the acolytes. The Temple is my home. I want to stay with you and Morgan and . . ."

The Bishop made a soft *tsk-tsk*ing sound. "It is beyond your control, Kalantha. It already has been arranged. You leave in two days with an escort of my men. They will take you to Dea Fortress in northern Uland. It is the foremost theological sanctuary on this continent, better—I am sad to admit—than anything available in Galmier. I am a personal friend of Bishop Gerald, who oversees the Fortress and the students. He will take exceptional care of you, and . . ."

Anger flashed across Kalantha's face and she dug her nails in harder. "I don't need anyone to take care of me, Bishop DeNogaret. I can well take care of myself. When Meven and I were away I . . ."

"Enough!" The Bishop spat the word as he rose from the bench. In a heartbeat he was standing behind her, hands pressed uncomfortably hard against her shoulders. She hadn't ever seen him move so quickly, nor had she ever seen him so upset. "I said it is decided, Kalantha Montoll." His words took on an almost venomous tone. "Bishop Gerald will take you into the sacred cloister until you learn your place in this world and until your soul is saved. You killed a man, remember? Bishop Gerald is far stricter than I, my treasure, which certainly will be good for you. Obviously I have been too soft, and my compassion has let you become willful and independent. Those are unfortunate traits. He will mold you into a proper young woman, subservient, a candle-bearer for the gods of Paard-Peran, an acolyte. You will marry the Temple, my dear. This Temple or Dea Fortress, it doesn't matter. However, what does matter is that you will lead a virtuous, religious, chaste life. Why, when Meven sees you years from now, he will be so proud of you."

"He will not recognize me," she muttered.

"It is for the best," the Bishop repeated, giving her shoulders a firm, almost painful squeeze. "As I said, the matter is decided."

"Meven will want me to be with him."

"No, Kalantha. Meven and I discussed this matter last night, and he agrees fully with me. This is best for you."

When he released her shoulders, Kalantha rose. She successfully fought to keep the tears at bay. "I will gather my things."

"No need," the Bishop returned. "This will be a fresh start for you, Kalantha. A bright, new beginning. There are no flower gardens at Dea Fortress to distract you, and no fine tailored clothes to make you prideful. Everyone dresses the same, and plainly. But there will be plenty of hard work. Studies. Discipline. You should look forward to this opportunity."

"I am to take nothing with me?"

He reached into his pocket and pulled out the coral necklace he'd given her on her tenth birthday. "Nothing save this. It will remind you of me."

Kalantha took the necklace, nodded, and hurried from the room, still fighting the tears. "I must see Meven," she said. She passed an acolyte, who smiled warmly at her. "Meven can't agree to this. He's the Prince. He can do something. He has power."

"Kalantha . . ." The acolyte got her attention. She whirled to face him. "Kalantha, your brother left for Nadir hours ago with the King's men. He said to tell you good-bye."

Kalantha stepped out of the Temple and tipped her face to the mid-morning sun. A lone tear rolled down her cheek and she sucked in great gulps of air. Her heart was hammering. There were clouds overhead, and by their shapes she imagined that they were mountain ponies thundering through her favorite valley.

~ ~ ~

Gallant-Stallion was relieved that Meven would be riding him to Nadir. The Finest had overheard a discussion in the stable his first day back that the acolytes wanted to keep him at the Temple to help work the fields. The Finest knew he was the strongest-looking horse at High Keep, and so he feared the acolytes might find a way to separate him from his charge. Because of that, he didn't leave the stable for the Finest Court, as he had originally planned. He stayed and schemed, trying to devise a way to keep near the Prince.

Steadfast, were you ever faced with such a situation? How can men play such a role in keeping a Finest from his charge? Gallant-Stallion didn't get an answer, but he continued talking, hoping that Steadfast's spirit was hovering somewhere close, listening, and might respond later. *Meven needs me to shepherd him. There have been no more assassin-birds, but I do not believe the threat is past. Something pricks at my withers and keeps my nerves on edge. Something bad will happen. Mara told me danger waits. I must find a way to stay with the Prince. And yet, I would like to travel to the Court for counsel.*

In the end, the Finest didn't have to scheme. Bishop DeNogaret decided that Gallant-Stallion was Meven's to keep. He made a formal gift of the horse early in the morning before Meven's trip.

"This punch has been with the Prince during his time away from us. Meven is used to riding him," he told the disappointed acolytes who ran the stable. The eldest of them had made a strong case for keeping the horse at High Keep. "There is a familiarity, and we need to honor that."

The Bishop denied Meven's request for the gray morab, the Temple's most impressive horse. "That was a birthday present to me from a northern noble, for whom I helped acquire some property from Uland. I would hate to see the noble's reaction . . . if he came to a service and to visit the stables and noticed his gift was elsewhere."

"Then what about the cutting horse? The one Kalantha took from the brigands?"

Again the Bishop disapproved. "That horse is tainted, Meven, and belonged to a vicious man. You do not want any part of that. Kalantha will ride that horse to Dea Fortress, and it will be used there for plowing. She can look at it often and picture the face of the man she killed. It will help her reflect on her deed and will help salvage her soul."

Meven patted Gallant-Stallion's neck. "This punch is not a handsome horse, Bishop DeNogaret. But he does humble me. And I think he saved my life in the mountains. So I suppose this is for the better."

The Bishop smiled and left a stable hand and Meven alone to saddle the punch. The acolyte led Gallant-Stallion out into the morning sunshine. There were one hundred soldiers on norikers waiting, reminiscent of the party that escorted Edan, but more formidable. These men were dressed in heavy plate mail instead of chain, and their shields were large and thick.

Meven eyed the procession from the stable door. "I will have one of those norikers when I am crowned Prince," he whispered. "And when I am eventually made King of Galmier, someone might give me a beautiful glavian like Nightsong. I will not need a punch to humble me then."

"Your highness!" the lead soldier waved to get Meven's attention. "We've a long ride ahead of us."

Meven rolled his shoulders and released a deep breath. *I'm not looking forward to another long ride,* he mouthed. With a nod to the soldier, he joined the procession and climbed onto Gallant-Stallion's saddle.

The Finest hadn't heard Meven's comment about a noriker or a glavian. He was listening to the soldiers and their horses, and looking across the grounds for Kalantha. He had become fond of her and used to her being around, and he wondered why she wasn't coming. Perhaps she would be arriving with the Bishop—he hoped that would be the case. The Finest heard the acolytes say that Bishop DeNogaret would be traveling to the palace in a few days to help crown Meven the rightful Prince of Galmier.

Steadfast, you were right. They are so easy to get attached to. But while he would miss Kalantha's company on this trip, her absence would make his task easier. Gallant-Stallion could concentrate solely on Prince Meven. There'd be no second person to keep his eye on. *I wonder what Nadir will hold for my charge and I. And will I be relegated to your stable? A place of my own?* He thought about that a moment, having a barn all to himself and someone assigned to groom only him. *It would be too quiet,* he said. *Horses may be simple creatures, but at least they are something to listen to and to watch.*

A cool breeze brushed Gallant-Stallion's muzzle.

And they can enjoy this world in a way we can never, Steadfast returned.

Then the breeze was gone.

The procession did not adopt as fast a pace as the one Edan had demanded on that ill-fated trip. It was an easy gait, one that Gallant-Stallion found almost monotonous. He turned his attention to the countryside as they left the Temple grounds.

Fields to the north were starting to turn brown, and he saw a variety of birds dipping low over them looking for corn and beans that the farmers missed. Some of the trees were starting to show yellow edges on their leaves, a sign that fall was coming. One willow birch was picking up quite a bit of color.

They passed an old cemetery that had more dead trees than live ones.

"My parents are buried somewhere in there," Meven told one of the soldiers. "They died when I was very young."

"Do you wish to stop and visit their graves, Prince Meven?" The soldier slowed his horse to afford Meven the opportunity.

Meven shook his head. "Perhaps some other time. I have never liked cemeteries."

Some of the plots were meticulously cared for and had flowers against the stones. But most were overgrown with weeds, and the stones were weathered and broken. Those graves had not seen visitors in a long time. Beyond the cemetery stretched another field, this one being plowed by three men and a half-dozen oxen. To the south were meadows and thin woods, and at the edge of Gallant-Stallion's vision, he saw a narrow branch of the Sprawling River.

They followed a road for several hours, but when it turned north and headed toward Uland, they cut across country straight east.

"We will have to cross the river tomorrow early, Prince Meven." The lead soldier rode back to discuss the route. "The river will be at its low point, and we know a shallow place that is effortless to ford. There is a road beyond it that will take us directly into Nadir. The King is anxious to see you."

"I've been told he is very ill. Rumors were thick in the village of Bitternut."

The soldier pursed his lips. "Ill, yes. He has never regained his health since word of Edan's death. But this is the worst we have seen him. We do not know if he will recover from his current malady. He has attendants keeping him cool and comfortable, and dosing him with herbs. But he is an aged man, Prince Meven, and his heart was severely weakened when he buried his son. You are the last of his family."

"Me and Kalantha," Meven said.

"Your sister? Will she be coming to Nadir with the Bishop?"

"No. But the Bishop will be joining us in a few days. He had some things to tend to at the Temple and could not come along now. Two weddings that I know of, and something about helping another noble with a land problem. Then he'll preside when I am crowned." Meven smiled wistfully at the thought. He would officially be Prince of Galmier then. *Prince Meven Montoll*, he mouthed. He truly liked the sound of that.

"Then what of your sister?"

"Kalantha is going to Dea Fortress to study with Bishop Gerald. She will miss the ceremony. She will miss a lot of things." He rubbed his thumbs across the reins and thought about his sister. "But it's for the best. Bishop DeNogaret said it is the best thing for Kalantha. The Bishop said my destiny lies in Nadir. Her destiny is elsewhere. And he said I need to concentrate on my own future and put Kalantha to the back of my mind."

STEADFAST, I UNDERSTAND NOW. YOU SAY HORSES ARE SIMPLE creatures who can enjoy Paard-Peran in ways we can never. So many of the animals who live on this land are unburdened, and so many of them run free. But men do not have such liberties, Gallant-Stallion said. *Neither Finest creations nor Meven and Kalantha have a say in their immediate futures—others have mapped that out for them.* So Kalantha was going somewhere to the north, Gallant-Stallion mused with some sadness. And

Meven was going to be ensconced in a palace in Nadir. *And I will be put in a stable. How am I to look in on my charge? How did you look in on the King?*

~ ~ ~

There was no village in a direct line between High Keep and Dea Fortress, and so four of the Bishop's men escorted Kalantha across farm fields and meadows. They were not dressed as finely as the Bishop's men usually were. They wore simple tunics of various colors—the only thing linking them to High Keep were similar cloaks of blue—and one carried a standard with the Bishop's colors.

On more than one occasion, the men tried to begin a conversation with Kalantha. But she didn't speak, she didn't want to talk about her situation. She didn't want to tell them that she hated this—it would be improper to speak ill of Bishop DeNogaret's plans for her. And she didn't want to lie and tell them she was looking forward to a strict religious life. So she let herself get lost in thought, and she listened to the cutting horse snort and toss its tail.

Kalantha had never been to Dea Fortress, but she knew with all of her heart that she didn't want to go there. She'd learned about it from her studies—the place was a castle built more than three hundred years ago when Uland's then-King was worried that the nearby island country of Qadira would go to war against him. The castle sat back a little from the high northern sea cliffs, and the land around it was rocky and very difficult to farm. About a hundred years ago it was deeded to a religious sect revering Paard-Zhumd, and now the fortress was under the auspices of Bishop Gerald. The students and acolytes supported themselves by farming under the harsh conditions, and relied on some donations from the present Uland King.

She remembered the very moment she was sent off on this horrid trip.

~ ~ ~

I do not want to go," she'd told Morgan.

The old gardener smiled weakly at her. The lines around his
eyes were deep and reminded her of deeply-grooved hickory
bark. Everywhere his wrinkles seemed to be more pronounced.

"I won't see you again, Morgan, will I?" She figured by the
time she was permitted to return to High Keep, he would be
dead. He would die and be buried in that cemetery that few visited. He must be well past seventy, she guessed, older than the
Bishop. That he was able to keep the flowerbeds so carefully
trimmed and weeded amazed her. "They will keep me at that
place for years."

Morgan held her fiercely and whispered in her ear. "Little
Kal, I'm not going anywhere. I fully expect to see you when
you return from Bishop Gerard's teachings. And I fully expect
you to survive that cloistered rock."

"I might be an old woman before they let me free."

He laughed and backed away a few steps so he could better
regard her. "I will miss you very much, Kal. You are the most
willful and independent girl I've ever known."

"It is prison, this Dea Fortress," she said. "A sentence as se-
vere as any a magistrate or noble might have handed down for
killing a man. No, a far, far worse sentence. No reasonable
man would have thought I committed murder, and no reasonable man would have assigned any punishment."

Morgan wagged a finger at her. "Such dark thoughts and big
words from a little girl."

"I believe I saved me and Meven when I killed that bandit.
And now I am being punished for it. I think the Bishop is keep-

ing me from Meven because he thinks I'll bring bad luck because of what I did."

Morgan touched the top of her head. "I'll see you when you return from the fortress," he said after a few moments. "You'll be much taller, I suspect."

~ ~ ~

She closed her eyes and trusted the cutting horse to stay with the Bishop's men. The rocking motion was relaxing, and she allowed herself to dream about the Galmier Mountains, the magical black pony, and the pudgy highland that liked water plums. She tried not to think of Meven, as it hurt too much to be separated from her brother. And so she pretended she was with the mountain ponies and was running barefoot across a meadow.

When they stopped for the night, she ate only a little; she was too busy thinking. Kalantha had decided she wouldn't be going to Dea Fortress after all.

"Willful and independent," she whispered with a faint smile. Again she avoided conversation with the men, and she pretended to fall asleep quickly. The Bishop's men posted only one guard among them. They were in safe lands, and the harvested farm field was devoid of predators. She listened to them. Two of the men snored quietly, and a third twitched during his sleep. The guard dozed on and off, and she took advantage of this.

The horses were sleeping too, but she was able to rouse the cutting horse without it making enough noise to wake anyone. Kalantha didn't bother to saddle the horse. She quietly led it far away from the makeshift camp and did not get on it until she couldn't see a trace of the men. She rode then, fast to the southeast. Kalantha was confident of the direction by the constellations. Morgan had taught her that in the late summer sky the formation of Paard-Zhumd was directly to the south. She rode until the sky was starting to lighten, then she stopped to give the horse a rest.

She was too far away to see the flock of blackbirds, starlings, kite-hawks, and bats descend on the Bishop's men after she left.

She didn't see the birds slay the men and the horses, then fly off triumphant, saying "Falafalafala. Death came. We will tell Falafalafala that we did not fail. Everyone died. No one escaped."

She didn't know she was supposed to conveniently die that night, and that Bishop DeNogaret had never intended for her to reach Dea Fortress. Neither did she know that her escorts were to be killed to help cover the Bishop's involvement and keep his hands clean. There would be no questions, as he would hardly have his own men slain—especially while they were taking his 'treasure' to such a famed religious sanctuary.

Kalantha planned to sleep only briefly, making a bed of her cloak atop a stretch of moss. But she was so tired the nap turned into several hours. It was afternoon when she woke, happy to find the cutting horse grazing nearby; she'd found nothing to tie him to.

"I will call you Thunder," she said. "For that's what your hooves sound like when you run."

Without the stars to guide her, Kalantha guessed at their course now. "We're going to Nadir," she told the horse. "To find my brother." And if she crossed paths there with Bishop DeNogaret? She shook her head and tossed that thought from her mind. She'd worry about that when the time came, or perhaps when the palace loomed into view.

26 · City Sights

The Finest must sympathize with their charges and strive to understand them. But let not a single Finest come to desire the trappings of people. Possessions only weigh down the soul, the gods decreed. And the more possessions people claim, the harder the task of their guardian Finest to lift their spirits toward salvation.

~The Old Mare, from the Finest Court canon

Initially it seemed no different than the village of Bitternut, just larger from a distance. First came small farms and goatherd residences, and then came narrow, dusty streets lined with simple homes. They were minor cottages mostly, made of river stones and logs, likely having two rooms at best for the one or two families that lived there. The roofs were made of thatch, and the entrances were either open or were covered with a thick curtain of common cloth. There were splashes of color, though, more than Gallant-Stallion remembered from Bitternut and Hathi, as the residents had small flower and vegetable gardens that were still being tended this late in the season. And frequently there were bits of trim on the house—a painted shutter here, a wreath of twigs and ribbons there, and occasionally something more elaborate, such as gaily-painted window boxes filled with pansies and marigolds and small sprigs of evergreen. The people were dressed in tunics and trousers that showed considerable signs of wear. And they looked tired and likely older than their years.

Moving beyond this, however, the city and the people changed, and it amazed Gallant-Stallion as much as it did Meven. Within the span of a few blocks the homes became larger and more elaborate, made of bricks and rising two or three stories. There were few thatched roofs; most of them had slate shingles or scalloped tiles. Trim was freshly painted, and no weeds grew against the foundations. Many of the windows had glass in them, and there were brocaded and beaded curtains tied back with shiny cords. In the upper window of a large white manor, a gray cat stretched on the sill and slowly regarded the procession. On that manor's small, manicured lawn were massive rose bushes that Meven knew would draw oohs and ahs from Kalantha. To the side of the residence was a carriage, eggshell white and embellished with pastel greens and blues on every edge, and behind it was a small barn that must have held the family's horses.

The people here were more fancifully dressed and were taking advantage of the scant remaining warm days. For the most part, the women wore gowns or flowing, sleeveless garde-corpes, with intricate head-rails or conical, veiled henins atop their heads. The men wore hose and doublets or jerkins. A few of the older men, Meven noticed, were wearing journades, very short beltless tunics, full and made of rich, thin fabrics. A long ivory pipe, the bowl fashioned in the shape of a bearded man, poked out of the pocket of a nearby gentleman. A silver and pearl clasp the size of a queen maple leaf was on the gown of the woman with him.

The people were standing on corners and in their yards, and some of them leaned out of the top-floor windows of their manors—all waving to him.

"Bow to Prince Meven Montoll of Galmier!" one of the soldiers shouted.

Cheers went up and everyone nodded or bowed, and women gestured with their lace handkerchiefs. Young ladies blushed as they tried to get Meven's attention.

"You will have your pick," the soldier nearest Meven said. "Unless the King arranges a marriage for you."

Meven scowled. He knew nobles were married off at an early age. But he considered himself a little too young. "I'm only fourteen. I'd like to wait a few years." He recalled Edan's conversation about the 'portly toad' that was likely Princess Silverwood of Nasim-Guri. Perhaps the King will die before he has a chance to make such an arrangement, Meven thought.

Gallant-Stallion had trouble taking it all in. The sounds were difficult to separate—conversations of the well-dressed onlookers; their coos and praises for the Prince; the steady clopping of the norikers' hooves; the nearest soldiers talking quietly to Meven, telling him about this or that family, and which manors he would likely be invited to first; the muted squeals of children playing streets away; the clanging of a bell; the shouts of someone hawking flowers; the strains of a flute coming from an open window; and much, much more he couldn't identify. And there was Meven talking too, asking question upon question.

"Everything is . . . beautiful here. Beyond those commoners' houses. Is it like this throughout the rest of the city?"

The nearest soldier shook his head. "This is the wealthy district, the one you will visit most often. Their taxes . . . everyone's taxes . . . keep up the city and the palace."

"And pay the wages for you and the other soldiers?"

A nod.

"And what about the rest of the city? What does it look like?"

"You'll see a good bit of it, as the palace sits at the edge of the eastern side. The King, were he a younger man and were he healthy, would probably build a castle elsewhere, to the north and east I heard him once say, where he could look at the Esi Sea and not see the slums."

"Are the slums considerable?"

The soldier pointed to the south. They were passing out of the wealthy district and coming into a section of modest homes. The buildings were somewhere between the manor houses and the cottages in size, and Meven guessed that the people were mostly laborers or shop owners. South of this, and lining a long street filled with ruts and gravel, were wooden buildings of indeterminate age. They'd clearly had no attention for quite some time, as they leaned or looked warped. Porches sagged and steps were caved in. Some of the buildings had been painted at one time, the faded chips curled and looking like fish scales. Broken chairs and crooked benches sat in front of boarded-up windows. Tattered women, stooped men, filthy children, and skinny dogs roamed up and down.

Gallant-Stallion could smell just how poor these people were. He picked out the tang of children who hadn't bathed in a month or more, the fetid odor of sweat dried long into clothes, and the scents of urine, rotting wood, and old cooking grease. That people could live in such squalor mere blocks from those who led grand lives was dumbfounding to him.

Steadfast, how can this be? Why can't the rich nearby help them? They must have plenty of food and clothes to share? Gallant-Stallion did not get a reply, and this time he did not expect one. He continued to absorb everything, saddened by the sight of the poor people, and in awe of the merchant district they had just come upon.

The buildings that stretched in all directions were more colorful than anything the Finest had seen and warred for his attention. Signs hung from most of them, one more vivid than the next. He couldn't read the words, but many of them only had pictures, for the people in the city who could not read either.

The building nearest the intersection they passed was painted pale orange and had a drawing of a frosted cake on a dangling wooden sign. Incredible smells drifted out from an open door, among them bread baking, which had become one of Gallant-Stallion's favorite odors. It was obviously a bakery, and beyond it stretched a brewer, butcher, cheesemaker, provisioner, blacksmith, and a cooper. On the opposite side were leatherworkers, masons, millers, potters, clothiers, glassblowers, jewelers, locksmiths, tanners, and weavers.

The procession traveled farther, and Gallant-Stallion noticed a furrier, bowyer, armorer, bookbinder, and an apothecary. Down another street were chandlers, cartwrights, barbers, scribes, tilemakers, seamstresses, and saddlers.

"I can hardly wait to visit these places," Meven gushed.

The soldier nearest him shook his head. "Prince Meven, that wouldn't be proper. When you've need of clothes or jewelry, or if you want to buy books, the appropriate merchants will be summoned to the palace. You do not go to them, they come to you."

"But what if I *want* to go to the shops? There's so much to see!"

The soldier's face took on a pensive expression. "Perhaps that can be arranged. If the King will permit it."

Meven let out a deep sigh and muttered under his breath: "Perhaps when the King dies and I am in charge I will do whatever I please."

All along the route, people turned out to see the Prince. Corner merchants passed flowers to him, and one woman handed a soldier a fresh-baked pie. Meven made it clear he wanted to keep that. From the highest windows people leaned out and waved long ribbons and pennants.

"It is good they welcome you," the near soldier said. "They do not always look so kindly on royalty."

"They consider you a fresh breath," another soldier said. "They see a change in the rulership coming, the King being so ill and all."

Meven sat taller in the saddle. "They will like me, I think. I will be just and honorable." Softer: "And I will visit those wonderful shops whenever I want to."

The cortege passed through another residential district, then turned south at a Temple larger than the one at High Keep. This one was made of pink and gray stone that had been chiseled into massive squares. The Temple covered nearly an entire block, and it was topped by a spire that Meven guessed was six or seven stories tall. A bell was ringing from that tower, and he felt sorry for the acolyte that had to climb all those stairs to get to it. The windows were made of blue, red, and green glass panels, fitted together to form images of what the people of Galmier thought the gods looked like. Paard-Zhumd had the largest window, and in it he was depicted as having the torso of a man and the body of a horse. A spear was in his right hand, and a shield in the shape of a shell was in his left.

"Does the Bishop of that Temple also come to the palace? Or is it proper for me to attend services there?"

"Prince Meven, I'm certain that both the King and the Bishop would be pleased if you worshiped there."

Meven reached forward and patted Gallant-Stallion's neck. "That is good. I am a religious man, raised at the High Keep Temple. I would not like to be kept from prayer. Besides, Bishop DeNogaret will insist that I keep regular worship practices."

"You speak highly of Bishop DeNogaret," the soldier observed.

"My father died when I was very young, and the Bishop took me in. I consider him my father in all respects, and I would not do a thing that would anger him, or would cause him to disapprove. In fact, I will ask that he become the Bishop of this Temple, and the other Bishop be assigned to High Keep. I will want Bishop DeNogaret near to help guide me. He will be my greatest counsel." Meven's fingers dropped to his waist. There was a new black belt festooned with carved wooden beads. Bishop DeNogaret had given it to him the evening before his trip. Meven closed his eyes and prayed now, for his sister, who he wished was here with him; for Bishop DeNogaret, who would arrive in a few days, and who he hoped would stay on permanently; and for the King. Though Meven didn't like the prospect of an arranged marriage and being sequestered inside a palace, he didn't want the King to die. "I am too young to rule this country."

"What did you say, Prince Meven?"

"I said that I am looking forward to eating that apple pie."

Gallant-Stallion stopped suddenly when the palace came into view. The soldier behind him had to haul back on the reins of his own horse to avoid colliding.

"Incredible. That is absolutely incredible." Meven said the words, but Gallant-Stallion was thinking them.

The palace was a breathtaking fortification on the extreme eastern side of Nadir, perched on a rise that overlooked the Esi Sea. There was a concentric pattern to it—the crenellated walls circled an egg-shaped complex of monstrous proportions.

"I thought the Temple was big," Meven said.

The palace took up a dozen times that amount of space. There were two lofty towers with cone-shaped tops, and there were windows and ornaments everywhere. Nearly all of it was made of grayish-white chiseled stone, but there was darker stone around the windows.

"That's a softer stone," the nearest soldier explained. "The builders had to use a softer stone to make the round and narrow cuts for the windows and arrow-slits. There are archers behind those slits, ready in the event the palace comes under attack."

"That wouldn't happen," Meven said.

"No," the soldier agreed. "The palace is nigh impregnable, and Galmier has no enemies. But the archers stay nonetheless. It is tradition." He pointed to the base of the walls. "Nineteen feet thick at the bottom. The main keep is a hundred feet high and has a stone dome ceiling, the only ceiling like it in all Paard-Peran. It took seven years to build everything."

The inside was even more impressive, and Meven dug his fingernails into his palm to keep himself from gasping at every turn. There were galleries filled with tapestries, sculptures, and golden statues, and paintings hung in gold and silver-edged frames. The lead soldier escorted Meven through a music room, where a young woman played a harp; a dining room, where three servants busily polished an impossibly long table; and a library that would easily hold both the High Keep library and the Bishop's private study, and have room left over. This route wasn't to show anything off to the Prince, the soldier explained, it was merely the most direct way to the King's chamber.

It was up a winding staircase, down the center of which ran a thick carpet. There were crystal sconces in iron fittings on the wall, and banners draped in the King's colors. The air was scented with jasmine, and faintly under that was the smell of meat roasting, a hint that dinner was not far away.

Meven's stomach rumbled. "My pie?"

"It has been taken to your wing, Prince Meven, along . . ."

"Wing? I have more than a room?"

"Yes, Prince Meven. The southern wing of the palace is yours. Your things have been taken there as well. If you wish, I can escort you there after your audience with King Montoll. Or I can have one of the servants take you."

"King Montoll. My uncle."

The soldier nodded.

"Bishop DeNogaret told me I was little more than an infant when the King saw me. I don't know what he looks like, and I never thought to ask Edan."

"He looks like a King," the soldier returned, as they climbed another staircase. At the top, he pushed open a heavy wooden door and gestured Meven inside.

It was a drafty room filled with cushioned furniture. At the far end was a bed big enough for any four men to sleep in. Animal furs were arranged on the stone floor so that their snouts pointed inward, forming a circle. Meven recognized the skins of a gray bear, a lion, a northern tiger, and a mountain cat. But there were two skins he had no clue about.

"The King." The soldier nodded toward the bed.

Meven hadn't noticed at first that anyone was in it—the room was so large, and the figure on the bed so small it was practically lost in the covers.

"My Uncle," Meven hushed. He heard the soldier's retreating footsteps, and heard the door close behind him. He had expected the King to be ringed by attendants, not to be alone.

"Meven?" The voice was a coarse whisper.

"Yes, Your Majesty." Meven shuffled forward, carefully when he crossed the animal furs. The air was scented with jasmine here, too. But as he neared the bed he smelled other things, unguents and acrid medicinal balms in open jars next to the bed, and the scent of sickness, the King decaying.

The King was smaller than Meven, all bony and pale, wrinkles hanging from his face and arms like the folds of overlarge clothes. His hair was the strongest feature about him. It was thick and steely gray, and it spread away from his face and across the silk pillow. With some effort the King sat up and extended a shaky hand, and Meven took it, almost recoiling to find it cold and feeling dry and unnatural.

"Your Majesty." Meven bowed as Bishop DeNogaret had showed him, and he held his breath when he kissed the back of the King's hand. He looked into the King's watery blue eyes, one of which was covered with a milky film. "I am honored to meet you, Uncle."

"Prince Meven," the King said. He broke into a smile and gently squeezed Meven's hand. "The Montoll line is not dead after all, Prince Meven. The gods have answered my prayers." Then he settled back on the pillow and fell asleep.

Meven sat with him for nearly an hour, until a serving girl came to fill a neck pouch with fresh herbs and to spread a pungent balm on his chest. The King continued to sleep through her ministrations.

"Isn't someone with him all the time?" Meven broached.

"He is a willful man, and that is not his wish. But there is a soldier, always, just beyond this door." She pointed to the wall near the bed, and Meven noticed an outline, a disguised door. "And there is often a priest with the soldier, should the King wish to seek counsel, or should the King . . ."

"Die," Meven finished. "I don't want him to die."

"I should think not," she said, as she rearranged the jars of balms and unguents. "Not before you get to know him in any event. I imagine you've a lot to take in, Prince Meven." She paused and brushed her hands on her apron. "You are a fine-looking young man. The people will like you."

"I will be just," he said. Then he stood and looked to the far doors past the animal skins. "I smelled dinner cooking."

"It will be served soon. They're preparing quite the feast in your honor." She frowned. "I had hoped the King would be well enough to sit at the table."

"Will you . . . will you show me how to get to the dining room? I'm afraid I don't remember."

"I will show you to your wing first, as no doubt you wish to bathe and dress properly."

My wing, Meven mouthed, still not believing his fortune. "I would be happy with just one room," he said softly. "And I would be happier if Kalantha was here."

27 · Finding Herself

The face of Paard-Peran is scarred by mountains and wrinkled by rivers. It is blemished by overturned crops and tanned by the sun. It is like the faces of all of its people~interesting and changing and worth studying . . . if only for a little while.

~*The Old Mare, of her final visit to Paard-Peran*

Kalantha sat at the edge of a stream, toes dangling in the water. Thunder grazed several yards away, ears twitching this way and that to catch the sounds carried by the brisk breeze. There was a trio of scarlet haws nearby, and she found their presence somehow comforting. She'd slept under them last night and dreamed of the mountain ponies.

"I'm not sure where we are, Thunder. I think we very well could be lost." The horse glanced toward her, then resumed grazing. "We went too far north, I think. And maybe I took us too far south to make up for it. We're to the east, I know that much from the stars at night, but I never studied geography like Meven. I don't know if we're near Nadir, or if we passed it." She hadn't paid enough attention to her studies to remember that Nadir was on the coast. "And I don't know if I care."

She thrust her feet all the way into the stream and let the chill water swirl around her ankles. Fall had taken a strong hold now, and the water was too cold for bathing. Still, it served well enough to wash the dirt off her feet. She would have to wear her boots from here on out.

Kalantha had only the clothes on her, and a cloak that was draped over a low-hanging branch. She'd not bothered to grab up a satchel when she fled the Bishop's men, and there'd been no place and no means for her to gain more clothes.

What she had on was dirty and smelled of her going too long without a bath. She guessed she'd been on her own and in these same clothes for a month or more.

"But who's to care what I smell like, Thunder, if I stay out here with you? I haven't heard you complain."

The horse raised its head and made a wuffling sound.

"But I'm going to need something warmer. Or I'll freeze to death before the first snow."

Maybe she would try in earnest to find Nadir, and thereby her brother. The Prince would make certain she had plenty to wear, and she'd ask him for a nice warm stall for Thunder.

"Or maybe I'll just look in on him," she mused, as she pulled her feet out of the stream and dried them in the grass. "Maybe he's with Bishop DeNogaret. And I don't want the Bishop sending me to Dea Fortress. I'd much prefer staying out here by myself."

She reached in a pocket and pulled out a small handful of dried berries. Her pockets were full of them. She'd dried them on a low, flat rock better than a week ago—after she came across a patch of late, wild blueberries and wanted to preserve them. When they were gone, she'd search for roots. She made it through one winter with the mountain ponies. She was certain she could make it through another without setting foot in a village . . . if she could keep herself warm.

But there was Meven to consider. She scolded herself for being selfish and thinking only about what she wanted.

"How is he doing?" she wondered aloud. "Does he miss me

as much as I miss him? Does he enjoy being the Prince of Galmier?"

She tugged at an errant thread on her tunic and instantly thought of the mad woman in Hathi who tried to unravel her skirt while Meven and she tried to get information. She dropped the thread and put on her boots.

"I really do miss him," she said. "I miss having someone to talk to. I miss Morgan, too."

If the world were different, she could be with the gardener now, tidying up the flowerbeds along the Temple before the cold set in deep. She'd be pulling up the dead vines and flower stalks and turning over the ground in anticipation of the spring planting. But the world wasn't different, and so she couldn't help Morgan. The Bishop would find her on the grounds and send her with another escort—this one considerably larger—to Dea Fortress. She wouldn't be able to escape them this time.

Kalantha shuddered at the thought as she shuffled toward Thunder.

"I need to know about Meven," she said, as she grabbed the horse's mane and pulled herself up. "But to do that, you and I will have to get ourselves un-lost and find Nadir. Maybe I can find myself along the way."

28 · Sorry Surroundings

The best place for a Finest to be is at the side of his charge. Any other place is not as pleasing and does not feel like home.

~*Steadfast, veteran Finest*

Gallant-Stallion was led into a stable easily triple the size of the one in Bitternut. There was a spacious area for grooming, and to store food and tack. He counted thirty stalls, and he knew there was another stable on the grounds at least this large. And from the soldiers, Gallant-Stallion learned a stable just north beyond the palace wall held the prized norikers and other horses used by the King's guards.

This stable was only half-filled, with dark brown akhal-tekes, chunky torics, a massive chestnut shire with substantial white feathering at its hooves, and a pair of bay heavy drafts with flowing manes and forelocks.

There was plenty of food and water, and Gallant-Stallion was brushed along with the other horses before sunset. It was a more practiced hand that plaited his mane and scrubbed the dirt from his legs, but the groomer did not speak to him or the other horses, as had the kind stable master in Bitternut. The akhal-tekes 'talked' to him, however, anxious to have a new tenant in the stable. They regaled Gallant-Stallion with tales of their long treks through Galmier, Nasim-Guri, and Durosinni. Akhal-tekes were noted for their endurance and love of extended trips. They were elegant and graceful, with long, muscular necks, high withers, and sloping shoulders that would lend them a soft gait. The Finest admired their form, and told them of his own travels with Meven.

They were comfortable surroundings, better than the stable in Bitternut, and better than the one at the High Keep Temple. But Gallant-Stallion considered them sorry surroundings, as they were far from Meven—so far that the Finest hadn't a clue what his charge was doing or if he was safe.

Fortunately, the Prince came to the stables after dinner, and Gallant-Stallion was excited to see his charge and to see that the King's men were taking fine care of the youth.

"They take good care of you, Rue," Meven said. He stroked the Finest's nose and looked up into the wide, expressive eyes. "And as you can see, they're taking good care of me. The palace is huge. I got lost in it twice today, and I had a hard time finding my way out here. Dinner was . . . I've never seen so much food. I came outside to escape dessert. I couldn't eat another bite." He leaned over the stall door and stirred the oats with his fingers.

"This is all too much for me to manage, Rue. I thought I was looking forward to the palace and Nadir. But everything is so big. And confusing! There are slums within a mile of this place. People who have barely enough to eat, when the table in there was filled to overflowing with every sort of food imaginable. Maybe I can do something about this, help the poor, give up some of this wealth. Melting down one little golden statue in the hall could provide enough coins to feed many of them for a year."

Gallant-Stallion realized Meven wasn't really talking to him. The Prince was merely talking to himself, while standing in front of the Finest's stall. So while it disappointed him that Meven continued to think of him as nothing more than a simple horse, it heartened him to know that Meven wanted to do something about the city's unfortunates.

"My coronation is in four days, Rue. It was to be late next week, but the King is getting no better. By the gods, I know he is dying, and that scares me. Being Prince is more than enough for me. Oh, I well admit to liking the attention, the thought of fine, fine clothes, a soft bed with all those pillows. Servants, people bowing to me. Who wouldn't like that? Living here will be much better than living at the High Keep Temple. In fact, I don't think I'll ever go back there. This is like a dream come true. But I don't want to be the King . . . not just yet."

Gallant-Stallion lowered his head and nuzzled Meven's hand. *Keep focused on the important things,* the Finest said. *Strength of character, a pure heart.* To guide such a young man without being able to talk to him was vexing indeed, Gallant-Stallion thought. *Meven, hear me.*

"I have an entire wing to myself," Meven said. "I wish Kalantha could see this. She wouldn't believe it. And the gardens! She would spend days there trying to learn the names of all the flowers. Where there was one gardener at High Keep, there are a dozen here—and someone to oversee them. I will never grow tired of this place." He stepped back from the stall and ran his fingers over the prayer beads. "To the gods of Paard-Peran, thank you for making me part of the Montoll family and bringing me to this amazing place."

The Finest closed his eyes. *Meven, you still have so very much to learn. But I have patience, and I will shepherd you well.*

"I'm going to sit with my uncle for a short while this evening. They say he wakes up about this time." Meven spun and left Gallant-Stallion, but he paused at the stall of one of the akhal-tekes. The horse had long legs and a deep chest, but was otherwise narrow. "You've a shallow rib cage," Meven observed. "And a long back. You're a beautiful horse, so well-defined. Your mane is like silk. You would do as well as a noriker, I think. They say I can have my pick of any horse in this stable. Perhaps I will choose you."

Gallant-Stallion nickered sadly. *You have no choice, Prince Meven. We are paired, charge and shepherd. There is no picking another.*

"I might very well choose you, beautiful horse. Though that ugly punch over there has served me well, and saved my life one night long, long months ago, I am tired of him. A Prince should ride a beautiful horse."

Steadfast, my task is considerable. A cool breeze found its way inside the stable and tickled Gallant-Stallion's nose. *Steadfast!*

The spirit of the elder Finest finally answered him: *Have patience, young one. Your charge is crucial to the future of Galmier.*

~ ~ ~

Four weeks passed, and Meven visited only once during that time—and on that occasion he took the akhal-teke out for a ride. He named the horse Pride, as he said the horse carried itself so proudly.

Gallant-Stallion knew Meven had been crowned Prince of Galmier some time ago in a formal ceremony attended by all the local nobles, and a few visiting royalty from Uland and the island country of Qadira. Meven hadn't told him any of this, the Finest heard stable hands and groomers talking. Not one of them had been invited to the ceremony, and so Gallant-Stallion had to imagine the pomp and circumstance. His form limited where he could go, his blessing and curse.

During the next week, he saw Meven again. The Prince ordered a groomer to ready Pride for a ride. He pointed to another akhal-teke and said that was to be saddled for Bishop DeNogaret. Meven said he was going to show the Bishop all of the Montoll property and wanted to consult with him privately about a few matters.

There was a touch of arrogance to Meven's demeanor, and Gallant-Stallion found it distressing. The Prince was becoming brasher and obviously loving the trappings of wealth. The Finest didn't hear him mention the poor people of Nadir; Meven only talked about parties and clothes and about some aspect of the palace he'd only just noticed.

Steadfast, it is hopeless, Gallant-Stallion said. *I cannot shepherd him because he will not let me. He considers me an ugly horse, and so does not even look at me anymore. You say he is crucial to the future of Galmier, and because of that I must leave him.*

The Finest paused, lifting his head and feeling the air inside the stable. He searched for the cool breath of a breeze that announced the arrival of Steadfast's spirit. But there was only musty, still air filled with the scent of horses and oats.

I cannot reach Meven. Perhaps I am too young and inexperienced to do so. Certainly I am too thick and unpolished. I will take my mystic journey to the Finest Court tonight when there are no stable hands or groomers or farriers about. And there I will beseech the Court elders to send a shepherd with a comely form in my place. If the Prince is to have a guardian, it must be a beautiful one, regal and acceptable to his royal eyes. He needs a Finest to help him lose that arrogance. There is so much good in him.

It was several hours before Meven and Bishop DeNogaret returned from their ride. The Prince continued to talk of the palace and surrounding lands, and of a trade treaty he must consider with Uland. Again there was no mention of the poor, or any of the people of Galmier for that matter.

"We must get ready for dinner," Meven said. "I requested pheasant and glazed yams. I know you are used to simple fare, but that is not how they do things here."

"I am sure dinner will be lovely," Bishop DeNogaret said.

"And afterwards the cooks want to discuss plans for my fifteenth birthday celebration. It is a few months away, but they say they need time to make all the preparations and to plan a guest list." He rolled his shoulders and ground the ball of his foot into the earth. "I don't know who to invite . . . from around here. And I doubt old friends from as far away as High Keep would want to come. There's Kalantha . . ."

"She will be in your thoughts, Meven."

"I haven't had a letter from her. Her birthday is a few months after mine." Meven raised his eyes to the stable ceiling. "Oh, Bishop DeNogaret, this party they will plan for me . . . I think it will be too much."

"Perhaps I can help with the arrangements."

"I would very much like that," Meven said.

"Is there time for us to visit the King before dinner?"

Meven nodded, and his face lost some of its shine. "Yes, Bishop DeNogaret. But he won't know we are there. He sleeps all the time now."

Gallant-Stallion strained to hear them as they strode from the stable and toward the palace. Meven was talking about a gallery of sculptures he wanted the Bishop to visit with him tomorrow. But the Bishop declined. He was head of Nadir's Temple now, and he said he had some matters to take care of there.

There is nothing here for me to take care of, Gallant-Stallion said. *There is no way I can reach Meven or help him, no way I can guide him down his life's path. Meven will have nothing to do with me. He has all but forgotten I am here.*

When night came and the last of the groomers left, Gallant-Stallion drifted as far back as possible in his stall. The horses were eating, some were nickering—talking about their day's ride or the treats of yellow apples they'd been given. One complained that the groomer was rough today, pulling too hard on his mane. Another asked Gallant-Stallion if he was ever going to be taken out of the stable for a ride—he'd not been outside once in these passing weeks.

Gallant-Stallion shut out the sounds and scents until he found a place of nothingness in the back of his mind. He was returning to the Finest Court. No noise intruded, no smell, and he concentrated further until he no longer felt the dirt and hay beneath his hooves. He pictured a pasture in his mind, brilliant green and speckled with tiny white and yellow spring flowers that delicately scented the air. There was a musical brook, and it led to a pond so still it reflected the perfect sky. He pictured himself running toward the pond, and he pictured the Court that stretched beyond it, and suddenly he felt like he was floating.

Gallant-Stallion was indeed on his way to the Finest Court. He knew no one would notice his absence, save perhaps a stable hand or groom, and they might think he'd been moved to another stable or was out for a ride. Another Finest would come to take his place, and they would notice this new horse. It would have an exquisite form and the Prince would select it as his mount and would visit with it often.

Gallant-Stallion began fading from the stall, his form looking ghostlike.

~   ~   ~

The boy ran toward the stables! I saw him!" The words were shouted and came from beyond the stable. The loud voice was distracting and was slowing Gallant-Stallion's journey, and so he fought to push the words out.

"He climbed over the palace wall and is somewhere around

here! Probably a thief who knows he'll be tossed in the dungeon to rot if we catch him."

"There! I think I see him! Running into the stable!"

THERE WAS THE SHUSH OF STEEL AGAINST LEATHER—SOMEONE was drawing a sword.

AGAIN GALLANT-STALLION TRIED TO FORCE OUT THE SOUNDS. Why were the voices intruding? Why couldn't he keep them away? He needed to return to the Finest Court and arrange for a replacement. The journey to the Court was far more important than being distracted by a thief that some guard claimed was running into the stables.

Or was it?

"THE THIEF WENT IN THERE! IN THE PRINCE'S STABLE."

GALLANT-STALLION ABRUPTLY ENDED HIS MYSTICAL JOURNEY, and his ghostlike form took on substance. The pasture disappeared from his mind, and he again felt the straw and earth beneath his hooves. The scent of the other horses and of oats filled his nostrils, and the voices of soldiers and stable hands and an irate guard became louder.

"CAN'T SEE HOW SOMEONE SLIPPED BY US SO EASY, CLIMBING over the wall and getting past the night sentries. An expert thief, the boy is. Probably come to steal some horses."

"Well, he might have slipped in, but he won't slip out."

GALLANT-STALLION OPENED HIS EYES. IT WAS DARK IN THE stable, but just enough starlight filtered in, through cracks in the wood and through an open door, that he could make out details. He focused his keen senses and picked up the rustling of straw and rapid breathing, the shuffling of feet against the earth. He stared at the shadows, and his eyes separated the shades of black and gray. A slight figure was pressed against the wall, inching toward the far end of the stable, where he and three of the akhal-tekes were kept.

There was something recognizable about the figure, and when it came closer, the "thief" gasped.

"Rue?"

It was Kalantha, thought a boy because of her tattered breeches and shirt and close-cropped hair. Her face was smudged with dirt, perhaps because she was trying to blend in with the darkness, or perhaps because of the way she'd been living. She smelled of sweat and dung, having run through the fields surrounding the stable and stepping in horse droppings along the way.

"Oh, Rue." She opened the door and rushed inside, closing it behind her and running her fingers through the Finest's mane. "They wouldn't let me in the gate," she said. "They didn't believe that I'm Meven's sister. They thought me a beggar or a thief and chased me away."

The sounds of soldiers searching for her intruded, and she crouched now at the back of Gallant-Stallion's stall, pushing a bale of hay in front of her.

"I could've sworn that thief ran in here." A stable hand led a pair of soldiers inside, lighting the way with a large hooded lantern. "Horses don't seem bothered, though. They're usually spooked when strangers are about."

The soldiers looked in each stall, then searched through the tack bins and oat barrels.

"Not in this stable. Let's try another," one of the soldiers suggested. He and the others gave up and moved on.

Kalantha didn't budge for several minutes. Eventually the voices trailed away and she stirred from her hiding spot.

"They wouldn't let me in the gate, Rue, and not even one of them would take a message to Meven. So I climbed the wall to get inside. One of the guards saw me, and hollered for soldiers. I was so frightened I ran and ran. I'm fast, you know, and I saw the stables and ran here. I thought I might hide for a little while, then go to the palace and find Meven."

Meven is lost to me, Gallant-Stallion said. *He does not visit and I cannot reach him. My charge needs my guidance. The Prince of Galmier needs shepherding.*

Kalantha was scratching the blaze between his eyes and pressed her face close to his. "I miss my brother, Rue. It took me weeks to get here. I was lost for days and days and days, and I never thought I'd find this city or the palace. Ever. I have to talk to him, Rue. I need to see him."

I need to see him also, Gallant-Stallion continued. *I cannot shepherd one I cannot keep an eye on.*

"Maybe when I see him, I'll talk him into coming out here, then you can see him," she said. "I'll tell him that his magic horse wants to know that he's all right. I agree with you, he needs guidance."

Gallant-Stallion snorted. *She hears me, Steadfast! Kalantha hears me.*

"Of course I can hear you," she returned. "You're magic just like that wonderful mountain pony."

29 · Passing the Scepter

I've learned in my long years that Finest and charge are music~dissonant at times, haunting and unharmonious. But when the melody blends and the pitch is exact, a concert is created that can compare to nothing on all of Paard-Peran or in the Finest Court. The partnership is faultless, and the charge is headed on the path toward perfection.

~Steadfast, former Elder of the Finest Court

King Montoll's face was as pale as snow. Bishop DeNogaret sat at the foot of his bed, and Meven hovered nearby. The attendant Meven met on his first day at the palace was filling the King's neck pouch with a fresh batch of herbs. Finished with that task, she rubbed a foul-smelling balm on his chest, then reached for the smallest jar of unguent and rubbed that pasty gray mixture on his arms. Her hands trembled faintly, and her expression was filled with worry.

The King's face and hands twitched, as if he was caught in a bad dream. Then his eyelids fluttered opened. She helped him sit up a little, fluffing his pillows. She continued to fuss over him, reaching for a glass of water and helping him take a few sips.

"Your Majesty," she began. "How are you feeling today?"

The old monarch chuckled, and then broke into a coughing fit that caused his body to bounce. When it had passed: "How am I feeling, Alora? I'm dying, is how I'm feeling. Been dying for some time. But I just wasn't ready to go until now."

She felt his forehead, and glanced nervously at Bishop De-Nogaret. "Nonsense, Your Majesty. You'll come through this malady and be moving around before all the leaves drop."

"Take care of Prince Meven after I'm gone," he told her. "And make him invite that Princess of House Silverwood for a visit. She's not much older than he, never married, and the alliance would do both countries good." He let out a papery sigh that sounded like sand blowing across a hard patch of ground. "I think I'll sleep now, Alora. Thank you for taking care of me."

He closed his eyes and instantly dozed.

"I can't say that he'll make it until morning," she said, moving to the Bishop and keeping her voice soft in the event the King was somehow listening. Carefully arranging the pots of balms and unguents, and putting the last of the herbs away, she stepped to the window and pointed at the night sky. "It's the constellation of Peran-Morab, the King's favorite. Until a year ago, he always called for an astrologer when Peran-Morab was in the eastern sky."

"What made him stop?" This came from Meven. He'd crossed to the other side of the bed and was leaning over, studying the King.

"Astrologers, though few in number, have always been meddlesome, devious folk. But they were nevertheless sought for their aptitudes. King Montoll had a bad experience with the last one." She walked to the disguised door. "There's a soldier just outside, and two novice priests from the Temple. And I will be back to check on him in an hour or so."

Meven pulled back from the bed and went to the window. "Bishop DeNogaret, I've not had much experience at being the Prince. It's all been dinners and parties, meeting nobles and signing a few unimportant decrees. I've not studied anything since coming here, and I've not read a single book—though I've pulled several from that incredible library. I've been living in luxury and letting everyone pamper me. I've been irresponsible. I know so little about this city. And I thought I understood politics, but clearly I am lacking. I am . . ."

"Frightened."

"And frustrated, Bishop DeNogaret. I am about to become King of Galmier. And I am not at all up to that task. I am only fourteen."

The Bishop made certain that Meven was still looking at the stars. He rose and glided to the table, looked at the jars and pocketed two of them. He would dispose of them at the Temple later, removing all trace of his involvement with the King's slow poisoning. His puppets in the palace had been very good about mixing the poison into King Montoll's medicine, and about increasing the dosage since Meven appeared. The dying had been slow and drawn out to make it look like an illness. And the puppets who had been so instrumental in it all would disappear tonight—keeping Bishop DeNogaret untouchable.

"Meven, I am here to help you. Surely you know that I will do whatever necessary to make you a good King. And . . . you are more than fourteen. You are a young man."

Meven pushed himself away from the window and walked to the center of the ring of animal rugs. He looked down and stared into the glass eyes of the bear. "Bishop DeNogaret, you're going to have to do more than just help me. I need you to be an equal partner in this kingship. While I've the desire to rule, I've not the wisdom. I'm too attracted to all this wealth. See? I admit my failing, and yet I do nothing to overcome it. I eat extravagant meals, I ask for the best clothes. This morning I selected an artist to render a portrait of me. I am like a man addicted to wine. He knows he should stop drinking, but he reaches for the next bottle, and the next, and the next. I need far more than just your help."

Bishop DeNogaret went to Meven, his steps slow and deliberate. He stretched out a finger and placed it below Meven's chin, raising it until their eyes met. "Meven, indulge yourself in these luxuries."

Meven's eyes widened. "Indulge myself? That's just what I've been doing, and I expected you to chastise me for it. A religious man should not embrace wealth like I'm doing."

"Dear, dear Meven, you have suffered much. You lost your cousin Edan, and you lived in the wilds like an animal. You are about to lose your uncle the King. Kalantha is . . . far, far from here . . . and you are about to be thrust into a role that is both terrible and wonderful. Enjoy what pleasantries you can for a time. You have earned the right to indulge yourself."

Meven's face relaxed. "That would not be so bad, would it?"

"It would be expected of you. A King should enjoy his wealth and his surroundings. And you've all these servants, attendants, and soldiers. Use them, Meven. It is why they are here. Continue to let them do things for you." The Bishop's voice was steady and hypnotic, and each drawn-out word increased Meven's ease. "Play the part, Meven. Be royal and glorious, and stand above the common people. It is expected."

Meven slowly rocked back and forth on the balls of his feet, his eyes never leaving the Bishop's. He was easily hypnotized. "Expected. I am expected to indulge myself."

"You are the King now, my child. You must be regal and aloof."

"Regal and aloof." Meven finally glanced past Bishop DeNogaret and noticed the King had stopped breathing. "I am the King now," he said flatly.

"Look at me." The Bishop used his finger to bring Meven's face back to focus on him. He kept his unblinking eyes locked on Meven's. "I will assist in all your decisions."

"Yes, Bishop DeNogaret. You will assist in all my decisions."

"From behind the curtains I will make the policies and set the alliances. I will plan the upcoming war with Uland."

"War. . . . Yes, you will plan the war."

"And all the while you will indulge yourself and keep yourself above the normal folk of Galmier. You will attend the parties and flirt with the noblewomen. You will make appearances at the Temple and wherever else I deem it appropriate and fortuitous. You are singular Meven Montoll. You are the King."

"I am the King."

"And the new King is in need of rest this night. You are so very, very tired. You will be crowned in the morning." The Bishop dropped his gaze, and Meven blinked.

"I suddenly find myself very tired, Bishop DeNogaret. If you don't mind, I'll go to my wing. There will no doubt be a big party tomorrow following my coronation, and I need to be rested for it. The day after we'll have the funeral for my uncle."

Bishop DeNogaret bowed deeply. "Of course, Your Majesty. Sleep well."

~ ~ ~

Meven walked back to his wing alone, declining all offers for escorts.

"He is like King Montoll," he heard one soldier whisper. "He does for himself sometimes."

I am King Montoll, Meven mouthed. *Why can't this be a dream?* He took the long way, going by a gallery that was filled with portraits of previous Kings and Queens, assorted royalty and their pampered pets. He stopped in front of a portrait of Edan. His cousin must have been ten or eleven when it was painted, and he looked happy, hands cupping a small tan puppy with round watery eyes. There were spaces on the walls for other portraits, and Meven tried to imagine one of himself hanging there.

"King Meven Montoll, High Lord of Galmier." He touched the frame around Edan's portrait. "You should have been King, cousin. And I should be at High Keep Temple, studying geography and history and praying every morning and night." His hand went to his waist, and he cursed softly to discover he'd forgotten to wear his prayer belt today. "I will put it on first thing in the morning. Before breakfast, and before the scepter is passed to me."

A last glance at Edan's portrait, then Meven left the room, following one hallway after the next, climbing a circular staircase, then entering the upper level of his wing. "My wing," he mused. "My palace come tomorrow. All of this mine."

His bedchamber was at the end of a wide, red-carpeted hallway. The door was open slightly, and he hesitated before going inside. "Is someone there?" Perhaps Alora was turning his bed covers down. He poked his head inside, and his legs locked.

"Kal?"

She was standing by a narrow window, and had been looking at the stars. She whirled at his voice and rushed to him. "Meven, I've missed you so."

He hugged her, then pushed her back to arm's length to take a better look at her. She was in man's clothing—breeches and a shirt, both too large and belted to keep them on her slight frame. The clothes were dirty and worn, as if they'd been discarded and she'd picked them out of the trash. Her hair, still short, had grown out some, and it was uneven and tangled. Her tanned face was smudged all over with dirt, as were her hands and neck. The ropy scar was still painfully visible. He wrinkled his nose at the horrid way she smelled.

"Kal . . . what happened? Where have you been? Why do you look like this?" *And smell like this*, he mouthed. "You reek!"

She smiled and wrinkled her nose in agreement. "It's so long a story I've to tell, dear Meven. I'm so sorry I don't look better. I've not had a bath in quite a few days. Weeks, actually. No money for one, and there hasn't been rain to shower in. I've been lost in this country."

He closed the door and pointed to a divan. He sat heavily and drew her down next to him. "Lost, you say? Bishop DeNogaret said you were going to Dea Fortress, and that his men were escorting you. Why aren't you at the fortress?"

Kalantha shook her head when he went to take her hands. She didn't want the dirt rubbing off on him. "I *was* going there, but I escaped from my escort during the night. I'm surprised the Bishop thinks I'm there. You'd think his men would have told him I'd run away." She glanced around his room and avoided his gaze. "I don't want that kind of a life, Meven. Locked away and praying all the time. I believe in the gods, but I believe I should have my own life. My life is not theirs."

"The Bishop doesn't know you're here."

"I'm certain he doesn't."

"He'll be furious with you, Kal. He'll send you to Dea Fortress and have you locked away for your own good."

"No doubt with a bigger escort to take me there, me tied to a horse perhaps. Maybe he'd even take me himself."

Meven sucked in his lower lip. "He couldn't take you, Kalantha. He's the Bishop of Nadir now, my most trusted counselor. He's in charge of the Temple here. But he'll have my soldiers take you to the fortress. He'll make sure you have an armed escort this time. He says a religious life is best for you. I believe he's right."

She straightened her back and her eyes flashed angrily. "No, I won't go there, Meven. I don't want to live at Dea Fortress."

"Kalantha, I have to tell the Bishop you're here."

"No you don't. It's a big palace, and I can lose myself in it.

Bishop DeNogaret would never have to see me." She stood and looked to the window. "But enough talk of me. You look well, Meven. Being a Prince suits you."

"I haven't been a very good one, I'm afraid. Too caught up in all of this." He gestured with his hands to indicate the palace. "But the Bishop will ground me and get me to see things from a proper perspective. He's going to make the important decisions, Kal. It's best for the country. When you come back, after spending a few years at Dea Fortress, I'll have you assigned as an acolyte at the Temple here. We'll be able to visit from time to time. Your life will have meaning."

Kalantha stepped away and was staring out the window. "Enough about my life and what you and Bishop DeNogaret have planned for me. Meven, Rue is in the stable and misses you."

"My ugly punch? I've forgotten he's still here. You've been in the stable?"

"He's not ugly, Meven. He's a beautiful horse. I don't know why you can't see that. He's a wonderful, magical horse and . . ."

"I have a new horse now, named Pride. He's a three-year-old akhal-teke, very handsome, and he rides even and fast. I suppose I have a lot of horses when you think about it. They are all mine now. If you were going to be staying at the palace, I would make sure you had an akhal-teke, also. Or one of those norikers. Maybe I'll give you an akhal-teke to ride to Dea Fortress."

She shook her head furiously. "I *am* going to stay here at the palace, Meven. I'm your sister, and you'll not send me away. You can't dismiss me like you would some cleaning woman."

He stood and continued to keep her at arm's length, nose still wrinkling at her smell. "All right, Kal. I'll not dismiss you just yet, not before a bath and a change of clothes in any event. And I'll let you stay for breakfast and my crowning."

She laughed at the comment, then her expression became deadly serious when she saw how his brows were knitted together and how his dark eyes shone.

"Yes, I will send you away, Kalantha. You will leave after my coronation in the morning."

Coronation? Meven? She gave him a look of disbelief.

"Uncle died this evening, just a short while ago. It is a pity you never got to meet him. He was a great man."

"Dead? The King is dead?"

"*I* am the King now, and *I* insist that you study at Dea Fortress. Bishop DeNogaret said that is best for you. The Bishop always knows what is best. Just think of it, Kal, no more embroidery stitches. Your life will have real purpose. You'll serve the gods."

She backed away from him and the window. "Meven, you can't be serious."

"Very serious." He stepped to the door and pulled a thin silver chain. It rang a bell in the hallway.

A heartbeat later an attendant was knocking on the door.

He opened it a crack. "Alora?"

"Yes, Prince Meven."

"King Meven," he corrected. "Uncle died a short while ago."

"Oh, I am so sorry."

"I need you to find Bishop DeNogaret."

"Yes, King Meven. Immediately."

"Tell him my sister has come for a visit."

"Yes, King Meven." She hurried down the hall.

Meven turned to face Kalantha again. "You'll stay for the coronation, of course."

Tears welled up in her eyes. "Go see Rue in the stable," she tried again. "He's magic, Meven, and he can help you. Oh, how you've changed. He can bring the old Meven back."

He stepped away from the door and settled himself on the edge of his massive bed. "I'm glad you're here, Kal. Really, I am. I'd been wondering about you, and worried because I hadn't received a letter. I've missed you. But this is really for the best. You'll see! You'll write to me, won't you? I've been told messengers travel between Dea Fortress and the various Temples in Galmier."

"Meven, you've truly changed."

"Yes, Kal. Of course I have. So much has happened. Listen, let me tell you about my trip here." He regaled her with the story of his arrival, and how he had gotten lost several times in the palace during his first few days. He stretched out the story, keeping her in place while he waited for the Bishop to arrive.

"Kal, I finally figured my way around the palace by looking at the tiles on the floor. There are patterns to them, and if you follow the tiles with swirling black lines, they'll take you to the library and the music room, and eventually to the largest dining hall. If you follow the tiles speckled with bits of granite, you'll end up in the kitchen and winery—and eventually in the servants' quarters. There are more than a hundred servants living here, Kal. And that doesn't count the people who tend the grounds and the horses, and the soldiers. This palace is like a city unto itself."

He told her about the parties and the various noble families he'd been introduced to, and about the expansive merchant district that offered wares from all over Paard-Peran.

She listened attentively, both because she was curious and because she was waiting for a trace of the Meven she once knew to emerge. Eventually she sat back down on the divan, noticing that she'd gotten dirt on it, and arranging the pillows so Meven might not notice.

"I am going to have my portrait painted. The artist I've selected is coming to the palace tomorrow afternoon. He's a fascinating man. I'd introduce you, but you'll be on your way by then. In fact . . ." He stopped when a soft knocking sounded on his door.

"King Meven?"

"Yes, Alora."

"I've informed Bishop DeNogaret about your sister. He said to tell you he is on his way here with his attendants."

"No!" Kalantha finally realized her brother had been stalling and waiting for Bishop DeNogaret. "Meven, you can't do this to me!" She bolted from the divan and ran to the door, throwing it open and sending Alora reeling. Kalantha ran by her and down the hall, Meven fast on her heels.

For a moment, Kalantha worried that she would become lost in the palace as Meven had, but she remembered his story about the tiles, and followed the ones with granite. She'd slipped in through the servants' quarters, as that was the part of the palace that was closest to the stables, and it had taken her nearly two hours of hiding and scurrying here and there to find Meven's bedroom. Her feet slapped over the floor, and she nearly lost her shoes—they were too large, and the toes were stuffed with strips of cloth. Meven had been right, she'd found the clothes and shoes discarded in an alley in Nadir. Though foul, they were better than what she'd been wearing.

She nearly tripped a man carrying a tray of mugs, and she knocked over a large vase on a pedestal. Meven cursed behind her, as stepping on the shards and vaulting over the fallen pedestal slowed him.

"I was always faster than you, Meven!" she called over her shoulder. "I only let you win."

His feet pounded after her, then they pounded over the grass when she burst out a rear door and shot toward the stable. "Kal! Stop! Be reasonable about this."

She was increasing her lead, as she hurtled rocks in a carefully arranged garden. Then she broke through a boxwood hedge and ran even faster. Her feet carried her into a meadow, and brought her near one of the stables.

"Kal, stop! Kal . . . look out!"

Meven's tone had changed, and she risked a glance over her shoulder to find out why. He'd stopped several yards behind her and was looking up at the sky. She slowed to a jog and looked up too, sucking in a breath when she saw hundreds of birds descending.

"The assassins. Meven, they've come back!"

"By the gods, Kal, after all this time I'd thought they'd forgotten us." He was rushing toward her now and flailing away with his arms to indicate the stable. "It's closer than the palace, Kal. Run for it!"

She stood spellbound by the birds for another moment, then she whirled and dashed toward the stable. "Rue! Help Meven! The assassins are back!"

The first wave swooped down before she reached the stable, and a large black hawk slammed into her back, toppling her.

"Death comes!" it screamed.

She rolled onto her back and saw it hovering a few yards above her, its cold evil eyes finding hers.

"You cannot escape it this time," the crow sneered. "Death comes for you now."

"Falafalafalafala," a blackbird high above called. "We will slay the girl for you!"

"Go after the Prince," Fala returned. "You missed this one on your last outing. I will finish her now."

The malevolent hawk swooped down, beak aimed at her heart and claws outstretched. But Kalantha was no longer frozen in fear. She rolled and rolled, then leapt to her feet, just as Meven came near.

A cloud of birds and bats instantly swarmed them, claws and beaks and tiny teeth digging in. Meven cried out, but not in pain, as he was pushed away from his sister.

"Guards!" he shouted. It was a strangled cry, as his throat had gone dry from all the running, and his side pained him from the exertion. He hadn't run since their time in the mountains. "Guards! Someone summon the guards!"

Kalantha doubted anyone could hear Meven over the racket the assassin flock was making. There was no stealth involved in the birds' attack this time, and they'd made no attempt to fly in the artful forms of men on horseback. They were cawing and screeching, and the bats were making a shrill whistling noise that bore into Kalantha.

She slammed her eyes shut and swung her fists at them. She connected with each swing, as they were so numerous and therefore impossible to miss. Her knuckles were bleeding from her efforts, and she knew she was bleeding from cuts along her arms and on her face. This attack seemed more vicious and hopeless, but Kalantha realized that this time it was only she and Meven. There was no wedding party to divide the assassins' attacks, and there was no herd of mountain ponies to come to their rescue.

"Rue!" she hollered, as she risked opening her eyes. "Save Meven! Save the King!" She prayed to the gods that the punch would somehow hear her through this cacophony. Perhaps the stable hands or groomers would hear the noise, or perhaps the soldiers that might still be looking for the trespassing thief were nearby.

The birds and bats were louder still, from the flapping of their wings to their cries, to their words. "Death comes at last! Death comes to you! Falafalafala we bring death for you!"

"Meven!"

The assassins were so thick Kalantha couldn't see through them and couldn't tell how close she was to Meven. She'd not heard him call for the guards again, and so she feared the birds might have killed him.

"Meven!" she screamed again, with all the volume she could muster. "Meven, where are you?"

She was forced to close her eyes once more when a trio of starlings started clawing at her face.

"Hurts," she said. "Hurts so much." She alternated between pounding on the birds and trying to pluck them away from her face. Her fingers were raw now, feeling as if she were dragging them across coals, then through ice. "Meven!"

~ ~ ~

Meven was faring better than his sister. The sheer number of birds had knocked him onto his back. They were buffeting him with their wings, preventing him from getting up, and they stayed just far enough back that he couldn't pummel them. Some had scratched his face and around his neck, and on the back of his hands. But none of the wounds were deep.

The assassins had been given specific instructions to injure Prince Meven—but not seriously. He was to emerge alive from this encounter, though his sister would not be so fortunate. It was supposed to look like both of them had been attacked.

"Kalantha!" he cried, again finding his voice. "Kal!"

~ ~ ~

Gallant-Stallion had retreated to the back of his stall and had closed down his senses. He was on his way to the Finest Court. For a brief minute Kalantha had given him hope that she would bring Meven to see him. But neither she nor Meven had arrived, and so Gallant-Stallion returned to his plan to travel to the Court and ask that they assign an elegant-looking Finest, one that had the form of a noriker or akhal-teke and that would be acceptable to Meven.

He saw an image of Mara, the pony from Bitternut who had filled his mind with visions. She'd told him his charge was crucial to the future of Galmier. She'd told him . . . Gallant-Stallion paused in his mystical journey. He recalled precisely his last visit with her. He'd been put in a stall by the kind stable master, given food and water. He smelled Mara, she carried a hint of cinnamon.

I knew you would return, Gallant-Stallion-called-Rue. The pony left the far corner of the stable and walked down the aisle between the stalls. She looked to each horse as she went, making a wuffling sound that some of them responded to. *I saw it in a vision that you would come back shortly before the snow.*

The snow is months away. Gallant-Stallion perfectly recalled the conversation.

The pony's gold-flecked eyes seemed to loom larger. *You came here with your charge.*

Of course. No doubt you saw Meven outside these doors.

Yes, I saw the new Prince. Your charge looks well.

Gallant-Stallion stopped the journey to the Finest Court. His eyes flew open. Mara had said: *Yes, I saw the new Prince. Your charge looks well.* She didn't say: *Yes, I saw your charge, the new Prince.* She'd made no reference to Meven being his charge.

And that is because my charge is not the Prince, Gallant-Stallion said. *My charge was never the Prince. I have been blind. My charge has always been Kalantha.* He cursed himself for not realizing it. He reared back in the stall and flailed out with his hooves in anger. *So thickheaded am I! So foolish. So utterly . . .*

Familiar sounds intruded—the nickering and snorts of the akhal-tekes, and the flapping of wings. The latter was growing so loud it sounded like charging horses. He faintly heard Kalantha calling for him, and heard Meven shouting for the guards.

The assassins! By the mane of the Old Mare, the assassin flock has found the cousins. Gallant-Stallion battered away at the door to his stall. Within moments, he'd broken it and was running from one stall to the next, and then he was running from the stable.

~ ~ ~

Bishop DeNogaret was high in one of the palace's towers. Though old, his eyesight was excellent, and he watched the flock of assassin-birds and bats descend on Meven and Kalantha. He knew the girl would run when Alora announced that the Bishop was coming. He knew Kalantha didn't want to see him and would leave the palace. And he knew the birds were waiting outside for her. They'd been perched in the nearby woods, attending Eyeswide and waiting for orders.

He had thought she'd been killed weeks ago on her way to Dea Fortress—killed with the men he sent as her escort. That she was alive angered him. It had been one of the sentry birds that spotted her going into the stable earlier this evening. The sentry alerted Fala . . . who in turn told Eyeswide . . . who minutes ago had told Bishop DeNogaret.

The owl was currently perched on the windowsill, his head swiveling to take in both the battle and the Bishop.

"It will be over quickly, Master," the owl said. He made a gesture that was the equivalent of a man rolling his shoulders. Then he shifted his weight first to his right talon, then to his left.

"Yes, I think it will be quick," the Bishop agreed. "The one person who could possibly jeopardize our plans will be dead. Then nothing can keep me from ruling this country."

"Through your puppet, Meven," Eyeswide purred.

"Yes. Yes. Through my blind and loyal puppet. Meven is clay for me to mold. Kalantha was always too willful to be of any use."

"And so you approved of my plan?"

"Ruling Galmier behind the curtains?" The Bishop's lips

turned up into a thin, tight smile as the cloud of darkness grew thicker around Meven and Kalantha. "Indeed. It was a good plan, Eyeswide. I am safe behind the curtain, untouchable. Nothing will be linked to me, and yet I will have all the power I've been wanting. Galmier first."

"Then Uland." The Bishop made a humming sound the owl knew meant yes. "Then Nasim-Guri."

"Yes, Eyeswide, gaining that country either through Meven's marriage to the Princess or—if necessary—through war."

"And all of the Old Forest and the Graywoods will be mine."

"That, and more, my old friend." The Bishop slipped back from the window, and the owl turned its full attention on him.

"You don't want to see the end?"

The Bishop steepled his fingers beneath his chin. "I must be with the novice priests who are preparing the deceased King's body. When word is brought to me there of Meven's injuries and Kalantha's death, I must appear surprised."

"And in the company of people. Witnesses and alibis."

"Nothing will ever be traced to me, Eyeswide. Nothing ever has been."

"Nor to me, Master." The owl took flight, streaking toward the woods north of the palace grounds.

Bishop DeNogaret started down the steps and toward the dead King's chamber.

~ ~ ~

Kalantha expected to die. She was in great pain and the birds had closed in so that her arms were pressed against her body—she couldn't lift them even in defense. She suspected Meven was already dead. And she was furious—not that she was going to die, she knew everybody died in time. But she was angry that she didn't know why it had to be now. Why were the vicious birds out to slay her and Meven and end the Montoll line? Who would stand to gain from their deaths?

"Meven . . . ," she gasped.

She felt the ground trembling beneath her, and she could tell the birds and bats were miraculously giving her more space. She curled into a ball and protected her face, and she listened to the sound of horses' hooves and the shouts of soldiers and stable hands.

Gallant-Stallion had freed the horses from the stable and begged them to help. The akhal-tekes were quick to comply, sensing something exciting happening. When the horses ran from the stables, the groomers and stable hands sleeping nearby were alerted, and they sounded the alarm for the soldiers.

Suddenly the field near the stable was filled with men and charging horses, and with the birds and bats under the direction of Fala. The big hawk saw the men and the "horse between" coming.

~ ~ ~

Falafalafala. Help comes to the cousins."

"I see them. Leave the boy," Fala instructed. "He is not to be badly hurt. Finish the girl and keep the men at bay. The 'horse between' is mine." The hawk launched himself at Gallant-Stallion even as the first of the akhal-tekes closed on the assassin flock.

Screams of men and cries of birds filled the air, mingling with the sound of beating wings and thundering hooves. The world was a wave of hurtful noise and twisting, flying shadows.

Kalantha uncurled herself and crawled out from under a swarm of assassins, batting the closest away with an arm as she went. "Meven?" At the edge of her vision, she saw him—on his back. Birds hovered above him, and she feared they'd killed him. But she saw his chest rising and falling regularly, and so she guessed he was only unconscious. "Praise the gods of Paard-Peran," she said.

Soldiers were swinging their swords at the flock, and more soldiers were coming. Lights were going on in the guardhouse, alarms were being raised all over the palace grounds. Stable hands and groomers were beating the birds away with pitchforks and other makeshift weapons. They were calling for more men.

"We are undone!" a starling shouted. "Again we fail! Too many men. Not enough of us. The overseer will punish us!"

The 'horse between' has indeed cut our numbers, Fala silently cursed, *and thereby made our flock weaker once more.* Despite new additions, the force was still not up to its previous strength.

"Fly! Fly to the north woods!" This came from a kestrel, who was banking away from a group of rushing soldiers. "I'll not die here!"

"Falafalafala! What do we do?"

"Fly? Fala, do we fly?"

The black hawk didn't answer; he was intent on the punch. Fala dove on the horse, beak pointed and body straight like a spear. He rammed into the horse's back with as much force as he could manage, then he rose and dove again, this time raking the horse's neck with his long, sharp claws.

Gallant-Stallion was prepared on the hawk's third pass, rearing back and striking out with his hooves. The Finest put everything into the blow, and was rewarded when he struck the crow squarely and brought him to the ground. Without pause Gallant-Stallion drove his hooves onto the body. Over and over, turning the hawk into a mass of bloody feathers.

Death came, Gallant-Stallion said. *Death came to you!*

"Flyflyflyflyfly!" became the new chorus. "Fala is dead! Flee!" The birds and bats climbed away from the battle as more soldiers arrived.

The akhal-tekes stomped the slowest of the retreating assassins into the ground. The field was littered with the bodies of birds and bats and a few fallen men.

"The Prince!" one of the soldiers called. "There's the Prince!"

Meven was sitting, shaking his head to clear his senses and squinting to take everything in. "Kal?"

She was on her feet, though she was wobbly. Her raggedy clothes were covered with her blood, and her exposed skin was heavily marred by welts and scratches.

"By the gods, Kal!" Meven motioned to the closest soldiers and stumbled toward her. "That's my sister. She needs help!"

"No!" Kalantha called to him. "I'll not go to Dea Fortress, Meven. I won't be shut away!"

You are Galmier's future, Gallant-Stallion said, though he knew she was too far away to hear him. *And I am your shepherd.* He galloped toward her, reaching her just before the soldiers and Meven.

She stretched up and grabbed his mane and hauled herself onto his back. "Get me out of here, Rue! Please take me away!"

His hooves pounded against the field, churning up earth and tossing the bodies of birds and bats in his wake. He headed toward a low spot in the wall that surrounded the palace grounds. There was a rise just before it, and he gathered speed.

"Hurry," Kalantha urged.

Gallant-Stallion hit the rise and leapt, extending his legs as he was carried over the wall. He came down on a slope on the other side and kept galloping, going faster than he ever had before and heading down one of the main roads of Nadir. It was the road he took when Meven was on his back when they first came to the city, so he knew it well enough that he didn't have to slow.

Lights were coming on in residences, alerted by the alarms at the palace and the sound of the fight. No doubt the battle-noise had carried well in the still air.

"Hurt so much," Kalantha said. "Why, why ever would someone want me dead?"

Because somehow you threaten someone, Kalantha, Gallant-Stallion replied.

"But I'm not a threat," she returned.

You must be to someone.

They raced through the merchant district with all its inter-esting and wonderful smells, then through a residential area, past the slums, then past where the wealthiest people lived. Gallant-Stallion considered slowing to learn if they were being pursued. But that was his curiosity urging him to do that. He shoved that notion away and continued at his relentless pace until he was well beyond the city.

He started south. Instinct? A random course? He wasn't sure, but he didn't alter his direction. A field stretched out in all directions. It was the field from Mara's vision.

"Where are we going, Rue?"

Someplace safe, the Finest answered.

"I am safe when I am with you."

Gallant-Stallion pressed on for hours until the field became marshy. In the distance, so indistinct because of the darkness, he thought he saw houses growing on top of trees. It was a vil-lage. Could someone there tend to Kalantha?

He slowed to a trot. He was exhausted, his chest on fire from the run. Kalantha was leaning against his neck. He felt her blood on him, and he worried that perhaps he'd been too late coming to her rescue, and had been foolish in taking her from Nadir where there might be healers who could help. But she was stirring, and after a moment he realized her breathing was strong.

"Why am I a threat, Rue?"

Gallant-Stallion almost didn't answer her this time. He was still puzzled why she could hear him. People weren't supposed to hear the voices of the Finest. Unless that was his gift . . . to be heard by his charge.

We will learn together why someone wants you dead.

Kalantha twined her fingers in his mane. "Together," she said.

Then she drifted off to sleep, and Gallant-Stallion walked slowly and carefully now, as the sky started to lighten. He'd lost sight of the village. The marsh was getting deeper, and he knew he was lost.

Steadfast, she is my charge, and I am to guide her on the path to perfection. But I do not know where that path lies. Danger surrounds this girl.

Yes. Danger and the future of Galmier surround this very important girl, Steadfast's spirit replied. *Guide and guard her well. The hope of Paard-Peran rides with you, Gallant-Stallion.*